ALL OF THEM WERE SCIENTISTS.

Roger Cortland, a famous man with a taste for virtual reality, came to the Orbital Complex to continue his life's work. Marissa Correa came to work with Cortland, and observe this theoretical Utopian society up close. Jhana Meniskos came to work in "Orbital Park," the station's biodiversity preserve.

But no Utopia is safe—from corruption, from sabotage, from corporate poison. And when this perfect world begins to unravel—attacked from Earth and from within—all three will have to fight to protect their work and their lives.

"In *Lightpaths*, Howard Hendrix gives us an exhilarating intellectual tour of both an amazing orbital habitat and a dizzying complex of ideas, from the scientific to the aesthetic to the utopian. I have a *future perfect imperative* for everyone who happens upon a copy: seize it—legally of course—and read it!"

—Michael Bishop, author of *Brittle Innings*

LIGHTPATHS

LIGHTPATHS

HOWARD V. HENDRIX

ACE BOOKS, NEW YORK

The material excerpted from *The Story of Utopias* by Lewis Mumford (All Rights Reserved) is used with permission of his estate.

This book is an Ace original edition, and has never been previously published.

LIGHTPATHS

An Ace Book / published by arrangement with the author

PRINTING HISTORY
Ace edition / September 1997

The Putnam Berkley World Wide Web site address is
http://www.berkley.com

Make sure to check out *PB Plug*,
the science fiction/fantasy newsletter, at
http://www.pbplug.com

ISBN: 0-441-00470-9

ACE®
Ace Books are published by The Berkley Publishing Group,
200 Madison Avenue, New York, NY 10016.
ACE and the "A" design are trademarks
belonging to Charter Communications, Inc.

PRINTED IN THE UNITED STATES OF AMERICA

10 9 8 7 6 5 4 3 2 1

ACKNOWLEDGMENTS

DURING THE AUTUMN OF 1990 THE TASK OF WRITING THIS novel forced itself on me—a long and lonely road, in prospect. I now realize, though, that because the boundary between life and art is a semipermeable membrane, I was never actually traveling alone. At the time of the book's composition, the world was wending its way into the Persian Gulf War. This novel responds, at least obliquely, to that political situation. Of more personal and direct concern, the body of my brother, Vincent John "Jay" Hendrix, had been found less than two years earlier. He had died just short of his twenty-seventh birthday. That loss led me to try to make some sense of his life and death. This book has been part of that sense-making process.

I am indebted to two friends I have met upon the road from time to time: philosopher Bruce Albert, for our discussions of the nature of consciousness, and gardener Stuart Straw, for his knowledge of horticulture. Any errors in these areas are mine, any strengths theirs. My thanks to David Hartwell for encouraging me to make another pass at the manuscript in 1994, and my especial thanks to Ginjer Buchanan for showing her faith in it by purchasing it for Ace in 1996. I hope this book also stands as a summing up of my debt to a century of science-fiction writers whose works have shaped my thinking.

Finally, I wish to thank my wife, Laurel, for her patience and support. No one could have asked for a better traveling companion.

ONE

LONELINESS LIKE EMPTY WIND MOANING THROUGH A UNI-versal blizzard of ashes and snow. Then, beneath the blatant, eternal white noise, another sound, a latent voice: "No, never put it all together, I'm afraid. Never completed the circle . . ."

Roger Cortland woke with a start, static in his ears and monitor snow in his eyes. He often fell asleep on shuttle flights—nothing new in that—but something, some sort of accidental access wave, had apparently knocked his personal data display off-channel. Now his wearable cyberspace was refusing to return to proper functioning. Grumpily he shut the system down, then turned it back on again for reboot.

As his monitors began to cycle up on his glasses, he thought about the strange half-dream he'd just come out of. Amazing what the mind in twilight sleep could come up with, the hypnagogic imagination imposing meaning where surely there was none, turning the mere nothing of white noise into loneliness and winds and cosmic anguish.

The voice, though, the words—Roger recognized those. His uncle Ed, his father's brother, had spoken those words. Ed had been deep in his cups at the wake for Roger's father. Otherwise he would not have said such a thing. Why had Roger thought of that—that suggestion of failure—now? True, things had not gone perfectly well on the recent trip to Earth, but the situation wasn't *that* dismal.

The virtual overlays on his glasses had now cycled over into a shifting saver/wallpaper mode, displaying what appeared to be a bright and perhaps mildly psychedelic stereogram—but one which, when viewed with parallel-eye technique, turned out to actually represent a 3-D-ified loop of Roger's favorite clip from his favorite old movie, the gypsy girls fight scene out of *From Russia With Love*. Though that period of history was over before he was born, Roger was an ardent Cold War nostalgist who longed for the grandeur of empires and the spy versus spy intrigue of those bygone days.

Yet not even that scene or the romanticized past it was part of could lift him from the mild depression that had settled on his spirit with that strange half-dream. Rather glumly he stared through the overlay scene on his glasses, out the window, into the blue-black of space beyond.

"Beautiful, isn't it?" said the young woman in the nearest lounge seat, apparently having noted his gaze. Roger had noticed her when they boarded: a tall, buxom woman with red-gold hair, dressed in a blue tunic and green tights.

"I suppose so," Roger replied. "If you like emptiness."

" 'The void, full of compassionate attention,' as Atsuko Cortland puts it," said the young woman, nodding enthusiastically, bright eyes flashing. " 'Like all times and places, if we could but see it.' "

Roger commanded his suit off, adjusted his eyeglasses on his nose rather pointedly, and peered more deeply through the shuttle viewport.

"That's not what I see, I'm afraid. Just an empty height, bright or dark depending on whether we're turned toward the sun or away, in the Earth's shadow or not. And hardly compassionate—hostile, rather. No matter what my dear mother says. Makes me thankful for the metal and polymer of these walls." He tapped a cabin strut. "Thin as they may be."

"Your mother?" the woman said, taken aback. "You're—?"

"Roger Cortland," he said, extending his hand. "And you are?"

"Marissa Correa," she replied, shaking the proffered hand. "I'm a postdoc, up from Earth on a full-year fellowship—the one named after your mother. I'm also going to be working in your lab."

"Ah," Roger said with a nod. "I thought your name sounded familiar. I must have signed some forms, I think. If I'm not mistaken, though, the Atsuko Cortland Fellowship is usually given in the humanities or social sciences. I don't quite see the connection to my research."

"They're not connected, exactly," Marissa said with a wry smile. "I got the fellowship because of an avocation of mine—an interest in utopian fiction. I'm sure you know that the Orbital Complex has the world's largest collection of utopian and dystopian materials—"

"No, I didn't," Roger said, thinking irritably that of course the Orbital Complex would have such a thing. He was not a particular fan of the social engineering the space habitat residents were attempting—his mother prominent among them. To his mind they were turning what should have been a straightforward scientific outpost into some kind of Fourierist theme park.

"Yes. First editions, manuscripts, notes to nineteenth- and twentieth-century texts. Micromedia and electrostorage of all sorts. A wonderful collection, from everything I've heard. But that's mainly a sideline, not my vocation. In real life my research has been in the biochemistry of aging, senescence. I don't know a whole lot yet about the mole rats you work with—except that they're unusually long-lived. I want to test the idea that, living in protected burrows the way they do, their lowered mortality has, over evolutionary time, tended to also cause an incidental retardation of the onset of senescence, even a lengthening of their telomeres as compared to other related Bathyergids."

"Good!" Roger said, genuinely enthusiastic, seeing for the first time the exotically beautiful grey-green of Marissa's eyes. "That sounds like the kind of rigorous scientific work I can appreciate. Now I know why I approved your stint in my lab."

"Thank you," she replied, perhaps a bit too quietly. Roger, though, was already back in the virtual space before his eyes, seeking out an article for his research.

• • •

So, MARISSA THOUGHT, THIS PASSENGER SHE'D SPOKEN TO, this handsome pale young man with a trim beard, dark hair, and very expensive Japanese suit—this was Roger Cortland. For someone who had accomplished so much, he was younger than she'd expected, mid- to late-twenties at most. Her lab supervisor, the son of an even more famous mother, the woman who had awarded her the fellowship that was now taking her to the space habitat. She desperately wanted to make the right impression—couldn't just let their conversation dangle off the way it had.

"Thin indeed, these walls—as you said," she went on, when she thought she had Roger's attention again. He grunted noncommittally, seeming to be only half-listening. "Whenever I was blowing soap bubbles, as a child, I used to wish and wish that I could blow a bubble big enough to enclose me, lift me off the ground and float me away in the summer sunlight, up and up, beyond winds, even beyond air, to some peaceful heavenly place." Marissa smiled and sighed wistfully. "Being in this bubble of spacecraft rising toward Orbital Park—it's my childhood dream come true."

The bearded young man said nothing to that. From her lounge seat Marissa wondered if she'd said too much. Had he heard her? Did she sound like a flake? If he was no longer in the mood for talking, was she making him feel trapped—from being in close proximity to a voluble fellow passenger?

Embarrassed, Marissa turned away, seeking solace in the wonderment she had been feeling at this flight up Earth's gravity well. For the crew and several of the more frequent commuters, this flight was, no doubt, ordinary and routine, but for Marissa it was described by neither of those words. For her the powerful g-forces of launch and the blood-draining, breathtaking surge skyward possessed an undeniable glamour. The globe suspended in the viewports now was something alive, motion-filled yet motionless, a still point inside a turning universe, a turning universe inside a still point, harmonious and *one*, the way a leaping cat, a living cell, and a smoothly toiling machine each and all are one, in the elegant union of their forms and functions.

From the high perspective of cislunar space Marissa saw that despite all the killing and dying and suffering that went on down there, the planet of her birth was manifestly built for life. In the viewport it shone brightly, a candle in heaven burning with a blue flame, a haloed orb of living fire and burning life aglow in a cathedral darkness vast beyond understanding.

She hoped that impression would stay with her always, but even in the moment of that hope Marissa saw the vision's magical newness beginning to fade into postcard-from-space mundaneness. She had to look away, afraid that familiarity would corrupt her initial, near-mystical appreciation of the wholeness and holiness of that world outside the window. What cynicism had so shortened the half-life of the awe-inspiring in her that she could take even this sight for granted if she looked on it for more than a few moments? She shook her head and tried not to dwell on it.

Glancing about the cabin, Marissa saw just across the aisle a woman of about her own age, with long lustrous black hair, dressed in the sort of sharply tailored charcoal-grey jumpsuit that Marissa had always admired but wasn't small or lean enough to look good in. She smiled, happy to catch the jump-suited woman's eye. If nothing else, she reflected, conversation could at least take her out of her own thoughts.

J HANA MENISKOS HAD BEEN TRYING TO READ WHEN THE conversation of two of her fellow passengers distracted her.

"Marissa Correa," said a grey-eyed young woman, extending her hand toward Jhana once she'd caught her eye. Caught was the word, all right: Jhana felt transfixed by the penetrating, almost manic brightness of the other woman's eyes, the absolute attention behind them. She shook the proffered hand and introduced herself.

"So," the grey-eyed woman continued, "what takes you to Orbital Park?"

"The 'ozone-safe' single-stage shuttle," Jhana deadpanned. Marissa laughed lightly.

"I mean, what business?"

"I'm going to be studying rates of speciation in isolation at the Orbital Biodiversity Preserve," Jhana said, using the Orbital Park's official (and, for her, always preferred) designation. 'Park' was such a nebulous word, and when it was used in reference to the Orbital Complex one never knew whether the user meant the parklike confines of the Preserve, or the industrial-park manufacturing areas of the Complex. "I'm interested in determining adequate gene pool sizes for controlling genetic drift in various species. Yourself?"

"Oh, nothing so scientific—officially." The ever-intent Ms. Correa then told Jhana about her interest in utopian literature— at some length.

"Really?" Jhana commented when Marissa had finished her spiel on her fellowship work. "I'm surprised I've never heard of the collection before."

"Yes, well, it's still in private hands," Marissa said, glancing down at no place in particular, "and usually open only to residents and specialists, I'm afraid. The founders of the Complex own it, in trust for the entire facility. They're very interested in ideas and speculations about creating better, more humane societies. I understand they've begun implementing some of these concepts in the culture they're developing, making great progress too—"

The bearded and bespectacled young man Ms. Correa had been talking to earlier snorted and looked out through his virtual overlays at them. Ms. Correa glanced at him.

"You disagree, Mr. Cortland?"

"One person's utopia is another person's hell," Cortland said brusquely as he turned back to his work. "All utopias are inherently authoritarian, precisely to the degree that they are under conscious human control."

"That might still be open to debate," Ms. Correa replied as pleasantly as could be, before returning her attention to Jhana.

"This must be quite an opportunity for you," Jhana remarked, trying to compensate for Mr. Cortland's bluntness. "A chance to see some of the ideals of utopianism being tested experimentally in an actual community."

"Yes. What more could I ask?" Marissa said with an awkward smile, glancing down briefly before continuing. "Just listen to me! Here I am telling you everything about myself and my work and I haven't even asked you what university you're with!"

"I'm not with a university," Jhana said politely. "I work for Tao-Ponto."

Mr. Cortland—he of the meticulously trimmed beard and less meticulous manners—suddenly became more interested in the conversation.

"You're with Tao-Ponto AG?" he asked.

"That's right. I'm in the biologicals division."

"You're a geneticist?"

Jhana shook her head.

"Population ecology's my specialty, actually. But I sometimes work with the genetics of population, as on this trip."

Mr. Cortland nodded and, drawing a holographically embossed business chip from his vest pocket, stood up carefully (gravity being what it wasn't) and leaned across Marissa to present it to Jhana.

"Roger Cortland," said the pale young man in the expensive suit. "You must come see us at our lab sometime—very soon."

Jhana took Cortland's chipcard. Ms. Correa seemed struck by a sudden flash of inspiration and, pulling a notescreen and electro-pen from her pocket, quickly jotted notes that the little machine dutifully converted to readable typeface. Jhana wondered what she was scribbling, but at that moment the image and voice of a woman—the shuttle commander—came up on the overhead monitors, informing passengers that they were approaching their rendezvous with the Orbital Complex.

M ARISSA KNEW THAT HER NOTESCREEN WAS DINOSAUR technology by most standards, but she had never liked implants or even wearable cyberspace—they made her feel too much like a peripheral attached to a vast machine, and she got enough of that on the job. She stared at the scribble-made italic type of her notes.

> *UTOPIA—akin to K's Absolute Paradox?*
> *—eternal coming into time?*
> *—testable in time?*
> *—testable by humans?*
> ****Is Utopia something for us to test—*
> *or something by which we are tested?****

What an odd idea, Marissa thought. Almost as quickly as the inspiration came, it seemed to fade. She sat puzzling a moment, her hand on her chin. Sighing, she put the notescreen aside and got up. With the odd, shuffling/floating gait of someone unaccustomed to the fractional gravity of a rotating spacecraft, she walked forward, following Roger and Jhana toward the main lounge, to view the shuttle's approach to the orbital habitat. Behind her, the notescreen, shining in shades of grey on the arm of her seat, began to drift slowly from its resting place. Remembering the little machine, Marissa turned and rescued it, pinning it beneath a seat restraint.

"Be it ever so humble: the Orbital Complex," Roger was saying, playing tour guide, as she arrived in the main lounge.

"Our home away from home," Marissa declared excitedly. Jhana sniffed slightly.

"It looks no place like home, as far as I can tell," she said.

"Still, it's permanent home to what—four thousand people?" Marissa argued. "It must have something going for it."

"Its geometry isn't nearly as straightforward as Earth's," Jhana said.

"Planetary chauvinist," Roger commented with a laugh, but Jhana was serious.

"Just look at it, the shape of it," Jhana pointed out, her esthetic sense much offended. "Like an antique ribbed transformer that swallowed a crystal ball and then was run through by a pole along its long axis."

"Ugly maybe, but it works," Roger said, slipping back into tour guide mode. "At the ends of that long 'pole' are some important functions. Clustered satellite communication arrays. Docking. Transport and industrial facilities."

Marissa recognized a fair amount of the detail as it hove into view—particularly the large solar energy panels which, from the shuttle's angle of approach, looked like a macroengineer's dream of windmills. Girding the middle of the entire structure was a Ferris wheel of swiveled mirrors incorporated into a larger, darker ring.

"Even if it does apparently work," Jhana said, pointing toward the Orbital Complex's middle, "that looks altogether a Rube Goldberg contraption. What's its function?"

"To let the good rays in and keep the bad rays out," Roger

responded confidently. "The mirrors are for gathering and focusing visible light. The dark ring provides shielding against solar flares and heavy primary nuclei."

"And that?" Jhana asked, trying to stump Roger, directing his attention to an X-shaped object—small but enlarging and unfolding—that swept by their shuttle at surprisingly close range.

"I can't really say," Roger replied, puzzled. "Probably some new powersat prototype."

Marissa, however, was keeping her eyes on the big picture. As the shuttle moved closer to docking—along reflecting sightlines near the "poles" of the ball—she could see into the Park enclosed by the central sphere, could see the blue of waters, the green of grasslands and forests, even the brown of tilled soil in the greenhouse tori to the "north" and "south" of the central sphere. On still closer approach she began to realize as well just how big the central sphere (let alone the whole Complex) really was: almost as if someone had taken a county from Earth and blown it into the interior of one of the big soap bubbles she'd wished for as a child.

A S THE SHUTTLE MOVED INTO FINAL DOCKING POSITION Jhana saw other craft already docked or in the process: floaters, mass-driver barges and liners, transatmospheric orbiters and tetherships—some national, but many bearing the corporate logos of the companies that had joined the High Orbital Manufacturing Enterprise, the consortium of nations and transnationals footing the bill for the continuing construction of zero-gee industrial parks, greenhouse tori, and the human communities and biodiversity preserves inside their High Orbital Manufactured Environments—HOMEs, of which the Orbital Complex was the first but would not long be the only one.

Oh, Jhana knew the broken-rhythm hype, all right. *Home, home on Lagrange / Where vanishing creatures still play / Where seldom is seen an unprofitable dream / And the sats beam clean power all day....* She should know it: her employer, Tao-Ponto Aktiengesellschaft, was a major member of the consortium, and among the craft hovering about the space colony now she recognized TPAG's streamlined glyph-heraldics emblazoned across the tailfin of a tethership.

From her rather skimpy training in preparation for this flight she knew a little about tetherships too—essentially high-altitude jets, as she recalled, with oddly angled attachments that enabled them to latch onto a skyhook dangled from a satellite platform, metal fish taking metal bait. She was glad the company tether had been all booked up, though. Even if the tetherships and mass-driver liners were cheaper and more efficient and less polluting, they were also, to Jhana's mind, far less exciting than the old rocket-tailed shuttles.

They had to return briefly to strap down in their seats for the final moments of the flight, but disembarking began almost the moment the shuttle was securely docked. As Jhana gathered her luggage, she bade Marissa Correa farewell and they assured each other they'd no doubt meet again soon. She also agreed to meet Dr. Cortland at his lab as soon as she got settled in—and before a week had passed.

TWO

WHEN SEIJI YAMAGUCHI HAD COME OUT TO LAKSHMI Ngubo's low-gravity residence among the industrial tori, he had presented her with an odd storage and retrieval request. Yamaguchi had brought with him the personal effects of his deceased brother, Jiro. Among a lot of legal records, sentimental junk, and odd debris—all of which Seiji clearly could not bear to throw away—there had also been three top-of-the-line LogiBoxes, each containing stacked arrays of microsupercomputers, massively parallel processed—and each worth high six-figure debt in the major world currency of one's choice.

"The Boxes were with Jiro when they found his body," Seiji said. "Since his death was ruled an accident, the Balaam police made only perfunctory efforts at hacking into them. You and your friends can talk to machines better than anyone else I know, Laksh. See if you can't get into them and find out if they might have something to do with why my brother died the way he did."

As a favor to her friend, Lakshmi had agreed to warehouse the physical effects and to try to hack into the LogiBoxes. To be truthful, though, her motivation in regard to the black columnar Boxes was not fully altruistic: she hoped she might be able to hack into them, transfer out all the information relevant to Seiji's brother, then keep the Boxes for her own use. They would be quite a prize.

But things hadn't turned out that way. A week ago she and Lev Korchnoi had powered the boxes up and hooked them into the habitat's network coordinating system, the Variform Autonomous Joint Reasoning Activity. Lakshmi's own creation, the HOME, had adopted it for coordinating all the machine intelligence activities associated with the functioning of the habitat. The coordinating system talked with everything, from the big expert AIs to the micromachines, the nanotech assemblers and mechanorganic cellular automata. But now she couldn't run *it*—or at least a part of it.

Slumping in her hoverchair, amid all its robot arms and actuators, she pondered. In the bright metal of an arm she saw herself reflected, a dark-skinned woman with wavy black hair, fortyish, her wasted body covered in the loose, flowing, earth-toned clothing that was her personal style.

I'm really not up to this sort of puzzle-solving, she thought. But she had no choice. Somehow she'd caused the problem. It was her responsibility to work on solving it.

The foreign system running on the Boxes had taken three days to go through some long, elaborate boot-up procedure. Lakshmi thought that was odd enough in itself—even wondered for a while if in fact the entire Box system might be trapped in some sort of infinite loop—but she decided to let it run and see if it straightened itself out. It had, with a vengeance. At the end of the long boot-up, Lakshmi discovered that the system-construct running in the Boxes had established links with her net coordinator at all scales. Every time she tried to hack into whatever it was that was running on the Boxes, she was confronted and confounded by a seemingly nonsensical blocking message: LAW WHERE PROHIBITED BY VOID.

Otherwise, the construct running on the Boxes hadn't done much—though what it had done was more than enough. Now it seemed fairly quiescent, content merely to identify itself with the habitat's coordinating system, sending heavily encrypted data-bursts back and forth along the laser connectors. That would probably have disturbed no one—except Lakshmi. She had designed the net coordinator as a sort of metapersonality.

The habitat's many systems and subsystems nominally functioned as semiautonomous psychoid processes within the superpsyche of the coordinator. Whatever was running on the Boxes should be *submitting* to the coordinating system—not identifying with it.

Her reverie was rudely interrupted when several of her workshop's robotic arms—down to milli- and micro-waldoes— began to swing into motion of their own accord. Lakshmi watched in startlement as the arms began reaching into and grabbing up items from the clutter throughout her workshop, but particularly out of the pile of Jiro Yamaguchi's personal effects, as if searching for something. This was too weird, she thought. She needed to talk to somebody about it, and fast.

Lev Korchnoi—he had helped her hook up the Boxes. Maybe he would have some explanation. Lakshmi called up the habitat's Public Sphere, the "marketplace of ideas" virtual construct where Lev spent a lot of his time, particularly in the "anti-Platonics" group area, pontificating and soapboxing to all who might be interested about how rigid specialization was what made Plato's Republic fascistic at base, how that was what led him to banish the polymorphous poets, how the city-state of this habitat must be the inverse of that, strongly anti-specialist, if it hoped to preserve its participatory democracy, etc., etc., blahdeblahdeblah.

WELCOME TO THE PUBLIC SPHERE, said a portal caption as Lakshmi popped up into the center of that virtual locale. The greeting was immediately followed by a quote from the philosopher Rorty: "A peaceful public sphere characterized by conversation is a utopian idea, but it's the best utopian idea we've got." For Lakshmi, it was calming, comforting just to be back in this virtual space—so familiar, functioning so smoothly. Knowing too some of the flaming discussions that had occurred in the Sphere, Lakshmi had to smirk at the "peaceful conversation" of that Rorty quote.

She scanned the virtual sphere around her. Every "speaker" or "auditor" was, from his or her perspective, always standing at the center, while the personas of everyone else logged in floated through the virtual space roundabout—a sphere with center everywhere, circumference nowhere. Lev wasn't currently logged in, but his personal system was on and monitoring. Lakshmi called up his persona-icon.

Transcript of L. Korchnoi statement, 10:04-10:10 GMT, 6.6.29.

No, you've got it backwards. What is counted as true is that which tends to perpetuate the reigning political power structure. Truth is politically constrained. The metaphysical is the political. Scientific materialism was developed by the middle and managerial classes as an ideological weapon for use against the tyranny of church and landed aristocracy. Think of all the great inventions and discoveries not as sudden bright ideas or revelations alone, but also as high points in a million-year-old revolutionary process, ideological weapons developed in the ongoing struggle against many forms of perceived tyranny. Think of the discovery of fire as a blow—

Typical Lev. Lakshmi had heard variants of this agitprop shtick more times than she cared to remember. She called up his personal number and sent him a message stating that she wanted to talk to him. He sent back, telling her to switch to holophone, which she did.

"Hey, Laksh," said the albino-blond man in the viewer. "How's the work coming on my skysign of soft advertisement? Hmm? The big Mob Cad show's sooner than we think, you know."

"Working on it, working on it. Look, Lev, something's come up with those LogiBoxes we brought on-line last week."

She told him about the way the system-construct on the Boxes was preventing her from hacking into their operations, about the way whatever was running on the Boxes was identifying and intermixing with the net coordinator.

"Is that all?" Lev said, nonplused. "You should be happy—at least it's working. That's more than I can say for my show robots. Even their bugs have bugs!"

"But there's more to it than that," Lakshmi pressed. "Just now several of my waldoes started doing things on their own.

It's like they're trying to do some kind of project. Other things, too, over the last several days . . .''

"What things?"

"Well," Lakshmi began, knowing she was into it now. "Over the last seventy-two hours there's been an increased rate of malfunction and 'defection' among some of the nano-tech assemblers and other mechanorganics, for instance.''

"Minor glitches," Lev said in his flat American English, rubbing his square jaw.

"Then what about the appearance of those little X-shaped things drifting down the gravity well?" Lakshmi wanted to know. "You've heard about them?"

"Pieces of space junk, that's all."

"But they're coming from the vicinity of the Orbital Complex."

"So? Laksh, relax. You're just being paranoid, seeing patterns that aren't really there."

"I hope you're right," she said with a small sigh, "but I have this gut feeling—"

"What? Feminine intuition, now?"

"Call it what you like. I think these isolated glitch events are somehow related to the construct that Seiji's brother Jiro left in the LogiBoxes.''

"Aw, come on, Laksh! That's the most paranoid—excuse me, *intuitive*—idea yet. You're making connections where there aren't any."

"Thank you for being so sympathetic, Lev."

"Okay, sorry, sorry. Look, why don't we get together in a couple days and see if we can't figure out some way to make Jiro's Boxes behave? Okay? Maybe I could come out there, or maybe you could come down here and help me work out some of the bugs in my shobots, first.''

"Maybe. We'll see."

"Keep in touch, all right?" Lev said.

Lakshmi said goodbye mechanically. Severing the connection, she wondered how long she'd stay peeved at Lev for his obtuseness.

•   •   •

CORTLAND HAD CERTAINLY SEEMED IN A HURRY ABOUT something, Jhana thought in passing as, picking up a free locator from an automated information booth, she programmed it with the address of the residence she was seeking. Maybe, though, that was just the way Cortland interacted with people.

Floating along the fractional gravity "smartpath" indicated by her locator, she finally stepped onto the slidewalk that carried the new arrivals toward the transport tubes. As she waited on the transport platform, the locator advised her that something called Ridge Cart 17 was due to arrive in four minutes.

"Excuse me," she said to a stranger who—judging by the ease with which he played the flooring against the low gravity—appeared to be a local. "I hate to sound stupid, but what's a 'ridge cart'?"

The Asian man with the bushy black Mennonite-style beard laughed.

"It's 'cartridge' spelled dyslexically, sort of. Local humor. The tube transport carriages are very stripped down and fast— like riding inside a bullet. Also, if the direction of gravity is 'down,' then the tubes, since they're at the lowest gravity, are the most 'up.' The tubes are 'on top of the ridge,' as it were, hence 'ridge cart.' "

"Oh. Okay. But I *can* take number seventeen to this address?" She showed the black-bearded man the address flashing in her locator.

"Sure. No problem. Just follow your locator's directions."

"Thanks," Jhana said doubtfully. No matter how good the technology of maps might get, she figured she'd still manage to find ways to get lost.

In the minute or so before Ridge Cart 17 arrived, she gazed around her, through the glass walls of the tube station and into the industrial facilities. It was a heavily automated realm, with very few people in view. She couldn't quite make out what all the machines were doing, but she knew that some of their activity must involve microgravity production of metals and ceramics for the solar power satellite network—the biggest project underway here, from all that she'd heard.

Despite its metal-bending connotations the manufacturing zone was ghostly quiet. Whatever noise there might have been was completely drowned out at that moment by the abrupt arrival of a bodysuited, face-painted youth at the other end of the platform, a wild child drum-pummeling the guardrail and singing along to his stereo implants, chanting the same lyrics over and over like a happy lunatic: *Between what is and what ought to be lies the Ecstasy of Catastrophe! The Ecstasy of Catastrophe!*

This was beginning to get on Jhana's nerves a bit when, fortunately, the ridge cart arrived, rising up out of the floor with a sigh of air into vacuum. Jhana, the painted boy, and the Asian man with the Mennonite beard all strode quickly into the cart's Spartan interior, which promptly resealed itself and dropped down into the evacuated tunnel of the tube. In seconds they were zipping through an airless space, propelled by invisible magnetic fields.

Inside the compartment the bearded Asian man sat quietly with his eyes closed, and even the painted youth had lowered his volume and varied his tune, now sharply whispering the words of a turn-of-the-century politirap classic even Jhana recognized:

> *Sitting in a hot tub staring at the stars,*
> *It's easy to imagine vacationing on Mars.*
> *Sitting in the south 'hood waiting for a bus,*
> *It's hard to imagine more than Them and Us.*
> *More than Them and Us, more than Them and Us.*
> *If you can't trust Them and Us, who can you trust?*

At least—she thought thankfully—he can carry a tune.

The ridge cart rose up to floor level and the doors popped open, revealing new passengers about to board. Behind them the living colors of crop-filled greenhouses curved away through the bright glare of mirror-bounced sunlight. The boy with the painted face tapped a pair of small disks above his ears, causing them to extrude a pair of bug-eye sunshades over his eyes. With dancing/floating steps he exited the bulletcart, distractedly chanting, *Surface tension is my dimension, my dimension is surface tension!* as he flowed around the entering passengers, or as they flowed around him—it was hard to tell which, for the young man's antics apparently didn't seem odd or out of place to anyone but Jhana.

In seconds she and her fellow passengers were moving swiftly and silently through the tube again, bound for the central sphere, the heart of the space colony habitat. The ridge cart popped to the surface, the doors opened, Jhana stepped out onto the platform, and . . .

Vertigo. She stood inside a glass-walled observation sphere in midair, hundreds and hundreds of feet from the nearest ''ground,'' but of course the ground was crazy too, for she was in the center of a rotating glass bubble within the center of a much larger bubble that she knew was also rotating (but didn't appear to be)—and when she looked up there were buildings and gardens and streams and ponds and forests and savannas growing on either bank of a sun-flecked river that hung above her like the Milky Way at night, yet this dayworld did not fall from the confused firmament but instead wrapped all the way around to right-side up and still inside out, houses and forests, boulders and grasslands, trees and the river wrapping all the way around like a snake swallowing its own tail without beginning or end and the contrived wilderness swallowing buildings in every direction and the glass latitude ahead shining with a light like the sun and children playing free-fall soccer and young people pedaling diaphanous—winged airbikes like creatures from a vision in a dreamworld—a dreamworld turned hysterical spherical mandala which she was trapped in the center of, inside a sphere of angels or demons the beating of whose wings roared in her ears, pulse pounding, hard sweating, white spittle, while in her head things unmoored, popped out of joint, detached from any known framework of the real—

What am I doing here? she thought faintly, severely disoriented. *What is this place—Subway? Metro? Mall? Airport concourse?*

Try to look around without falling into the sky. A folded note fluttered to the ground from her pocket. She bent quickly to pick it up, trying not to look wherever ''down'' might be.

DIAMOND THUNDERBOLT, read one line. WORTHWHILE PROJECTS said another. The circumstance of the note-taking flashed into Jhana's head as clearly as if her boss, the eminent Balance Tien-Jones, were standing in the hanging vastness with her.

"Certainly after what you've been through this year you deserve some sabbatical time away from the company," Dr. Tien-Jones says with a slight nod, taking off his glasses and polishing them scrupulously. "But while you're doing research at the space habitat we expect you nonetheless to serve as a sort of unofficial observer for Tao-Ponto. . . ."

Look around, not down. Everybody with shopping bags and briefcases and baggage, refugees all, men and women permanently in transition, endless clangor of voices—

"As you know," Tien-Jones continues, leaning forward over his desk and staring at her with myopic directness, "our firm has a considerable investment in the Orbital Complex. Though the homesteaders up there have been allowed a good deal of freedom, we do prefer to see the habitat operating in accordance with sound corporate principles. . . ."

Around her always, everywhere, the unfathomable echoing depths of angelic public address systems speaking in a language she almost knows, announcing closeout sales or departing/arriving trains or jet flights or something—

"Over the last two days we've begun to hear rumors of something called Diamond Thunderbolt," Dr. Tien-Jones says squinting at his upheld glasses one last time. "No one seems to know exactly what it is, but it might well cause some stresses, shall we say, in the relationship between Earth and the colonists. From that name—and from a certain trideo game that's started to appear on Earth over the last day or so—the scenarists in our military products division believe that Diamond Thunderbolt may be some sort of space-borne weapons project intended to allow the settlers to break away from Earthly control. . . ."

She can't tell which is now and which remembered, which blatant and which latent, as the words cascade over her, distorting and echoplexing toward the demonic, taking with them on fallen angel wings little pieces of her acceptable mask of sanity—

"I hope that is not the case," says her boss, sighing and putting his glasses back on his nose. "All the companies involved have been so careful not to give anyone here on Earth cause for offense. Consider how thoroughly we've worked out the multiethnic composition of the settlement community—

trying our best not to leave any major group feeling left out. And certainly we don't want anyone down here to feel threatened by anyone up there. . . ."

She feels herself becoming less a person than a place being traveled through by all these travelers—

"Everyone who has applied for permanent residency in the space habitat has been carefully screened and tested for their dedication to nonviolent methods of conflict resolution," the bespectacled Tien-Jones says, leaning back in his chair, staring at the star-tiled ceiling of his office suite as if it weren't there, as if his executive X-ray vision were seeing clear to the space habitat turning in cislunar space, even through and beyond that. "The High Orbital Manufacturing Enterprise has not done this out of any love it might feel for idealists but rather as a precaution against precisely the sort of military adventurism now being bruited about. To maximize production efficiency and keep down administrative costs, we've been screening for bright, dedicated, peaceful, hard-working types. . . ."

She is sore afraid these travelers might see her naked face, feel the ticking time-bomb pressure in her head—

"That bunch of Gandhians and Quakers and Buddhists and Peace Churchers and psiXtians up there," Mr. Tien-Jones says, smiling and waving a dismissive hand toward her, "they should be the last people in the world or off it to be building some sort of secret weapon. Look into it, though, won't you? 'Perfect paranoia is perfect awareness,' as the old saying goes."

Her head is about to go off in a skull-splitting mind-shattering brain-scattering blood-fountaining display right on the esplanade avenue concourse platform—

"Oh, and Ms. Meniskos," Tien-Jones says without looking up from his large marble-topped desk, "if, while you're there, you come across any worthwhile projects of particular interest to Tao-Ponto, be sure at your earliest convenience to inform me of them directly. I've provided an encryption keycode so you can contact me quickly over a secured channel, if necessary."

All those around her, what will they think of her explosion? Will they be horrified? Will they applaud?

''Hey,'' said the man with the Mennonite-style beard, coming up beside her where she stood, white-knuckled grip on the railing, breathing hard. He waved his hand before her eyes. ''Are you okay? You don't look so good.''

She focused on him, trying not to see the mandala world beyond, trying to control her breathing, her pulse, bring everything back under control. Slowly the self that had exploded out of her head and seemed to fill the whole bubble of space around her began to filter back into her skull. She nodded mutely. A moment more and she turned away from him, staring fixedly at her hands upon the railing.

''Anxiety attack,'' she said quickly, her back to him. ''The height, the low gravity, the culture shock from all—this, I guess. Training didn't quite prepare me for it. I'm okay now.''

The man with the Mennonite beard nodded sympathetically.

''I remember my first days up here. Sensory overload. If it starts getting to you again and you need someone to talk you through it, don't hesitate to give me a call. Name's Seiji Yamaguchi. I'm listed.''

''I will.''

Taking Jhana at her word—even though she had yet to look up from her hands on the rail—Seiji Yamaguchi turned and went on his way. She was thinking, thinking that it was more than sensory overload or vertigo or an anxiety attack that had done this to her. She smelled burnt almonds in the air—a scent she had read was characteristic of cyanide, but which she had known personally only once before: almond cookies burning in the oven on the terrible night that her lover Mike died.

No, it was more even than that, more than just some olfactory trigger that had done this to her.

It was memory.

AFTER DISEMBARKING FROM THE SHUTTLE, ROGER HAD briefly watched his new postdoc, Marissa, wandering about confused, then offered to show her down to his lab, where she too would soon be working—at least some of the time, anyway.

Roger and Marissa took the low road to the research station in the desert biome. The subsurface maglevs tended to be less crowded than the ridge-cart tubes and were just as fast to the lab, even if neither were private enough for Roger's taste—especially now, when he was still wound tight from the uncertainty of the way things had gone on Earth.

Behind him a girl with a shaved head and painted face was whispering the chant of some Möbius Cadúceus pop tune playing on her implants. Glancing over his shoulder, Cortland saw that the girl, her eyes masked in wraparound VR shades, was also playing some sort of portable trideo game—VAJRA presents BUILDING THE RUINS!—in which (as nearly as he could tell from his furtive glances) nightmare fighters and assorted waves of chaos dove at a cybernetic City of God, a heliarc-bright Heavenly Kingdom that even Roger had to admit was beautiful, in a fractally complex sort of way. The girl, thoroughly caught up in her game and her music, paid Roger and Marissa no heed and just kept playing and chanting. Roger caught the refrain—*All my depth is on the surface, all the surface is in my depths! Surface tension is my dimension, my dimension is surface tension!*—before he turned away, shaking his head, mercifully able to screen it out, drop the lead shutters of his mind and bring up the internal security monitors to play on the backs of his closed eyelids.

Marissa seemed tired too, certainly not as loquacious as on the flight up the gravity well, so Roger remained in his shutdown quasi-meditative state until the car arrived at their stop. Exiting with Marissa in tow and in impolitic haste, he made his way automatically up the ramp, then along another level to the entrance of the Desert Biome Research Station, beneath the Preserve.

By the time they reached his lab, Roger had threaded them through a considerable maze of passageways and corridors. That was only appropriate, he thought, given the complex burrowing of the creatures he studied—and the increasingly labyrinthine character of his own research.

The retinoscope scanned his eyes and let him in, and together they programmed the security system to accept Marissa's retina scan too. As this was a Sun Day—the only day of the week that all three HOME zones overlapped on a similar daylight schedule—they could expect to have the place to themselves.

Once the sensors clicked on the lights, they saw there in front of them the subjects of Roger's research. Inside the main chamber, between the thick glass panes, naked (or at least very nearly hairless) grey-pink things squirmed and writhed and slept, or ran from chamber to surface along the tunnels they had excavated, or in groups dug still more tunnels.

"They're so ugly they're cute!" Marissa exclaimed, watching this bustling slice of underground life. "It reminds me of ant farms I saw as a kid."

"They're the mammal with a social structure most like the eusocial insects," Roger explained, nodding, pleased with her response.

"Except for their size and those big yellow incisors," Marissa commented, walking around to the other side of the glass enclosure for a better angle, "they could almost pass for newborn mice—blind and naked. Or, maybe, newborn humans!"

Roger walked around to where she was standing.

"You'd be surprised how many altricial characteristics they share with humans," he said. "You know what they remind me of? Newborn mutant sausages!"

Marissa laughed. The grey-pink mole rats were indeed sausage-colored, and about the size and shape of uncooked links—only these links had legs and eyes and teeth and a brief comma of tail.

"What got you interested in them?"

"The best laid plans of mice and men," Roger muttered, then cleared his throat. "Seems to me they present ways to solve so many of our problems as a species—not just another weak half-measure like this utopian space colony up here. I've gambled a lot on these critters. Even returned here, because the project seemed so perfect."

"Perfect?" Marissa asked, a bit confused by Roger's elliptical way of speaking. "How?"

"Perfect for providing a real and ultimate solution," Roger went on, glancing thoughtfully at his creatures, making sure that they had not suffered during his absence on Earth. "A solution that will take conscious decision-making right out of the picture. An organic social construct—not authoritarian because not conscious."

"But a solution for what?" Marissa asked, trying to keep

the exasperation out of her voice as she too watched the eso-
teric creatures going about their lives behind glass, seemingly
unaware of any human presence.

"The answer to overpopulation, of course," Roger said,
"and with it an answer to habitat destruction and mass extinction, loss of biodiversity, resource depletion, the whole
bundle."

"That's a lot of answers."

"Yes, but I'm sure they'll provide it all. Naked mole rats,
Ethiopian sand puppies. NMRs, ESPs, as I like to call them."
He crouched down, looking directly into the mole-rat colony's
main chamber. "They're misnamed, you know. They're not
rats, they're not moles, and they're not really naked. *Heterocephalus glaber*. Smooth other-headed ones. Hairless, differ-
ent-headed creatures. The perfect gene source for creating
transgenic, less problematic humans."

"Transgenic?" Marissa asked, at least as fascinated as she
was repulsed by the idea.

"Human genetic stock engineered to produce people capable of surviving fossorially," Roger said, still carefully observing his charges. "Without free water, without technology.
Lower metabolic rates, slower growth rates, the ability to self-
regulate population, everything. 'Sandmen' as a survival hedge
against global heating and ecodisaster. Or even creatures capable of surviving the rigors of life on a distant planet."

"These things can provide genes for all that?"

"And more," Roger said, nodding and smiling. "Naked
mole rats are native to the desert country of the African Horn,
lands that regularly experience surface temperatures as high as
any on Earth. Yet the extensive communal burrows of mole-
rat colonies always remain within a few comfortable degrees
of their own optimum body temperature. Their environmental
and behavioral control of temperature is so good they've
evolved away from warm-bloodedness. As close to ecto-
thermic as a mammal gets. Their burrowing activities even
foster the spread of the geophytes they subsist on—a nice feedback loop—and their population is self-regulating."

"But a lot of that sounds behavioral—" Marissa ventured,
cautiously, not wanting to offend her new supervisor.

"True, true," Roger admitted, "but struck off a genetic

template. If you want straight genetics, well then, their genes contain code for hemoglobin with an extremely high affinity for oxygen—an evolutionary response to living in sealed burrows heavy with carbon dioxide, but one that also might be handy for Diggers living on a world in the process of being terraformed—like Mars, say.''

Reaching up and swiveling in a hovering magnifier, he began pointing to attributes of the little creatures as he spoke of them.

"In the desert, you see, their lack of tear ducts and sweat glands, combined with the moist underground-tuber diet they subsist on—that has pretty much eliminated their need for free water. Their lack of body hair facilitates rapid heat transfer with their burrow microclimate. Their short conical digging claws, their tendency to form collaborative digging chains—all these adaptations make them perfectly suited to existence in a harsh environment that's challenging even for humans with the best tools.''

"Why study them here, though?'' Marissa asked. "Why not in the field, on Earth?''

"Because,'' Roger said sourly, "during the past fifty years, white Western scientific interest and black African population growth have come together in a bad synergy, destroying mole-rat habitat to the point that they only survive in captivity now—the largest colonies being those here in Orbital Park's high desert. A colony inside a colony, an oasis inside an oasis in the desert of space. But everything that was true of *Heterocephalus glaber* on Earth—no sweat, no tears, no overheating or overeating or overpopulating fears—''

"Like Adam and Eve before the Fall!'' Marissa said, struck suddenly by the resemblance.

"Yes,'' Roger agreed, "all of that's still true of them here. That's why, finally, as much as I dislike 'living at HOME with Mother,' I had to return here. No place else where I can study them in adequate depth.''

"Do you actually live with her?'' Marissa asked. "With Atsuko Cortland, I mean?''

"No, no.'' Roger laughed. "I have my own place. It's hardly all bad being up here. I mean, I have access to some great toys.''

"Such as?"

Roger glanced around, as if to make sure no one was listening.

"I've got Cybergene machines to play with," he said impishly, flashing a bright smile as he saw Marissa's eyes light up.

"You're kidding!"

"Not at all. Follow me."

They walked out of the lab and down a short hallway to a door labeled Computer-Aided Molecular Design (CAMD) and placarded with aggressive No Admittance—Authorized Personnel Only signs. Roger led her inside.

"Here it is," he said, turning on the virtual-reality simulators, then locating two pairs of trideo display wraparounds and force-feedback gloves. "Prime MIME—Military Industrial Medical Entertainment."

"How's that?" Marissa asked as she slipped on the gloves and the wraparounds.

"It's all here," Roger said happily. "The military-derived simulation space—operable even by joystick if you want, like the ghost of a long-lost fighter jet. Computer algorithms originally designed to enable cruise missiles to find their targets—now devoted to recognizing molecular shapes. Industrial robotic arm programs, rewritten to describe the orientation and motion of molecules. Morphing programs originally designed for movie special effects but later used for everything from advertising to military and industrial design. Military, industrial, medical, entertainment."

Roger could sense Marissa's fascination as he called up examples, mostly prepackaged, and highly specialized computer graphics software for molecular designers and genetic engineers. Graphic representations of molecular structures—information from X-ray crystallography, nuclear magnetic resonance spectroscopy, scanning probe/scanning tunnel microscopy. Even the short interactive computer movie he had put together himself, to illustrate the dynamics of virus/chromosome interactions—using the most interesting time steps from the best simulations.

"I see it!" Marissa said excitedly. "Military industrial medical entertainment. It's like—the whole world system, all the pieces swapping back and forth so easily—''

''Of course,'' Roger said confidently, ''because they're all part of the same technorationalist consciousness, the same total system of meaning. A system that works—despite all the nay-sayers up here and their complaints about it.''

Watching Marissa pilot her way through a simulation, Roger felt good. He was in his element—and certainly not above playing the successful bachelor with the expensive toys, if that's what it took to impress this attractive coworker.

THREE

STILL DISORIENTED BUT FEELING SOMEWHAT BETTER, JHANA was secretly thankful that her local hosts were not there to meet her when she reached her temporary residence. Instead she found a note attached to the door:

Jhana:

Sorry we're not here to greet you—something has come up. But about 8:00 local time this evening we'll be having a little get-together at our place with some friends to celebrate the arrival at the lab of new visiting researchers like yourself. Purely informal. Hope this leaves you enough time to relax by yourself after the flight up from Earth.

> *Looking forward to meeting you personally,*
> *Sarah Sanchez, Arthur Fukuda*

P.S.: The door's unlocked but can be scoped to your retinal print if you want the house secured.

Taking down the note, Jhana opened the door and trudged inside. Somewhere in the living area behind her a wall screen came on, flaring with infotainment fodder from Earth. Dimly she realized the guest house must have been programmed to greet arrivals in this fashion—specifically herself, in this case, for the program that appeared in the bedroom as she walked in was in English.

"What?" said a whey-faced young sitcomedian with an exaggerated shrug and knowing smile. "You think 'cause it's the end of the 2020s everybody's got perfect vision?"

A laugh track dutifully cranked out a string of mixed chuckles and chortles from another place and time. Jhana dumped her luggage at the foot of the bed, recalling as she did that the 2020s line had quickly become the comic's personal trademark, the tag line of the decade, before it became just another outdated rerun. But if it was such a funny line, then why did the viewing audience have to be told it was funny? Or was everybody just supposed to keep laughing along, herd-style, because once upon a time anonymous people had been anonymously recorded in the act of laughing?

That was the spooky part: much of the "source laughter" on the tracks had been recorded fifty or sixty years ago, and many of those laughing were now dead, gone to ashes or worm's meat. When Jhana laughed along with the tracks, she was laughing with the dead in one big happy haunted human comedy. . . .

What a morbid thought! She must still be overwrought from the trip—she could tell, for though she was bone-tired she could not bring herself to lie back upon the bed and close her eyes.

"I'm not in the mood for comedy right now," she told the house, presuming it was smart. "Another channel. Something straightforward. Factual. Boring."

"—of Samosata," a female narrator's voice intoned from the wall screen, "or Edward Everett Hale's story 'The Brick Moon,' published in 1869. But thoughtful consideration of the colonization of space—as opposed to the colonizing of planetary surfaces—probably only began with the work of Konstantin Tsiolkowsky in the first years of the twentieth century, and the work of Robert Goddard and J.D. Bernal somewhat later. Throughout the war-torn middle of the century, only the image of the 'space station' lingered—and usually only in boys' books and science fiction. Even during the 1960s, the decade that saw humanity's first landing on the moon, the space colony idea was largely forgotten.

"Oddly enough, it was during the late 1970s that the space colony concept began to be given serious and practical consideration, at precisely the time when the American manned-space program seemed a spent force, exhausted by the successful moon-landing effort of the previous decade. That the concept of the 'humanization of space' could germinate and begin to grow even in such an inauspicious season was largely the work of one man, a Princeton physics professor named Gerard K. O'Neill—''

Great, Jhana thought, leaning back on her elbows on the bed. A documentary on the history of the space colony. Tourist propaganda. If that couldn't put her to sleep, nothing could.

During the "long, rocky road to realization of the colony" she found herself slipping in and out of troubled, restless, dream-filled sleep. From the screen, history played on.

"Through the economy-shattering militarizations and failed spaceborne defense proposals of the eighties the L-5 Society—''

Her lover Mike's shining hovercycle bent and twisted and smashed under the glittering sun, his blood on the asphalt all the way to the curb, dyeing all the world, all the sun blood-red, everything blood-red and dying . . .

"—end of the Cold War and—''

Shivering in the sun with the shock of guilt, responsibility, sorrow . . .

"—fall of the hypermilitarized superpowers to the status of praetorian guards shielding the planet's billion or so 'haves' from its four- and then five-billion 'have nots'—''

Christmas. After church Mike in his new Air Force uniform presents her with the ring, asks her to marry him. Damsel in distress at this request from knight in shining armor but Yes, she says yes . . .

"—the resource conflicts and redistribution wars at the century's end, often masked as ethnic or neotribal clashes—''

Mike, black and flashy and ambitious. Training to be a transatmospheric fighter pilot. His father dead years before in an Indo-Pak skirmish when Mike was ten. His parents' marriage remembered by him and rewritten by his mother as a state of perfect bliss with never an argument. A standard Jhana is expected to meet and match . . .

"—seeds of the new in the demise of the old. As early as 1990 the first man-made Biosphere was tested privately in Arizona, and a decade and a half later came the return to the moon, not by any nation, but in the form of the Space Studies Institute probe, Lunar Prospector—"

Always ministering to Mike. Are you enjoying the party, dear? Finding enough people to talk to? Wherever they went . . .

"—ecopoiesis in space, interrelations of biogeochemical cycles, mechanisms of biochemical adaptation, ecosystem stability—"

Sure, I can wait till you finish your graduate work, Jhana. But I think we should have at least three kids, don't you? And it's best for them that you leave work for at least a year when each one is born. . . .

"—the sustainability realignment with its emphasis on spaceborne solar power stations and the development of prototype nanotechnology replicators—"

Always Mike's satellite. The reflected glamour of the pilot's girl. Another pampered and polished decoration on the sleeve of his uniform. Barely conscious of her situation until she meets Rick, quiet blond student coworker, who knows of her engagement to the "flyboy," loves her in patient quiet defiance of it . . .

"—the 'break out' of investment capital into space after the turn of the century, particularly after the War Mite Disaster with its hundred and twenty-five million dead from escaped military nanotech—"

Last year of undergraduate studies, with Mike training far away, Rick close at hand. Seeing each other more, her feeling for Rick deepening despite her pledge to Pilot Mike. Love! Love. Love? Rick wants her to be who *she* wants to be, follow her own choices and career, but is that what she wants? He respects her more than true-knight-of-romance Mike does. But no. Despite Rick's corporate job success fresh out of school, he's bland, a pale shadow, not as flashy as Superpilot—must be lacking ambition. How can she respect a man who truly respects her . . . ?

"—to the banning of 'large-scale nanotech' from Earth's surface. Nonetheless the War Mite infestation, the Nanogeddon, spurred the nations and transnationals to the cooperative effort that has resulted in the creation of the High Orbital Manufacturing Enterprise—"

Jhana and Mike and Rick, a ballet of distance and time, not smooth but jerkily tugging, silent-movie spacewalk-awkward. That she loves Rick is proof of the incompleteness of her love for Mike. And the funding cuts coming too, the ones that will sack Mike out of the service, out of the work he's prepared for all his life . . .

"—deep recognition that 'Earth was too small a basket for the human race to keep all its eggs in' was all that was needed to overcome the so-called Westfahl objections. Construction on the first colony began within a century of Tsiolkowsky's inklings and imaginings—"

Mike's sudden backhand exploding across her face as he breaks into tears. How can you do this to me? I don't want the fucking ring back! We were perfect together! You're the only person I'll ever love! I can't live without you and now you tell me you don't want to live with *me*. Why are you doing this to me? Turning me into nothing—into shit! Throwing me over for some blond Aryan creep. That's it, isn't it? The old race thing. Good enough to defend this country but not good enough to marry one of its light-skinned daughters . . .

"—a cosmocentric theory of intrinsic values coupled with the triumphal march of human settlement on the new frontier—"

No no no she sobs from the floor, but he isn't listening, has already slammed the door. Almond cookies burning in the oven. She hears the hovercycle choke and roar away. Then, faintly the banshee screech of monster lift-truck airbrakes slamming down, the dull, hollow crunch of death's metal jaws clamping shut.

"No!" She sat bolt upright in bed.

"—living proof of the truth of the words of Robert Goddard: 'The dream of yesterday is the hope of today and the reality of tomorrow.' "

Jhana stared dumbly at the wall screen, at the ending credits of the program whose phrases had slipped and slithered, blind worms and confused snakes of language, through her half-dreamed memories. She rose from the bed and, still half asleep, began slinging her hangered garments onto hooks in the closet. A folded note fluttered to the floor from a pocket, the same note that had fluttered out earlier, like a living thing, some bird not wanting to be caged.

DIAMOND THUNDERBOLT. WORTHWHILE PROJECTS. Both were scribbled in her own hand, above an encryption keycode number: 105366.

Yessir, yessir, yessir, she thought. Heading for the shower now, remembering restless sleep and restless waking, her aching head spun with the difficulty of distinguishing dreams from memories, hopes from fears, reality from nightmare.

"HERE, LET ME TAKE ONE OF YOUR BAGS," ATSUKO Cortland said, closing her facsimile copy of Lewis Mumford's *The Story of Utopias*. Rising to grab a large bag and direct Marissa to her lodgings, Atsuko gazed at Marissa with a glance the younger woman could not interpret. "So you met my son."

"Yes! Met him—and now you! I've read all your books! And it's all happened so quickly! Amazing!"

"Oh, not really," Atsuko responded, striding quickly away into the greenery of the Archive grounds, where they had agreed to meet. "Even including visiting scholars and professionals, we're just a small town, population-wise. And I'm afraid I wasn't here just to meet you. I do help manage our archives."

Marissa nodded. She almost had to run to keep up with the swift pace her escort set through the thickets of bananas and lianas, ginger plants and bird of paradise flowers. She was more than willing to sweat a bit, though, having been so lucky as to meet one of the famed Founders so soon after arriving on the habitat.

"Tell me, what did Roger think of your research project?"

"He liked my side project with mole rats just fine," Marissa said, winded, "but he didn't much like the topic of my fellowship research. Said something about utopias being inherently authoritarian."

Atsuko smiled sadly and shook her head as they toiled up a small but surprisingly steep hill.

"He still can't get it out of his head that we're trying to create some sort of utopia here."

"You're not?"

"Most definitely not," Atsuko said thoughtfully. "We've looked at a lot of social engineering documents, certainly. But what we are is an experimental station in the fullest sense—an ongoing experiment on many levels."

Absently slipping the Mumford into her large shoulder bag, Atsuko sat down on the mooncrete bench they had come to at the top of the small hill.

"We make no claim to having any sort of 'whole' or 'final' truth. Personally, if you asked them, I think most people here would tell you they believe in the truth of incompleteness and the incompleteness of truth."

Marissa, glad of the chance to rest, sat down on the bench, too. Now that she had a moment to take Atsuko Cortland in, she saw that the older woman's long black hair was streaked with grey and white.

"But certainly there are some basic principles you follow here?"

"Of course," Atsuko replied. "Societies inevitably generate structures, more open or more restrictive as the case may be—but always something. On that spectrum of structures, though, we're on the opposite end from most utopian proposals and actual communes. From my research into the subject—and maybe from yours too, Ms. Correa—it seems clear that most so-called utopian communities have rigid social structures and highly restricted technologies. They're essentially monocultures, like wheat fields or cornfields or vineyards or orange groves—spaces of land planted entirely with a single crop.

"Our case here is just the opposite: we have looser social controls than most communities on Earth. We actively encourage each other to explore the new social potentials made possible by our developing technology and novel situation. Look around you. See all the different species? Over fifty thousand of them here inside the sphere, many endangered. Hear the birds, the insects? Take a deep breath. Smell the flowers, the green scent in the air? It's brave and it's new and it's a world, but it's not a brave new world.''

Marissa nodded quickly, reminded of how Atsuko's son, Roger, had described naked mole rats as not really naked or moles or rats. Maybe it was a family way of speaking. . . .

"All our strength and all our sweetness rolled up into one ball," the spry, greying woman said, standing and striding onward all too soon for Marissa's tired muscles. "We've taken for our biological model not the monoculture but the natural community—a thing of diversity, like a rain forest, or chaparral, or savanna, or desert. We have functioning examples of all of those biomes here." She reached into her shoulder bag and pulled out some fruit. "Would you like an apple, Ms. Correa?"

"Certainly," Marissa replied, gazing around at the lush greenery of the jungle landscape they were passing through on their way to her temporary residence. "Just so long as I have your assurance that this is not Eden—and you're not Eve."

Atsuko laughed lightly, a sound like distant wind chimes.

"Rest assured. Everything you see around you has been achieved by the sweat of our brows—and that's the only way it can be maintained. There have to be gardeners, even for a hanging garden in the sky."

She handed the apple to Marissa, who took it and ate it, juggling her luggage hand to hand as they walked.

"Adam and Eve, you know," Atsuko said as they went along. "Before the Fall they must have had the 'bliss of bees or wristwatch calculators,' as my friend Cyndi Easter once put it."

Marissa almost laughed. "I'm sure there are theologians who would disagree strongly with that idea," she said with a smile, trying to keep pace.

"Cyndi was a filmmaker," Atsuko said with a shrug. "Her daughter lives here now, but she's a ship designer."

"I don't quite follow how you come to that theological conclusion then—"

"Straightforwardly," Atsuko said, in the sort of mentorly tone Marissa knew all too well from graduate school. "In their prelapsarian condition, Adam and Eve were supposedly fully one with God, one with all the universe—and therefore could 'know' nothing in the way that fallen human beings like ourselves 'know' things."

Atsuko had stopped to look at a particularly beautiful flower blooming in a pathside garden—fortunately for Marissa, who was having trouble keeping up in more ways than one.

"I still don't quite get your meaning," she said, winded once more.

"The philosophers complexify it a bit," Atsuko said, setting a blessedly slower pace at last, "but it's a simple idea, really. To view something as an object of knowledge, to *know* it, is to see it as something distinct from oneself. Our 'first parents,' however, because they were fully one with divinity and all creation, could view nothing as separate from themselves and therefore could not *know* anything. Adam and Eve lacked the alienation inherent in the process of knowing—what philosophers call an epistemological space. Without that distance they could only *be*; they could never know. We are doomed to knowing, as well as being, so all our paradises can only be artificial."

"Including this one?"

"Especially this one."

Atsuko turned down the pebbled walk toward a garden apartment. Marissa realized with a start that they had reached their destination. The door to the small but well-appointed residence stood open, in anticipation of her arrival. She entered and, peering about, nodded approvingly. Returning to the door, she found Atsuko standing in the midst of a garden that seemed to combine the best of the English and Japanese landscape styles. Atsuko was watching the twitching, lingering flight of dragonflies there—wings like shivered jewels upon the wind, bodies like blue neon.

Marissa's gaze strayed beyond her mentor to the meadows and forests, the streams and houses rising beyond, up and up and around, above the thin wisps of cloud floating in the mirrored sunshine that filled the habitat sphere with a light like late morning on Earth. Occasionally she saw the glint and glimmer of wings high above—airbikes flashing in the sun. Hanging gardens, with dragonflies.

"Artificial or not," she said at last, her gaze returning to

Atsuko and the dragonflies hovering over the small pond in Marissa's' garden, "there's a beauty—a joy—to this oasis in space that can't be denied."

"True," Atsuko replied with a small nod. "But also an undeniable sorrow."

"How's that?"

Atsuko eyes swept her surroundings in a long, slow, melancholy arc.

"Oh, not so much in itself as in its implications. For there to be an oasis there has to be a desert. We find it easier to build expensive imitation Earths than to voluntarily limit our own selfishness on the world we come from."

For Marissa that word, *selfishness*, seemed haunted by the ghosts of other words left unspoken—more specific terms like "habitat destruction" and "extinction." Though Roger and his mother didn't seem to agree on the solution, Marissa sensed that at least they agreed on the problem. Before she could mention that to Atsuko, however, the older woman had shrugged her shoulders, seeming in that act to also throw off the depression that had settled upon her momentarily.

"But," Atsuko went on, "it's a truism that technological change always proceeds faster than cultural or spiritual change, I suppose."

"Ah, the spiritual!" Marissa exclaimed, her eyes lighting up. "I would most definitely like to talk about that!"

Atsuko smiled and waved her off.

"Another time, my dear Marissa. I really must be getting back to the main archives. Walk about and familiarize yourself with our home here. Oh, and you might want to read this," Atsuko added, reaching into her bag and pulling out the Mumford book. "Sorry it's marked up, but I lent it to Roger once—and he likes to keep up a running commentary in the margins."

"That's all right," Marissa said politely. "It'll be interesting to see what his responses to it were."

"Yes," Atsuko agreed, somewhat distractedly. "When we see each other again we'll have more to talk about. If you feel the need to lock your door for privacy, it's keyed to your retinal scan." She gestured toward the plants at one side of the walk and the small pond on the other. "Keeping up the garden, by the way, is your responsibility while you're staying here.''

''But I, er, I've done very little gardening,'' Marissa stammered, genuinely bewildered.

''There's an instructional program in the house memory. Certainly a young woman of learning can learn.''

Smiling enigmatically, Atsuko turned and walked away. Marissa went inside, thoughtful. Calling up the instruction program, she hoped, and very nearly prayed, that she would prove a quick study.

Excerpt from *Keeping the Green Fuse Lit: Gardening for a New World* (transcript).

Human civilization begins with agriculture, but horticulture is older than agriculture, older than civilization. Like cattle (which were first domesticated for ritual sacrifice, and only later raised for meat and milk and hides), plants too were kept for ritual and sacramental purposes long before they were grown as food crops. That has been the human pattern—from profound to profane, mysterious to mundane. Our relationship with plants has been typical of our relationship with the entire natural matrix out of which we sprang and of which we are still a part: first we feared our world, then we fought it into submission, then we took it for granted. Only lately have we learned that we must also foster it and nurture it. Nowhere have we learned this more powerfully than here. . . .

Marissa watched, intrigued. She wondered whether the supposed greater antiquity of horticulture than agriculture might be anthropologically incorrect but, she reflected wryly, Adam and Eve had been gardeners, not farmers, right?

''DAMMIT!'' LEV KORCHNOI CURSED AS A SWIVEL ARM on one of his show robots froze up in mid-arc. ''Another glitch!''

''What now?'' Aleister McBruce said telepresently. A lifelong denizen of the virtual deep, Aleister did just about everything telepresently. If Lev hadn't met him in person, hadn't seen his bald head and greying beard and fleshly bulk, he would have doubted there was really a person to meet.

"Something ate a chunk of my code," Lev said, having pulled down the relevant code-object for examination, "and shat out a bunch of garbage. A virus—a damn virus!"

"Temper, Lev dear, temper!" Aleister said with a chuckle. "Self-replicating software, if you please—'virus' is a pejorative term. Shoot me the garbage and I'll run it through an interpreter and see if anything pops out."

Lev shot the chunk of junk code to Aleister. Waiting, he felt the urge to twiddle his thumbs but, remembering he was wearing force-feedback gloves, thought better of it.

"Got something here," Aleister said at last.

"Let me see."

Aleister dutifully shot a 3-D thing like a spiral staircase to Lev's virtual overlays. Where it should have had stairs, however, it had keywords instead. TETRAGRAMMATON, Lev read. MEDUSA BLUE. WORLDGATE. APOTHEOSIS. UTEROTONIC. ENTHEOGEN. TRIMESTER. RATS. SEDONA. SKY HOLE. SCHIZOS. BALANCE. COMBINATION. ANGELS.

"What's that supposed to mean?" Lev asked, but at that moment the foreign construct fell apart—leaving behind what Lev suspected might be a reinstatement of the original code.

"Not to mean," Aleister said, laughing, "but to be, or not to be. It does, and then it was. A self-consuming artifact, like your—"

"Performance robots," Lev said, getting but not appreciating the joke. "Who do you think our little jokester is? I mean, the source code was all object-driven stuff taken from the net coordinator, the VAJRA. That's always clean. It was sent as quantized information packets, and QUIPS can't be virused like that."

"Ask Lakshmi," Aleister said with a shrug. "She's the VAJRA goddess. If you find any more of these self-replicating software forms, though, send them to me. I haven't run across this species before."

"If I'm unlucky enough to be plagued with them again,"

Lev said, "I'll be happy to let you play epidemiologist to your heart's content."

Aleister disappeared, leaving Lev to hope that Lakshmi would see fit to stop by soon and work this through with him.

FOUR

J HANA THOUGHT HER HOST FAMILY'S OWN HOUSE WAS one of the most comfortable-looking places she'd ever seen. Computer-redesigned for more efficient use of space, the Spanish villa-cum-courtyard overlooked levels of gardens punctuated by pocket meadows, small streams, and copses of trees.

As she jangled the antique doorbell, Jhana heard the sounds of twelve-tone classical music, Tibetan overtone singing, and many voices in spirited conversation. Sarah and Arthur answered the door together, a couple perhaps twenty years older than herself, smiling a bit uncomprehendingly at her. Once Jhana had identified herself, her hosts led her toward a sunny atrium living room, bombarding her with inquiries about and sympathy for her trip up the gravity well, while she complimented them profusely on the beauty of their home.

"Thanks," said Arthur Fukuda with an Aw shucks-t'weren't-nothin' shrug. "It's all just mooncrete, you know— luna-cotta tiles on the roof, the 'stucco' on the walls, the slabmix beneath this Corsican mint—everything."

Jhana looked down. She'd thought she smelled mint. She was standing on it.

"What an interesting idea," she exclaimed. "A living rug!"

"Yep," Arthur said proudly. "Photosynthetic floor cover, gene-engineered for resistance to foot traffic, and for thriving on lower light and water levels. It was my friend Seiji's idea. He's the local garden wizard.''

"The only thing the house really lacks," said Sarah Sanchez as they walked down a few steps into the main living area, "is wood. The trees we have here are a bit too young and valuable yet to be turned into lumber, and the tank-grown stuff never looks right to me. Another thing I miss from the old world."

"Hardships are a part of frontier life," Arthur said with a wry smile as he gestured for Jhana to be seated, a light scent of mint still hovering in the air from the crush of their footsteps. "Sarah and I have discussed it quite a bit. We gain and we lose."

"Do you miss anything?" Jhana asked him.

"Me? Oh, certainly." Fukuda ran a hand through his grey hair, then absently picked up a bottle of wine. "We're a rather small and isolated community as yet. For all their over-crowding and craziness, Earth's cities still have a certain loony energy I miss sometimes. Individually, the people up here are at least as intelligent and energetic as the best you'll find anywhere, but you have to have a certain critical mass for Earth's sort of urban energy. We don't."

He poured them a red wine made from grapes grown locally in the greenhouse tori.

"I miss a good mature wine now and then too," Arthur went on. "What we can't mine on the moon or grow in the greenhouses we have to ship up the well from Earth—and that's prohibitively expensive. Bulk luxury items like wines are absolutely last on the priority list."

"Everything's so new up here," Sarah explained, "including the vineyards and viticulture. All our wines are, alas, quite young yet."

"But they'll mature," Arthur said fervently, "like everything else."

Jhana sipped some of the wine, well aware that her hosts were watching for her reaction—even if they were politely gazing elsewhere, pretending disinterest.

"It seems fine to me," she said after a thoughtful pause—to her hosts' obvious relief. Perhaps the wine was a bit shy in terms of crispness, a bit too long-lingering on the palate, but it was certainly passable.

There was a lull in the conversation, during which Sarah stared past the guests partying in the courtyard, over the gardens and up the curve of the world to where the reflected sun was dimming, bringing night to the third of the habitat her home stood in.

"The sun sinking into the Pacific—I miss that," she said at last, over her wine, fading light glinting in her long dark hair, making in her wineglass a soft-edged ruby, slowly dimming, like the thermograph of a failing heart. "High orbit is a world of light, and in a world of light you can do a lot with mirrors—but not everything. Don't get me wrong: the engineers have done a good job. The promotional videos promised Hawaiian climate here, and since we used to live on the islands, I think we can say they've matched the climate pretty well. But they just can't match those Pacific sunsets."

From the large bowl-shaped lounger in which he'd taken a seat, Arthur nodded.

"The stars too, strangely enough," he said, swirling the wine in his glass meditatively. "I remember sleeping under the stars way out in the sticks one summer when I was kid and we were vacationing in Manitoba. The moon wasn't going to rise until late. When my eyes adjusted to the dark, I saw the sky was different that night. All the stars were golden; the Milky Way was a thick river of gold flowing across the heavens. Each star seemed bright and close and warm. Some of them were red-gold, some blue, and I swear, with some of them I wasn't seeing points but actual disks of light. "

Jhana looked up from studying the patterns of the Corsican mint growing on the floor.

"And you've never seen another sky like that? Not even up here?"

"Nope," Fukuda said, shaking his head slightly. "I've seen stars big and beautiful and colorful and clear—and in greater numbers than ever before, no doubt about that. But when falling stars shot through the sky that night in Manitoba, they weren't the usual pale streaks—they were great golden sword slashes. Some of them calved and split fire, and I could hear them popping and breaking and burning." He looked away, wistful. "Maybe I only *thought* I heard that—but I know I've never seen that gold again, any time or anywhere else. Maybe it was something in the Earth's atmosphere that night that made the stars shine golden. Maybe it was something in my eyes, or my memory, or my imagination—"

"Dear," Sarah interjected, "how many times have you already told that story in the Public Sphere? Come now, we don't want to monopolize our guest with stories of the 'old country.' Let's introduce her to the rest of the party, shall we?"

Arthur laughed, and they all stood. Walking through an archway, they came into the courtyard, where all the lively music and conversation had been coming from.

"Everyone!" Sarah Sanchez called as they made their way to the center of the darkling courtyard. Not everyone but at least five or ten heads turned toward her, away from the music and the food, and that was good enough for the party's hostess. "This is Jhana Meniskos, one of the visiting ecologists in Arthur's lab! She just arrived today, so let's make her feel at home!"

Scattered shouts of welcome and the thin patter of applause greeted this announcement. Shaking Jhana's hand, Arthur and Sarah took their leave, with apologies for having to return to the kitchen for more hors d'oeuvres. In the gardens beyond the courtyard, a maze of pathway lights came up slowly, followed by soft lights around the periphery of the courtyard itself. Jhana moved through the knots of people gathered around the food and drink tables.

"All drama is essentially family conflict," proclaimed a flush-faced young man—in doublet, hose, codpiece, cape, and multi-neoned hair—to a group of more or less interested listeners round a wine table. "Just depends on how broadly you define family—even up to the family of humanity, or the family of all living things. Now, if conflict is what arises in any situation that's less than perfect, well, we know no family situation's perfect, so conflict is unlimited, drama goes on and on—"

Her wineglass full, Jhana moved on. She'd met enough drama-jocks in high school and college to recognize the type. She had no interest in listening to the flamboyant artiste holding forth to his admirers. From her correspondence with her hosts, Jhana seemed to recall that Sarah was involved in the arts in some way. The drama-jock must be one of her friends.

Walking past musicians oblivious to everything save their performance, Jhana made her way toward tables laden with platters of goat cheese and crispbreads, canapes, sushi, and melon.

"The right mythologizes, the left explains," said a heavyset man, bald, bearded and bespectacled, to a lanky younger man in wraparound shades beside him. "How can you possibly expect to move people in a more progressive direction through myths or stories or performances, Lev? The idea that 'it's just a story' always prevents them from recognizing the link between the simulation and consensus reality. No connection, no critique. The medium distorts the message."

"Not necessarily!" replied tall, pale Mister Shades forcefully, around a mouthful of sushi. "Granted, the myth or story format is inherently conservative, self-satisfying, flattering the audience by affirming values they already hold. But self-consuming works exist too, dialectical works that purge the audience by scrutinizing and disturbing its values. The wall between myth and explanation isn't all that complete—to some degree, myths are explanations, explanations are myths. In Möbius Cadúceus's performances, we can create myths and stories that are self-satisfying in form but self-consuming in function, virus programs, as it were, telling the truth but telling it slant—"

Having placed on her plate samples of whatever looked most appetizing, Jhana drifted quickly away through the music. More of Sarah's friends, she presumed. The younger man smelled vaguely of machine lubricant. Artsy types, she thought, shaking her head. She'd never understand them.

Walking and eating, she moved out of the courtyard and down some steps toward the quiet of the gardens beyond. A man and woman, oblivious of her presence, flowed up the steps past her.

"—and two large solar panels, like wings," said the woman. "The mass driver between the panels has two long drive tubes extending out aft, beyond the panels. All completely automated. Because of the tug's shape I call my design The Swallowtail.''

"Sounds like the perfect vehicle for mining the asteroids," her companion said, nodding sagely yet enthusiastically.

"Or at least the Apollo Amors. I'm hoping the HOME consortium and the colony council will approve a test run of the prototype within the next few weeks.''

When the twosome had passed, Jhana at last had time to herself in the garden. As she strolled the mazelike paths, she heard frogs croaking, insects buzzing and chittering, various birds making their evening calls, dragonflies whirring softly, someone intermittently humming and whistling a short distance away. Farther off, the band was playing a worldbeat salsa mix, but she had to strain to hear it. The water of the stream and the leaves of the bushes and trees seemed to soak the music up like a green anechoic chamber.

Eschewing the benches she saw here and there along the path, she sat down at last on a large flat rock to finish off the canapes remaining on her plate. She could still see most of the garden around her fairly well, for though it was "night" in this sector of the colony, it wasn't nearly as dark as a clear moonless night on Earth. The ambient overflow of the reflected light shining on the "daylight" sectors made the light-level in the garden unusual, a bit brighter than a full-moon night, yet a bit darker than a long midsummer twilight she'd once seen, in the Sierras back on Earth. She found it a very pleasant and restful light, one that softened colors without reducing them to shades of grey.

Sitting there, Jhana felt her breathing slowing as she relaxed. In front of her in the thin liquid light stood flowers, tall pink blossoms and shorter yellow ones, a scent of wild onion and honey and musky perfume in the air. Becoming ever more fully aware of the world around her, she noticed the leaves, how intricate and subtle and complex they were in their myriad variations. Among them, insects sang their tiny chitin calliope songs, while a small stream chuckled stones slowly to sand. So wonderful—just to relax, in a place that did not demand guilt or forgiveness, success or failure.

"Beautiful," she said, her eyes half-closed.

"I like to see people appreciate my garden."

Jhana's eyes flew open and her head swiveled in the direction of the voice. Before her stood the man with the Mennonite beard, examining day lilies.

"Yours? I thought it was Arthur and Sarah's."

The man picked one of the blown lilies and slowly ate it.

"Oh, it's theirs, all right. They maintain it. But I designed the grounds. Turned the moon dirt into soil by adding natural nitrate sources, trace metals and minerals, the right mix of soil bacteria, fungi, nematodes, worms—you name it. Put in all the bulbs and perennials—or drew up the ground plans for Arthur and Sarah to do it, anyway. Designed and helped install the micro-irrigation system, and the water recycling lagoon—there, with the meandering stream and catchment ponds. I designed it freelance for my friends, but I still have a paternal interest of sorts."

The man stepped forward slowly, extending his hand. "Seiji Yamaguchi. I work in ecodesign and solar power utilization."

Jhana stood, brushing her clothes lightly.

"Jhana Meniskos," she said, not bothering to parade her specialist credentials. Yamaguchi frowned slightly, but Jhana, unable to determine any reason for that change in expression, went on. "Haven't we already met? On the ridge cart, earlier?"

"That's right," he said. "Are you feeling less anxious now?"

"I was, until you popped up and startled me."

Yamaguchi smiled, slightly abashed.

"Touché. Sorry to interrupt, but I was curious. When you said 'Beautiful,' I presumed you meant the garden."

"You presumed correctly."

"What about it struck you that way, particularly?"

"I don't know. Everything. The colors—" she said, pointing. Yamaguchi nodded. "And the smells."

Yamaguchi walked to the flowers she'd indicated.

"These pink ones are varieties of *Allium*, flowering onions," he said, plucking a few of the blown flower heads, almost in a sort of reflexive grooming action. "These yellow blossoms are *Oenothera missouriensis*, evening blooming Missouri primrose—sweet-scented."

"And the flower you were eating? A lily?"

"A day lily, actually. *Hemerocallis*. These scarlet and white ones over here are *Lilium*, Asiatic true lilies, a musky-scented variety."

"And that blue flower there?"

"*Platycodon*," Yamaguchi said, kneading soil in the palm of one hand, then brushing both hands off. "Japanese balloon flower. But what else did you find attractive in the design?"

"Something about the leaves," Jhana said, looking about her, almost feeling as if she were being quizzed by a benevolent, very enthusiastic teacher. "Different shapes, patterns. And the way all the plants go together, in levels, from the low-growing plants and bushes and flowers up to the bigger bushes and the fruit trees. The way it all blends, you can't tell where the gardener leaves off and nature begins."

Yamaguchi, smiling happily, bowed slightly.

"Thank you. You've just given me the finest compliment I could possibly hope for. That's exactly the aim of my design, that blend. The paradox of contrived naturalness—just like this whole habitat." Together they began to walk forward slowly. "You named the first two elements right off—color and scent, particularly the way the colors and scents play off against each other. The third item—the shapes of the leaves, the look and feel of them, the heights and shapes of the various plants, the way their levels interact visually—that I call texture. The poet Shiki describes it in an old haiku: 'Roses: / The flowers are easy to paint, / The leaves difficult.' In translation it loses the standard haiku form, but that captures the sense of it, the meaning. You've got a good eye, picking out the texture factor—much subtler than I was, in interrupting your appreciation of it. Again, my apologies."

"That's okay," Jhana said with a wan smile. "But if you feel the need to atone, you *could* do me a favor."

"Name it."

"Since you're the designer of this garden maze, maybe you would be so kind as to show me the quickest way back to the courtyard from here?"

"No problem. Follow me."

Jhana smiled politely as Seiji, who of course knew the garden layout quite well, led her unerringly through all its multihued, multiscented, multitextured complexity.

From another path she heard someone twanging an amplified reverb guitar and a woman's voice singing, *The global
Brain has gone insane and now seeks suicide to end its pain*—
to a jaunty Gilbert-and-Sullivanesque tune. The song had been
a morbid little hit in some avant-garde quarters a few years
back. In Seiji and Jhana's path, coming toward them, were
two men with maniacally bright eyes, dangling conversations
over an abyss only they seemed to appreciate.

"A day is a mushroom on the mycelium of time, maaaan—"

"Yeah! And the mycelium of time grows in the night soil
of eternity! I cog it."

" 'Eternity. It's as real as shit.' "

"So true, so true. The Huxter never wrote truer words."

Jhana stared questioningly at Seiji, who flashed an embarrassed grin and glanced down at his feet.

"A couple of our amateur mycologists, I'd guess. Some of
the coprophilic fungi in the waste degradation system possess,
um, hallucinogenic properties. They seem to have discovered
that."

"You mean they're eating magic mushrooms from around
the sewer lagoon?"

Seiji nodded. Jhana shook her head in disbelief.

"We have no controlled substances here," Seiji said with a
shrug. "Our only requirement is that anyone who plans on
partaking of any mind-altering substance be thoroughly informed as to the nature and effects of that substance—and that
he or she assumes full responsibility for usage, in no way
imposing that usage on other members of the community without their stated agreement. Informed consent, improved quality
of life, ordinary politeness—you'd be surprised how far
they've gone toward transforming substance abuse into a non-
problem here."

They started up a flight of steps leading to the opposite side
of the courtyard from which Jhana had descended to the gardens. She was aware of the musicians playing again, but they
were farther away and not nearly as loud as they had been
earlier.

"—ecocatastrophic overcrowding of Earth and the suffering
of all the billions we've left down there," said a black woman

to the listeners gathered around the paté de foie gras as Jhana
and Seiji came up to the table. Jhana wondered briefly if the
paté could be real, here in Textured Vegetable Protein land.
More likely it was paté de *faux* gras. "Ozone burnout, heat-
trap atmosphere, the Big Red Tide, cyclonic 'dissipative structures,' rising sea levels, increased police-state totalitarianism,
religious extremism—my sister's usual catalog of ecolapse and
doomed humanity. I told her I was only going to be up here
for a year and the year was almost up, but she kept coming at
me from all those thousands of miles away. So I shrugged and
told her, 'Hey, where do you get off thinking humanity is so
important? We're just another species, one that'll go extinct
like any other.' That shut her up."

"It usually does," Jhana muttered, remembering her own
conversations with Chicken Littlers of various stripes. But
Seiji, who seemed to know something of the situation, would
have none of it.

"Not a good answer, Ekwefi," he said, spreading the os-
tensible paté on a cracker as he sat down at the table. "Your
sister was right: as a species we face enormous problems that
must be dealt with—continually. Easy biologist's cynicism is
no answer at all."

The woman Ekwefi, still standing, gave him a condescend-
ing glance.

"Oh? And how would you have responded, O Wise Seij?
Hm?"

"First off," Seiji said, taking a bit more paté and filling a
glass with wine, "I would have agreed with her that too many
people and too much per capita consumption are indeed the
root problems. We can't do much without a curb on our
growth- and greed-rates as a species. Then I'd tell her that
we're trying to build enough artificial paradises up here so we
can eventually alleviate Earth's population burden somewhat
through emigration. Two more space habitats even larger than
this one are scheduled to open within the month—and they'll
be coming faster, now that we can use micromachine assemblers and replicators to make active surfaces."

He paused to take a sip of wine—quickly, continuing before
Ekwefi had a chance to jump in again.

"Someday there might even be enough space habitats to

absorb Earth's annual human population increase,'' Seiji said,
''if that increase slows enough. A bit further down the line,
Mars will be ecopoiesed and there'll be enough habitable area
in space so that we can begin actually reducing Earth's population, eventually to well below the one billion mark, where
it belongs. Once that has happened we can start the recondi-
tioning process, let the Motherworld start healing herself, re-
verting to whatever new natural state ol' Gaia can come up
with—''

Someone had brought over another bottle of wine from one
of the other tables and Seiji refilled his glass, barely pausing
in his discourse. Jhana had the distinct sense that he knew
Ekwefi well, and that they'd had this conversation before.

''—and during the whole restoration process we'll be rein-
troducing all the species currently being preserved live, or cry-
ogenically, or in the genome banks in the zoos and arks and
our own biodiversity park. Once Earth is at last restored, it'll
be a holiday world, a vacation planet where human beings are
primarily just tourists, grown children occasionally visiting
their mother.''

Ekwefi threw back her head and laughed.

''That's the rosiest scenario I've heard in a long time. You
know what my sister Denene would say to that? She'd say
databits and freeze-dried remnants do not a species make—the
animal and its context are fundamentally connected, and to
truly re-create an animal you have to re-create its entire environment—''

''And she'd be right,'' Seiji agreed quickly.

''She'd also say this place is a college campus in the sky
and we do too much ivory tower theorizing. She'd say we
have too much faith in technological progress. She'd start talking about how we're a rich and privileged elite in the ultimate
castle on the highest hill. She'd say all HOME's claims of
multiethnicity are bull. She'd sound off about Master Race in
Outer Space types fleeing to an orbital suburb of Earth City,
a lifeboat for the powerful, another technofascist nonsolution
to human problems—''

Ekwefi took a quick sip of wine, her index finger held up
to indicate that she still had more to say and did not want to
be interrupted.

"—and I don't know if maybe she doesn't have a point after all. I mean, doesn't it seem sort of odd that all of us up here who are so dedicated to peace and social justice and world-saving are at the same time so isolated from the world we're trying to change? A plot to wall off activists and dissidents and idealists in a big, isolated holding pen couldn't have done a better job of getting all of us up here! To the people living in the trashlands down there, an elitist paradise in space must look pretty hollow."

Ekwefi took a long pull on her wine. Frowning deeply, Seiji brushed crumbs from his pant leg while the people around him waited for a response, spectators at a conversational tennis match waiting for the serve to be returned. He put his wine-glass down and stared straight at Ekwefi with a frankness that made Jhana suspect they had once been intimate—and not so long ago.

"Ekwefi, your sister's still alive. Be glad of it. You know damn well I've seen the sacrifice zones outside the cities back on Earth, the areas you call the trashlands. I've seen the cities of people living in steaming mountains of rubbish and filth and debris, scavenging from womb to tomb in the garbage. I've seen them building their houses of trash, feeding off trash, finally becoming just more trash to be body-bagged and incinerated when they die. That was how my brother was lost. A refugee living in a smoldering wasteland. In an ancient abandoned refrigerator he'd hulled clean and rigged to lock from inside. Coming out only at night, rising in darkness from a white coffin, convinced he had already died or forgotten how to live. One of the living dead, a vampire, a very sallow, failed, shivering Christ."

A tension, a trapped feeling, began to envelop Jhana. Sensing it also in the body language of the other people within range of Seiji's voice, she wondered if they too were feeling as if the political had suddenly become personal, too personal, as if they'd accidentally walked in on someone else's very private and particular nightmare.

"You know I think about all of this a lot, Ekwefi," Seiji continued in a somewhat different tone. "About how stupid and abstract it seems, trying to save the world when I couldn't even save my own brother. But I have to, because I'm still alive. Up here we can't take our brothers and sisters for granted—not any of us. Up here we're absolutely interdependent. A shell in space can't afford to let people fall through the cracks, because it can't afford cracks to begin with. We must be the keepers of our garden, our brothers' and sisters' keepers, because it's the garden and our brothers and sisters that keep us alive. That's a feedback, a message even a hollow sphere in the sky can send back to Earth."

Someone coughed uneasily. Seiji grinned, swirling the wine in his nearly empty glass slowly, carefully, before making an awkward attempt at recovery.

"I must be drunk, to be going on so! Excuse me for getting so personal."

The tension dissipated and people eased away. Jhana lingered, for reasons she could not at that moment fathom. So too did Ekwefi.

"Sorry to have reminded you of your brother's death," Ekwefi said quietly.

"Sorry I dragged his corpse out. Again."

"I have to know, though," she said. "You're not some simple-minded gung-ho technological optimist. Do you truly think an artificial paradise can give people real hope?"

Seiji stopped his careful centrifuging of the lees of his wine and stared thoughtfully into an indeterminate distance.

"Yes. I have to. Humanity may be just another species, but it's mine, it's ours. I have to believe in the Future Perfect Imperative."

Ekwefi smiled and squeezed his hand, and in those actions Jhana thought she could read again a shared history that had ended and yet not ended.

"You told me that story, Seij. No language in the world has a future perfect imperative."

"Then we'll just—" he said, pausing to stand, "we'll just have to create a language that does."

Excusing himself, he crossed the courtyard and disappeared into the house, leaving Jhana and Ekwefi standing alone beside the table. As if at some unspoken signal, they both sat down. They exchanged introductions, then sat in silence while they nibbled the remains of what looked and tasted very much like the liver of a fat space-raised goose that had died for their dining pleasure. Even here in TVP land—where Jhana had heard that almost everyone was a vegetarian of one stripe or another—not everyone eschewed meat, apparently. Either that, or they'd developed the best substitutes for flesh and fowl she'd ever come across.

"I didn't mean to eavesdrop," Jhana said at last, her curiosity getting the better of her accustomed reserve, "but you mentioned a story that Mr. Yamaguchi told you. What was it about?"

Ekwefi Muwakil looked at her through fatigue-veiled eyes.

"Ask him yourself. He'll tell just about anybody just about anything about his life." Ekwefi smiled to herself, as if at some remembered mischief. "When we were all hot and heavy and involved, that extreme openness used to get on my nerves. Got me so angry once, I told him he suffered from flatness of affect, as the psychs call it."

"Does he?"

"What? Oh, no. He's probably one of the sanest people I ever met. Too sane. That's why his brother's madness and death still disturb him so much."

"Yes," Jhana said, nodding. She had sensed a very personal affinity, a sympatico feeling, for such grief in herself. "I picked up on that right away."

Ekwefi looked at her oddly, with a depth of penetration that was somehow almost mocking.

"Really? Are you disturbed too? Or are you like the rest of us—too disturbed to admit you're disturbed?"

Jhana shrugged her shoulders and raised the palms of her hands, gesturing Who can say? But there remained something, well, *disturbing* about Ekwefi's question, even after they'd said their goodbyes. It would not leave her head but instead resonated there like a struck tuning fork, until she felt increasingly tired, wrung out, and longed for sleep so deep no alarm could ring her from it.

FIVE

ROGER CORTLAND OPENED THE LAB DOOR ANGRILY AND entered. Marissa gave him a startled look, which he returned. He hadn't expected to find anyone in yet, least of all his newly arrived postdoc.

"Roger! You're up early!" she said. He noticed that she was dressed casually—no lab coat. Obviously she hadn't expected to see him at this hour. "My internal clock is all off from the trip up the well, so I thought I'd get to work. Did you hear back on your funding requests?"

Cortland groaned.

"Yeah. Just got the news. One mention of 'transgenic humans' seems to have practically sent them diving under the conference table. I'd heard there were a bunch of forward-thinking psiXtians among the directors. You'd think they, of all people, would understand—living in those solar-powered underground homes in the desert, walking around in hemp robes and rope sandals preaching 'light-livelihood' and 'minimal impact economy.' But I might as well have been talking to a bunch of medieval clerics."

"None of the Digger scenarios appealed to them?" she asked with concern, moving closer, checking temperatures on a telomerase reaction she was running.

"Diggers, Sandmen—it didn't matter what I called them. Settling new planetary surfaces was too blue-sky for them, apparently.'' Roger began to pace distractedly around the glass panes of the mole-rat colony. He shook his head savagely without breaking his pacing. "They didn't buy it. Acted like they doubted the results would really be human. And you know what was worse? The whole time I was on Earth I could almost hear them thinking, 'Why would we need to settle planet surfaces, anyway? His own mother and the rest— haven't they proven the space colony concept is workable? We have a lot invested in that already, don't we?' Damn but it's frustrating to be the offspring of somebody everyone *else* thinks is a genius!''

"Hey," Marissa said, putting her hands on the shoulders of this man who suddenly looked ready to kill or to cry. She began to massage the tensed up muscles between his shoulder blades. "Relax a little. Your face is clenched like a fist. Here.''

She took his head in her hands and with the tips of her fingers worked to smooth the furrows from his forehead and temples. Roger resisted her ministrations at first, then slowly yielded to them. He felt the tightly coiled spring in him unwinding a turn, two turns. Eyes closed, he stopped spinning on his thoughts and slowly calmed, becoming aware of his surroundings, the quiet hum of machinery, the scrabbling of mole-rat claws, the warmth of Marissa's fingers on his face, the scent of her perfume—all making him feel so relaxed, even drowsy.

The scent of her perfume . . .

"Of course!" He fairly leapt from beneath Marissa's fingers. "Why didn't I think of it before!"

Marissa stared at him, an obscure disappointment rising in her features as she slowly pushed back a dark-rooted red curl from her forehead.

"Think of what?"

"Pheromones! Your perfume made me think of it! There's a chemical key to mole-rat social organization, not just a physical or behavioral one—no matter what those who follow Faulkes's behavioral/physical explanation say!"

"Wonderful," Marissa commented, with evident sarcasm. But Roger Cortland was already off in the world of his head, calling up articles on *Heterocephalus glaber* via a soft keyboard on the arm of his lab coat.

• • •

"L EV, ARE YOU SURE THESE THINGS ARE SAFE?" LAKSHMI
asked hesitantly, staring up at the two machine assemblages towering toward the warehouselike ceiling of Industrial Torus 2.

"Absolutely—or they will be, at least," replied the lanky figure safety-belted into a cranny about a third of the way up the Scylla, as he called the particular mechanism he was working on. "I'd stake my life on it."

"You may just be doing that," Lakshmi said with a wry smile.

"Nonsense!" Korchnoi gave a small dismissive wave as he began to rappel gracefully down the side of the mechanism. "It'll be completely safe, once you've helped me work out some of the programming glitches. All just theatre, remember? Bells and whistles and special effects."

Lakshmi watched as the thin albino-blond man slipped out of his climber's harness and walked toward her with the fluid movements of a veteran dancer. The man undeniably had a certain style, a *sprezzatura* about him. Maybe too much.

"But the advance press release says these things"— Lakshmi gestured with her eyes toward the towering performance robots—"will be throwing missiles and bullets and bombs at you."

Korchnoi sighed as he plucked his work gloves from his fingers.

"I make it a point never to read my own hype," he said calmly, taking off a pair of wire-rimmed welder's specs and carefully cleaning them with the shining silk handkerchief that had appeared almost magically from the pocket of his stained and spattered work coveralls. "The PR is true, but only to a certain degree. Stage fireworks, remember? Yes, missiles and such will be firing—do you know what kind of hassle I had to go through to get permission for that?—but everything'll be soft-nosed and programmed to *miss* me, if we get rid of the glitches in time. As for the bombs, they'll only be smoke and carbon dioxide, maybe a hint of carbon dioxide and methane. Just machine flatulence."

The lanky man gave Lakshmi one of his shyly crooked

smiles then—the same winning smile she'd seen in all the media.

"Oh my," Lakshmi said, falling into mock-slavish adoration, "what a tremendous honor it is for little old me to be working with the eccentric and enigmatic Lev Korchnoi himself, the habitat's most renowned performance artist and robotheatre impresario, the mind behind Möbius Cadúceus—"

"All right, all right," he said, laughing. "Put a cork in it. How about that new skysign symbol you were going to develop for the band? Have you got anything yet?"

"I've got something, all right," Lakshmi said, nodding as she subvocalized commands to her hoverchair's holojector. Immediately a beautifully complex form sprang into the air before them, a thing of self-consuming rainbow serpents—and much more.

"Wow! This is great!" Lev said, totally enthralled by what he was looking at. "Möbius Cadúceus was just a clever name, a vague idea in my head, but this—this turns it into *something*. What is it?"

"You tell me," Lakshmi said evenly.

"It's like the two ancient snakes that intertwined themselves about the staff of Hermes or Asklepios," Lev replied, walking around the hovering, twisted halo of the thing, "but at the same time it suggests—I don't know, a model of the interlocked base-pairs of the DNA double helix. It's like a complex serpent-knot from the *Book of Kells*, or an illustration of the topology of three-space manifolds—both, and neither, *at the same time*."

Lev shook his head, trying to break the form's spell.

"It's hypnotic!"

"Yeah," Lakshmi deadpanned. "You might say that."

"What's it supposed to be?" Korchnoi asked.

"I don't know," Lakshmi said, pausing, deeply thoughtful. "It's sort of a Rorschach tesseract—it's what you make of it. Maybe it's an ancient pair of tail-swallowing Ouroboroi. Or a new symbol for the infinite recycling of universes, taken from a cosmology yet to be invented. Who can say?"

"Come on, Laksh, you can, can't you? I mean, you created it, right?"

"No, I did not."

"What?"

"I made some tentative steps, trying to combine the idea of
the Möbius strip and the medical symbol, the caduceus, but I
wasn't getting anywhere. I left it running and went to get some
coffee. When I came back, that thing had appeared in my
virtuality. Full-blown."

"How?"

"I'm not sure. Something came out of the net coordinator,
the VAJRA, and constructed it for me."

"You been feeding the brownies and the little people
lately?" Lev asked, giving her a quizzical look.

"Hardly. I tried tracing the intrusion back to its point of
origin. I think it came out of the LogiBoxes Seiji Yamaguchi
gave me—the ones his brother Jiro owned."

"Not that Jiro stuff again," Lev said, grimacing. "Okay,
okay. I can see this is all just an elaborate ruse to get me up
to your place to troubleshoot the installation job I wish I'd
never done on those damn Boxes. Look, help me debug some
of my robot programming first, and transfer this 'skysign of
unknown origin' into the big holojectors, then I'll get up to
your place as soon as I can, all right?"

Lev turned away then, muttering. Lakshmi smiled to herself.
Lev might grump about it, but at least he was knowledgeable
about machine intelligences, and could confirm or deny some
strange possibilities she was beginning to suspect.

J HANA WAS DISTURBED BY HER FIRST MEETING WITH HER
immediate supervisor in Fukuda's lab, a diminutive, can-
tankerous, white-haired senior scientist named Larkin, who eschewed lab coat and smock, preferring instead the politically
self-conscious prole-drag of denim workshirt and jeans.

"So Tao-Ponto's your tribe of cash-flow hunter-gatherers,
eh?" he said, staring quizzically at her as she followed him
through the Genetics Lab. "They still big into Tetragrammaton
and Medusa Blue?"

"I'm afraid I've never heard of that, sir," she replied, trying
to be polite.

"Yeah," he said, giving her an appraising look. "You are
pretty young. I don't suppose they'd want to talk about it to

their employees, either—black mark and all. A potential Worldgate—scandals and conspiracies always used to be called gates back then—but they covered it up good. Only place you could probably even find a reference to it would be in an old copy of *Covert Action Information Bulletin*, or some source like that. See, Tetragrammaton's the big long-range survival plan. A living fossil from the Cold War days, when the shadow governments—the CIAs and KGBs and Mossads and MI-5s—played such a big role in running the planet. Before they went to work for the big corporations. Your corporate hierarchies are even worse, you ask me. They were the ones let the black hole sun thing happen at Sedona.''

He stopped and sneezed. Jhana hadn't a clue as to what had set Larkin off on his diatribe—he was a biologist and cryonicist, after all, not a political scientist. Maybe he was some sort of obsolete politico? She tried to remember her history. Didn't the old Right fear Big Government, and the old Left fear Big Corporations? Larkin seemed to be paranoid about both.

"Been spending too much time in the coldboxes," he said, mopping at his nose with a frayed and faded handkerchief, then striding purposefully onward. "But I guess we shouldn't bite the hand that feeds us. It's only on the governments' and corporates' sufferance that we have our little cislunar Dreamland here to begin with. The Consortium keeps our biodiversity preservation projects funded—at least enough to get by— so I guess I shouldn't complain too loudly, now should I?''

The little biologist turned a corner, Jhana following close behind, despite Larkin's rapid pace.

"Good PR for the money and power types—'We prevent extinction. See how much we love Nature from the bottom line of our hearts?' Good business too. Never know when these Orbital gene reserves might provide something valuable: another potent Amazonian analgesic, spidersilk organic steel, transgene micromachines. Ah, the profit motive. Greed works, in a limited sort of way.''

Larkin asked her to step forward and look through a retinoscope peephole beside a door. Its scan completed, the door unlocked and opened automatically, revealing a tidy, empty cubicle beyond.

"Your workstation," Larkin said blandly. "Your access code for the genome library has already been authorized. The library database has genome maps for all endangered species preserved here, as well as subdirectories of sex-linked, maternal organelle-linked, and parentally imprinted genetic traits. You can interact with the system via keyboard and screen or through a virtual reality construct. If you have any questions, give me a call."

Larkin left the cubicle, closing the door behind him. Jhana sat down at her workstation, placing on her head a connection circlet, which resembled wraparound sunglasses. The tiny embedded jacks and electrodes of the computer's diadem whispered tingling pins and needles of static electricity across her skull. Adjusting her throat mike and dual viewscreens—one for each eye's field of vision—she popped in her personal virtuality construct based on the Martha Shrine in what was now the Cincinnati Ark.

When she was a little girl, her parents had taken her to the Cincinnati Zoo to see the monument to Martha, the last passenger pigeon. The bird had once lived there at the zoo, her every heartbeat tolling like a feathery bell until, on a morning when World War I raged far away, her keeper found her (and her species with her) dead at the bottom of her cage. Over ninety years later Jhana's parents had showed their precocious girl-child the monument the zookeepers had built to Martha's memory: a stone pagoda shrine, more appropriate to Nagasaki than to Cincinnati. It was there she'd first realized what extinction meant.

Now she pumped HOME's database through her own virtuality, her memorial to a memorial. As images and gene maps of frozen ghost species hovered before her in virtual space, she thought of other ghosts, true ghosts in that long-ago shrine. Out front had stood the life-sized statue of Martha, in bronze more lasting than life, and colder—too cold to thaw, a death from which there had as yet been no technological resurrection. Inside, on three walls of the shrine, she remembered displays depicting the extinction of the once unbelievably numerous passenger pigeons. The fourth wall had been covered with descriptions of extinctions ongoing throughout the world—a display out of date before it went up. All of that she had incorporated into her personal virtuality, her House of Extinctions.

Jhana's parents had been old enough to remember the times before the zoos became arks, old enough to remember when most of the animals caged in the zoos still roamed free somewhere in the world. During her parents' lifetimes, though, the zoos had increasingly become home to animals that existed only in captivity. More and more the zoological gardens became museums, stuffed-creature mausoleums, graveyard monuments to the Great Extinctions: Madagascar, Australasia, Amazonia, the great globe itself.

So many species' names were there, she realized as she looked at the lists in her virtuality. The living dead, the *in vitro* remnants, microforms haunting laboratories and gene banks. She tried to recall how long cryogenics facilities had been freezing germ plasm down to end-of-the-universe temperatures, tried to recall how many genome maps were stored in the infosphere's memory banks. She couldn't remember the exact numbers and dates but she knew that, in this Limbo roll call before her eyes, science's fantastic voyage was complete: life reduced to information, the leap of the gazelle on the veldt transformed to quanta-hopping circuit gaps.

The final judgment on the threatened and endangered species of Earth had stood suspended for decades now. Suspended *in*animation. Living death row. Theirs was a "virtual" reality as surely as this computer construct she looked into now. In one corner of the construct floated the Ark symbol of the Biodiversity Preserve—a creature-filled boat afloat on a sea of humanity. An odd symbol, she thought: the human flood keeps the Ark afloat, but isn't that same flood what makes the Ark necessary in the first place? And when that people-sea grows stormy, what then?

She tried not to think about that. She was just here to do her job, to find some way of preserving against genetic drift the genetic material of these tenuous species, while still allowing for change, diversity, evolution. In itself it would not be an easy task; add to it Mr. Tien-Jones's *sub rosa* requests, and her personal problems still in need of working out, and it would all make for a busy business-sabbatical indeed.

She might as well get going. Scanning through the virtual

space of the computer memorial hovering before her eyes, she pulled up the genome map of a likely candidate—an obscure organism by the name of *Heterocephalus glaber*—which, judging by the log-in list, someone had been giving considerable attention to even within the last twenty-four hours.

DESPITE BEING TIRED FROM THE WORK SHE HAD ALREADY done in Roger's lab, Marissa had made what she considered a breakthrough in her other researches, her fellowship research for Atsuko—and she had made it while grabbing a quick late-afternoon nap.

It had first occurred to her almost in the form of a dream in that time between sleep and waking—just before her earplug alarm went off. Somehow she had seen her imaginings of the characters in Huxley's novel *Island* falling onto the two pans of a balance, a set of scales—then not just the characters but entire worlds dropping onto that balance. One scale was the descriptive world, the world-as-it-is; the other was the normative world, the world-as-it-ought-to-be. The key to *Island*, she thought—and hopefully to hundreds of other utopian/dystopian texts—lay in a balancing, an almost ritualistic exchange, of what she thought of as "hostage" characters: people held hostage by the circumstances of their birth and upbringing in one or the other of those worlds. . . .

She was so caught up in her theorizing that she was completely unaware of the beauty of the early evening light around her as she walked toward the archives, planning to pad among the stacks in search of a copy of More's *Utopia*. Abruptly her thoughts were cut into by the persistent calling of a bird nearby. Turning, she saw not only a black and orange bird she could not identify but also a young couple, strangers sauntering hand in hand, and a group of men and women dressed in white, practicing what looked like tai chi or perhaps aikido.

Marissa smiled awkwardly to herself. Living in her head again. Here she was preoccupied with bookish utopias while this world lay before her, a world in which the inhabitants, her fellow inhabitants, were doing their best to realize the dream of a better, more humane society. *Be here now*, she thought, reminding herself of the old Buddhist admonition.

Always so hard to live in the moment—not in the past of memory or the future of expectation but just here, just now. Watching the young couple disappear from the Archive grounds, Marissa decided her analysis could be put on hold for a spell, given time to age and "season" while she tried to get back in touch with the rhythm of the life going on around her.

She strolled along the evening-damp grounds and sat down on a stone bench, thinking of quiet times like this on Earth, times she'd spent watching the moon in the afternoon, the ghost moon burned away by the harsh light of day. The melancholy of that remembered sight settled in her soul, making her pensive.

Images of her life back on Earth came to her, thoughts of course-loads and committee work and research and publications. She pondered her likely future, all the impedimenta of the hoped-for tenure-track job, of becoming the "ladder faculty member" trying to keep moving upward or at least not falling down any rungs of that all-important ladder. She'd thought about it many times already, until even academia—the only field she'd ever been able to tolerate, much less enjoy—began to seem to her what it had seemed to some of her professors: less a ladder than a vertical treadmill of constant turf-battling, grant-grubbing, conference-connecting, log-rolling, and string-pulling.

In her bleak times Marissa nearly lost her faith in the almost unconscious mysticism of her callings as student and teacher. The essential myths of academe failed her and she felt scarcely better off than the vast majority of Earth's men and women, hating her job and her situation until she felt the full enduring ache of the long illness called life, knew the pain of having a poet's heart trapped in a scholar's hide, the agony of a soul knotted and fastened to the dying animal of the body—morbid thoughts she was supposedly too young to have, but also thoughts that had somehow led her to study aging on the right hand and utopia on the left.

To hold onto Hope she'd have to let go of Fear. She knew that, intellectually, but the pain of being torn apart by the widening gap between those two worlds of "ought" and "is" was not lessened by such intellectual knowledge. So damnably difficult to let go, to make that leap from one to the other for herself.

Perhaps, she reflected, it was difficult for the whole world, too. Earth's people seemed overwhelmed by that gap between the worlds, paralyzed by it or turning their backs on it, turning their backs even on hopes like this space colony, as if muttering, Better the Hell we know than the Heaven we know not.

She could talk about research grants, think about possible jobs and possible promotions, argue her need for material available only in the Archives or Roger's lab, but those weren't her real reasons for being here. She was here because of a fervent hope that this world, this place, would be everything and more than she could have wished for.

She closed her eyes, trying not to think of anything, trying not to reflect on things but rather to let them reflect on her. She longed to become like still water reflecting the moon, a bubble of silvery mercury suspended between worlds, a mirror-mind floating on the surface of the past and the bottom of the future, a meniscus of Now, a liquid crescent moon—

Marissa shook her head. She had never been as good at meditation as she would have liked, no matter how hard she practiced. Images only got in her way, and even the idea of blanking her mind was always just another image. Opening her eyes, she stared around her at the splendid, colorful shining bubble she sat inside, and wondered. This world as it is— might it be the world as it ought to be?

Sighing, she opened her backpack and took out the Mumford text Atsuko Cortland had given her—the copy Roger had read and decorated with his marginalia. No time for the blues, Marissa decided. She had work to do. The fact that she would be reading Roger's private notes made the task more interesting, perhaps even made her heart beat a little faster. Certainly he was handsome and brilliant, in his own quirky way, but she was growing fonder of him than even those features would merit. She tried to tell herself that it was because they seemed to complement each other well: laserlike Roger with his sharp but narrow focus, and she, more like a flashlight, illuminating a broader range, a polymath, a Renaissance woman. . . .

• • •

ATSUKO CORTLAND WAS HOT. TOWELING OFF THE PER-
spiration she'd raised on her body during the aikido class,
she wondered for the hundredth time if these refresher courses
in civilian-based defense—required of all habitat citizens—
were really all that necessary. The NonViolent Direct Resistance (NVDR) program was, even down to the word suggested
by its acronym, based on the premise that someday the habitat
citizenry might have to face an "invader"—an eventuality
Atsuko considered highly unlikely.

In the colony council she had initially opposed the NVDR
program, fearing that the training might well bring on the invasion it was, hypothetically, supposed to resist. Even after it
was made clear to her that the sort of defense arts that were
to be taught would be thoroughly "local" and had no real
offensive component—that they were only a small part of a
much larger overall program intended not so much to directly
oppose invaders as to make it difficult for an occupying force
to maintain its hold on the colony—even after all that, she still
had qualms. Once the council reached a consensus in support
of NVDR, however—and it became as close to "law" as was
to be found up here—Atsuko had dutifully joined in the training. It was good exercise at the very least.

As she slipped back into her street clothes, the datasleeve
of her blouse began to ping softly, announcing an incoming
message. She took a quick look at herself in the dressing room
mirror, then swept out of the building beneath the Archive
playfields, still trying to determine whether she wanted to deal
with "the world" just yet. Finding herself in a fairly private
situation as she strode along over the fields, she decided to
take the message as she walked.

"Message recorded for Atsuko Cortland, from Global Trade
Authority," her PDA (personal data assistant) said quietly. Atsuko grimaced. She knew she should never have agreed to
accept the post of colony council liaison to the GTA—an organization which she always thought of privately as the Global
Trade Autocracy. Descendant of the GATTs and G7s and
WTOs of the last century, the international trade-coordinating
body had grown into quite the behemoth. She should have
known better than to liaise. She had, after all, formulated one
of the primary laws of political life in the habitat, the Principle

of Reciprocity: Those who accept the responsibility also must accept the power, and those who accept the power must also accept the responsibility. Serving as GTA liaison meant having more power and more responsibility than she really wanted just now.

"Abstract and condense it for me, please," she told the PDA, thinking once again of what her husband (ex and late) had told her—how that acronym had meant something quite a bit different when he was a teenager. She sighed inwardly for a moment, remembering a long-ago snatch of warm human contact, then returned to the present, thinking that any number of acronyms had meant different things at different times. CD had meant everything from certificate of deposit to compact disk to civil disobedience. Maybe it should also mean context-dependent.

While she was thinking, her PDA was busily working. For a pocket artificial intelligence it was fairly smart and soon had GTA's undoubtedly long bureaucratic text distilled to its most relevant points.

"How many key points?" Atsuko asked.

"Two."

"Give them to me one at a time," she said, not breaking her stride as she continued her usual post-aikido cool-down walk to her residence.

"First, the GTA is concerned about the unauthorized design, manufacture, and distribution of a trideo game called Building the Ruins," the PDA said levelly. "It is being made by a number of micromachine flash manufactories in several countries. GTA has traced the original design, manufacture, sales, and distribution structure to the orbital habitat, specifically to the Variform Autonomous Joint Reasoning Activity, the net coordinating intelligence. The individual trideo game units are capable of two-way communication with the habitat VAJRA. Said coordinating intelligence appears to send upgrades to the trideo software on a regular basis. GTA wishes to remind the colony council that the manufacture, sale, and distribution of this product violates numerous trade agreements. GTA demands that the High Orbital Manufacturing Enterprise cease and desist from further production of this item."

Atsuko frowned. This was strange news indeed. She'd have

to contact whoever was currently in charge of the habitat's net coordinator and get some background on this before she took it to the council.

"What's the other key point?" she asked the PDA.

"Second, the GTA requests information concerning the reasons for deployment of several small satellites of previously unknown description. These objects originate in the vicinity of the orbital habitat and are currently headed toward Earth orbit. The GTA wishes to remind the colony council that the orbital habitat has no contract or authorization for the production and deployment of these satellites. Their unauthorized deployment is a serious breach of international and interorbital law."

Atsuko walked in thoughtful silence for longer than she would have expected. The unauthorized trideos were bad enough, but these satellites or whatever they were—those could be a much more significant problem. She had lived on Earth long enough and learned enough history to know that there were many people down there—particularly those of a military bent—who considered space the ultimate high ground. Hadn't that been a big part of the motor that drove the first space race to the moon? These people would not do well with the prospect of unidentified satellites deploying to Earth orbit from the habitat. She needed to talk to someone in powersat production, and soon.

"Hope it's just the usual space junk," Atsuko said—aloud, but to herself. Looking around, she realized that she was already in her yard. Glancing up at the other side of the ensphered world of the habitat arcing far above her, she wondered with a shudder if the scenario underlying the NVDR program might not be so far-fetched after all.

"I STILL CAN'T FIGURE OUT EXACTLY HOW THOSE GLITCHES might have arisen in the net coordinator," Lakshmi said to Lev as they worked to transfer the Möbius Caddúceus skysign into the memory of a photorefractive holographic projector—one of Lev's most prized stage-pyrotechnic devices. "The keyword mention, though, particularly 'schizos', that has to have something to do with Jiro Yamaguchi's connection to all this."

"Whatever floats your boat," Lev said with a shrug, not

wanting to get into it. "At least we've got all the corrupted code out of my shobots. I'm sure Aleister's having a great time with it."

"Looks like the skysign's all loaded," Lakshmi said, checking a display screen and turning her hoverchair toward where Lev's special effects holojector would soon be projecting. "Set it free."

Lev spoke a machine command, sotto voce. The Möbius Cadúceus symbol leapt into the warehouse space before them, giant-sized, a rainbow redesigned by a mad topologist, a Rorschach skyscape.

"Oh yeah," Lev said, unable to take his eyes from it. Lakshmi remained silent, staring, the beautiful complexity of the thing forming a singularity from which her words could not escape.

SIX

"HERE AGAIN SO EARLY, MARISSA?" ROGER SAID, JOINING her in the Cybergene virtuality. "Already at work, too. You spend much more time here and we're going to start calling you The Girl with the DNA Eyes."

Marissa laughed. She was, after all, dealing with DNA, and when she had her virtual wraparounds on, anyone looking at her would see two images of that molecule where her eyes were supposed to be.

"I'd consider that an honorable title," Marissa said, shagging back her red hair. "You were right about this being a user-friendly toy. Got right into it. I'm dealing with the dynamics of reverse transcriptase and with a well-known location on Human Chromosome One, so there's a good deal of prepackaged graphics material available on those."

"What're you doing with them?" Roger asked in her implants. "I thought you were working on longevity's link to lowered mortality and delayed senescence in naked mole rats."

"I am, but I've broadened it beyond just mole rats," Marissa said, initiating a graphic sequence. "Here, I'll show you." She switched on the large-scale display and the two of them moved within it, interacting with the submicroscopic world.

"Let's move down into The Notch," she said, causing an area of chromosomal surface to grow into canyon around them. Via feedback, they "felt" their way among the forces acting on the molecular landscape through which they moved.

"There it is," she continued, "the part of Chromosome One where aging and death are. This is the genescape my viral vector will have to target and modify."

"What exactly are you trying to do?" Roger said, sounding genuinely curious.

"Well," Marissa began, taking a deep breath, wanting to impress Roger and hoping he wouldn't shoot her idea down from the start, "my research with your mole rats indicates it should be possible to design viral vectors to speed up the evolutionary pace of the immune system, supercharge its rate of reactivity. At the same time, it should also be possible to use reverse transcriptase's ability to translate viral RNA into host-cell DNA—as a means by which to vector into the genome the immortalizing capability from teratoma tumors. A noncarcinogenic telomere alteration. These immortalizing vectors can then be targeted at, among other places, Human Chromosome One—particularly at the gene series on that chromosome which programs senescence and allows death to occur."

Roger was silent a moment. Marissa hoped that merely meant he was thinking carefully about what she'd said.

"You want to take traits from the so-called immortalized cancer cells of teratocarcinomas and use them against aging?" he asked.

Marissa nodded mutely. Perhaps he felt her nod, but at any rate he went on.

"Well, I don't think you can overcome aging and death quite that easily," he said, "but it would be a step in that direction, certainly. Using engineered viral vectors to transfer the immortalizing trait from teratoma sources into the human genome—that's quite a novel approach. Potentially dangerous too, however, even if you do beat the cancer factor. If human longevity were to be greatly increased, but without any corresponding decrease in birth rate or the rate of survival to sexual maturity—just think how that would ratchet up the population problem! That's a consequence you might want to consider carefully."

Marissa smiled, for in Roger's voice she could hear that he

was indeed impressed—almost despite himself—and was taking her work quite seriously.

"I'm nowhere close to developing the vector yet," Marissa said. "Don't worry. I have no intention of unleashing an Immortality Plague upon humanity."

"I didn't think so," Roger said with a laugh. "My own work may be a little closer to fruition, though."

"Show me," Marissa said eagerly.

Roger promptly logged them out of Marissa's Cybergene graphics sequence and into his own. They moved along another chromosome, watched and felt it grow into canyonland around them, then stopped along a particular length of it. Roger quickly overlaid the site with all pertinent chemical information.

"What's here?" Marissa asked.

"A gene that gives rise to important receptor molecules in the vomeronasal nerve," Roger said proudly, "maybe even in the brain itself, of the naked mole rat. I've always believed that behavioral and physical controls are inadequate to account for the level of reproductive suppression in the mole rat. There must be a chemical component, a pheromone. The receptor molecules this gene leads to are exactly what the mole-rat pheromones would have to bind to. Using gene machines like this one, I'm generating thousands of hypotheticals—scenario-compounds—and testing them. Speeded-up mutation, as it were. With the receptor cloned or even just simulated, we can test those compounds quickly to select the appropriate active ones. Mutation and selection: all we basically need for directed artificial evolution."

Now it was Marissa's turn to be impressed. They clicked out of the virtuality, exited the CAMD facility, and headed for the main lab, busily exchanging insights into each other's work. They were still thus caught up when they walked into the lab.

"Good morning, Roger. Hello, Marissa."

They looked up to see Atsuko Cortland standing in the doorway of Roger's office.

"Hello, Mother," he said with a grimace. "What brings you to my lab?"

"Nothing in particular," Atsuko said, absently fingering the end of a thin braid that drifted from her flowing hair like a rope in a waterfall. "I heard you had returned from Earth. Not that you'd tell me yourself, of course." She paused, as if awaiting some response. Roger only clicked off the terminal he'd just turned on and stared at her. "I also heard your funding hunt didn't go so well."

"Hearing things is a sign of deteriorating mental health," Roger said, standing abruptly and walking stiffly past his mother. "You should really have that checked into, Mother."

"Ah, that's more like the Roger I know!" Atsuko Cortland said, walking out of the office, following Roger into the center of the lab. Her gaze lighted on the squirming naked mole rats in their glass-walled colony. "You're still working with these little grotesques, hm? Whatever do you see in them?"

Roger began to talk about self-regulating populations and feedback loops and the only mammal with insectoid eusocial organization—

"No, no," his mother interrupted. "I've heard all that. What is it, really? You've been obsessed with them for years. It's even less healthy than my 'hearing things.' "

Roger said nothing, merely fiddled with genome map graphics and pretended not to have heard.

"Oh, very well," Atsuko sighed. "Then at least you can tell me what direction your research is going to take, can't you? Now that you've lost most of your funding?"

"I haven't lost most of my funding," Roger said in exasperation, turning to monitor the output of an automatic nucleic acid synthesizer that hummed and clicked in an alcove. "I just didn't get the new funding I wanted. We're restructuring our researches."

"How?"

Roger summarized the gene/receptor molecule/pheromone binding scenario he'd just given Marissa.

"Seems like an awful lot of work," his mother remarked with a shrug when he was done, "just to find out what turns some obscure endangered sand rats on or off."

"It would be—if that were where I intended to stop," Roger said quickly, pride creeping into his voice once more. "But I don't. I have a strong suspicion that the pheromone active in mole rats will be a strong structural analog of one active in humans too.''

''Oh, I see what you're getting at!'' his mother said, turning her gaze from the rat burrow. ''You're going into the perfume business, just like your father did before he branched out.''

Roger glanced down at the floor of the lab.

''I hadn't thought of it in exactly those terms, but yes, I guess you could say that.''

''A word to the wise then, dear. Making sweet smells is a dirty business. Your mole-rat pheromone—where do you think it comes from?''

Marissa sensed that Roger already knew where she was headed but was going to answer anyway.

''Urine, scent secretions on the skin, fecal matter—''

''See?''

Roger shook his head in frustration.

''So? Ambergris is whale puke. Civet is cat stink—''

''My point precisely. A dirty business. Good luck, but try to keep your nose clean. So to speak.'' With a burst of her shattering wind chime laughter she breezed toward the exit door of the lab. ''Goodbye,'' she called as she left. ''See you later, Marissa.''

Roger stood cracking his knuckles nervously, until he realized he was doing so. Then he stopped. Somehow, Marissa felt sorry for both of them, wondering what it was that could ever have driven mother and son into such an antagonistic relationship.

ATSUKO CORTLAND KNEW SHE HADN'T BEEN AT HER BEST with Roger. She had really intended to console, not to taunt, but the moment they saw each other, that expression appeared on his face—as if he blamed her for everything that had ever gone less than perfectly in his life! It was maddening!

It wasn't as if she didn't have enough to worry about already—what with the illegal trideos and space junk satellites souring relations between the colony and Earth. She really didn't need Roger giving her further cause for alarm right now.

She needed some time to herself to think. Some time when she could be someone other than the respected and recognized

Atsuko Cortland, someone anonymous and seemingly new to life up here, someone through whose eyes she could look without having to pass everything through the distorting filter of Atsuko Cortland's reputation.

Following her own private admonition that she should have first-hand knowledge of all the workings of the space colony, she decided to try the Prince and the Pauper routine just this once, to see if people truly understood the sort of new world they were trying to build up here. Acting on that decision, she donned dark glasses and a sun hat and immediately set off to visit the agricultural production toroids, outside the main sphere.

The trip by bulletcart up to zero gravity was uneventful (even if she did always find zero-gee somewhat disconcerting), but the view back into the great sphere was stunning, as usual.

"*For the world is hollow—*" Atsuko thought as she tried to take in that view, remembering an old line from somewhere, "*—and I have touched the sky.*"

Turning, she entered a ridge cart that shot her along either transparent or mirrored tubing (depending on her location), eventually disgorging her into one of the doughnut-shaped tori which, stacked in twelve levels on each side of the sphere, constituted the space habitat's zones of primary agricultural production.

The plaza area she stepped into reminded Atsuko of nothing so much as the great glass and steel conservatories of the earth-bound botanical gardens she had visited as a child. The same green, humid, living smell permeated the air. The "conservatories" here, however, stretched and curved away in arcs the greenhouse workers of previous centuries could hardly have imagined, and outside their walls lay not just some inclement Northern winter but the cold airlessness of space itself.

"May I help you?" offered a thin woman of indeterminate age and dishwater blond hair, speaking in Slavically accented English. The slightly incongruous name of Lex was printed on the ID space of her dull-orange uniform coveralls.

"Er, yes," Atsuko began, slightly startled and trying to ground herself for the role she was supposed to play. "I'm recently arrived from Earth and trying to learn more about the space habitat. Do you provide tours of this area?"

"Nothing formal, no. But everyone who works out here is required to be familiar with the way the agricultural tori function—so I can show you around, if you'd like."

Atsuko brightened.

"Could you do that? I wouldn't want to take you away from anything important—"

"Don't worry," Lex said, setting aside a coil of thin irrigation tubing. "I can have someone look after my station for a while."

"Are you sure it's not too much trouble?"

"No trouble at all," the blond woman assured her, unclipping a small phone from her belt and speaking a few words into it before turning back to Atsuko. "Most everything here in food production is automated, anyway."

They walked from the plaza down a path toward where an electrical harvesting machine hummed and slashed through what looked like a wheat field. Atsuko introduced herself as Karen Ohnuki.

"Alexandra Petrunkevitch," said the young woman, shaking Atsuko's proffered hand. "Lex or Lexi to my friends."

"How do you like working here, Lexi?" Atsuko asked as they took a meandering path among a polycultured field of myriad plantings.

"About as much as everybody else, I guess. It's not my only job, you know. All permanent residents are required to do at least two months' agricultural production work out of the yearly cycle. Mostly machine tending and crop monitoring, but there's some H and K work too."

"H and K?"

"Hands and knees," Lex said, unfolding her hands and showing Atsuko the day's dirt and calluses. "I'm on a day-a-week plan in ag, though some people take their ag work all in a lump. By trade I'm a software engineer, so this is very much a change of pace. Hard, sweaty, sometimes dirty work—though not bad work, overall."

They walked beside the edge of an apple orchard interplanted with stands of various perennial grains.

"Young apple trees," Lex said, noting Atsuko's gaze, "but producing already, see? And these Rome trees were seedlings less than three years ago."

"That's fast, I take it?"

"Very," Lex said with an enthusiastic nod. "There are some real advantages to farming in space." She reached down and picked up a handful of dark, slightly damp-looking soil. "All our ground is shot up from the moon via mass driver, so it's quite sterile. What we add to that moon dirt to make it soil is a completely controlled process. No pest species here, no harmful microorganisms."

Lexi walked over to the trees, picked a ripe red apple for each of them, and brought them back.

"Since it's so expensive to ship anything in bulk up the well from Earth," she went on, "most of our plant material arrives in the form of seeds or clonal tissue cultures—all quarantined and scrupulously inspected. Pest control again. No messing with pesticides or fungicides or herbicides anywhere near the growing areas."

As they walked along, Atsuko's eyes strayed up through the transparent roofing to what looked like a great fluorescent light bar hanging in the sky.

"What about lighting?"

"Oh, that's all controllable too. We can control levels of light intensity, photoperiod, day/night cycles, you name it—just by using screens on the lightpaths."

"Lightpaths?" Atsuko asked, feigning ignorance. "Like the light bar above us? Is it some kind of new technology?"

The wiry woman in coveralls looked at her strangely.

"New technology? I don't think so. New use of an old idea, maybe. The purpose of lightpaths is to bring light into darkness. That's one thing we have a lot of out there—light. This habitat is in high circular orbit, above the Earth's radiation belts and below the moon, so eclipses are very infrequent. We have virtually unlimited sunlight. The lightpaths are paths of reflected sunlight. All the light in the agricultural tori is sunlight reflected from the mirrored surface of the space colony's central axis—what you're calling a light bar. The light inside the big central habitation sphere is reflected sunlight too, only instead of the lightpaths bouncing off the central axis they bounce off the mirrored surfaces around the sphere itself and come in through the light zones or glass latitudes near the 'poles' of the sphere."

Atsuko nodded, as if beginning to understand. A pungent odor assailed her nostrils. Onions?

"Yes, I read something about all this before," Atsuko said, "but I still don't quite understand. Excuse my weakness in science, or in visualizing this, but how can you let light in without letting in everything else the experts warn about— dangerous radiations like solar flares and heavy nuclei and cosmic rays?"

Ms. Petrunkevitch was at the moment stooping and looking at rice plants growing in an experimental hydroponic polyculture, apparently evaluating the kind of yield the crop was producing. Straightening, she turned to Atsuko, with her index finger raised.

"The key thing is that it's *reflected* light," she said enthusiastically. "We have so much radiation shielding above, below, and around this habitat that if it weren't for the way the mirrors are placed and their lightpaths directed, this whole place would be dark as the inside of a cave. But that's just the point: the mirrors reflect the good part of the electromagnetic spectrum—mostly the visible range—down to us here and in the sphere, but not the bad part, the dangerous part. That part is absorbed or deflected by the radiation shielding."

"I see," Atsuko said with a nod. That idea of letting only the 'good part' in both pleased and puzzled her. Was that what they were doing in terms of the HOME culture as a whole? She hoped not, for cultural homogeneity of that sort, though it might make things easier in the short run, might lead to fatal rigidity in time. Better to cope with the reality of the darkness—or the "bad light"—rather than try to screen it out.

Atsuko's gaze lingered on a tight patch of structures that looked to be more than just agricultural outbuildings. "Are those homes? I thought everybody lived in the central sphere."

"Most people do," Lex replied. "But some—about a sixth of the colony, I guess—find living in the greenhouses lighter, airier."

She paused, bending down to examine the green tops of a field planted in various tubers and underground starch-storers. The one Atsuko recognized was labeled POTATOES in several languages.

"That combination of shielding and mirror and lightpath I just told you about makes it possible for us to work and even live in these greenhouse agricultural tori, safely. No unexpected frosts or droughts or deluges. Because of the conditions here we can make good and increasing use of techniques like green manuring, biodynamics, polyculture cropping, extensive permaculture.''

Lexi gazed around until she spotted an example of what she was trying to explain.

"That area there, for instance, the one that looks like a field gone wild? That's based on Native American milpa polyculture, corn and beans and squash all growing together. The high-growing corn plants shelter the more delicate beans, and the squash vines grow from mound to mound among and between the corn and bean plants. The squash provides good, moisture-preserving cover for the soil, while the beans in turn fix nitrogen in the soil and aid in the growth of the corn and squash.''

Spreading her arms to encompass the plantings around her, Lexi turned to her visitor with a smile in which there flickered more than a little pride.

"Our fields are a mosaic of monocultural and polycultural strategies. We do multiple planting in some places, seeding one or more crops shortly before the previous crop has been harvested. We can pull off a phenomenal number of crops per twelve-month cycle. Even without the use of gene-engineered self-nitrifying cereal crops, these ag lands and hydroponic plots around us here would already be, on average, productive enough to support over two hundred people per hectare.''

Listening to the crowing of a rooster somewhere nearby, Atsuko was reminded that she really should spend more time boning up on agricultural practices—but she clearly remembered the implications of that level of productivity.

"Amazing!'' she exclaimed. "But that would mean you could support the entire colony's population, permanent and transient, on only twenty hectares—''

"—and we have a good deal more than twenty hectares under cultivation,'' Lexi said with a nod, still stopping to look at this plant or that as they walked along. "Yes, I know. All our granaries, silos, storage facilities—they're all full. I know it sounds a bit like carrying coals to Newcastle, but recently we've begun sending fully laden grain barges down the gravity well to Earth, as humanitarian aid to help alleviate famines and starvation shortages.''

"Really?" Atsuko stared at her, as if genuinely surprised. "But I hadn't heard of that!"

"No, you wouldn't have," Lexi said, as if confiding a secret. "It's being done very quietly through several international philanthropic organizations."

"But why hasn't it been publicized?" Atsuko wanted to know, playing her role to the hilt. "The HOME consortium should be shouting such good public relations to every satellite dish and rooftop antenna on the planet!"

Lexi smiled awkwardly, pushing a recalcitrant lock of grey-blond hair back from her brow. As she spoke, however, the expression on her face grew gradually more serious.

"You'd think that, wouldn't you? But it's not the case. I'm afraid there are some rather powerful groups on Earth opposed to our philanthropy, even if it is for a good cause. The major grain and food agricorps don't want us upsetting the market, even though what we're sending down is only a tiny fraction of Earth's production."

Lexi paused, crunching a piece of clotted dirt to dust under the toe of her boot. She snapped off a slender grass stalk and twirled it between her fingers a moment before clamping her teeth round the butt of it.

"And then there are those powerful people who, if they knew of it, would feel what we're doing is not a good cause— that it's counterproductive. They'd say what they've said before in similar circumstances: why feed people who are only going to breed more people who will also need to be fed? By alleviating the suffering of the living, we are only creating more suffering, greater numbers of the suffering among those, as yet unborn, whom we will one day be unable to feed. Even up here there are some who say that we should be 'an island of plenty in a sea of want,' hoarding what we have, letting all those born in less fortunate times and places starve and die."

Lexi turned suddenly toward Atsuko, the grass stalk dangling from between her lips. Was her face flushed from emotion, or was it just high color from healthy work?

"They've got a point," Atsuko said. "Quality of human life versus quantity of human life . . ."

"Yes," Lexi acknowledged, sighing abruptly and turning away. "But I wonder sometimes if their argument is so altruistic—or if it might not be motivated at some level by the selfishness of race or place, greed or creed."

She began walking quickly along a looping route that was taking them back toward the plaza where Atsuko had met the ag worker.

"But we can't just let them starve," Lexi continued passionately as they strode quickly down the path. "Not if we still have compassion. Not if we really believe that through human reason we can learn to control the growth of our own population. Not if we really believe we can break out into space, that we can build enough homes in the sky to save the world we came from. Not if we still believe in ourselves."

After Lexi subsided, there was only the sound of their footsteps on the path for many minutes. No word passed between the two women until they finally stepped back onto the small plaza near the transit station.

"Thank you very much for the tour—and the conversation, Ms. Petrunkevitch," Atsuko told her, shaking Lexi's hand as she prepared to leave. "It gives me hope that we might someday find a way of doing with human nature what you people have managed to do with the radiation of space—to let all that is good in it shine through, and absorb and deflect all that is bad."

Smiling, Lexi released Atsuko's hand, then removed the slender stalk of grass from between her teeth, staring thoughtfully at it for a moment.

"You'll have to ask other people about that one," she said, tucking the green blade firmly between her teeth once more. "Where I pull a weed, I try to plant a seed, but pulling up darkness from the human soul is a bit out of my league." She thrust her hands in her pockets and looked down at the ground. "I'm just a part-time farmer in the sky. Besides, we have no weeds up here—only plants sometimes growing where we don't want them to grow. Maybe the same is true on Earth. Nice meeting you, Ms. Ohnuki. I hope you enjoy your stay with us."

Atsuko would have loved to say more—to have told Lexi

how pleased she was with her answers, even to have revealed her true identity—but at that moment her bulletcart pulled in, so she could only wave and run, flying into the cart that would take her back up to the ridge, into the zero-gee corridor sheathed in light, and away.

J HANA SAT IN HER EXTINCTION HOUSE VIRTUALITY, LOOK- ing at the data as she already had, time and again. She watched the graphs rise and fall as the computers ran the numbers through Schliessen-Schwann and Hardy-Weinberg transforms, through chaos screeners, through decomplexification equations, the works. Still the problems raised by *Heterocephalus glaber* remained. What constituted an effective population size among naked mole rats? Average colony size was what—about seventy? Yet there were records of colonies comprising four hundred individuals. How big a threat was genetic drift to their viability? Their strategy of consanguineous mating was so complete that members of a colony were essentially clones—sharing more genetic material than lab mice that had been inbred for sixty generations. That incestuous mating strategy was a great help toward making mole rats eusocial, but how did it fit in with population expansion through colony fissioning?

Trying to take it all in, concentrating so intensely hour after hour, gave Jhana a headache. Commanding her virtuality off, she got up and left her cubicle. At first she thought she'd just stretch her legs, but soon enough she found those legs carrying her toward the lab lounge, and coffee. When she got to the lounge, she was glad to find it empty, which meant she could remain alone with her thoughts.

On one of the lounge's trideo units she called up an image of Earth viewed from the habitat, real time and 3-D. She sat staring at the picture for quite a while, trying to make sense of it, and herself, and where she was now.

Unfortunately the lounge didn't remain empty long enough for her to come up with all the answers. She'd barely finished her first shot of caffeine when the gnomish Paul Larkin, dressed in yet another variant of his usual denim prole-wear, came in and poured himself a cup, intent on striking up a conversation—or at least intent on hearing himself talk.

"Feeling a little homesick, Dr. Meniskos?" he asked, sitting down across the table from her and the 3D-ified Earth floating between them.

"Yeah, I guess I must be," she admitted. "I've been sitting here comparing the space habitat to my memories of Earth."

"To the habitat's disadvantage—am I right?"

"You are," she said, nodding in agreement. "This place, it has no rugged mountains or deep canyons, or broad oceans—"

"No mysterious hidden spaces of underground caves," Larkin interjected. "No vistas of unlimited stars overhead, no sense of Earth's impersonal vastnesses of land and sky. None of the crazy riskiness of walking on the outside of a body spinning in space. I know the feeling well."

"Does it bother you sometimes?" Jhana asked.

"Sure," Larkin said. "Here everything is thoroughly *inside*. Safe, like the womb. A totally humanized space, artificial, created and maintained absolutely by human beings. A clean, well-lighted cave among the stars, a hollow earth, with gardens. Pastoral, bucolic, even beautiful—but I doubt it could ever be sublime. For that you need something that isn't human, something wild and unconquered. 'In wilderness lies the preservation of the world,' as Thoreau said. I used to wonder what he meant by that, until I came here."

Jhana stared at him a moment. Larkin really *had* done some thinking about this.

"Don't you think there might be a danger in that?" she asked, swirling her coffee a bit.

"What do you mean?"

"I don't know," she said, though actually she did know. "It's just that, in my work, I have to think about isolation and genetic drift a lot. If these habitats are successful, what happens when generation after generation has lived in them? What if the residents eventually don't want to leave the womb anymore? What if they think it really *is* crazy to walk around on the outside of a body spinning in space, like Earth?"

"Ah," Larkin said with a nod, "the Plato's Cave problem. The Flatland problem. But that can only happen when there are no more adventurous souls, when the wilderness *within*, the final frontier inside each of our heads, becomes as conquered and domesticated as the wilderness *without*. Me, I prefer to keep seeing as much wilderness as I can in either direction."

"But how can you see that here?" Jhana asked, curious almost despite herself.

"Because, for all its mountains and oceans and canyons and caves," Larkin said, staring hard at her, "Earth's in much the same condition as we are. 'Generations have trod, have trod, have trod; And all is seared with trade; bleared, smeared with toil; And wears man's smudge and shares man's smell,' as the poet Hopkins put it. All of that world has been touched by our machinations, no matter how vast and desert it may look. In a sense, we're a laboratory up here, where the same experiment that's already going on down on Earth is being repeated— except we're doing it in microcosm and under more controlled, more 'scientific' conditions. The wilderness *without* doesn't factor in much, here. Only the wilderness *within*."

Jhana didn't know what to say to that. She drank more coffee and thought about it.

"Tell me, Ms. Meniskos," Larkin began again, seemingly on another topic, "in your research, do you encounter living fossils much?"

"From time to time," Jhana admitted, brushing a long lock of silky black hair into place behind her ear. "They do have some relevance to questions of genetic drift and population ecology."

"That they do," Larkin agreed, sipping at his coffee. "I've been fascinated with living fossils for years. Darwin himself coined that term, you know. For the sole survivors, the creatures frozen in time. Survivors like the Shark Bay stromatolites, the ginkgos, the nautiloids, the horseshoe crabs—"

"*Lingula* clams, coelacanths, cycads, dragonflies," Jhana said, willing to add to the list—for in truth she too had had a secret fascination with living fossils ever since childhood. "Scorpions, tuataras . . ."

"Yes," Larkin said, smiling. "Such creatures have always struck me as undying memories, long-lived memes in the mind of Life. Do you know what a meme is, Ms. Meniskos?"

"I've heard the word," Jhana replied, feeling as if she were being quizzed on some arcane forty-year-old term—one current when Larkin was her age. She decided to cover the awkwardness of the situation by getting another cup of coffee. "I can't say that I really remember what it means, though."

"A meme is an idea that takes on a life of its own," Larkin

said, "replicating itself through minds the way a gene replicates itself through bodies. Lots of our big ideas are memes. Paradise, apocalypse, utopia—those are memes. The idea of a world savior, a Christ or a Buddha—that's a meme. Most of what Jung was talking about in terms of archetypal imagery and the collective unconscious—those are memes and constellations of memes, too. At some deep level, the most successful memes seem to be fundamentally related to biology, to the experience of being born, growing up, living and dying as a biological being. So deeply related that they seem almost genetic."

"I don't quite get what you mean," Jhana said, not really wanting to encourage Larkin in his rambling discourse yet doing so anyway, curious as to where this might be leading. "Generic maybe, but genetic? How?"

"Think of the idea 'Be fruitful and multiply and have dominion over the earth,' " Larkin said, looking at her from under arched, quizzical eyebrows. "Most people would agree that's been a successful meme, replicating itself through minds over several thousand years. But isn't there a biologically driven component—even a genetic program—involved in the success of that meme? Can a meme or a gene in fact become *too* successful? If conditions change but the gene doesn't, what then?"

"The gene can be neutral, 'dead weight,' " Jhana replied, "or it can become deleterious."

"Precisely. Harmful to the continued existence of the individual or even the species. Some memes, some ideas, are like that too. They may have been good ideas at one time, but conditions have changed. The Genesis Plan of 'be fruitful and multiply and have dominion' has become the Holocaust Plan: Consume the Earth until there is nothing left to consume. Consume so-called inferior species out of existence to make room for the 'master' species, *Homo sapiens sapiens*—much the way the Nazis attempted to consume 'inferior' races out of existence to create *Lebensraum* for the 'master' race. Most species on Earth now go extinct not from hunting or trapping but from habitat destruction. Plant and animal habitat is destroyed to make way for human habitat. Species lebensraum."

Jhana finished the last of her second cup of coffee, toying with the cup and with an idea.

"But that hasn't been true of this habitat, this space colony," she said, shutting off the 3D real-time image of the Earth. "No life-supporting environment existed here prior to the construction of this colony."

"True," Larkin agreed. "No species died so that we might live here, in this beautiful—but not sublime—place. However, even this colony is just a part of another meme-constellation, the Exodus Plan. Mass-migration off Earth. Tetragrammaton is a star in that larger constellation, a part of that larger meme. It's an idea still very much—"

Larkin's time-cuff began ringing. He rose quickly from his chair.

"Nice talking to you, Jhana, but I'm afraid I must run back to my work. Duty calls."

Jhana waved goodbye to him. When he was fully out the door, she sighed with relief. His secret not-secret Plans, and that Tetragrammaton stuff—he was veering into that obsolete paranoid politics thing again. She was thankful to have been saved by the bell.

*S*O MUCH TO LEARN, SO LITTLE TIME, MARISSA THOUGHT, looking out through a study of altriciality in humans and mole rats she'd just finished scanning in overlay, looking beyond it to the Archive's peaceful grounds. *If for no other reason, increased longevity would be a plus for lengthening and strengthening the human learning curve.*

With a series of eye-blinks she scanned through an index of articles on mole-rat behaviors. Stopping at one that looked interesting, she called it up and began to read it on her overlays.

Excerpt from "Sex and Death: Gender-linked Intracolonial Aggression in the Naked Mole Rat:"

Though there is little aggression among males of *Heterocephalus glaber*, the violent fighting among the larger females in a colony has long been noted. Most often this violence occurs after the established queen and sole breeder for a colony has died. At this point, several of

the previously sterile, nonbreeding females grow suddenly larger, become sexually and reproductively active,
and aggressively battle one another—often to the death—
to replace the deceased breed-queen.

Marissa stopped. Reading about the mole rat's female-on-
female aggression made her slightly queasy, largely because it
reminded her of something she'd seen years before. Once,
walking home from high school, she'd seen female classmates
fighting in a nearby parking lot, three against two, pulling hair
and punching each other viciously. Never having witnessed
anything like it before, and having always been an entirely
nonconfrontational person herself, she'd stood there dumb-
founded, becoming almost physically ill as she watched, until
a security guard showed up and the group of three jumped in
their white car and sped away, leaving their black-eyed and
bloody-nosed opponents behind.

Years later, when she'd told her college roommate the story,
the roommate remarked that Marissa had been too accepting
of the patriarchal programming that "women should be passive and men should be aggressive"—and that Marissa's
sickly response denied women the right to fight if they wanted
to, denied them the right to express their full range of emotions, including anger and aggression. Still, Marissa had wondered if "patriarchal programming" was enough to explain
the very personal, very visceral response she'd suffered at the
sight of seeing her classmates' female-fight.

There had been much in her childhood that had been equally
sordid. "Squalor" and "filth" were terms too genteel and
vague to describe the deeply personal organic funk that permeated all the places where she'd grown up. Ancient miasma
compounded of damp rot and green-black mold and mildew
triumphant. The unquiet ghosts of stale cooking odors, the
stench of dead men's cigarettes and bad plumbing, always
hovering around the shotgun-shack alleys, the spare-tire-roofed
trailer parks, the cheaply remuddled alumisided prefab row
houses of her girlhood. The smell of too many people living
in too small a space on too little money for too many years.
A stink that lingered on your fingertips if you brought them
too close to your nose, the persistent perfume of poverty un-

original as sin and seemingly inescapable as death.

No, "mortality rates" and "overpopulation" and "poverty statistics" were not numerical abstractions, for her. They were as real as her life. The source of her optimism about the larger world came somehow from her success in overcoming the obstacles in her own life. Perhaps too, that was part of the appeal of the space habitat for her: so clean and new, full of sweet smells and peaceable people—so different from the world she'd had to move beyond.

Not wanting to think about it anymore, she eye-blinked her overlays off, and removed her wraparounds. Looking in her bag, she found the copy of *The Story of Utopias* that Atsuko had given her, marked up by Roger with a running commentary. Paging through the book, Marissa found that most of the marginalia and highlighting seemed to be in Chapter 12, and she decided to read through these passages in particular, thinking they might give her some insight into the way that Roger's mind worked.

Highlighted excerpt from Mumford's *The Story of Utopias*:

While the classic utopias have so far been nearer to reality in that they have projected a whole community, living and working and mating and spanning the gamut of man's activity, their projections have nevertheless been literally up in the air, since they did not usually arise out of any real environment or attempt to meet the conditions that this environment presented. This defect has been suggested by the very name of Utopia, for as Professor Patrick Geddes points out, Sir Thomas More was an inveterate punster, and Utopia is a mock name for either Outopia, which means no place, or Eutopia—the good place.

Marissa almost smacked her palm against her forehead on reading the highlighted text. Of course! How could she have forgotten? The inherent duplicity of language! Too often she fell back into the habit of treating language as if it were some product, complete and stable and fixed—instead of a process inherently incomplete and in flux. She thought of Nietzsche's admonition: "We shall not have gotten rid of God so long as we still have faith in grammar."

Indeed. Roger the annotator had clearly been less trusting of the words, in his marginal notes disputing the reading of *eu-* as "good" and instead emphasizing its meaning as "true—as in eusocial, truly social," like his beloved mole rats.

Marissa thought of the static, locatable Word of institutional religion, as opposed to the divine Word of the mystics, the divine Ground that is a sphere with its "center everywhere, circumference nowhere." Language was the same sort of thing—for what word could be the center of language, what word its circumference? She read on.

Highlighted excerpt from Mumford's *The Story of Utopias*:

Our choice is not between eutopia and the world as it is, but between eutopia and nothing—or rather nothingness. Other civilizations have proved inimical to the good life and have failed and passed away; and there is nothing but our own will-to-eutopia to prevent us from following them.

Marissa saw that Roger, the "author of the marginalia," had noted at this point in the text, "cf.: Buckminster Fuller's equally questionable contention, choice facing humanity is between utopia and extinction." Marissa wondered why Roger should find that idea of Fuller's questionable, but, flipping pages, she scanned onward.

Highlighted excerpt from Mumford's *The Story of Utopias*:

The problem of realizing the potential powers of the community—the fundamental problem of eutopian reconstruction—is not simply a matter of economics or eugenics or ethics . . . Bacon looked for the happiness of mankind chiefly in the application of science and industry. But by now it is plain that if this alone were sufficient, we could all live in heaven tomorrow ... More, on the other hand, looked to social reform and religious ethics to transform society; and it is equally plain that if the souls of men could be transformed without altering their material and institutional activities, Christianity, Mohammedanism, and Buddhism might have created an earthly paradise almost any time this last two thousand years. The truth is ... that these two conceptions are still at war with each other: idealism and science continue to function in separate compartments; and yet "the happiness of man on earth" depends upon their combination. ...

Roger had starred "man on earth" and written in the margin (as a mock-political correction), "Evil sexist earth chauvinist—should be 'Humanity anywhere'!"

As she read further in the highlighted Mumford text, Marissa wondered how much of Roger's bad-boy stance was in response to the fact that his mother, Atsuko, in her works, often preached the idea of a "new science" and new scientists—embodying the very idealism Mumford wrote of and Roger, apparently, rejected. Reading on, Marissa wondered if it was the fate of every generation to inevitably rebel against what their parents believed.

Highlighted excerpt from Mumford's *The Story of Utopias*:

... So it follows that while science has given us the means of making over the world, the ends to which the world has been made over have had, essentially, nothing to do with science ... When science is not touched by a sense of values it works—as it fairly consistently has worked during the past century—toward a complete dehumanization of the social order. The plea that each of the sciences must be permitted to go its own way without control should be immediately rebutted by pointing out that they obviously need a little guidance when their applications in war and industry are so plainly disastrous. ... Knowledge is a tool rather than a motor; and if we know the world without being able to react upon it, we are guilty of that aimless pragmatism which consists of devising all sorts of ingenious machines and being quite incapable of subordinating them to any coherent and attractive pattern.

Seeing the asterisks and stars beside some of these statements and recalling Atsuko's writings on the gap between knowledge and wisdom, Marissa was becoming increasingly fascinated with the idea that she was reading the unguarded comments of Roger Cortland himself. Looking up from her reading, she wondered why it should matter so much to her that it was Roger's mind behind these scribbled responses to the words of a man long dead. Was she becoming like some lovesick girl mooning over a trifle that the hand of her beloved had touched? Was this intense desire for insight into the workings of Roger's mind merely the more abstract form lovesickness was taking in her? A moonstruck scholar doting over her beloved's asterisks?

Looking at the world that had been blown into being all around her, though, she thought that perhaps such doting, transmuted into love and respect, might not be such a bad thing after all. What else but a desire to *preserve* drove lovers to dote on seeming trifles—and what else but love and respect for the seeming abstraction of "biodiversity" had driven scientific idealists and idealistic scientists to create this habitation in space?

Yet it had to be something more than just preservation involved here, more than just saving what's left. A lover—whether of another human being or of the natural world itself—could seek to preserve something of the beloved purely out of the fear that it would otherwise be lost, but the danger with that would always be that by the time the lover got around to thinking of saving that something, it would already be too late to preserve it in any meaningful way. Such had been the case with far too many species during the twentieth century.

Better, then, to want to preserve or save something for its own sake, she thought. Save it in recognition that that beloved something had value in and of itself, independent of its value to the lover. But then, that assumed the lover and the beloved were somehow truly independent, subject and object. *That* sort

of denial—of the fundamental unity underlying all things—
would just get everyone back into the same mess.

Another paradox, Marissa thought, as the birds sang and the
streams flowed and animals and insects moved among leaves
and trees of the enclosed-garden world around her. This place
was full of paradoxes: an attempt to save what was left but
likewise an attempt to create something more, something new;
a preservation but also a new creation; an artificial world
meant to preserve the natural; the human construction of a
habitat in space intended to redress the human destruction of
habitats on Earth; a pragmatic venture of nations and corporations that was creating something other than nations and
corporations, something communal and eutopian and experimental and "in process," in Atsuko's sense of all those words.

Marissa was startled out of her reverie by the appearance of
Roger Cortland proceeding up the sun-dappled path toward
her. She rose from the bench, the blood rushing to her head
slightly.

"Roger—this is a surprise!"

"Yes. Working on utopia again? I suppose you've found a
good deal more fiction on it in there," Roger said with a somewhat disdainful gesture toward the Archives buildings, "than
factual realizations of it out here."

"Oh, I don't know," Marissa replied, weighing her words.
"My research today has just reminded me that utopia means
not only 'no place' but also 'good place.' This place seems
like a good place, to me."

Roger laughed somewhat sourly.

"No place is a good place," he said, heading toward the
nearest entrance, "but you have a good afternoon, anyway."

After a few steps, Roger called back to Marissa just as she
was sitting down again on the bench.

"Is my mother inside, do you know?"

"No, I'm afraid not."

"Ah."

Watching a shattered rainbow of butterflies drift among the
flowers of the Archive gardens, Marissa could detect neither
pain nor pleasure in Roger's "Ah." Still, there was something
about his presence here that she just couldn't pin down. Maybe

it would be best not to pin it down, but to just let it be, let it drift along like these butterflies. She thought lazily of the Chinese philosopher—who was it, Lao-Tse?—who said that one day he fell asleep and dreamed he was a butterfly. The dream was so vivid and real, however, that on waking he was much perplexed as to whether he was a man who had dreamed he was a butterfly, or a butterfly who had dreamed he was a man. Thinking of such things, her eyes following the easy flitting of the butterflies from bud to bud, Marissa herself almost began to drift off.

"*Watching* butterflies isn't much of a pastime," Roger said when he came out of the Archive, an optical disk in hand. "How'd you like to *be* one?"

"What?" Marissa asked, wondering if she were really awake and hearing things right.

"Be a butterfly," Roger said, "or at least fly like one."

"Oh—sure, I guess."

"Then come with me," he said, offering her his arm. "I'll show you."

Taking the proffered arm gently but firmly, she walked with him to a ridge cart station where they caught a carriage for the low-gee zones. Even before they entered the ridge cart, though, she was already as light on her feet as if someone had cut off all local gravity. Phrases—*dancing on air, swept away*—floated into her head, demonstrated their inadequacy, and quickly disappeared.

Such light-footed romance did not prove eternal, however. It didn't last very long at all, in fact.

"So many damned old people," Roger complained sotto voce to her as they waited in line for a couple of the safety-chuted airbicycles the locals called paraflyers. "Why don't they just stay back on Earth?"

"Because living in low gravity increases their longevity," Marissa said placidly, but with a tactful look around to be sure no one was in earshot. "If they were still back on Earth they'd probably be dead by now."

"And good riddance to them too," he said seriously, his impatience growing. "Look at that pair of greyheads—the airbike instructor must be explaining everything to them at least half a dozen times!"

Marissa grimaced.

"Roger, come on. We're all going to be old someday, if we live that long. And those who are already old won't be taking up space much longer. No reason we can't be courteous. Show a little understanding, a little compassion—"

The elderly couple, at least ninety years old, took off gingerly from the low-gravity platform, pedaling their human-powered two-seater airbike slowly up toward the zero-gee axis.

"Compassion is one commodity I will not waste on the incompetent and unqualified," Roger said firmly as he and Marissa stepped up to the instructor. "Compassion, compassion, compassion. That's something else I've noticed since I came back from Earth: everybody up here parrots that word too damn much."

Roger pushed off, pedaling down into a speed-building dive and swooping back up in a roll around the nonagenarians as they pedaled their paraflyer in slow, steady fashion toward the vista complex at the center of the sphere. Still back on the platform, Marissa shook her head in bafflement at Roger's behavior, then pushed off as well.

There was no way she could keep up with him as he executed rolls and Immelmann turns and falling-leaf stalls, the hollow world spinning and twisting and turning about him, axis and vista complex standing more tightly nearby, thickets and young forests and veldts and streams and gardens and houses farther away, above and below and around.

He swooped back down toward Marissa, slightly above and to the left of her as they pedaled in a more gentle arc near the habitat's axis corridor, giving a wide berth to parasuited young people playing three-fall soccer there.

"Maris, I was just thinking," Roger began, smiling impishly, "that maybe it's good those old people want to live up here in low grav. I mean, they're too weak to bug us down in higher grav, right? They've voluntarily had themselves committed to a low-gravity prison!"

Marissa just shook her head.

"And that idea gave me another," Roger continued as they pedaled, knowing he was getting to her. "When we start having crimes and criminals up here, we can confine the criminals in very low- or even micro-gravity. After a couple of months their bodily systems will have atrophied to such an extent that they'll be unable to escape to higher gravity without risking death. A prison without walls, without even the need for guards or electronic monitoring systems. Rehabilitation will finally mean something, because it will have to be literal. They'll have to have physical rehabilitation just so they won't die when they attempt to rejoin the mainstream of society in normal gravity. Of course, that would still leave them able to prey on the old people, but maybe that'd be a way of killing two old birds with one stone-cold convict—"

"Roger Tsugio Cortland," Marissa said, staring at his slyly smiling face in disbelief, "you have a special genius for the perverse and morbid."

"I also have a genius," Roger said with a laugh, "for knowing how to push your buttons!"

Marissa put her paraflyer into a slow, looping spiral.

"Maybe. But you've forgotten one thing, Roger dear. Everyone has pretty much equal access to the necessities of life and to what few luxuries the habitat can afford. You have no crime and no criminals here."

"But we will!" Roger said, banking away steeply to the right, toward the night sector of the sphere. "Even if I have to become the first one myself!"

"You've spent too much time on Earth!" Marissa called after him.

Pedaling furiously, he was already almost out of earshot. Marissa picked up her pace, trying to catch him.

IN THE SPHERE'S UNSETTLING REGION OF ARTIFICIAL TWI-light, Roger did a small, swift series of loops and rolls, daylight and green life and business as usual above, twinkling lamps and house lights below—

"Wha—?" Roger gasped in shock. Into the air before him, quick and bright as linked thunderbolts, had leapt two immense writhing snakes banded in shimmering reds and greens and yellows and blues, snakes intertwined like those on the insignia of the medical profession, yin-yang snakes of light swallowing their own tails, a snake circle but one that inverted with a subtle twist like something out of Escher, a single-sided snake

Möbius strip, a serpentine infinity sign, relaxing, opening toward O. . . .

*He was far away, flinging himself from a tower, into the
wind. Below him monks and novices and clusters of townspeople stood with their mouths open in awe. Soaring like bird
or angel, he rose above winter-grey earth just turning green
again, the westering sun bright on his backside, the cold wind
rushing through his hair. In a glance he could see clear from
the Cotswold Hills to the meandering headwaters of the River
Thames. Above him stretched only the endless dome of heaven
pocked with a few broken clouds, while below stood his mo-
nastic brethren, their tonsured heads turned skyward, craning
their necks and gawking at him, looking foolish and innocent
as the yardful of chickens he'd seen in the rain earlier that
day.*

*He felt like a great and mighty hawk in the sky above them
until, a furlong from the tower, the wind seemed to grow violent and the air to whorl as he struggled more and more
desperately to control his gliding air vessel. No matter how he
fought to correct the motion of his flight in the wind his vessel's fractiousness worsened until he was wobbling and bouncing wildly, finally spiraling headlong for the rain-softened
earth—*

He landed with a thump. In grassland, in light. As his orange
parachute drifted to the ground, he unstrapped himself slowly.
Expecting to a certainty that he would be wearing a bloodied,
coarse monk's robe over shattered legs—and astonished that
he was not, that his legs were not—he stood slowly, stunned
that he was once again inside the habitat, no longer living on
the outside of a world turning through a different space and
time. The blue dome of heaven had disappeared, replaced by
the wraparound sky-county of the habitat's interior.

Staring at that inside-out sky, he slowly remembered himself
and began to gaze about purposefully, looking for something,
a shimmering slithering intertwined something, a thing with
neither outside nor inside. But it too was nowhere to be seen.

He had almost finished the embarrassing task of folding up
the flyer's chute by the time Marissa and a paraflight instructor
arrived on the scene.

"Roger, are you all right?" Marissa asked.

"Yeah," he said with a terse nod. "Must have blacked out or something. I don't remember."

"The chute deployed automatically when you went past the half-grav mark—just like it's supposed to do," said the thin young black man with the G. SMITH, CHIEF INSTRUCTOR badge, who now began breaking down and folding up the airbike itself into a portable size and shape. "You're lucky it did, or you wouldn't be here to not remember it."

"You've been working too hard," Marissa said to Roger, as much for the chief instructor's benefit as for Roger's own. "That must be what's behind it. You're usually a natural with human-powered vehicles, right?"

Roger said nothing. The instructor, having reduced the flyer to backpack size, slipped his arms through a pair of straps and, bidding them goodbye, walked away over the windy green-gold grass of the veldt, headed for the nearest cart station. Marissa and Roger followed after him, at a slower pace.

"Marissa," Roger said tentatively as they approached the small station, "you didn't happen to see anything strange before I blacked out, did you?"

"Strange? In what way?"

Roger averted his eyes.

"Like a pair of snakes intertwined in a twisted circle in the air."

"Oh, that!" she said, smiling in relief. "That's just a sky-sign for that band that's so popular, that performance troupe—Möbius Cadúceus, I think they're called. I saw an announcement about it in the local media earlier this afternoon. They've got a concert coming up sometime soon."

"But the tangled snakes in the air—" he said, a quaver of remembered horror in his voice.

"That's their symbol, their logo. I think they use one of those big new projection holos to make it appear in the sky like that." She looked at him suddenly as they boarded a bulletcart. "Hey, you did fly awfully close to it—you don't think you might have gotten zapped by one of their lasers, do you?"

"No, I don't think so," Roger said uncertainly. He didn't know what to think, but he could not shake the idea that he had somehow, for a moment, gazed upon an event a thousand years old—through the eyes of the monk who had lived through it.

Compared to that, lasers and high technology seemed a most mundane magic.

J HANA TOO HAD GLIMPSED THE MÖBIUS CADÚCEUS SKY-sign, but she was so exhausted from working around the living fossil Larkin all day that she'd barely noticed it. About the only thing she'd accomplished the rest of the day was learning that the local expert on mole rats was Roger Cortland, the man she'd met on the flight up from Earth. That wasn't much to show for all the hours she'd put in.

On arriving home she immediately prepared for bed, still feeling time-lagged as she undressed. As she fell asleep she thought dreamily of what an arbitrary, localized thing the human telling of time was—merely the sequence of light and shadow on a small planet a certain distance from its star. When was high noon on the sun? Always? Never? When was midnight for someone floating halfway between Earth and the moon, or among unshadowed, uneclipsed Lagrange points? Arbitrary, she thought as she tumbled over the edge of sleep, all so arbitrary....

Mike and Rick fighting naked before her, dark and light, black and white tangle of armholds and leglocks and pummeling fists and blood streaming from noses and lips and herself caught up in the ineluctable grasp of time-transcending dreamvision, powerless to break free, becoming less a person than a place, less the object of battle than the battlefield itself, suddenly flooded with people in the dress of a million times and places running to and fro over the shoreless ocean of time, screaming sobbing crying shouting people. Sirens wailing and singing, singing and wailing over a vast darkling plain where Mike and Rick transmogrify into stormwaves of men smashing against each other in ever vaster oceans of blood, where ships and sailors explode and sink and drown and projectiles and jets and starfighters boil madly in the heavens raining ever more hellish destruction upon the burning Earth until all the land is fiery charnel quagmire and the sea and sky endless firmaments of blood.

A bubble of froth afloat upon the seas of blood and fire, powerlessly she watches machineries of construction and destruction proliferate bloom and die and proliferate, again in ever larger numbers, building destroying rebuilding redestroying, until it is impossible for her to tell the building from the destroying, humanity devouring everything and always already itself on a disposable planet, a womb to be callously forgotten just as soon as the umbilical cord can be cleanly cut, but she is that world, that womb, that woman on a death-mound bed of skulls and bones and skeletons big as forever under skies redolent of blood and fire, being taken against her will again and again by a man with burning wounds for eyes, a man alternately light and dark, making fevered sickmonkey love with her under bloody sheets, where pain and pleasure, love and death, always and never fuse into—

Screaming, Jhana woke to the buzzing of her front door. Coming out of the nightmare, she threw her robe about her, walked out of the bedroom and through the living area to the front door. The wall screen flashed 6:01, 6:01, as she walked past.

"Jhana Meniskos?"

"Yes?" she said groggily, staring at the thinly mustached, brown-uniformed young man at her door.

"Sorry to have called on you at this early hour," said the tall thin man with some embarrassment. His uniform tag said LOSABA and he spoke in the rich tones of a black South African. Jhana vaguely recognized his uniform as being that of the Intersatellite Courier Service. "But we received this very high-priority private message from your employer and we felt we should relay it to you as soon as possible. If you'll just look into this retinoscope here—"

The courier handed her the computer clipboard and she gazed into the scope, wondering if the bloodshot condition of her eyes would affect its readout. But no, a bell-like tone sounded and the courier nodded, handing her a sealed packet with a datawire inside. He bid Jhana a pleasant if somewhat hasty goodbye and she closed the door behind him.

Without opening the packet or pulling the datawire from it, Jhana walked dazedly back through the living area, into the bedroom. Returning to the scene of the dream, she sat down on the edge of the bed, wondering if she needed to see a therapist. It would be so easy to write it all off as just a dream—except for the fact that, for most of her life, she hadn't been bothered by her dreams, seldom remembering them because she rarely thought them worth remembering. But these recent dreams lately—they were so different, so strange and vivid. That impression of being hardly aware of herself—feeling herself only a place in which sensations and emotions were held for a moment as they poured through from nowhere to nowhere—that was so unprecedented she desperately wanted to make sense of it, of everything so disturbing in these night visitations.

Had she—deep down, in ways she'd never admitted to herself—really wanted to see Mike and Rick fight over her? Had she wanted to enjoy the spectacle of it? Their pain and struggle for her pleasure and entertainment? She'd never imagined there could be that much of the voyeur and the sadist in her. She hoped there wasn't.

It had, in any case, not worked out that way. Mike was dead in an accident, or a suicide, accidental suicide or suicidal accident—whatever—for which she undeniably felt guilt. And yet, despite that guilt, when she had gone to Rick for solace that evening after the funeral, they not only comforted each other—they also made love, furious love, as if on top of Mike's grave, upon his so very newly interred coffin. Why? Was it guilt over Mike's death that had driven her to that—or the desire for revenge, sexual vengeance for his denying her the fulfillment of some fantasy from which her conscious thoughts and words recoiled?

And to what avail? The dead felt no punishment, and the living could gain from it only a most guilty pleasure. Rick—Rick who had grown tired of waiting for her to make up her mind about Mike—he had already begun seeing another woman, the woman he would eventually throw Jhana over for and marry, but not before Jhana herself had first learned how it felt to be one of two satellites circling a single body.

Disgusted by her memories she tore open the packet, snapped flat the wire, and inserted it into a reader.

TO: Jhana Meniskos, Ph.D.
FROM: Balance Tien-Jones, Ph.D. TPAG Dir. R/D
(Bio)
RE: Worthwhile Projects

Stresses and tensions between here and there are increasing. Strongly suggest you look into mirror projects, SSPS. May prove valuable as diamonds or ephemeral as lightning.

That was cryptic enough. Delivered by security courier, no less. Unwilling to trust the message to the habitat's wide-open, nonencrypted broad- and narrow-cast channels.

Jhana found herself less and less in the mood for cloak and dagger games, but she supposed she'd better play along. Her job might depend on it.

"Diamonds" and "lightning" could pretty obviously be combined into a reference to that supposed secret weapons project, Diamond Thunderbolt. No doubt the professional paranoids of the Weapons Division were bothered by something to do with mirrors and the satellite solar power stations.

Dressing for the day, she thought again of the tides of blood that had flowed through her dream and devoutly hoped all that sort of thing was coming to an end. We have been sick monkeys for such a long time, she reflected. Still, there were increasing signs of health. Except in the entertainment media there were no orbital forts or starfighters like the ones in her nightmare, and even the transatmospheric fighter program had been phased out—much to Mike's grief. Life and reality were at least going a good deal better than her fearful nightmare. The world's sickness, though chronic and sometimes even acute, had not yet proven fatal.

Checking herself over one last time in the bathroom mirror, she hoped that Diamond Thunderbolt would prove to be only a fiction, the product of overwrought hyperparanoid minds desperate for the excuses of Fear and Money to prime the slowing machinery of death and destruction. Nevertheless, it would probably be best to keep her superiors happy by at least going out to the solar power satellites and taking a look around. Undoubtedly Tao-Ponto and the other consortium members had much more experienced "unofficial observers" already snooping about, but she would do her part—if only to keep them off her back.

How, though? Under what pretext? Who could provide her with a legitimate entry to that realm? Setting out for the day, she racked her memory until she suddenly recalled the first-night party and Seiji Yamaguchi. Hadn't he claimed to be connected with the solar power utilities somehow?

She'd have to look him up—but not before she got in touch with Roger Cortland. How odd that the man she'd met on the shuttle coming out had some considerable connection with her real work, in the form of his own research into that threatened species with the common, unappealing name of naked mole rats.

Her official observations as a scientist came first—unofficial observing could wait a bit.

SEVEN

"LAKSH," LEV KORCHNOI SAID, LINKING IN FROM A POD module in near-space, "sorry I've been so long getting back to you and your LogiBoxes up there, but have you ever noticed the way problems don't come singly—they come in clusters? I mean, it's not bad enough that we're under all this time pressure with the Mob Cad show and we're still getting glitches in the shobots. Now the team leader at my Communications day job has a bee up his butt about this space junk, so at this very minute I'm on my way to take a close-up look-see at the stuff—just to make sure Communications isn't implicated. As if that weren't enough already, I get a query from this woman, Marissa somebody, wondering if our skysign might have accidentally zapped her friend Roger *Cortland*, because he had an 'adverse reaction' to it in its first public appearance!"

Lakshmi nodded gravely.

"I know exactly what you mean. I just got a message from the other Cortland, Atsuko herself. She's current council liaison to the trade-gods on Earth and they're all upset about some trideo game thing the VAJRA is supposedly involved in manufacturing. I'm going to have to stall her until I can figure out exactly what's going on with the big spider I built for the habitat's web. And that's not the only problem. My workshop is now certifiably haunted."

"What?" Lev asked, surprised even out of his self-pitying funk.

"You'll see. Park your pod by my port after you're done scouting around out there."

"Will do. See you then."

As he signed off, Lev saw that he was within range of one of the X-shaped pieces of space junk he'd been sent to investigate. Maneuvering the pod into position, he saw that the X—smooth, reddish-orange and flecked with black, like a multicolored fun-house mirror—was only about the size of his vehicle. He did a series of scans of the thing: all wavelengths, and at scales rang-ing from visible-light photography to electron-micrograph ul-traclose-ups. He scanned it with gamma-ray lasers, low-energy collimated particle beams, scanning-tunneling X-ray micros-copy, stereomicroscopy, electron and positron emission scopes. Milliwaldoes and microwaldoes attempted to tease samples out of it.

Despite all the mechanical ministrations, to Lev's eyes the thing appeared inert—certainly it didn't seem to be responding to his scans in any way. Its inertness, though, turned out to be an illusion of scale. At the submicroscopic level, the thing was bustling with activity, innumerable micromachines swarming over it, making it 'grow' like some strange mechanorganic flower.

The micromachine stuff wasn't too surprising—a small per-centage of nanoassemblers always glitched and made debris. This X-shaped flower, though—it looked far too purposeful to be random garbage. Some of what the micros were growing appeared to be solar exchange film—which was good, since that made it Power Utility's problem. A lot of the X's surface, however, looked like microlasers and photorefractives—some-thing like the tech he and Lakshmi and Aleister had used to make the skysign shine, only much smaller and more sophis-ticated. That was bad, because that might make it Communi-cations' problem.

There was nothing Lev could do about what he was seeing except send on the data and his observations to his team leader in Comm. He wondered vaguely where the micromachines were getting the mass and materials to build and extend their constructions, but he didn't have time to puzzle that out at the moment. He had done his job. He'd gotten the higher-ups the data; now it was up to them to do something with it. He kicked in the pod's thrusters and headed toward Lakshmi's shop out in micro-gee.

When he arrived, Lakshmi was waiting for him just past the airlock. No sooner was he inside than she quickly ushered him into the bowels of her workshop. In her hoverchair she could move quite fast when she wanted to, and he had to hurry to keep up. Abruptly they stopped in the center of the shop.

"Where's this 'haunting' you spoke of?" Lev asked. "All I see is the usual clutter of your stuff drifting around."

"Look more closely," Lakshmi said, arrowing a thin beam of light from her hoverchair to indicate a corner of the lab. Lev saw it now: robotic arms acting cooperatively, sorting through a pile of stuff. He walked closer to it, Lakshmi following slowly and silently.

The arms were building something, attaching pieces to an assemblage or mobile. He saw a mandala, a tantric ritual object, a small piece of what looked like African tribal art, a Catholic scapular medal, a rosary, and a lot of stuff that looked like straightforward junk and debris, all assembled into a vaguely animal-like form connected by microthin optical wire. As he watched, the arms—which did move in a rather abnormal, "ghostly" fashion—opened up a leather pouch with a biohazard trefoil done in bead work and began extracting simple objects: feathers, dried flowers, bones, beads.

"Where's it getting this stuff from?" Lev asked, walking around the construction.

"Some of the African and Asian stuff is mine," Lakshmi said, "but the majority of it is stuff the arms have sorted out of Jiro Yamaguchi's personal effects. I've tried to tell you about this before, but you haven't been very willing to listen."

"And you know why?" Lev said. "Because you're going to tell me that there's some sort of artificial consciousness running on Jiro Yamaguchi's LogiBoxes—and that it's what's responsible for the problems we've been having lately. I don't buy it. Since when has human malfunction become a computer function? Jeez, the way we scapegoat machine intelligences, you'd think they were secret manifestations of our own ids, some kind of externalized subconscious—"

"But what if the construct running on Jiro's Boxes *is* involved?" Lakshmi persisted. "What if, before he died, he was able to transfer something of himself into them?"

"What—computer-aided apotheosis?" Lev scoffed. "I don't believe in the 'ghost in the machine,' Laksh. Mind is more than just electrified headmeat. You can't just go beaming it from place to place like an old radio program—"

Lev was interrupted by a message coming over his PDA. Looking down, he saw the plump visage of Aleister McBruce.

"Ah, I'm glad to see you're there too, Lakshmi," Aleister said. "This concerns you as well. I've pinned down what these odd self-replicating bugs are on Lev's shobots. You've got rats, Lev. RATs. Realtime Artificialife Technopredators. Funny thing is, they aren't supposed to exist anymore. Supposedly they were all destroyed with their creator, a guy who called himself Phelonious Manqué. At Sedona. Seems they're not extinct after all—and the VAJRA has a pretty good case of them. Check it out, Lakshmi. They're stealthy and pretty unobtrusive at the moment, but they're there."

"Great," Lakshmi groaned, calling up search protocols on her overlays, looking through them at Lev. "Are *these* ghosts allowable in your philosophy, Mr. Korchnoi?"

"Problems," Lev said with a smile and a shrug. "They never come alone. . . ."

"No," Lakshmi agreed, busily scanning through her overlays. "They always come in clusters. Herds. Multitudes."

MARISSA HAD LEFT A VIRTUAL-MAIL MESSAGE FOR Roger, explaining that she was taking the morning off to look at a monument down by Echo Mirror Lake. The inscription, she had explained in her note, was relevant to her fellowship work for Atsuko. Really, though, she needed to decompress, spend some time away, and swimming in the little lake seemed a good way to do that. So she walked, her guilt draped over her left arm in the form of a bathing suit.

And she did feel guilty. Guilty about taking the time away from Roger, especially after the airbike incident. Perhaps it was guilt too that had made her fire off a query to the Möbius Caduceus people about their skysign and its effect on Roger.

It was definitely guilt that had her reading what Roger had highlighted in the Mumford text as she walked along a branching path amid a stand of foxtail pines. As she walked and read, she saw that the notes and highlighting became more fragmentary as they went on.

Highlighted excerpt from Mumford's *The Story of Utopias*:

... a local synthesis of all specialist "knowledges" ... common tissue of definite, verifiable, localized knowledge is what all our ... utopias and reconstruction programs have lacked ... Regional survey is the bridge by which the specialist whose face is turned toward the library and the laboratory, and the active worker in the field, whose face is turned toward the city and region in which he lives, may come into contact; and out of this contact our plans and our eutopias may be founded on such a permanent foundation of facts as the scientist can build for us, while the sciences themselves will be cultivated with regard for the human values and standards, as embodied in the needs and the ideals of the local community ... we must return to the real world, and face it, and survey it in its complicated totality. Our castles-in-air must have foundations in solid ground ...

Marissa stopped awkwardly, flicking a pine cone off the path and back into the woods with the toe of her shoe, then went on with her reading.

Highlighted excerpt from *Mumford's The Story of Utopias*:

There is no genuine logical basis ... in the dissociation of science and art, of knowing and dreaming, of intellectual activities and emotional activities. The division between the two is simply one of convenience; for both these activities are simply different modes in which human beings create order out of the chaos in which they find themselves ... cultivated few/mutilated many ...

plans for a new social order have been dull as mud because, in the first place, they have been abstract . . .
Where the critics of the utopian method were, I believe,
wrong was in holding that the business of projecting
prouder worlds was a futile . . . pastime.

Locating a tree-shaded bench, Marissa sat down, finding the
bench cool, almost cold, beneath her. She glanced up at the
world-sky arching through the firmament above, trees and
streams and gardens and grasslands and small clusters of buildings. Castles in the air, she thought with a smile. Something,
a spot among the branches of the foxtails, caught her eye.
Concentrating her gaze, she saw a dark flash move with incredible speed and agility along a bunch-needled branch. A
pine marten, she realized. Nearly extinct in the wild on Earth,
but apparently there was a good little colony of them thriving
here. For a moment she became aware of the wonderful fresh
smell of the trees around her, even as she returned to the book
in her lap.

Highlighted excerpt from Mumford's *The Story of Utopias*:

These anti-utopian critics overlooked the fact that one of
the main factors that condition any future are the attitudes
and beliefs which people have in relation to that future
. . . as Dewey would say, in any judgment of practice
one's belief in a hypothesis is one of the things that af-
fects its realization . . .

The importance of the will, then, in any realization of a
better human social condition. Huxley and Callenbach had
named the protagonists in their eutopian novels "Will," she
remembered, wondering if there might be any significance to
that. Intrigued, she rose from the bench and walked along the
sandy path a while, listening to the silence, watching the light
filter through the trees around her, smelling the pines' perfume
floating in the air. At last she turned back to her book and
read further.

Highlighted excerpt from Mumford's *The Story of Utopias*:

The first step . . . is to ignore all the fake utopias and social myths that have either proved so sterile or so disastrous during the last few centuries . . . In turning away from obsolete and disastrous social myths I do not suggest that we give up the habit of making myths; for that habit, for good or bad, seems to be ingrained in the human psyche. The nearest we can get to rationality is not to efface our myths but to infuse them with right reason, and to alter them or exchange them for other myths when they appear to work badly.

Roger the annotator had heavily starred the section on myths, and beside the phrase "right reason" had written "What does this term mean? Is reasoning ever unequivocally 'right'?" Marissa was surprised to see that. Such notes seemed to her evidence more of Atsuko's propensity to emphasize the uncertainty and incompleteness of thought and all systems thereof—rather than what she'd perceived to be Roger's simple rebelliousness. Maybe Roger and his rebelliousness weren't so simple after all.

Without breaking stride Marissa snatched a pine cone off the trail and gazed at its complexity a moment, then turned back to the book as she walked.

Highlighted excerpt from Mumford's *The Story of Utopias*:

Among the utopians . . . as land is a common possession, so is work a common function; and no one is let off from some sort of labor of body or mind because of any inherited privileges or dignities . . . the inhabitants of our eutopias will have a familiarity with their local environment and its resources, and a sense of historical continuity, which those who dwell within the paper world of Megalopolis . . . have completely lost . . . We shall not attempt to legislate for all these communities at one stroke;

for we shall respect William Blake's dictum that one law
for the lion and the ox is tyranny . . .

Among the stars and exclamation points surrounding these
passages Roger had remarked, "What of equality? Is equal
justice only equal tyranny? Can we give the lion and the ox
different worlds in which to live? Will solving this conflict
only generate new ones?" Reading on, Marissa could appreciate the tenacity with which the annotator took the text to task
rather than merely accepting Blake or Mumford as "authori-
tative."

Marissa saw that she was coming out of the forest into a
meadow-lined bowl. At the bottom of that grassy depression
lay a small round body of mirror-smooth water, reflecting the
tree-lined ridges that surrounded it on every side and, farther
away, those parts of the other side of the Sphere that were also
in light. In the meadow nearer at hand stood the small pedestal
monument that she'd been looking for. She walked toward it,
trying to finish up her reading as she went.

Highlighted excerpt from Mumford's *The Story of Utopias*:

If the inhabitants of our eutopias will conduct their daily
affairs in a possibly more limited environment than that
of the great metropolitan centers, their mental environment will not be localized or nationalized . . . The notion
that no effective change can be brought about in society
until millions of people have deliberated upon it and
willed it is one of the rationalizations which are dear to
the lazy and ineffectual . . . the foundations for eutopia
can be laid, wherever we are, without further ado . . .
when that which is perfect has come, that which is imperfect will pass away.

Following much asterisking and exclamation-pointing,
Roger, the anonymous commentator-within-the-text, in response to the last statement, had noted, "The perfect is always
coming, the imperfect is always passing away. The perfect can
never be fully come, and the imperfect can never be fully

passed away. If perfection means the end of change, then perfection is death. If nothing changes, everything dies. If everything changes, nothing dies.''

That clinched it for Marissa. The highlighter of the text, the
author of marginal notes upon it—he had to be the same person who was bothered by the potential of her immortalizing
vector—and a more complex person than he so often seemed.

Marissa closed the book and stood staring at the plaque set
into the top of the pedestal. It was still new enough for its
words to glint sharply in the late morning light:

THE POLITICS OF THOSE WHOSE GOAL IS BE-
YOND TIME ARE ALWAYS PACIFIC; IT IS THE
IDOLATERS OF PAST AND FUTURE, OF REAC-
TIONARY MEMORY AND UTOPIAN DREAM, WHO
DO THE PERSECUTING AND MAKE THE WARS.

—from Aldous Huxley's *Perennial Philosophy.*

As Marissa stood there puzzling and frowning over the pedestal and its inscription, someone took her by the arm—suddenly, familiarly.

"How goes the research?" Atsuko said, smiling at her.

Caught out, Marissa wondered for a moment, Which research? Then she thought better of it and decided not to mention her work with Roger, as that seemed somehow always to
involve her in the ideological tug-of-war between mother and
son. Instead she rapidly tried to outline again her ideas of the
normative world-as-it-ought-to-be and descriptive world-as-it-
is, particularly the normative world as an hypostasis of the
pure soul and the way *that* tied utopian fiction into the apoc-
alyptic tradition, into teleology and ethics. Feeling that she was
blathering on, she finished by pointing to the inscription on
the plaque, telling Atsuko that she'd seen a reference to it in
the Collection, so she thought she'd come and take a look.

"I see. Tell me, Marissa," Atsuko said, in a voice of mock-
interrogation, "what exactly is the efficacy of a swimsuit to
the reading of inscriptions on monuments?"

Marissa glanced down at the bathing suit draped over her
arm and laughed.

"You've found me out. I thought I might like to take a

noontime dip too. But I really was going to read the inscription first.''

"I don't doubt it," Atsuko began, coming up beside the monument and reading the plaque. "I was headed to the lake myself. Seriously, though, your interests should make you quite the person for evaluating what we're trying to do here. Have you begun to understand the nature of our experiment yet?''

"I thought I was starting to," Marissa said with a sigh of frustration, "but every day I find something new that puzzles me all over again. I come to look at this inscription—and what do I find? The quote is under a diagram of the space habitat here, on a disk calibrated like a sundial—but there's no gnomon, no style, to cast a shadow on the dial. As a timepiece it's useless, a contradiction—just like placing that quote about a 'goal beyond time' being preferable to utopian dreams under the image of this habitat and all you people are trying to do here. Contradictory—or at least paradoxical.''

"Then you haven't yet learned the experimental and tentative nature of our work," Atsuko responded, smiling enigmatically as she turned Marissa toward the beach and beach tents nearby. Marissa allowed herself to be led. "We're not interested in some product, some final stable state. Process and flux and a certain level of chaos are much more interesting. The chaos of science is the science of chaos, after all—even if I still do have to make my bed every morning.''

"But all those things take place *within* time!" Marissa said fervently as they stopped in front of a dressing tent. "Huxley talks about a goal *beyond* time.''

Atsuko's eyes looked past the green near-distance of the meadow to the shining water beyond.

"The goal is necessarily outside time," she agreed with a small nod, moving toward the other side of the tent. "We can never reach it—woe to us if we could. Think about it this way. Hawking once said that scientific progress mainly involves replacing one wrong theory with another theory that's more subtly wrong. Maybe that's what human history is about too.''

Marissa lifted the flap on her side of the dressing tent as Atsuko entered the other side.

"Are you saying," Marissa began incredulously as she undressed, "that all your projects here are to some degree doomed to failure?"

"Of course. Aren't all projects?" She could hear Atsuko through the canvas, and though she couldn't see her, Marissa thought her mentor must be smiling that enigmatic smile again. "The universe is inherently a place of relativity, incompleteness, uncertainty, at least according to the physicists. No single perfect final anything anywhere in it. Who knows? They might be right."

Hearing a croaking sound inside her tent, Marissa glanced down, momentarily distracted by a frog she could not identify. Oddly, the creature seemed to have bright yellow legs. As she watched, she thought it must undoubtedly be a concrete, living example of another of those threatened lines of life that the orbital habitat was trying to preserve.

"That's all well and good on an abstract theoretical level, I suppose," Marissa replied, pulling on her swimsuit top. "But if I knew that what I was doing must ultimately fail, then what would be the point of trying?"

Even as she said it, Marissa wondered if she might be revealing her misgivings about her own double-headed research projects here. She stuffed her clothes into a hanging sack on the wall and stepped outside to wait for Atsuko.

"Well, it only fails to some degree," Atsuko said from inside the tent. Was there a hint of something maternal in her voice at that moment, or was it only Marissa's imagination? "At the very least, one can learn from failing—even if what one learns is only how to fail better next time. Realizing *that* is a form of enlightenment."

"How's that?" Marissa asked, gazing toward the lake which, to be honest, looked as if it might prove to be more than a little cold.

"Being able to say, 'I don't have the perfect final answer, I can't have it,' " Atsuko replied. "That it's a presumption to assume I can get it. That it's egotistical to think the little piece of the truth I've managed to get in my short span is more important than anyone else's. Coming to that sort of realization is good for one's humility, I think."

So saying, Atsuko—dressed in a snug black one-piece suit—stepped lightly from the tent. Marissa noticed with surprise that she was in quite good shape. As a woman who had just begun the long years of striving against the ravages of time and gravity herself, Marissa admired the older woman's effort.

Atsuko moved awkwardly under Marissa's frank appraisal for a moment, then smiled impishly.

"Speaking of humility," she began, suddenly shifting to verse, "Dr. Correa, quite abstracted, how does your garden grow?"

"With oaths and yells that cursing swells," Marissa rhymed in grimaced reply, "but learning as I go."

Atsuko laughed and clapped her hands as they moved toward the water's edge, creating echoes that bounced off the lake and around the bowl for several long moments before dying away.

Standing at the sandy edge of the water, Marissa noted the way the shore fell steeply away, only a short distance out, the lake clear and suddenly deeper to the water weeds on the bottom, among which supple trout swam, flexible green steel flashing in a flickering verdant shade. The water looked mountain-trout cold, too.

Atsuko abruptly dove in with a big splash, resurfacing quickly with a great intake of breath.

"Come on!" she called and waved as she swam off. "We've got the lake to ourselves! That won't last long—dive in!"

Marissa sprang off from the shore. The chill water when she hit it slammed the air from her lungs and the thoughts from her head like a blow from an icy fist. Her heart had stopped. It did not start beating again until she rose to the surface with a loud whoop. Shivering as she tread water, she began to laugh.

"What's so funny?" Atsuko shouted, splashing some distance away.

"I was just thinking how absurd this all is!" Marissa called, floating on her back, trying to catch some reflected sunlight on her chest and stomach in an attempt to get warm. "I spent my whole life on a green and living world and I never learned to garden! I haven't been swimming in a pure mountain stream or lake since I was an undergraduate! I had to come into space, into a completely artificial world, to get back in touch with what is natural—with the whole world of things we didn't create, of creatures that aren't us!''

Atsuko swam closer.

"That's it,'' she said, smiling even though her teeth were beginning to chatter. "That's the fundamental absurdity of our situation here in this habitat. But absurdity's built into progress too—into the attempt to fail better. Civilization is fundamentally absurd. Even the universe itself. The odds are at least as good that the universe shouldn't exist as that it should, right? It's absurd that the universe should exist, that we should be here to talk about its existence. But here we are.''

Marissa nodded, struck by a sudden thought.

"You know, I can't help thinking—despite everything my research tells me—that maybe at the heart of this world-as-it-is lies the world-as-it-ought-to-be. If we could only see it, only remember how to stop eclipsing its light!''

Atsuko looked as if she suddenly wanted to reach out and take her shivering (but wonderfully perceptive) student in her arms and kiss her—and Marissa would have welcomed that gesture of approval from her mentor. Reluctantly, though, they held themselves back; the water was too deep and they were both afraid they might sink if they stopped swimming.

"I'M HAPPY TO SEE YOU AGAIN,'' ROGER CORTLAND SAID, opening the door to his lab. He'd been surprised to find Jhana Meniskos waiting for him in the hall when he returned from lunch. "You say you're interested in *Heterocephalus glaber*? What is it about the little buggers that interests you?''

"As the most eusocial mammal,'' Jhana said as they walked into the artificially lit confines of the underground lab, "there's been a great deal of genetic research done on them already. They've been DNA-fingerprinted for forty years. Wild and captive groups have been thoroughly charted, and their DNA prints demonstrate heavy inbreeding and a kin-selected colony structure.'' She gestured toward the glass-paned slab of soil and the squirming digging living things inside—creatures that seemed somehow out of place in the sparkling, orderly cleanliness of the lab. "Are these the mole rats? I've just read about them—never seen them alive.''

"That's them, all right," Roger said with a nod. "The 'little grotesques,' as my mother calls them. But you still haven't said what you hope to learn from them—"

"What I want to know," Jhana said, without turning her fascinated gaze from the bustle of the mole rat colony, "is how, given their tendency to form isolated, heavily inbred colonies—how have they remained recognizably a single species, with a remarkably high genetic similarity even between distant colonies?"

"A good question," Roger said, leaning lightly against the rat colony's glass enclosure. "But where does that tie in with the sort of genetic drift research you're engaged in?"

"Everywhere!" Jhana said, flashing him a quick, intense glance. "It opens up all the questions. Usually there's a loss of diversity associated with heavy inbreeding within a highly limited gene pool. Have mole rats successfully managed to avoid that? Is their burden of deleterious mutations lessened through unusually low mutation rates? Or is genetic variability itself purposely kept down?"

Jhana walked around to the other side of the glass case, apparently trying to locate the mole-rat queen. Roger followed slowly behind her.

"Answering those questions," she continued, "finding mechanisms to ensure species diversity, establishing firm numbers for adequate breeding populations—all of those things are of great importance, I would think, to projects like the Orbital Biodiversity Preserve. Not only for the animals but, over the long run, for humans isolated in space colonies, too."

As she turned toward Roger again, he was once more struck by the fineness of her features, particularly her dark eyes, almost as dark as the black silk of her hair. He also noticed that, beneath her businesslike blue-green lab coverall, she had the slim, wiry body of a former gymnast or ballerina. He glanced around, almost unconsciously reassuring himself that Marissa was not there. Certainly his redheaded coworker was attractive in a more voluptuous sort of way, he thought, but—compared to Jhana, here—she had something of the galumphing cow about her. An odd impression, because in fact the two women were probably fairly close in weight and height.

"How about you?" Jhana asked.

"What?" Roger said, suddenly shaking his head and straightening up from the table he'd been leaning his tall frame against. "Excuse me. My mind wandered for a moment. What was your question?"

"How did you become interested in the mole rats?"

"Oh. Saw them in a zoo when I was about fifteen or sixteen, I guess. From the start I was fascinated by how the whole structure of naked mole-rat society is maintained. The only known mammal that possesses a colony structure truly similar to that of the social insects, all that sort of thing."

To make his point, he gestured to the system of tunnels and chambers excavated from the soil inside the glass.

"Within each colony there are three castes, what I like to call queen, courtiers, and peasants. The queen, the breeding female, is generally the largest in size and the most protected. Then come the nonworkers and infrequent workers I call the courtiers, then finally the frequent workers, the peasants, which are generally the smallest in size and the most readily expendable. The peasants cooperate in burrowing, gathering nest material, and bringing food to the nesting chamber for the dominant female and the courtiers, there. Some specialists call that big chamber the 'breedhall.' The male and female courtiers defend the colony. Only the queen breeds, and always only with a courtier male."

He crouched down and stared closely through the glass at his blind, squirming, grey-pink charges—shriveled sausages come to life.

"Individual nonbreeding mole rats are not irreversibly sterile, though," he continued. "And still they have a self-regulating population. That's what fascinated me when I was a teenager. If naked mole rats appreciate the long-term significance of *not* breeding no better than most humans do, then why don't they breed? Why does only the queen breed?" He absently traced the outline of the breedhall chamber with a fingertip on the glass. "The answer I learned in college was that once a particular female becomes dominant, she somehow *behaviorally* suppresses breeding by other females. The older version was that the suppression was achieved through the use of pheromones. Either way, the others in the colony have no choice in the matter."

He came out of his crouch, in the quiet of the lab his knees (the ghost-sounds of an old skiing injury) clicked audibly as he straightened up.

"Unfortunately, no one succeeded in isolating the essential pheromone of a chemical suppression, so the Faulkes orthodoxy of behavioral and physical rather than pheromonal suppression stood." He turned toward Jhana and fixed her with a steady gaze. " 'Behavior'—so vague. I felt I might just as well have been learning that the queen suppressed breeding by magic. But all that's changed now. I believe we've isolated and synthesized the long-sought pheromone here, in this lab. Field tests are proving it out. The Faulkes orthodoxy will be overthrown. I've already finished my paper on it for the *Journal of Mammalogy*."

"Congratulations!" Jhana exclaimed, genuinely impressed. "That's a monumental accomplishment!"

He dismissed her excitement with a wave of his hand.

"I'm already at work on something bigger, *much* bigger," he intimated proudly, his eyes shining. "Quick—give me a list of the world's problems."

Jhana looked at him oddly. Seeing that he was absolutely serious, she shrugged her shoulders and began ticking off the usual litany on her fingers.

"Ecodisasters, mostly—global heat-trap effects, phytoplankton mass extinctions, ozone depletion, losses of biodiversity, worldwide desertification and famine, storm systems of unprecedented severity and duration arising from the recalibration of the planetary heat machinery—"

"Right, right," Roger said, cutting her off. "Poverty and starvation when more food is being produced than ever before. Increased levels of violence as overcrowding generates conditions of behavioral sink. Pestilence and suffering and resource wars—all the age-old plagues, which we have the technological know-how to eliminate but can't."

Absently he ran a hand through his hair and turned his gaze toward the floor, as if trying to stare through it toward the occluded Earth below.

"All the signs indicate that catastrophic environmental effects induced by humans have become not only cumulative but also synergistic, multiplying and dominoing like mad," he continued evenly, a heavenly judge calmly pronouncing the final doom. "We've very nearly exceeded the ecosphere's capacity to regenerate itself—at least in a form that will support humans. And what lies at the root of all those problems, hm?"

Jhana, feeling like a prisoner in the dock, took time to think before she answered.

"I've heard different people say the basic problem is patriarchy, or transnational capitalism, or any world system based on growth and more growth," she hedged—realizing how politically loaded Roger's question was—before coming around to her real thoughts at last. "As a biologist, though, I suppose I'd have to say the root cause is population."

"Exactly!" Roger said, affirming it forcefully with a finger pointed skyward. Jhana felt as if she'd just been given a reprieve from the general doom. "But no one wants to see that or really do anything about it. The essence of tragedy is willful blindness to certain facts or realities. Our situation is tragic because most of our world's governments, religions, and economic systems have remained willfully blind to the increasing likelihood of *human extinction*. As a result, most of the world's people remain ignorant of this likelihood."

"Extinction?" Jhana looked at him as if he'd suddenly sprouted two new heads. "But there are over seven and a half billion human beings on that planet down there—despite every population control method tried. We're hardly a 'vanishing animal.'"

"Yes," Roger said, pacing slowly, thoughtfully, back and forth. "In fact we've been too successful. We're birthing ourselves to death. If you have eyes to see it, it's clear that we're caught in a classic boom/bust cycle. We're quickly becoming the victims of our own success. The only thing that can keep us from finally going past the point of no return is a drastic decrease in human population."

Jhana shook her head, turning her gaze back toward the busy mole rats in their glass-walled slab of habitat.

"Now you're the one talking magic," she said at last. "Or lots of death and suffering and Malthusian mayhem."

Roger spun suddenly on his heel.

"Not at all! I'm talking pheromones, *human* pheromones! Think about it, Ms. Meniskos: a subtle perfume containing a sexual attractant pheromone that acts on human fertility—the denser the concentration of people, the more powerfully the pheromone reduces fertility. A paradox, but there are precedents, you know. Examples of feedback systems by which other species self-regulate their numbers. Epideictic displays among birds, for instance. Think of the advantages. No government would have to force people to undergo vasectomies or tubal ligations. A form of population control, yes, but one not dependent on laws or political decisions or demographic shifts or levels of education. Purely and abstractly responsive to population density, and at the same time inseparably caught up in the whole essence of sexuality and sensuality. ''

A paradox so perfect immediately caused objections to rush into Jhana's mind.

"But it would be so—so unnatural!"

Roger Cortland looked at her with furrowed brow.

"My dear Jhana, we are at this moment living inside an artificial world hanging in space between the Earth and the moon—a habitat as contrived as that mole-rat slice of life you're staring at. What could be more unnatural than that?''

She could only turn and stare at him, still turning over in her mind the potential pitfalls of his scheme. He took her silence for acquiescence and made his checkmate move.

"Even more importantly," he said in a hushed, slightly paranoid manner, "if I can develop such a pheromone, might your employer be interested in it?"

B EFORE ATSUKO AND MARISSA HAD EVEN FINISHED THEIR short, chilly swim and headed back to shore, they no longer had the beach and Echo Mirror Lake to themselves. A group of perhaps half a dozen youngsters had appeared on the other side of the lake, naked, holojam box in tow, projecting trideos onto the lake's surface and exploiting the basin's echoing acoustics to noisy effect.

Excerpted lyrics from Möbius Cadúceus song "Socrates":

The old man urged his students then,
"Make good use of your reason."
But the Athenian state
Called his teachings treason.
Still better to be Socrates than a happy pig.
Far better to be Socrates than a happy pig . . .

Over the noise Atsuko tried to explain to Marissa that the lake shore was, by recently established consensus, divided roughly into sectors that accommodated mixed nude swimming, same-sex nude swimming (male only and female only), mixed swim-suited bathing, and all overlapping gradients of cladness and uncladness in between.

"I know it smacks of 'the oversocialization of the Left'," Marissa heard Atsuko say clearly as their neighbors across the lake finally turned the music down, the volume of it having apparently proven too much even for their young ears. "Or 'the limits of segregation are the limits of toleration.' But openness to diversity is always much needed here. "Toleration of alternatives, combined with a respect for the individual's right not to have his own beliefs infringed upon so long as his beliefs and actions don't infringe upon the rights of others. Always a challenging balance."

"My right to swing my fist ends at your nose?" Marissa asked pleasantly as she lay on the beach, drying off in the sunlight beside Atsuko, who nodded. "But how do you instill that tolerance?" Marissa continued. "The presence of those kids across the lake has gotten me to thinking—particularly about the way you educate and plan to educate your young people here."

"What about it?" Atsuko asked, adjusting her wraparound sunshades.

Marissa thought a moment. More words and music about hemlock and Socrates and happy pigs drifted over from the far shore, but the younger kids seemed intent on some trideo game they'd projected upon the waves. The word VAJRA flashed over the water, followed by a symbol like a shining multifaceted thunderbolt; then a City of Light appeared which, as nearly as Marissa could determine, was being besieged by the forces of darkness. She seemed to remember the word "vajra" from someplace, though she couldn't quite recall where. She shook her head and shrugged.

"Well, if everything is so situational and incomplete and uncertain as you say," Marissa said, trying to put her thoughts into the right words, "then how can one possibly have an ethics?"

Atsuko smiled, beginning to make a game of the conversation.

"That's easy. One can't have an ethics—one *is* an ethics. That's the problem: everybody treats ethics as a product rather than a process." Atsuko paused, thinking it through. Across the lake the song told of a trial and sentence of exile. "That's the problem with ethics generally: so teleological, so oriented to a product external to life rather than inherent in the process of living itself. What I hope we're teaching the children here is that, in a very real sense, the journey *is* the goal—the treasure, the pot of gold, lies not at the rainbow's end but in the chasing of the rainbow. I hope we're teaching the kids to find meaning in the search."

" 'Persistent striving,' as Kierkegaard calls it," Marissa said with a nod. "Not striving for something, or to be somebody. Striving as an end in itself."

"Right," Atsuko agreed, flicking sand off her arm. "A product-oriented ethics, a teleological ethics, is no ethics at all. Any ethics you can *have* isn't worth having."

Sitting up on the sand, Marissa realized that the song of Socrates and the happy pigs was ending, though the game of the shining city floating on the waves still seemed to be going strong.

"But then what do you replace ethics with?" she asked.

Atsuko flipped the wraparounds up off her eyes and looked at Marissa carefully as she answered.

"With nothing. With just being. Letting the stone roll away from the heart, allowing the moon to slide away so the sun can shine."

"Very poetic," Marissa said, "but how does one do that? Through showing compassion?"

Atsuko sat up, brushing sand off her suit.

"Not just showing it. Being it. Living compassion. Existing in a lived recognition of the metaphysical unity behind and underlying and connecting all things." Atsuko laughed lightly.

"That sounds too mystical by half, but it's the best way I can think of to put it—and it's still a lot easier to talk about than it is to do."

Sounds of whistling, shouting, and clapping from across the lake drew the women's attention to the group of youngsters, who were pointing toward the axis of the sky. Looking up, Marissa and Atsuko saw the immense dual snakes of the Möbius Caduceus skysign shimmering and writhing, self-consuming rainbow serpents—

"Good heavens!" Atsuko exclaimed. "What's *that*?"

"Beautiful, isn't it?" Marissa said quietly over the continuing shouts and whoops coming across the water. "I saw it the other day. Roger passed out when he saw it—might've gotten hit by their projection lasers, I think. No real harm done, though, apparently. It's to publicize a performance by that band the kids were listening to. They must be fans. See? There's the skysign where their trideo game was. Or maybe that's just a reflection?"

Atsuko turned from the image in the sky to its reflection in the lake's smooth surface. It seemed even stranger and more exotic mirrored in the water.

"I'm surprised you haven't heard the publicity," Marissa replied, turning toward Atsuko.

"I haven't heard much of anything, lately," Atsuko said, "except rumblings from Earth, that is."

Atsuko neither elaborated nor turned her gaze from the skysign, and Marissa didn't press her. When at last the symbol had disappeared from sky and water, when at last even the echoes of the applause and the shouting had ceased, she turned to Marissa.

"Can there be so mundane, so *profane* an explanation for that symbol?" Atsuko asked, still lost and wondering at the vision in the sky. "It makes me think of that line in Yeats's *Second Coming*—'a vast image out of *Spiritus Mundi* troubles my sight.' And it *is* troubling, too. So archetypal—it makes my head explode with associations! Ancient and modern, past and future, time and timelessness—and all for what? Advertising a show!"

After the fiery eruption of her words, the look of disdain that subsided onto Atsuko's face seemed so curmudgeonly and

out of place that Marissa had to laugh. Atsuko suddenly realized why Marissa was laughing.

"Hah! Listen to me! We hardly need to drive the sacred
and the profane any farther apart than they already are, do we?
And here I am doing just that!"

Atsuko moved off toward the changing tent then, her final
words echoing over the lake and deep inside Marissa. True,
she cherished her theory about the world-as-it-ought-to-be and
the world-as-it-is, but Marissa could never quite forget Hume's
law: No *ought* deducible from *is*. Abruptly she was swept by
the fear that as long as she believed in her *ought's* and *is's*
she was doomed to an Arnoldian limbo, wandering between
two worlds, one dead, the other powerless to be born. Had she,
albeit unconsciously, already consigned the Earth to the first
category, the space habitats to the second? Why her personal
fascination with utopian literature—with what had never been
born from the womb of time? From what longing could such
an obsession have arisen in her?

She suspected that her sudden self-doubt had something to
do with those "rumblings from Earth" Atsuko had mentioned.
As Marissa moved slowly over the sand from the cold water
to the dressing tent, she was not comforted by such thoughts.

SINCE HIS COWORKER JHANA WAS TO BE GONE FOR THE
rest of the day, Paul Larkin thought he'd indulge in a little
media-surfing. A short ride on the "Planetary Fear Machine"—the plenum of all Earth's infotainment and news
broadcasts pumped into his lab's best VR hallucinatorium—
always made Paul feel that, despite living in the orbital boon-
ies, he was still able to keep in touch with what was really
going on down there.

Not that what was *really* going on was to be found openly
talked about on the Fear Machine, Paul thought as he walked
into the big VR room. He knew better than that. He tended to
view the whole constellation of what got pumped out on the
Earth's nets as a sort of planetary ego, a reality principle con-
sciously wailing against the void. He was actually more interested in the planetary id and superego, the unconscious parts
of Earth's noosphere—those parts of the planetary mind that,

with luck, he could read traces of in all those conscious mediations, like a therapist interpreting dreams or slips of the tongue.

To help him see through the wash of surface data he had an entheogen, the mushroom *Cordyceps jacintae* he'd brought back from Caracamuni tepui so long ago—along with some pure KL 235 from the same mushroom species, recently extracted in his lab. He'd never been so gutsy as to let the mushroom take its full twelve years and form a mature myconeural symbiont with his central nervous system—the way the indigenous people of the tepui had. Still, he had a two months' growth of the fungus in his head now, and that, with a new ingestion and the pure extract, should be enough to trigger the chaos in his brain necessary to fully overcome the constraints of the dorsal and median raphe nuclei, the "reducing valves" on brain activity.

Once those impediments were overcome, he could mediasurf at greater than flash-cut speed, which would in turn serve as an information trigger for "going elsewhere," entering that different structure of possibility where he could see the meaningful patterns slowly shifting behind the seemingly meaningless random scatter of world events, entertainments, spectacles, reportage. He always knew when he got to elsewhere, for he could see the patterns of the future already present in the present, could see them clicking into shape like a three-dimensional image rising out of stereogram dot-scatter.

His friend Seiji called it paranoia-tripping, but Paul preferred to think of it as electronic shamanism, aerial voyaging to another realm. Strapping himself into the gimbaled swivelstand and looking about him at the full 360° virtual surround, Paul remembered what work they'd gotten this fancy toy for: identifying, analyzing, and interpreting raw ecological imagery, creating an electronic forest to stand between the thing of dirt and cellulose and sunlight, and the thing of numbers and bytes and electrons. It had not been designed for the use he was now going to put it to, but he knew it would do that well, too.

He slowly chewed the *Cordyceps* fungus, washing it down with the KL extract mixed in papaya juice. He started pumping the material from Earth's infotainment nets into the virtual

space around him, still keeping manual control over the first
thousand channels and the rate of switching. It would be a
quarter of an hour before the entheogens kicked in and his
mind opened out enough so that he could up his data feed and
go to automated switching.

He saw the usual news. Ongoing food riots in at least a
dozen nations. Refugees pouring from one overcrowded camp
to another due to wars civil and uncivil, unrests political and
impolitic. Monsoons in the Bay of Bengal. Heavy storms over
Europe and North America. Forest fires here, flash floods there,
tornadoes and earthquakes thrown in for good measure. Sheep-
herders putting sunglasses on their flocks in Patagonia—the
usual ritual, intended to prevent cataracts resulting from increased UV coming down out of the depleted ozone. Death of
the last wild Florida manatee, in a speedboat encounter. More
marine mammal beachings. Two corporate-sponsored resource
wars in southern Asia . . .

His gaze lingered on a fundamentalist siege of an ark/zoo
facility:

"Before this night is through," booms some folksy white-
maned media holy man, *"the Lord's own wrath will raze this
ark of Satan and lay low every evolutionist, ecoterrorist, and
Gaia worshiper therein!"* Choruses of *"Amen! Amen!"*, and
a wave of applause breaks over the preacher, who smiles be-
nevolently upon his people like a greeting-card grandfather
smiling upon his large, holiday-gathered happy family. The
image cuts from the pastor's words to the actions of his flock—
an overhead twilight shot of thousands upon thousands of
wrathful zealots wearing crosses and cartridge bandoliers,
shooting and shouting and milling round a sandbagged perim-
eter defended by private security forces in riot armor. The
nattering of small arms fire and the occasional whump of mor-
tars can be heard in the background, where smoke rises from
shattered buildings.

Larkin grimaced. Nearly eight billion people on that rock
down there, the one with the blown ozone layer and the cyclonic storms marching across its face, the one with the unhappy isles of seacoast cities huddled behind high dikes,
castellated walls, and moated oceans, the one with the continents of buff-brown desert where once there had been globe-

girdling forests—and all so many of them could still think of was being fruitful and multiplying, clinging all the more tenaciously and in all the greater numbers to the very fundamentalisms that exacerbated the situation.

Crazy—but crazier still if these attacks, now being allowed on the arks and zoos, came also to be allowed upon the Orbital Biodiversity Preserve itself. He knew that many of the religioids thought of the space habitat as a techno-Babylon, an orbital abomination. Were these increasing attacks a sign of some growing betrayal? The Orbital Complex was merely a big investment, after all. Investment strategies could change, if costs got too high. What if some Terran baron got impatient to move stock and began to play the middle between the temporal lords of space and the increasing number of ''spiritual'' rulers on Earth? The habitat's untrammeled Easter garden, its endless springtime world, its lake and marsh and meadow and forest and jungle in space, where ghost species were becoming enfleshed again, a resurrection of all those scattered bodies— this secret-garden world continued to exist only on the sufferance of some very powerful forces on Earth. . . .

He was starting to see the faint gold traceries in his peripheral vision that indicated the entheogens he'd ingested were beginning to take effect, though not yet at full strength. He scanned further:

''We find the addictive popularity of this Building the Ruins game very disturbing,'' said a Korean trideo industry spokeswoman. ''We've already gotten many complaints about it from parents' groups. We want to make clear that responsible Earthbound trideo companies bear no responsibility for the game or its manufacture. In violation of trade regulations it is being designed and updated by someone or some group in the HOME habitat and then flash-manufactured and networkmarketed by questionable business groups here on Earth. Also disturbing is the fact that these addictive game-units are broadcasting back to space, presumably to enable the quick upgrades characteristic of this product and its users' need for constant novelty—''

Larkin's visual field became completely filled with entoptic shimmering, networks of light glowing like spiderwebs of molten gold. He felt himself transforming from a person into a place through which threads and lines of bright energy and information were flowing, creating structures of possibility that he examined not so much with his eyes as with his mind. Some part of him far away snapped the channel-switching mode over to automatic infosurf and removed the thousand-channel limit. Data fell into him at greater than flash-cut speed—not just open broadcasts and public information, but encrypted material, business and government and military. Stock transactions, diplomatic communiqués, troop movements and transport preparations and readiness status. Tetragrammaton and Medusa Blue back-channels, intelligence webs operating behind "bought" governments and corporate fronts like Tao-Ponto and ParaLogics, all squawking about games and unidentified satellites and other strange matters. As much of the Earth's infosphere as he could process was being crammed into Paul's head, randomly and meaninglessly at first, but soon with meaning and pattern rising and growing out of it.

When, two hours later, he had completed his electronic shamanic flight to elsewhere, he knew that the pattern was an ominous one. The forces behind the Plans were marshaling—Holocaust and Exodus, demons and angels, and something, some inevitable but surprising third thing that was both and neither of those oppositional powers. And the focus of that shape of time he'd encountered! It was as if the flat-looking starfield background of the universe had turned into a three-dimensional mountain made of stars—a mountain the peak of which was pointed precisely at the orbital habitat itself.

Switching off the virtual surround, Paul realized the machine was still jittering madly with images. But then, so was he.

J HANA RETURNED TO HER RESIDENCE IN AN AGITATED state. She knew that her employer, Tao-Ponto, would undoubtedly be interested in a pheromone perfume like that which Roger Cortland was working on. Dr. Tien-Jones would definitely consider it a "worthwhile project." She felt equally sure, however, that in their hyping of such a perfume neither Roger Cortland nor Tao-Ponto would be emphasizing its fertility-decreasing aspect. If a perfume could be developed that contained a powerful human sexual attractant—and could also generate tremendous profits without causing immediate cancer in the wearers—she was sure everyone at TPAG would be all for it.

Yet something about the whole scenario still disturbed her— so much so that she felt the need to take her mind off her visit with Roger. She had viewed the instructional tape on the up-keep of her garden area and now decided that a little green therapy might do her some good. Locating a small pair of pruning clippers and some envelopes for seeds, she went out to trim the blown roses, then to remove and store the seeds from the poppies and columbines.

Working her way among the plants, Jhana got sweaty and dirty and itchy with plant cuttings and debris. Despite that, she still marveled at the way this artificial world worked, and won-dered why the world below and its people did not work as well. The gardens here flowed easily (if not effortlessly) into the designated "wild areas," those special habitats for the en-dangered and threatened species of Earth that were being pre-served in space. Looking about the Sphere now, with her feet on the "ground"—looking toward that diversity which, com-bined with height, had so overwhelmed her upon her arrival— instead of seeing something fearful she was now beginning to see a world that was beautiful in its complexity, despite its inside-out strangeness.

Some of the beauty was plainly visible: the multiplicity of environments, the streams that meandered down from the poles through marshes and ponds and then onward to the river gird-ing the Sphere's equator, all flowing into and out of the small natural-looking reservoir called Echo Mirror Lake. Houses and other small buildings were set into the landscape/skyscape, usually in small tight clusters. In the case of single units like the Sanchez-Fukuda place, they were constructed in such a way that rather than being imposed upon it like a city planner's nightmare, the residences seemed to flow up out of the mazed landscape like a geomancer's dream.

As she finished pruning the blown roses, Jhana thought how different the cities of Earth looked, viewed from low orbit or that unsure boundary where airspace ends and outerspace be-gins. Even before she came up here she'd flown over L.A. and

Tokyo and Mexico City, seen computer-enhanced reconnaissance photos of cities around the world, and they'd always reminded her of one thing: a biochip vat-spill gone out of control, some malignant metatumor, half supercomputer microcircuitry and half fungal colony, spreading across a petridish planet, an informational spawn-complex bedding out through mycelia of highways and railroads and sea lanes and flight patterns, trade and exchange, lines of print and code, power lines and telephone wires, broadcast channels and fiberoptic cables and information winging out to satellites. When she'd flown over Earth's cities after dark, or seen shots of them nightside from space, they had not reminded her of glittering diamonds but rather of great electronic fungal colonies glowing and burning like graveyard foxfire, a luminescent pox on the face of the darkness.

Rubbing columbine seed pods mechanically between her fingers so that the black seeds fell into an envelope, Jhana's mind was far away, thinking how different her homeworld would look if this habitat were everted and spread upon the Earth, in place of the human habitations that were already there. Certainly an Earth so inhabited would be almost invisible from space, day or night—the presence of human settlement harder to detect because it would be shedding so much less light and heat into the surrounding environment.

Even as she looked at the Sphere's cavernous interior now, she supposed that most of its real beauty—or at least its elegance and efficiency—was almost invisible here too. Despite her initial misgivings, she was beginning to develop a grudging respect for the place. Its virtues were that way: invisible, subterranean—not sensational or spectacular.

Nearly all of the habitat's trashstream was fully recycled—so? The soil in the farming, wild, and habitation areas was always given time to regenerate itself—who cares? All the gases of organic decomposition were utilized and all the possible pollutants of living or farming or manufacturing were eliminated at the source or fully reclaimed for other uses—eh, big deal. None of that was sexy, none of that would ever show up well in a tour-brochure-from-space description. Yet it was really what this place was about.

When she'd heard, before she came up here, that the

weather in the habitat was pretty much always perfect, Jhana had thought, My God, whatever do people find to talk about? Yet clearly they found plenty—as if, once the actual weather was no longer a topic of conversation, every other kind of weather—political weather, religious weather—could be discussed. Not that that distanced them from dirt and wind and water, though. Working in the garden, it was becoming clearer to her that people here had to live in careful harmony with their environment because if they didn't, they'd die. This place was a lifeboat compared to the luxury liner of Earth, but as a consequence of their stricter confines the passengers here seemed much less inclined to take their world for granted.

She thought about that passage in the Bible that says it is easier for a camel to pass through the eye of a needle than for a rich man to enter the Kingdom of Heaven. Here, in this peaceable kingdom in the heavens, it seemed equally difficult to live luxuriously and wastefully—because everyone was always aware of the narrowness of the needle's eye. Yet, despite the constraints, the lives of the settlers were still rich, as rich as that of nearly anybody on Earth, though in less tangible ways. Crushing dried, ripe poppy capsules between her fingers for the tiny seeds that rained out of them and fell into her collecting envelope, Jhana thought that this sort of world, spread upon the Earth, might not be such a bad thing after all.

Standing in the midst of the garden she closed her eyes and inhaled the thick, sensual blend of scents around her. The action of this perfume, she reflected, was very different from that of the perfume Roger Cortland proposed. She knew that the scientific reason for all the green plants in the habitat was nominally that they pumped more oxygen into the air and encouraged an ion balance more favorable to human contentment. The scents and colors, though not much talked about in the technical reports, were a superfluous grace everyone appreciated.

The idea of scents, however, dragged her mind determinedly back to Roger's work. Besides its sexual attractant powers, the other property of Roger's proposed perfume, the secret one that no one would be talking about—would that be a superfluous grace too? Or something else?

Her eye caught Seiji Yamaguchi's as he walked past on a

garden path nearby, jaunty in an anachronistic pair of blue overalls. Jhana waved and he came toward her, the two of them making small talk about gardening and Seiji's landscaping work for one of her neighbors, until he changed the subject.

"You seemed deep in thought when you first turned toward me," he said after he'd joined Jhana in her garden. "Hope it wasn't anything I said or did."

"Oh no, no," she assured Seiji, then stared a moment at him. Something about the man's look of quiet expectancy removed any barrier of "confidentiality" she might have felt toward Roger what he'd told her. "I don't know if I should tell you about this ..." she began, then went on to tell him about Roger's proposed pheromone plan, spilling out the disturbing issues it raised for her, continuing as she did so to absently deadhead flowers and cut newer blooms to bring inside.

"If the settlers here have no choice but to live in harmony with their environment or die here," she said, finishing up, "then does Roger's scheme to reduce Earth's population differ all that much from the space habitat designers'? And, if he can really develop what he's working on, Roger's plan will take effect much more quickly. In the short term it would be more efficient, too."

Seiji frowned and shook his head.

"It's not that simple though, you know," he said, taking an armful of her cut flowers, both of them thinking about it as they walked from the garden. "The main difference between the 'constraints,' as you call them, associated with Roger's plan and those associated with the hopes surrounding the space habitat come down fundamentally to an issue of choice."

"I don't see how," Jhana said as they walked inside her house.

"People make a *conscious* decision as to whether or not they want to live in a space habitat to begin with," Seiji insisted as they began gathering vases for the flowers. "We make an informed choice as to whether we want to put ourselves in such a restricted situation. We have a choice of worlds, more so than any previous generation of humanity. The system of space colonization will take longer to reduce the population burden on Earth than Roger's plan would, true. Space habitats are more long-term, arguably more 'wasteful' of time that humanity and the Earth's ecosphere can ill afford to waste. Yet, no matter whether it succeeds or fails, at least our long-range plan is a humanitarian means to a humane end.''

"And you don't think Roger's plan would be?'' Jhana asked, filing away the packets of seeds she'd collected as Seiji puttered about, absent-mindedly arranging the flowers.

"If people are kept uninformed about the pheromone perfume's secondary effect, if they're deliberately kept unconscious of it,'' Seiji said, puzzling it through, "then the element of informed choice will be left out of the equation. Denying people that choice means denying them part of their role as autonomous adults, diminishing their humanity by diminishing the role of choice and will in their lives.''

"So Roger's perfume proposal reeks of chemical authoritarianism,'' Jhana said, unable to resist teasing Seiji a little as she made a few changes in his flower arrangements. "Stinks of olfactory fascism, of leading people literally by the nose?''

"Now, I didn't say that,'' Seiji protested, holding his hands up before him. "Why would anyone want that? From everything I know about him, Roger Cortland just doesn't seem the type of person who lusts for power in that sort of Big-Daddy-knows-best style. I wonder what's driving his interest in this pheromone stuff?''

Seiji looked at his watch, then glanced around the room as if trying to remember something.

"Oh, I've got another appointment,'' he said suddenly. "I must be going. Perhaps we could get together and continue this conversation again sometime soon?''

"Yes, I'd like that,'' Jhana said, walking with him to the door. "Over lunch, maybe? Let's keep in touch—I'd like to learn more about your work with the power satellites, too.''

Seiji agreed and they said their goodbyes. Jhana watched him go, thinking that it didn't require pheromones to make Seiji Yamaguchi attractive to her, in his kindly, distracted sort of way. He was in very good physical shape, probably from all his gardening work. She'd hate to think she was just using him as a source of information.

Standing in the living area, looking at the flower arrangements and smelling their perfume in the air, Jhana pondered her next course of action. Should she—based on what she only suspected and could not prove, about a biochemical that hadn't even been synthesized yet—should she keep Roger's work hidden, neglect to pass the information on to her superiors? She had promised Roger she'd let Tao-Ponto know about it. Should she go back on that promise for the sake of protecting strangers from some as-yet-obscure harm—or would with-holding information make her a Big Mommy, guilty of de-nying people the possibility of choice? As unethical as Roger and Tao-Ponto would be themselves, if they ever marketed the stuff and purposely neglected to inform the public of the pher-omone's secondary effect?

Abruptly, Jhana felt as if Roger had handed her the olfactory equivalent of nuclear bomb plans. The roles offered her now—spy, accomplice, whistle-blower—were none of them very comfortable.

No, she couldn't hide his proposal. Doing that would deny her TPAG superiors the possibility of informed choice—the very thing which, she had to agree with Seiji, was so wrong about Roger's plans. If it was wrong for Roger to use such covert means for the supposedly lofty end he sought, then it would be equally wrong for her to use such means to accom-plish her ends.

Checking the time in Balance Tien Jones's zone on Earth, Jhana gave his office number to her wall screen. She did not feel good about doing her job in this way, but she did it. Getting only his answering computer on the line, she was ob-scurely relieved that she could leave the information as a mes-sage for him without having to actually converse with anyone about it.

WONDERING IF HE HAD TOLD JHANA TOO MUCH, AND UN-sure of her reaction to his project, Roger was working late, determined more than ever to promptly complete the syn-thesis of the human pheromone that had become his obsession.

With the help of his information manager program or IMP (which he'd customized to look and act like an on-screen mole rat), Roger had finger-walked through innumerable virtual li-braries on Earth, scanning myriad relevant selections from the scientific literature relating to pheromones and sexuality. He

had stumbled on the relationship of the olfactory sense to
memory, to theta rhythm, to REM sleep and the rise of dreaming in mammals one hundred and forty million years ago—
learning, in the process, a great deal more about dreaming
itself, both as information reprocessing and as survival strategy.

"Everything in the literature fits the plan for the proposed
pheromone," he mused aloud to his mole-rat IMP, "except
for one thing: theta rhythm has not been demonstrated in
higher primates in this context."

"Yes," the IMP confirmed. "Available evidence suggests
it disappeared when vision replaced olfaction as the dominant
sense."

"Okay," Roger said, sending his IMP on a new search.
"Our pheromone will have to be a potent one, capable of
reawakening some of the olfactory sense's underlying, ancient
powers. Examine further the scientific literature on the deep
relation of olfaction to sexual excitation—focusing particularly
on this memory trigger issue."

"Will do," said the IMP, tunneling away mole-ratwise into
the infosphere.

Roger felt too tired to think and analyze further—but still
much too fidgety with nervous energy to consider going to
sleep. Wandering through the lab a bit aimlessly, he saw that
Marissa was working late too, playing the Girl with the DNA
Eyes on one of their CAMD facility's Cybergene machines.
As he stopped outside the door, he saw her unsuiting, clearly
frustrated.

"How goes it?" he asked innocently—though he stared less
innocently at the coppery waterfall of her thick hair as she
removed her wraparounds.

"Not well," Marissa said with a sigh. "Getting this immortalizing vector to even *begin* to function is turning out to
be a lot more work than I suspected."

"I was thinking of taking a little spacewalk to unwind,"
Roger said nonchalantly. "Maybe you'd like to come along—
if you're at a good break point too, that is."

"Are you kidding?" Marissa said. "Even if I were on the
verge of a major discovery I'd take a break to do that."

"Then follow me."

Via ridge cart they made their way to the docking facilities and then to the pod bays. Boarding Roger's small private craft, they donned a pair of his custom maneuvering suits as the little ship, traveling on autopilot, left the bays and the docking area, then slowed and stopped a hundred kilometers off the main traffic lanes leading to the habitat. Since they had to strip down to get into their opaque suits, Roger politely turned his head as, back to back, they dressed in the small pod. When he had checked over Marissa's suit and they were safely at their destination, Roger ordered the hatch open and they drifted into the vast blue-black womb of the universe.

"This is fantastic!" Marissa said over the intercom, nervous excitement in her voice. "Like being angels in heaven!"

"Ah, but if a heaven is to be safe for astronauts," Roger said as he stepped from the airlock behind her, "it must be devoid of angels."

"What?"

"Just think of all the trouble angels would have posed to the opening of the space frontier," Roger said, mock-serious as he instructed Marissa in some basic tandem maneuvers. "Splatting on portholes. Getting sucked into scramjets. Fouling the lines of lightsails. Getting blasted to pieces by mass-driver projectiles. Winged by space junk, to fall down the burning sky, helpless feathery meteors smashing into the Earth's thick walls of air . . ."

"That," Marissa said, "is a truly perverse image."

Roger laughed.

"Maybe," he said, "but not historically unprecedented. Think of dodos and passenger pigeons, or aborigines and American Indians, for that matter. If angels did exist, it would be necessary for us to exterminate them. Angel killers, like the stool-pigeoners and buffalo hunters of old, blasting away at huge flocks of the heavenly hosts, lasers splashing red on their pearly wings and flesh. Have to be sophisticated hunters too— 'What sport, eh? Back in the hypersaddle again, riding the range on the final frontier!' "

Roger cut in his suit's maneuvering and attitude jets. In the thin, flexibly responsive gossamer armor of his livesuit, he did feel a bit like a conquistador surveying new worlds to conquer, though certainly he was not so bloody-minded as those angel-hunters he spoke of. He had to admit, though, that he *did* like to tweak Marissa's sensibilities a wee bit. She moved more slowly behind him as he zipped along, but she was a fast learner and was quickly catching on to how the maneuvering suits worked.

Coming up above the space colony, he saw the bright mass of Earth, blue-white big sister in the womb of night. He saw the anorexic moon further on, and the great fireball of the sun.

"There it is," Roger said, always somewhat awestruck by the power of that fireball. "A hydrogen bomb exploding endlessly, eight and a half minutes away, far enough for terror to become beauty and death to become life."

"Why, Roger," Marissa said, "I'm surprised. I do believe there's a poet trapped somewhere down in that soul of yours."

"Stick with me, kid," he said, imitating a twentieth-century film icon, "and you'll never get bored."

They pivoted slightly. Ringing Earth like a necklace, the solar power satellite stations floated in the void before them, glinting in the sunlight of an eternal day, sending vast streams of gigawattage invisibly to Earth in the form of microwaves, powering up the dawn of the so-called Solar Age. Arrays of metal-film reflectors stretched upon frameworks a kilometer square each, they were the space colonies' reason for being—both this colony below and behind them now, and the two scheduled to open soon.

"See that?" he said, gazing carefully. "You can just make out one of the new colonies in the distance—doughnut-stack tori along the axis of a completed sphere, see? The other colony must be occluded by Earth and shadows, at the moment."

"I'm just so impressed by what's being done out here," Marissa said, following him as he moved from vista to vista, "especially by what your mother and the rest of the colony founders are doing."

"Hm," Roger grunted and swung around toward the colony. "All this great tech, and still they want to waste their time on ridiculous social engineering schemes."

"What? Don't you believe in the possibility of bettering ourselves?"

"My dear Marissa, I am certainly a firm believer in the revealed religion of Inevitable Technological Progress—more so than either of my parents. What else is there to believe in, in the long run?''

''Human beings, maybe?'' Marissa ventured, suspecting what sort of response that idea would get.

''Nonsense! Too unpredictable!'' Roger said firmly as they floated into better view of the long axis of the space habitat. ''Just look at the ridiculous shams of politics and political science and sociology. I have a good deal more faith in engineering specs than in the 'nature' of my fellow mortals. There's a technological solution to every human problem, if only enough time and money were put into searching for that solution—and if it were allowed to be implemented.''

''I can't believe you're that naive a technological optimist!'' Marissa exclaimed, even though, at that moment, she was also quite well aware of how dependent she was on the impressive piece of technology keeping her alive and functioning in this environment that was so inimical to unprotected life. ''You can't eliminate the human factor—''

''That's just the problem!'' Roger said, truly exasperated as they drifted along in their sublime surroundings to which, for the moment, he was thoroughly oblivious. ''Within a relatively short time, the need for satellite solar power stations will drop, because the stations already in place will be providing all the energy humanity needs. Eventually such energy wealth will help bring about the demographic shift that might lead the population growth rate downward—but when? Once human numbers have hit ten billion? Fifteen? At some point along that trajectory, ecocatastrophe will kick in and take an enormous toll. Then, when humanity needs the space habitats most, where will they be? The government/corporate consortia will have already stopped building the habitats because our major product, the satellite solar power stations, the SSPS, will have already ceased to be profitable!''

''But I've been reading the works written by your mother and the other founders,'' Marissa objected, wishing she could reach out, grab Roger by the arm, and say, Wait a minute!—but settling for narrowcast argument instead. ''They claim that the space habitats will become valuable in themselves—regardless of whether they turn out a profitable product like the SSPS. According to the founders, the construction of space habitats themselves will become a valued enterprise—''

''—'and this will drive a momentum growth phase, during which habitat construction will, over time, outstrip human population growth, eventually reaching the point at which emigration to the space colonies will be so great that Earth's human population will actually start to decline!' '' Roger said, sententiously and sarcastically. ''I've heard that song and dance before. I wish I could believe it, but I just don't buy it.''

''Why not?'' Marissa asked, maneuvering up in front of him. She really wanted to know, since she thought it was a hopeful scenario that might even work.

''Where will the demand for new habitats come from?'' Roger asked, intent on demolishing what he perceived to be her illusions. ''Before the majority of human beings will ever want to live in a floating botanical garden in space, things will have to have already gotten pretty damned lousy on Earth. And by then it will be too late.''

''Do you have a better suggestion?'' Marissa asked, a bit peeved at what she regarded as his technological arrogance.

''Yes, as a matter of fact, I do. Better to trust in solutions that take human decision-making out of the loop. Like my pheromone research. If my idea works, then human population can be made realistically resource-dependent. If humanity never fully breaks out into space, that will be all right—human numbers will be self-regulating and thus will never push the Earth's life-support systems into ecocatastrophe.''

''And if the breakout into space begins to happen anyway?'' Marissa prodded. Much about Roger's whole scenario struck her as downright dehumanizing—even if it did seem to solve a lot of critical problems.

''That'll be fine too,'' Roger said happily. ''A pheromone-shifted humanity will be more amenable to, and more easily spread by, the same process of colony fissioning or budding that's seen in mole rats.''

''You seem to have all the answers,'' Marissa admitted as they jetted along through the silent void between the space colony and the nearest satellite solar power station. She tried to change the subject—hopefully not too awkwardly. ''I don't share your absolute faith in tech, but I must admit—these spacesuits we're wearing, they're quite impressive. I've never seen suits like them before."

"That's right," Roger agreed, beaming. "Here we are, naked inside them, separated from the killing emptiness by only a few millimeters of transparent helmet and opaque, rubbery, slick material."

"It feels so sheer," Marissa enthused, believing what she was saying even if it did sound like an advertisement, "that I almost forget I'm wearing anything. Like being naked to the universe."

"But still fully protected, breathing clean fresh air," Roger said. "It's a livesuit, possessing a programmable active structure. Nothing like the bulky armor that protected fragile humans when we first came into space. This is all active nanoelectronics and nanomachinery. Microscopic motors and computers, combined with the suit's three-dimensional weave of diamond-based active fibers. Makes you quite capable of wrestling with angels or grasping the head of a pin. In sunlight the suit functions like a one-person ecosystem, absorbing light from outside and your own exhaled carbon dioxide from within the suit, to produce fresh oxygen from the two, almost like a plant. In case of emergency, it can break down other wastes into their constituent molecules and reassemble them into foodstuffs."

Marissa could have done without hearing that last yummy bit of technological goshwowery, but she was still undeniably impressed.

"Why haven't I heard more about these supersuits?" she asked, executing a full somersault that she wouldn't have imagined she had the grace to complete so flawlessly.

"Because," Roger said, exhaling heavily, as if the question had punched him unexpectedly in the solar plexus, "it was inside just such a prototype supersuit, as you called it, that my father died."

Marissa abruptly stopped doing somersaults.

"He was walking at the bottom of the Marianas Trench," Roger said. "Kilometers underwater in the Pacific. One of his companies had developed the livesuit. There was no reason for the suit to fail—even under such extreme conditions. I still don't believe it was the technology that failed. It was people.

Someone, somehow, programmed that suit to collapse, or at least to allow itself to collapse. The moment the suit failed, my father died.''

Roger began to move slowly back in the direction of the pod they'd come out in, now on a line with the space colony and its space docks. Marissa moved beside him, carefully matching his slow speed.

"My father had already given me a pair of the prototype suits as a birthday present," Roger went on. "I always try to wear one, without fear, whenever I'm out. Still, I can't shake the memory associated with it. I guess Dad's executives haven't shaken it either. For them the livesuit is a deathsuit. They've never marketed it."

He put himself into a slow 360° turn. Maneuvering alone in free space was as close as he ever came to a meditative state, but he'd had enough of contemplation for now, he thought, as he came face to face with Marissa.

"It gets to me too, sometimes," he said quietly over the intercom. "No matter how much I trust the tech, no matter how often I come out here protected by it alone, I sometimes feel haunted in the suit, like I'm wearing my dead father's clothes."

Without so much as a word, Marissa came to Roger and hugged him—a strangely sensual embrace, in the livesuits. He did not attempt to free himself from that intimate contact. Slowly, as they turned together in space, their motion became a sad waltz among the heavens, a dance unutterably mournful, though their brows were wreathed with stars, and planets stood at their feet.

Trying to dismiss the thought from his mind, Roger spun slowly out of their long embrace. Just as he was completing his turn, however, he thought he saw from the corner of his eye a flutter of tremendous shimmering wings, all around the Earth. Snapping his gaze back toward it, he could see only the glint of some of the new mirroring structures, the X-shaped things he'd noticed on the flight up, though now there were many more of them, rapidly abuilding near all the SSPSs.

Shifting his attention back to his return trajectory and taking

Marissa by the hand, he wondered vaguely what purpose the new structures might serve. The thought left him as they re-boarded his small craft and he and Marissa began stripping out of the livesuits, face to face this time, not back to back.

EIGHT

A S LAKSHMI APPROACHED THE BACKSTAGE AREA WHERE
the members of Möbius Cadúceus were building their set,
she eavesdropped on the comments being exchanged through
the closecomm Public Sphere. Such philosophical remarks
bounced among them that they made her wonder a) if the cast
and crew had been indulging in a bit of mind-alteration this
early in the day and b) what had ever happened to that Hitch-
cockian era when actors (and, by extension, all performers)
were "cattle."

"—paranoid alienation is the basis of science and the scientific method," said a woman whose voice Lakshmi didn't
recognize.

"But the knower must not only be alienated from, but also
related to, the object of knowledge," an unfamiliar male voice
said. "If the knower weren't related to it in some way, how
could he or she know it at all?"

"Think about it this way," said a voice Lakshmi definitely
recognized as Lev Korchnoi's. "Knowledge is recognizing
that 'I,' the subject, and the 'Other'—it, the object, you—are
not one. Wisdom lies in understanding that, despite appearances, I and the Other are one, is One."

"Metaphysical unity of all beings?" said a new female
voice. "Then what's the difference between wisdom and com-

passion, if it's all just the shift from the 'I-it' to the 'I-thou' relation?''

"True," Lakshmi heard Lev agree, "but it's more than that. Creatures with no epistemic space, no alienating self-awareness, could never know 'I' nor 'it' nor 'thou.' Alienated, self-aware humans know 'I' and 'it' quite well—just look at our obsession with personal or tribal power, dominion over the Earth and our fellow creatures, all that. Maybe we even know a bit about 'thou.' Generally, though, we find it really hard to live inside the idea that I and it and thou are actually one.''

"A cycle, then?" asked another unfamiliar voice. "From an unconscious unawareness of self or other, to a conscious awareness of self and other, to a superconscious awakening to the idea of the fundamental inseparability of all things?''

"Not so much a cycle as a spiral, I think," Lev said slowly. "Or some sort of circle with a twist maybe—''

"Oh, no," groaned one of the women. "A Möbius strip again!''

"Whatever shape we try to cast the idea in," Lev said, trying to regain control of the conversation, "it's still pretty clear that if wisdom equals knowledge plus compassion, then as a species we're very knowledgeable but not very wise. Higher than the snakes but lower than the angels. That's really what our performance is about, ultimately.''

Lakshmi, now within sight of the set builders, had been stopped by Security.

"Pretty highfalutin talk," she called out to Lev, "for a guy in a fake soldier suit.''

"This is not a *fake* soldier suit," Lev said, waving her in past Security, then executing a perfect spin off the high scaffolding where he'd been working, coming to rest in a gymnast's landing. He walked toward Lakshmi as she hovered in.

"This armor was the very latest in stealth-soldier *haute couture*, circa 2014," Lev continued, in mock fashion-show-host tones. "A Mitsui/GenDyn joint venture. Superdense Kevlar lined in EMR absorbent material that also reduces both noise *and* infrared signature. It offers extensive musculature augmentation, stands impervious to all kinds of small-arms fire and shrapnel, and is fully covered in computer-sensored chameleon cloth—camouflage adaptable to any level of light, any pattern in the surrounding environment, or programmable for special missions. The helmet is similarly top-of-the-line, equipped with fully integrated telecommunications and heads-up targeting electronics for the suit's shockwave gauntlet. It also features a mechanically activated C4 self-destruct capability, for those sticky social situations.''

Lakshmi heard some of the crew up in the scaffolding laughing and snickering, but ignored them for the moment. She watched as Lev did Superman leaps in his costume, and she tried to remember what he'd said about musculature augmentation.

"It looks real enough," Lakshmi had to admit.

"It is," Lev said, bounding about like a Wehrmacht gazelle. "Absolutely real. Genuine enhanced stealth battle armor."

"But what's it for?"

"What do you mean?" Lev asked, trying a roundhouse kick, and smiling in satisfaction when it lashed the air with inhuman force.

"First you do that heavy study in stage combat," Lakshmi said, the edge of concern creeping into her voice, "and now this."

"Authenticity," Lev said, leaping a dozen feet straight into the air. "And added safety. All for the show. Besides, with the right programming, what I'm wearing will not only adapt to surrounding spatial patterns, but also temporal ones."

"What?"

"I can program it to simulate battle costume from any period in history I choose—and that's key to the performance."

"Well, just don't become too enamored of this macho-boy stuff," Lakshmi cautioned. "There's a world going on outside your Möbius Cadúceus performance, you know. And it's getting stranger all the time. Aleister pulled some interesting stuff out of the RATs that you need to see."

"Okay, okay, but first let me introduce you to the band," Lev said, then turned to call up to the crew he'd left behind on the set construction. "Everybody! This is Lakshmi Ngubo, the person who, after much effort, finally completely debugged the shobot Guardians! Laksh, that guy on the fastener gun is our woodwinds maestro, Adewole Umoje. Those two, hanging flats there, are Mary Nakulita and Liselle Merukana, keyboard and string interfacers, respectively. The gentleman hanging lights is Liu Xang, brass master, and the woman under the spot-welding mask is my co-star—Eve to my Adam, Bliss to my Will—Cana LaJeunesse.''

Lakshmi and the band members waved and nodded to each other. When that was done, she and Lev moved off to a corner of the playing space, out of the worst of the construction noise.

''Since you dumped the LogiBox problems into your friend Aleister's lap and ran off to work on your show, Lev dear,'' Lakshmi said, her voice a level purr only slightly louder than the sound of her hoverchair, ''we've made some progress. You'll be glad to hear that your LogiBox installation is not responsible for the problems—''

''Hah! I knew it!''

''But there are other matters which might still concern someone with a day job in Communications—or have you forgotten that part of your life?''

''What other matters?'' Lev said grumpily.

''Oh, little things—like the fact that the majority of the dataflow between Earth and the Orbital Complex is no longer going through recognized channels.''

''What?''

''The thing in the Boxes, Lev. The consciousness you said couldn't be a consciousness. Whatever it is—let's call it an intelligence—it's out of the Boxes, now. We couldn't shut it down if we wanted to. It's 'distributed' itself, largely through the RATs, but in other ways too. That distributed consciousness—excuse me, distributed *intelligence*—it's behind the spread of this Building the Ruins game. I've played it, Lev. *Very* strange. Even stranger is the fact that the information from all those playings of that game is being sent up the well, along with one helluva lot of other data. Informationally speaking, the Orbital Complex has become a hot spot. At the current rate of dataflow, in a day or so we'll be hotter than any single city on Earth—hotter than most countries, in fact.''

Lev stared at her.

''But where's all that data *going?*''

''Not to us,'' Lakshmi said quietly. ''Aleister and I aren't sure, but we suspect those X-shaped satellites have something to do with information storage, among other things. They've been built by micromachines acting 'autonomously.' But the distributed consciousness is deeply intermingled with the VA-JRA—''

''And the VAJRA coordinates with all the micromachines,'' Lev said, chewing his lower lip nervously. ''Aw Jeez. What have you told Atsuko Cortland about this?''

''Just that we've located the source of the problem and are working to correct it.''

''That's true enough,'' Lev said, trying to put a hopeful spin on things. ''You got the thing in the Boxes to stop glitching my shobots, at least.''

''Right,'' Lakshmi acknowledged. ''Or maybe it was just finished getting our attention that way. Something's still building that weird 'spirit-animal' sculpture in my workshop, you know.''

''But otherwise the distributed whatever-it-is seems harmless enough, right?'' Lev continued in his hopeful vein. ''The only damage I can really think of that it's done is sour our relations with Earth a bit, that's all.''

''That,'' Lakshmi agreed, ''and some of the micromachines have been raiding the mass drivers—for materials to build those X-satellites, is our guess. But there's something else. Aleister's found this extreme redundancy in the RATs, all repeating the same nonfunctional sequence of code. It's a list of names.''

Lakshmi shot the list to Lev's personal data assistant and the list appeared on his wraparounds. Six names. Two he knew well enough by reputation—both Cortlands, Roger and Atsuko. Two he knew vaguely—Seiji Yamaguchi and Paul Larkin. One he knew not at all—Jhana Meniskos. And one he could never get to know—Jiro Yamaguchi.

''Strange list, isn't it?'' Lakshmi said cryptically. ''We don't know how they tie into the RATs. None of them have ever been to Sedona, where the Real-time A-life Technopredators were developed. None of them ever had any connection with the Myrrhisticine Abbey and its network manager, the ex-phreaker Phelonious Manqué. Some weren't even born when it happened.''

''When what happened?'' Lev asked, lost for a moment.

''This,'' Lakshmi said, shooting Lev's PDA another feed.

An old-style video image appeared on his wraparounds, amateurish, someone's unsteady hand moving the viewfinder. A red mesa or butte—Lev couldn't remember which term fit—topped by a complex of Neo-Gothic buildings.

"The abbey," Lakshmi said, following along. "Here it comes. Watch."

Above the abbey on the mesa a flash of light burst, but didn't go away. Instead it quickly became a point of light, then a hole of darkness rimmed by light like the "diamond ring" stage of an eclipse. The light-rimmed hole grew rapidly, until it was clear that it wasn't ringed by white light but by myriad rainbow fires dancing over its whole surface. What looked like points of light glowed inside it too. It blotted out the abbey, then most of the mesa, then disappeared as quickly as it had come, leaving behind only a bowl of broken stone.

"What the hell was *that*?"

"We don't really know," Lakshmi said quietly. "Aleister's still searching. Sensationalist media at the time called it the 'black hole sun' and 'Tunguska II.' Scientific theories ranged from meteoritic impact to anomalous seismic event to the sudden appearance of a microsingularity. Religionists claimed it was a 'rapturing'—mainly because the Myrrhisticineans were slow apocalyptists."

"Looks like they got their wish," Lev said cautiously. "Does it have anything to do with what's going on up here?"

"We don't know that either. The RATs are the only connection. But the man who called himself Manqué didn't survive. No one who was on that mesa that day has ever been heard from since. The only Myrrhisticineans who survived were those who were away from the abbey."

One of the band crew called Lev's name. Apparently his advice was needed on some aspect of the construction.

"Look, Laksh, I've got to go," Korchnoi said, already moving away. "But keep me in the loop on this—especially if anything else affecting Comm comes up."

Lakshmi watched him leave. He still bounded away, but his bounding wasn't as light. Superman, with burden, she thought as her hoverchair turned slowly away.

•   •   •

M ARISSA HAD STEPPED OUT OF THE LAB ONLY BRIEFLY for coffee, but when she got back the ideological tug of war between Atsuko and Roger was well under way. She should have known better than to suggest that Atsuko meet her at the lab.

"—and this work is hyperspecialized and reductionist in the extreme," Atsuko was saying pointedly. "Working with these perfect little monsters from the id, these naked mole rats."

"I'm surprised at you, Mother," Roger said sarcastically. "Isn't it you who's always preached the inherent worth and value of every species? Why else preserve biodiversity?"

"But these creatures strain even *my* tolerance. Blind, hairless, incestuous, subterranean, shit-eating little beggars!"

Marissa burst out laughing at the obvious distaste in Atsuko's voice. Seeing who had laughed, Atsuko managed a slight smile.

"Why are you laughing?" Atsuko asked. "I didn't mean for it to come out as profanely as it did, but it's all literally true, you know. They *are* blind. They *are* hairless, or virtually so. They spend their entire lives underground—'completely fossorial,' as the scientific articles put it. The researchers may speak primly of inbreeding and consanguineous mating, but that's just a nice way of saying incest. The young, the pups, when hungry 'beg fecal matter from the adults,' which the mole-rat experts term coprophagy. They also engage in autocoprophagy—they roll their own, and then they eat it!" Now Atsuko laughed, too, at quite some length.

Marissa found herself laughing along.

"Undeniably," Roger said at last, when his mother's childish laughter had subsided, "but they're as worthy of scientific research as anything else—"

"No doubt. Maybe more worthy, than most things. All I'll say is that Jennifer Jarvis, the 'mother of naked mole rat research,' must have possessed an incredibly detached scientific objectivity while she was working with them."

Marissa smiled, leaning forward.

"You seem to have learned more than a little bit about them yourself."

"Yes," Atsuko said, her tone growing more serious. "A mother likes to know what her son is up to—even when the son and mother are as *loving* as Roger and I are. It helps me figure out certain things. Knowing, for instance, that Jarvis worked at the University of Cape Town, turning it into the world's great center for the study of eusocial mammals—that helps explain why Roger spent several of his graduate-school summers there. It also explains why he's working up here now.''

''Not to be closer to my mother?'' Roger put in, *faux naive*, hugging his mother with an almost painful ferocity.

''Hardly,'' Atsuko said, extricating herself from her son's embrace. ''The Preserve has the largest collection of wild-caught naked mole rats anywhere, and some of the best facilities available to biological researchers, as you well know. It's not filial love that brings you here. It's your own obsessions—though why you should be obsessed with those little monsters, I'll never know.''

A silence fell between them then. Marissa strove to fill the awkward emptiness.

''Weren't we going to the gym?'' she said to Atsuko. ''Then on to the Archive?''

''That's why I came here,'' Atsuko said, none too obliquely. They bid Roger goodbye, Marissa smiling knowingly over Atsuko's head. Roger returned the knowing smile gratefully, thankful to have Marissa's help in ushering his mother onward and out of the lab.

Roger returned to reviewing the material his mole-rat IMP had scavenged from all over the infosphere, but after about ten minutes he found he couldn't concentrate. Maybe it was just a hangover from his spacewalk with Marissa, but he found he kept thinking about his father.

Evander Cortland had been a financial genius, Roger reflected, staring down at the lab's richly polished mooncrete floors. A brash, arrogant man, too. Roger could never figure why Atsuko had married him—they were so different. During his childhood, he remembered, the three of them had seemed the happy family, living all over Earth, playing the games of the international set for several years.

Eventually that became aimless, pointless. The whole time that slow realization was coming, though, his father was becoming more and more successful. Ev's speculations in leading-edge technologies paid off, his millions became billions. About that same time, Atsuko started joining organizations like the Global Futures Fund, the Space Studies Institute, the Space Frontiers Foundation. What better way to fill the void of being A Successful Man's Wife than joining organizations planning literally to fill the void through the colonization of space? His mother took up that vision as her crusade, and his father— who had connections everywhere in the high-tech industries— took up Atsuko's crusade as his own new vision. Together they had been instrumental in putting together the HOME consortium.

Roger remembered, though, that as the lobbying and proposal-making dragged on and on, his father had become increasingly pragmatic about "the project" while his mother became increasingly idealistic. His father used to always address the vision in practical terms: Who would ante up? How could they generate enough corporate 'will' to open up the corporate wallet? His dad had never been very happy with the idealistic elements of the project—great for selling it to the public, sure, but the reality for him was the bottom line. He wanted a moneymaker, a cash cow in the sky that could be milked for a long time.

As the space habitat became more and more of an actuality, his mother began to spend more time with the people who were going to settle in it—the "nuts and flakes" as his father took to calling them. Ev had tried gamely to fit in with the new crowd. He even lived up in the habitat for a brief period while the central sphere was being constructed, but he found it far too restrictive. Roger could understand that: on Earth his father was a king, he could do anything he wanted, have anything he wanted. Here he had to play by the same peon rules as everyone else.

That wasn't his father's way at all, something that became quite clear when—just to prove Ev Cortland didn't have to play by anybody's rules—he took to "swooping" some of the younger women colonists. Naturally his father found the swooping easy, and naturally his mother became justifiably enraged, hurling invective about Evander's "male-pride midlife crisis" and how the "raft" of his conquests—all those women he'd bedded to "salve his ego and gratify his lust"—

would sink the habitat project. In reality, though, the project had already gotten bigger than Roger's father, bigger than his parents or their problems, bigger in fact than all the players put together. By then it had picked up so much momentum that it really couldn't be stopped. It had a life of its own.

His parents' life together, though, was over. Three months before the space habitat was officially opened, they divorced. Roger had been just short of fifteen at the time. Because he'd known the space habitat only as something endlessly under construction, he'd opted for good times on Earth with his father. His mother decided to move into the habitat. Roger hadn't really felt the separation to any great extent; even when they were supposedly still living together, his mother hadn't been around that much for him anyway, toward the end.

He remembered the rest of his teen years as something of a blur. He'd continued to excel in school, entering Oxford at fifteen and taking his degree at seventeen. Graduate work in France and South Africa and at Tsukuba Science City outside Tokyo, before finally taking his doctorate at Stanford when he was twenty-one. He hadn't seen his father a lot, but Ev gave him plenty of money and everything it could buy. Hovercycles, private jets, sports cars, hydrofoils, all manner of supertoys. For his eighteenth birthday Ev gave him the production rights to the first true supercomputer-on-a-chip, the prototype developed by one of his corporate subsidiaries. Roger was still making money from that.

He had become his father's son. What you can buy, what you've accomplished, is who you are—his father's credo, which he had made his own. He was as revolted as his father ever was by the "idealistic" life of this habitat, the "voluntary simplicity" of the local "lifeways." He'd even gone so far as to have a cosmetic surgeon reconstruct his face and eyes so he'd look less Asian, more Anglo like his father.

He and both his parents had all been together for the last time at Roger's Ph.D. graduation ceremony, his doctoral hooding. Three years ago, now. Then, a month later, it had all ended. The deep-sea diving "accident." While there had never been real proof, persistent rumor said it *wasn't* an accident, that it was the result of a conspiracy among his competitors. Roger had clung to that theory. The other option—that Evander Cortland, billionaire world-conqueror, empire-builder and eminently successful man, had in fact committed suicide—was a thought more chilling than the cold at the bottom of that deepest sea where his father had died.

A thought cold enough to send Roger back to his research, in earnest, and with no more memories before his eyes.

WHILE AT THE LAB THAT MORNING, JHANA RECEIVED A pair of virtual-mail messages. One was long-link and encrypted from Earth—Balance Tien-Jones thanking her for the information she'd forwarded concerning Dr. Cortland's research and also reminding her of the rising tensions between Earth and the colony. The other message originated closer at hand—Seiji Yamaguchi agreeing to meet her for lunch. He suggested they meet in one of the townlet shop-clusters near her lab, at a small cafe called Chameleon on a Mirror.

When Jhana arrived at the gossamery, tentlike reflecting structure of the Chameleon, Seiji was already seated at a stone table beside a stream, waiting for her.

"Hello, Ms. Meniskos. Good to see you again. If I remember right, the last time we met I was holding forth about God, the universe, and everything."

"Not quite everything," Jhana said, smiling politely as she sat down, noting the glass panels set into the stone table's top. "And please, call me Jhana."

"All right."

The owner, a black-haired, walrus-mustached man whom Seiji introduced as Ehab Alama, stopped at their table with glasses of water and spiced tea, and flatware wrapped in cloth serviettes. Seiji seemed to have some sort of business relationship with the man.

"The sulfur shelf and oyster varieties were very good this week," Ehab said. "Not as rich as the morels and truffles, of course, but the customers like them very much, anyway. I've been using the sulfur shell in omelettes and as a substitute for chicken. The oyster mushroom, the Sajor Caju, is working wonderfully in seafood salads, and the enokis and shiis are still a hit."

"Good, good!" Seiji said, pleased. "I've got a few others

for you to try next week. I think I've got the shaggy mane's deliquescing problem licked, and we can probably go to the pink-bottoms and portobellos instead of the button agaricus you've been using.''

''Excellent. I look forward to cooking with them. Your menus are mounted in the tabletop,'' he said, the latter primarily for Jhana's benefit. ''I'll be back after you've ordered.''

Alama bustled away quickly to attend to the luncheon customers at other tables. Jhana pressed a small stud mounted in the tabletop and a menu appeared in the glass inset.

''What was all that about?'' she asked, perusing the electronic menu.

''Well, since raising beef cattle is far too land- and water-intensive for a space habitat, Ehab and I are conducting an experiment in what you might call 'cuisine design,' '' Seiji said, leaning back in his chair and counting creatures off on his fingers. ''We have some pigs and goats and sheep, plus rabbits, chickens, partridges, pheasants, and other fowl out at the agricultural tori. Lots of trout, pike, eels, carp, catfish, scads of other fish in the watercourses here—but they all make their demands too. The cost of live protein, in time and labor, seems to grow dearer all the time. Their dung is a partial payback as manure, but mainly they're a luxury item for our visitors and tourist trade. It's astronomically expensive to ship foodstuffs up the well—though what we have an over-abundance of we do sometimes ship *down*. Are you ready to order?''

''Yes,'' Jhana said, caught a bit off guard by the way he'd switched tracks so fast. ''Are the kebabs good?''

''Very. Ehab makes great kebabs. Good choice. I think I'll have the same. Just speak or punch your order in—there—and they'll make it up in the kitchen tent.'' Seiji took a sip of tea. ''So anyway, as I was saying, there's a need sometimes to stretch fish and fowl with supplements, and provide substitutes for flesh in general. You can do an awful lot with textured vegetable proteins, but I've been working a different angle: the fungi.''

''Mushrooms?''

''That's right. Basidiomycetes and ascomycetes both. They've long been underused, particularly in the West, where mycophobia is a centuries-old tradition. You're from North America, right? Have you ever eaten a sulfur shelf?''

"No, I can't say I have."

"You don't know what you've been missing! It's a bright, yellow-orange, shelving fungus that grows on trees just about everywhere. You must have seen it. You probably passed by hundreds of them when you were a kid and never once thought of them as edible."

Jhana looked at him oddly. It almost seemed as if the rather blandly patterned tent material of the Chameleon was assuming three-dimensional shapes behind her luncheon companion. She shook her head to clear away the impression.

"To be honest, Seiji," Jhana said slowly, "if I came upon a bright yellow-orange thing growing out of a tree stump, my first impulse would hardly be to stick it in my mouth. I suppose you've eaten them? What do they taste like?"

"Like chicken—''

"Oh no!'' Jhana laughed. "Rattlesnake tastes like chicken. Frog legs taste like chicken. *Everything* tastes like chicken— sometimes even chicken!''

"Okay, okay,'' Seiji said, smiling wanly. "So I should have been more specific. But one of the popular names for it *is* chicken of the woods—not to be confused with *Grifola frondosa*, hen of the woods. But a sulfur shelf really *does* taste something like chicken that's been crossed with a mild cheese and a firm tofu. It's great in omelettes.''

"And it's bright orange, you said?'' Jhana asked skeptically. "Right. Sure. Sounds just yummy. No thanks. I'll stick with what's safely sold in the stores, thank you.''

"Suit yourself,'' Seiji said with a shrug. He was about to say more, when a bright green chameleon fell from one of the trees to the terrace and scampered off in splay-footed fashion. Watching the chameleon, Jhana once again had the odd sensation that, beyond the scurrying creature, three-dimensional shapes were flashing out of the subtler patterns on the pavilion walls. Before she could ask Seiji about it, however, Ehab arrived with their kebabs on white-noise-grey stoneware plates, which he placed before them.

"Now the mushrooms on this are more my speed,'' Jhana said, pointing to the clearly recognizable button variety interspersed among what looked to be chunks of meat, sliced red and green peppers, whole miniature tomatoes, and pieces of pineapple and other fruit. It looked delicious and tasted even better.

"Do you like it?" Seiji asked after a time.

"Wonderful," Jhana said. "The lamb is excellent, and this other meat, which I can't quite place, is marvelous."

"Tastes like a good steak cooked over a macadamia-nut fire, maybe?"

"Exactly! What is it?"

Seiji smiled a Cheshire cat grin that lingered and grew until she thought it would swallow his whole face.

"You don't mean—"

Smile unwavering, Seiji nodded his head.

"Okay. I give up. What kind of mushroom is it?"

"A morel," he said proudly. "One of the last important delicacy species to become mass-producible, if not mass marketable."

She took another bite of the morel "meat." Despite knowing what it was, she still found it delicious.

"Maybe you're right," she conceded reluctantly. "Maybe I have been missing something."

Ehab came to refill their tea and water glasses. They drank and continued to eat, Seiji going on about still more obscure fungi: lion's manes and fairy rings and swordbelts, blewits and namekos, paddy straws and stropharia. Jhana tried to pay attention but, throughout the meal, she kept getting fleeting glimpses of three-dimensional images emerging from the walls of the pavilion—geometric figures like stars and crosses and pyramids, rippling waves, peaks and valleys, but also animals, particularly lizards, birds and butterflies—a veritable hallucination of jungle camouflage. When a spiral vortex like the Milky Way suddenly appeared out of the white-noise pattern of her by-then-empty plate, she had to say something.

"Seiji, are any of the mushrooms we've been eating, uh, hallucinogenic?" she asked, a hint of nervousness just barely audible in her voice.

"Not at all," he said dismissively, still finishing his meal. "One of the cardinal rules up here is that you're not supposed to alter other people's consciousnesses without their knowledge and permission. Why do you ask?''

"Because I've been *seeing* things," Jhana said, cautiously but firmly, after making sure no other patrons were in earshot.

"What sorts of things?" Seiji inquired, almost managing to keep a straight face.

Jhana described the images she'd seen appearing and disappearing in the walls of the pavilion, in the furniture, even in the plates. She was sure she was seeing them, and she wanted to know why.

"Because this is the *Chameleon*, that's why!" Seiji said, unable to keep from laughing. "Because Ehab is a devoted fan of stereograms and anamorphic devices. They were popular toys around the turn of the century. Almost every surface here is covered with particular patterns that are perceivable at more than one level. At the obvious, the 'blatant' level, they're just pretty patterns or colorful random noise. Seen in the right way or from the right angle, though, a deeper, 'latent' level appears, three-dimensional figures and images emerging from the blatant background. You're lucky. A lot of people can't see the latent stuff unless they've been told to look for it—or they've been drinking heavily. I've always thought of the three-dimensionals here as a great visual joke, a prank on the unsuspecting, but don't tell Ehab that. He's very serious about his 'art.' ''

"I've heard of stereograms before," Jhana said, "though I've never had much exposure to them outside of virtual reality constructs."

"He generated most of this stuff on his computers," Seiji said with a nod, "even claims he's invented a new technique that combines anamorphics, color-field, random-dot, and wallpaper stereograms—God knows what all. For him, I think they're a sort of visual koan—optical meditations reminding us that things aren't always what they seem."

Seiji's explanation was reassuring. Jhana was relieved to hear that the images were coming purely from that "mushroom" of brain inside her skull—unaltered by the chemical constituents of the shish kebab mushrooms that had been on her plate.

"This whole habitat is like that," she said at last. "Everything more than it seems. Always what it is—and then something else, something more.''

"How do you mean?" Seiji asked.

"Why is it, for instance, that so many of the permanent residents up here wear so many different hats?" Jhana said. "I mean, how do you know so much about mushrooms when you're a landscape architect—and why are you a landscape architect when your academic training is in energy systems and you're officially employed by the HOME consortium as a solar power engineer? I took the liberty of checking.''

Seiji smiled over his jawline-fringing Mennonite beard.

"Lots of us move beyond our specialties," he replied, "both out of necessity and inclination. Not for wealth, certainly. We've pretty much succeeded in de-linking social status from material consumption. But even here, where most of us are dedicated to lives of voluntary simplicity in some form, there's still more work than there are specialists to perform it. So we double or triple up. Take Ehab, for instance. He came up here for the initial engineering and construction of the habitat, then decided to stay on—as a restaurateur, among other things. All of us have to assume at least some responsibility for basic policing, educating, and paramedical training, and everyone has to spend some time in the agricultural rings. In my own case, working out there revealed a green thumb part of my nature that I never knew existed. Working in the agricultural areas, I became interested in landscape architecture. From there I became fascinated with the role of decay and the breakdown of complex materials into simpler components in the soil, through the action of soil organisms, saprophytes—the fungi, particularly.''

"But how do you find the time and energy to do all of it?"

Seiji, having at last finished his main course, too, put down his knife and fork.

"Not everybody does. Your friend Roger Cortland, for instance—in the Public Sphere I've heard him rant on and on about how our required 'green time' is just a new version of the Cultural Revolution, with his mother as Madame Mao! To be honest, though, I look on it less as a lot of 'hats' than as a lot of opportunities. Most of the heavier grunt work is automated, so that saves both time and energy. Quite a number of us are single, too, and many who are married are voluntarily childless or are beyond childbearing years. You'd be surprised how much adult energy is freed up from the demands of child-rearing here—and how much that freed-up energy can accomplish for the betterment of the community and the individual.''

Jhana tapped her fork lightly against her plate, thinking.

''But those couples who *are* having children,'' Jhana began, ''don't they feel that those who choose not to are being self-ish?'' She had often heard that argument on Earth.

Seiji laughed, lifting a chameleon off the tabletop, onto which it has just dropped.

''Were medieval European nuns and priests, Tibetan monks, and Siberian shamans considered selfish by their contemporaries for electing not to have children? People in those cultures seemed to have accepted the fact that those who chose to be childless were following a different calling than those who chose to be parents. It's only relatively recently in human history that having children has come to be thought of as something that all adult human beings somehow *ought* to do. I know it's a big issue down on Earth, but it's really pretty much a non-issue here.''

''But how has that been accomplished?'' Jhana asked, watching the charge for the meal flash up on the electronic menu. She inserted her credit needle and its ID chip into a slot to cover her part of the lunch, before Seiji could even think about paying for both of them. They had agreed to ''go Dutch,'' after all. Apparently the inhabitants hadn't yet gotten completely beyond currencies and credits, though she'd heard they were working on it.

''Many of us who are child-free also voluntarily serve as part of extended family networks,'' Seiji continued, ''supporting and helping the child-rearing couples with their needs. I'm doing a fair amount of that work next month. If you ask me, a child born here in the habitat is lucky.''

''How so?''

''Kids born here have a better shot overall. A lot of places on Earth, you've got a withered educational system side by side with an overstuffed prison industry. Here, we'd rather educate sooner than incarcerate later—just the opposite of Earth. The boy or girl born here has dozens of nonrelated aunts and uncles and grandmas and grandpas, too. Parenting itself, like teaching, is becoming a more communal activity here, less of the psychological pressure of the mom/dad/kids nuclear family.''

Jhana still wasn't convinced.

"What about the person who has no interest in having children and no interest in tending someone else's little rug rats?" Jhana asked, watching as Seiji "chipped" in for his part of the meal and gratuities. "Is that sort of selfishness allowable?"

"Certainly it's allowable," Seiji said with a nod as he fished his credit chip expertly from the pay slot. "Considering how overpopulated it is down on Earth, you could argue that by choosing not to have children, by deciding that the continued *quality* survival of human and other species is more important than the survival of one's own particular genetic material, the nonreproducing person is in fact engaging in more altruistic behavior than those people who choose to have children to begin with. But nobody really gets that self-righteous about it in the habitat. We're working the middle way here, between the extremes."

Getting up from their table, they waved and called goodbye to Ehab. Walking out of the cafe, Jhana filled Seiji in more fully on her recent work with *Heterocephalus glaber*. His mention of altruism had reminded her of the little beasts.

"—and your 'extended family networks' sound a lot like what's called alloparenting in mole rats," Jhana said, finishing up (without further mention of Roger Cortland's work) as they approached the bulletcart station. "The nonbreeding animals in each colony demonstrate a high degree of sociobiologically determined altruism, probably in response to environmental constraints—the aridity of the regions in which they live, the difficulty of tunneling through the hard-packed earth, the patchiness of their geophyte food sources."

Together they glided down on an escalator into the center of the station, Seiji standing beside Jhana, quiet, thoughtful.

"An interesting paradox," he said as they stepped off the escalator. "The harder life is, the more it encourages altruistic behavior, at least among mole rats. You'd think it would be just the opposite. I wonder if it might be true not only for mice but also for men? I mean, look at us here in this space habitat.

The mole rats and us—we both live in deserts, only ours is the high desert of space. We both live in colonies. Our population, too, will spread by budding off colonies to a distance, the way you say mole rats already do.''

He gazed briefly at the few other people in the station with them and then at Jhana. She thought she saw in his eyes a flash of something—fascination with his own theorizing? Or something deeper, something his theorizing was meant to camouflage?

''And in both cases environmental constraints encourage altruism,'' he said, gesturing toward the whole of the sphere. ''The difficulty of bringing things up the gravity well is our version of the difficulty of tunneling. Our food reserves aren't *that* tight, but we can't take for granted an already-existing ecosphere, one that will provide us with food and crops and everything we need for survival. We have to work at it. Because we had to build our ecosphere ourselves, we know how fragile and interconnected it is.''

They sat down on a bench and awaited the arrival of the next bulletcart. In a bush nearby a bird gave a trilling call. High in the sky above them, children dove and swooped in flying suits. Higher still, it was night.

''But what about the future residents?'' Jhana asked. ''Eventually the builders and the building of this place will be only a legend—what's to prevent future generations from taking it all for granted?''

Seiji stared down at his hands.

''I've thought about that some. I don't have an answer. There's no guarantee they won't duplicate Earth's whole overpopulation/ecocollapse scenario on a small scale right here. All I can hope is that they'll still be so caught up in the process of keeping this place whole and alive that in some sense they'll never be able to forget what it is we're up to—because they'll be living it every day. If we're lucky, their sense of place will continue to make this a place of sense.''

They both smiled at his turn of phrase. In the station, lights began to flash softly, indicating the impending arrival of the next bulletcart. That different sort of flash passed through Seiji's eyes as he glanced at Jhana again, but then he was looking away, burying it all in words once more.

"I guess that's where we differ from the mole rats. You said the breeding female of the colony suppresses the breeding of all other females of the colony—a top-down suppression, an enforced altruism. Turn that into a human society and it would be the equivalent of an authoritarian state based on the idea that the rights of the individual must always be subordinated to the social order. That's the sort of stuff your friend Roger is always warning against in his Public Sphere diatribes. Yet you say it's in fact what he's actually working on, in his pheromone research. Strange."

Jhana wondered about that "your friend Roger" phrase—particularly the subtle querying tone behind it. She wanted to respond, but found Seiji looking at her, openly, frankly, not averting his gaze this time as he spoke.

"Involuntary—that's the big difference," he said adamantly. "What we're trying to do here is voluntary. It's an altruism based on the idea that individual freedom and social responsibility are equal and inseparable, that it's impossible to truly have either without the other. That one change, from voluntary to involuntary, would turn our dream here into a nightmare. It would guarantee our experiment's success—and its failure."

The bulletcart appeared. Seiji glanced away. Jhana rose from the stone bench, surprised that Seiji, upon hearing of the mole rats' eusociality, had so quickly returned to those problems of freedom and responsibility that had also troubled her. Though she had mentioned nothing further of Roger Cortland and his plans, Roger seemed to hover near them, present even in his absence.

Jhana shook hands lingeringly as she parted from Seiji, wondering how Tao-Ponto would respond to the implications of Roger's work. Walking away from the solar power engineer, the thought of Tao-Ponto and his "need to know" reminded her that she would need to meet with Seiji again, to pick his brain about the strange satellites growing in nearby space.

"But I didn't get to ask you about the 'future perfect imperative'!" Jhana said, turning around, calling behind her as she moved toward the bulletcart. She'd have to ask Seiji for a tour of the solar power facilities outside the habitat next time they got together—that is, if there were a next time. "At the party Ekwefi said you could tell me that story."

"I can," he called back, looking relieved that this parting might lead to another meeting. "I will. How about tomorrow evening?"

"Sounds great! I'll give you a call."

Waving, Jhana settled into her seat as the cart closed around her, separating her from Seiji. She sighed. Somehow her conversations with Seiji had become like the stereogram patterns in the Chameleon—blatantly about one thing, latently about something else, something deeper, something more. She was beginning to enjoy Seiji's company entirely too much. The thought that she was merely playing him for information, that he was supposed to be nothing more than a source, was becoming increasingly distasteful to her. She sighed a second time. This Mata Hari stuff just wasn't her calling.

HOURS LATER—LATE INTO THE EVENING, IN FACT—ROGER was at last finishing his overview of the materials his mole-rat IMP had gathered for him. After going through so much of it, he was now far more optimistic about the success of his project. Evidence of the still powerful but usually latent power of olfaction in human sexuality was everywhere in the literature, and he dutifully squirreled away comments and notes. Having come at last to Krafft-Ebing's *Psychopathia Sexualis*, published in 1886, he felt he had gone as far back as he needed to. Krafft-Ebing's work definitely marked a hinterland boundary of some sort, for the book often seemed less a work of science than a collection of anecdotes on aberrant sexuality.

From the electronic text of the old book, Roger excerpted relevant passages by cursor, or point-and-shot them into note-form before throwing them into a notepad memory file.

Excerpted notes and sections from Krafft-Ebing's *Psychopathia Sexualis*:

Althaus—sense of smell important re: many species' reproduction. Almost all species at time of rutting emit a specially distinct odor from their genitals.

Schiff—extirpated olfactory nerves in puppies. As animals grew up, male unable to distinguish the female.

Mantegazza—removed eyes of rabbits. Defect constituted no obstacle to procreation, proof of importance of olfactory sense in sexual life of animals.

Many animals (musk ox, civet cat, beaver) possess on their sexual organs important glands which secrete substances having a very strong odor.

Cloquet—calls attention to sensual pleasure excited by odour of flowers. Richelieu lived in atmosphere redolent of heaviest perfumes in order to excite his sexual functions.

Zippe—cites both a passage in Song of Solomon ('And my hands dropped with myrrh, and my fingers with sweet-smelling myrrh, upon the handles of the lock') and the esteem in which geographically disparate peoples hold pleasant perfumes for their relation to the sexual organs, as proof of olfaction/sexuality link.

Most, professor in Rostock—"I learned from a sensual young peasant that he had excited many a chaste girl sexually, and easily gained his end, by carrying his handkerchief in his axilla for a time, while dancing, and then wiping his partner's perspiring face with it."

Krafft-Ebing—"The case of Henry III shows that contact with a person's perspiration may be the exciting cause of passionate love. At the betrothal feast of the King of Navarre and Margaret of Valois, [Henry] accidentally dried his face with a garment of Maria of Cleves, which was moist with her perspiration. Although she was the bride of the Prince of Conde, Henry conceived immediately such a passionate love for her that he could not resist it, and made her, as history shows, very unhappy. An analogous instance is related of Henry IV, whose passion for the beautiful Gabriel is said to have originated at the instant when, at a ball, he wiped his brow with her handkerchief."

Jager—regards the sweat as important in the production of sexual effects, and as being especially seductive.

Ploss—holds that attempts to attract a person of the

opposite sex by means of the perspiration may be discerned under many forms in popular psychology.

—love of certain libertines and sensual women for perfumes indicates a relation between the olfactory and the sexual senses.

—tribal custom among Philippine Island natives: when it becomes necessary for an engaged couple to separate, they exchange articles of wearing apparel as tokens of faithfulness. These objects carefully preserved, covered with kisses, and repeatedly smelled.

—histological conformity between nose, genitals, and nipples: all have erectile tissue.

Roger left off scanning, surprised to observe that his own tissue was demonstrating some erectility. Strange, for none of these descriptions should have aroused him that much. Contrary to the olfactory emphasis of his research, his personal kink was quite visual, as he was well aware.

He knew how politically incorrect his kink was—especially for the son of a noted peace and social justice activist. The "progressive" types his mother had hung out with for the last twenty years were hardly perfect human beings, though—as he himself had learned. For a brief time at Oxford, Roger had tried to devote himself to the sort of Leftward causes that his mother would approve of—almost as if, for just a while, some of that maternal programming had clicked in. That didn't last long, however, especially when he found that his ideas, his very thoughts, were devalued or ignored because he had "too much testosterone from that Y chromosome" and "too little melanin" in the layers of his skin. It was the worst sort of biological essentialism—the very thing the rads inveighed against, yet were guilty of themselves.

Oh, he could use the trump card of his middle name and Asian blood, but then they'd use that too, not his talents or abilities, just the tokenism of his "positive" biological markers. That's what it came down to, too often: being used, the faculty rads using the graduate rads using the undergrad rads, all in the name of undeniably enlightened and highly moral causes.

Even to get a date he had to wade through all the faulty

logic, the faulty generalizations of the Sex Wars: Men who blamed women in general for their own specific failures with certain individual women. Women who blamed men in general for their own specific failures with certain individual men. At one extreme stood the Androciders and Xtatix, who felt testosterone was a toxic poison that threatened the survival prospects of the species and could only be eliminated through the all-female reproductive process of ovular merging—as a result of which process no more males would be born and humanity would be saved. At the other extreme were the Gynociders and cYclones, who felt that estrogen was a toxic poison that threatened the survival prospects of the species and could only be eliminated through the all-male reproductive process of cellular Y-cloning—as a result of which no more females would be born and humanity would be saved. A plague on both their houses, Roger thought. He was glad to be shed of the whole lot of them.

Thinking of all this reminded him of the holodisk he'd picked up on Earth but had yet to view because he'd been so busy since his return. He began checking drawers in his desk, seeming to recall that he had stashed the disk in there somewhere. Yes, here it was: *Free Fall Free-For-All.*

As he turned over the pornholo package in his hands, he thought, Why not? I've put in a lot of hours tonight. No idea what time it is, but there's no one about, and there's a player in the conference room down the hall . . .

Getting up from his chair, crystal disk in hand, he padded out of the lab and down the corridor. In the dark of the conference room, the player's control pad glowed dimly. Locking the door behind him, he walked forward, slid the small disk into the player, physically thumbed Play and Projection Display, and waited for its contents to spring forth in glorious "virtual three-dimensionality."

After a nice exterior establishing shot of a space habitat, the scene cut immediately to an orgy in low gravity, a moaning squelching squishing grunting knot of happily intertwined bodies making the beast with many backs—all in slightly off-color 3D. The low-gravity simulation was just wrong enough to remind Roger that the film had not been shot on location in space but on the cheap in some Earthside studio.

Watching, Roger soon saw that the holo was yet another Earthbound fantasy about what life was *really* like in a space colony. The habitat culture's greater respect for the rights of consenting adults was, as usual, exaggerated out of all proportion and translated into the accepted Earthside mythology of space-colony life as an unending carnival of sexual license. Somewhere in the popular imagination, space-colony sexual freedom seemed to have gotten tangled up with the sensual heaven of Islam—and gone that heaven one better with the introduction of the much-overrated "zero-gee sex."

As the performers in virtual space before him feigned sexual ecstasies unknown to mere mortals, Roger felt like laughing. Watching orgies—zero-gee or otherwise—was not his particular kink anyway. He was glad when the action moved on to Commandante Professor Florio's attempt to extract tall, dark, and glandsome hero Brock Rio from out of the moansquish pile—in order to assign him an Important Mission and get the Plot under way.

Plot summary of *Free Fall Free-For-All*:

Professor Florio explains at great length to Brock Rio that Earth has long since become a howling wasteland. The human population boom there went bust centuries before. Under the successive scourges of a generalized ecocatastrophe—with some midscale nuclear and biological wars thrown in for good measure—mere anarchy was loosed upon the Motherworld, and the habitat severed all connections with the home planet. Now, however, in the interests of Science and the Future of All Humanity, Professor Florio has become convinced that poison levels have fallen enough on Earth that it is worth the risk to send One Brave Individual down the gravity well to Earth's surface, to make contact with the few humans who remain, learn about and report back on their culture, and (without coercion) bring back one of the natives for examination—all to determine just how heavy a mutation burden the survivors of Earth's catastrophe might now be carrying.

Without hesitation, hero Brock, outstanding space-pilot/anthropologist/ecologist/linguist/athlete/cocksman, accepts the mission. Bidding his coquettish blond most-frequent sex partner Gwen Blanc a long, passionate, crotch-grinding farewell, he's off in his spaceship to visit Mother Earth in her decay.

All does not go as planned, however. Despite the fact that Professor Florio has programmed into ship's memory the coordinates for that area on Earth's surface which (according to satellite observation and computer analysis) is most likely to still be populated and least likely to be "genetically burdened," Brock's ship malfunctions, crashing in the Poisoned Lands several hundred kilometers south of his destination.

Wounded and dazed, all communication gone between himself and his home, he struggles for survival against fierce mutant beasts and even fiercer mutated men and women whose particular genetic alterations seem mainly to have multiplied their erogenous zones, so that supernumerary lips and breasts and buttocks and penises and vaginas are very much on display. Captured and kept as a sex slave, Brock is worn down almost to death by the sensual needs of the overendowed indigenes.

Escaping at last, he wanders in the desert until—falling unconscious and on the very brink of death—he is rescued by the leader of a Komodo-dragon caravan that's carting the remains of his ship northward. Regaining consciousness under the ministrations of dark and beautiful caravan leader Morchella Esculenta, Brock quickly learns her language and explains to her about his ship and his own origin in the space habitat. Knowing of the space colony only through legends and superstitions, Morchella is at first skeptical, but gradually, as they travel toward her home in the city-state of Dodona, she comes to believe Brock's story, even begins to fall in love with him. At the same time Brock is coming to truly appreciate her and her world—to enjoy living on the surface of a planet rather than in a hollow sphere in space. The broad bowl of the sky, the sense that this world, so damaged, is slowly renewing itself—all of this appeals to him. So too does the barbaric civility of Morchella's ways.

As he watched, Roger could see the pattern forming up for the payoff on his kink. The "true love" developing between Brock and Morchella (remarkably chaste up to this point, for a porno) seemed in the best traditions of women's romance fiction, but back home in the orbital habitat, Gwen was waiting—the triangle was forming. Triangles were old news in the traditionally female matter of romance—only this time they were tricked out in the traditionally male garb of action-adventure science fiction.

Plot summary of *Free Fall Free-For-All*, continued:

Brock and Morchella reach Dodona, where Brock learns that Morchella is in fact the adventure-loving daughter of the High Priestess. Brock proves that he is the Chosen One From The Sky by fulfilling the legendary test of sexual stamina (satisfying the sexual desires of all the temple virgins in a single night). He then further astounds the rulers of Dodona with his ability to read and translate the Sacred Book, Guaranty's *Myth's Edge and Nation*, a dream text covered in gaudy metallic-purple adorned with lavender knot-work.

Using materials gleaned from the Dodona Antiquarium, Brock the Chosen succeeds in restoring his transceiver to working order. Informing Professor Florio and the space colonists that he is still alive, he requests a rescue ship capable of carrying himself and (gazing approvingly toward Morchella) one other passenger.

Preparations are made and the ship from space arrives with Gwen Blanc piloting. Leaping from her craft and striding past the assembled dignitaries, Gwen plants a fervent kiss on Brock's mouth. Brock awkwardly introduces Gwen and Morchella to each other. From the sudden shift in her body language and her increasingly pouty demeanor, it's clear that Gwen has immediately surmised that Morchella is the Other Woman. The handshake that passes between the two women is strangely prolonged, almost as if they are testing each other's strength.

As they return to the ship, Morchella and Gwen, in their ceremonial finest, walk ahead of Brock, very briskly and very straight-of-spine, almost as if participating in some strange foot race where each competitor not only has to reach the finish line first but also has to stand tallest while doing so.

The performers playing the dark woman and the blonde stood almost exactly the same height and looked to be about the same weight, Roger noticed, though Morchella was fuller in the shoulders and chest while Gwen was heavier around the hips and thighs. An even match, he thought, his arousal growing.

Plot summary of *Free Fall Free-For-All*, continued:

Brock takes the controls of the three-seater and pilots the craft off Earth and up the gravity well, trying to ignore the tension behind him, where the two women sit at opposite ends of the back cabin like fighters in their corners. From his expression it's clear Brock expects them at any minute to hear a bell and leap at each other.

But they do not. The tension of the triangle continues to build and build as Brock, following their return to the space habitat, spends more time with Morchella than Gwen will excuse, even in the name of Science. Finally one day, when the three of them are alone together in the padded confines of a low-gravity gymnasium, the tension explodes into action.

This was what Roger had been waiting for: contrasting female bodies rushing together with an audible smack; enraged cursing and yelling; stinging slaps; red-faced fury; murder in the eyes; circling, wary, crouching stances; hands extending like claws, grabbing hair and scalp and yanking savagely; women kneeing and kicking each other; female fighters clinching in hostile embrace, breast against breast, snared in each other's arms; solid headlocks; chokeholds; muffled grunts; short shrieks; arm-locked upper bodies; half and full nelsons; leg lifts; hip throws; scissors holds; hand clenches; long raking scratches; strangleholds; popping, stinging blows; the tangled ball of intertwined arms and legs; straddles; pins; submissions—all the impedimenta of his kink without a name—half voyeur's spectacle and half sadist's pleasure at seeing others' pain—being played out in the virtual reality before him.

Roger privately thought of himself as a *scopogynomachia-phile*—his own coinage for his nameless sexual obsession. He had been one for as long as he could remember, his kink like a dark twisted root anchored deep, irremovably, in the soil of his soul. He didn't know where the obsession came from—his mother arguing with his crazy aunt? a girl-fight seen in grade school?—but he did know it was making him come now.

Behind him a cardkey scrabbled in the lock of the door to the conference room. Putting himself quickly and sloppily back into his pants, Roger turned to see Marissa standing wide-eyed in the doorway. In the pornholo's virtual reality, the fight played on, life-sized.

"Oh, sorry," Marissa said, embarrassed, closing the door again quickly.

Roger sat, slumped and pondering. The new day must be beginning. He must have stayed in the lab all night. He felt numb somehow—too numb to get up and turn off the porn-holo.

Plot summary of *Free Fall Free-For-All*, concluded:

Morchella, Brock's true love, defeats her blond opponent. The habitat scientists determine that Morchella is not genetically burdened at all. When she opts to return to Earth, Brock decides to go with her—to monogamy and a settled life on an inside-out world. They ride off, not into the sunset but down the gravity well, new Adam and new Eve bent on reestablishing Heaven on Earth.

As the pornholo credits flashed up, Roger found himself wondering how much of it Marissa had seen—how much of his secret kink she might even now be figuring out. Would she make the connection between it and his other obsessions—mole-rat society, the human pheromone project? The thought of it made him curse his own stupidity. Twice in twenty-four hours, once intentionally with that Tao-Ponto woman Jhana and once accidentally with Marissa, he had let too much of himself show, let his plans and desires be nakedly exposed to others. Who knew how all these nonviolencers up here—especially his mother—might react if they became aware of a particularly crucial side effect of the pheromone he was trying to develop? Would they banish him? Send him into lifelong exile, never to return?

He should be so lucky. What would be so bad about getting away from all these overpolite idealists, really? People who would hardly admit they belched or farted or did anything physical and human, much less admit to their own dark sides? If, amid all their public chatter in this Happy Isle In The Sky, the only true private, individuating event was a guy watching a pornholo, then so be it. That said less about him than about the sad state of their so called "diversity" here. He would be glad to be free of the tight constraints of their insufferable good manners, their intolerable tolerance.

Still, he would have to guard carefully against such thoughtless self-revelation in the future. He had jeopardized his project enough already.

NINE

"THE RATS HAVE CHANGED AGAIN," ALEISTER SAID, APpearing with Lakshmi in Lev's virtual overlays. Korchnoi was in virtual space already, doing research in military history for Mob Cad's upcoming performance, which he and the band had now agreed to officially title *The Temple Guardians*—more to meet publicity deadlines than anything else.

"How so?" he asked.

"Here," Lakshmi said. "We'll shoot you an extract."

Passage embedded in RAT code:

Paradise always has been hollow. The word 'paradise' itself is from the Avestan *pairi-daeza*, meaning the wall around. That's the paradox of paradise: paradise *is* the wall around, the boundary. In that sense the inside-out world of the orbital habitat is the perfect paradise, a world that's wall all around, a spherical wraparound wall world.

"Seems pretty harmless," Lev said with a shrug, perusing a Sumerian war chariot in another part of his virtual space.

"Try this one," Aleister suggested, shooting another marquee of three-dimensional words into Lev's virtual space.

Passage embedded in RAT code:

A Spanish philosopher once claimed that human consciousness is a disease. Maybe Earth would be better off if humanity quarantined itself. Maybe the only way Earth can be a paradise again is if humanity walls itself out of that world.

"Sort of like quirky fortune cookies," Lev said, scanning a diagram of Greek hoplite armor. "Interesting, though I can't say much for fortune-cookie philosophy."

"Better not speak too soon, Lev," Lakshmi warned. "There are hundreds or even thousands of these encysted or embedded bits of text. A lot of them are coming out of the Public Sphere. As near we can tell, all are being taken from pre-existing sources—including your song lyrics."

"Well," Lev remarked, moving around information on Roman short swords, "even cyber-toothed rats can show good taste, I suppose."

"The RATs don't show much of anything," Lakshmi said. "Their autonomy is pretty limited. Aleister's found out more about their history. They're just being used."

Sensing that Lakshmi was going to start talking about the "distributed consciousness" again, Lev decided to head her off.

"So, Aleister," he asked the man he knew was lurking somewhere behind the web-spider icon with the pudgy face, "what *have* you found out about the RATs and where they came from?"

"The abbey where they were developed was a pretty interesting place," Aleister said. "Turn of the century New Agers who believed in 'mental singularities,' portals in the sky, a gradual, Gnostic version of the end of the world. The 'Rainbow Door' opening into the 'World of Light' on the 'Day of Doom'—that's what they talk about in their literature. What I don't get is why a lot of high-powered information-industry types listed themselves as Myrrhisticineans and donated scads of money to the abbey."

"What about this guy Manqué?" Lev asked, examining diagrams of pikes and halberds in another section of his virtuality, "the one who created the RATs?"

"According to the surviving members—the ones who were

off the mesa the day it was destroyed—Manqué was something of a heretic. While the Myrrhisticineans generally were more or less gradualists, Manqué was an immediate apocalyptist. He believed the Earth itself could be the rainbow door in the vault of heaven—that any day could be doomsday, every day a Judgment Day. He was in favor of a 'technological push' to open the door so they could walk into the world of light *right now*."

"And that was tolerated by the rest of the brethren and sistren?" Lev asked, scanning specifications of blunderbusses and early musketry.

"Certainly," Aleister replied. "I've scanned some Myrrhisticinean texts. The ex-nun who founded the group, Alicia Gonsalves, had an interesting hodgepodge of influences—mystical scientists like Arthur C. Clarke and scientific priests like Pierre Teilhard de Chardin, for instance. She believed humanity's role on Earth was to create the conditions for the manifestation of the divine. The role of the Myrrhisticineans in particular was to midwife the birth of a technology so advanced as to be indistinguishable from divinity."

"But what's that got to do with the RATs?" Lev asked, pausing from his overview of the evolution of small arms and light gunnery.

"I'm not sure yet," Aleister admitted, "but I do know that the Myrrhies were particularly big into a Teilhardian notion of evolution. Not long before the disaster happened, a team from Kerrismatix installed an ALEPH, an Artificial Life Evolution Programming Heuristic, on the abbey's ParaLogics systems. Manqué was the abbey's network manager, its web spider, so he had to be involved. Given what I can figure from the RATs I've decrypted, he developed them using the ALEPH's predation subheuristic—"

"But the RATs aren't what they used to be," Lakshmi interrupted impatiently. "Manqué developed them as a joke: A-life with nasty habits. From the survivors' reports, we know that Manqué released them in the abbey net, where they took to devouring a user's mannequin, the old-style virtual body in electronic space—while the user just happened to be inhabiting said mannequin."

"That must have made him popular with the locals," Lev said with a smirk.

"Hardly," Lakshmi continued. "Even the serene brothers and sisters of the abbey didn't much take to being virtually eaten alive."

"They sent a bunch of messages flaming down to Manqué," Aleister put in. "Eventually—all dolled up in a Pied Piper of Hamelin mannequin, according to the reports—Manqué piped away and the RATs followed him through the abbey virtuality, until they were all drowned in a buffer 'river.' "

"Then ours aren't the same RATs?" Lev asked, looking over from a display on cavalry charges.

"There's a *lot* of evidence in the actual code that says ours are highly related to his," Aleister said firmly, glancing toward Lakshmi, as if they'd had this discussion before.

"But our RATs *do* behave very differently," Lakshmi demurred. "We're only finding the ones that *want* to be found—with messages *something* wants to communicate. I've gotten a bunch of inquiries from industry friends on Earth. All the new information being beamed into cislunar space has not escaped their attention. Those trideo game things were the initial vector, but it's spread. Sudden shifts in machine memory-usage suggest, to my contacts at least, that stealthy forms of self-replicating software—the RATs—have thoroughly infiltrated almost all of Earth's infosphere. Now, though, it seems they're less rats than retrievers, fetching and sampling quantum information packets, then returning the QUIPS almost instantly to the infostream."

"And now you're going to tell me," Lev said, unable to dodge the inevitable any longer, "that the master those retrievers are fetching for is your 'distributed consciousness.' "

"That's right," Aleister said, intervening. "There's just too much evidence for it, Lev. I think Manqué's work didn't end with the RATs. I think he was working toward that 'technology indistinguishable from divinity'—but something went wrong and the Sedona disaster, the abbey event, happened. Someone saved the black box from the wreckage, though—or beamed Manqué's work off-site and stored it before the disaster. I think our distributed consciousness found where that work was stored."

"And *how* did it do that?" Lev asked, frustrated at the particular electrometaphysical turn the conversation was taking—and by the fact that it had now fully taken him away from his military research for the Mob Cad performance.

"The same way it's monitoring everything we're saying and doing right now," Aleister said, very quietly.

"Aw, come on!" Lev exploded. "*Net* stands for 'no easy transcendance,' remember? What are you saying? That this thing's omniscient, like God or Santa Claus?"

"Not omniscient," Lakshmi said thoughtfully, "but it does have a really *big* database. And a vast array of sensors, too."

"Not omnipresent either," Aleister added, "but it's got lots of remotes, peripherals, and actuators, if it needs them. Body electric—and a big strong one at that. You ought to come and see the latest progress on what it's building at Lakshmi's place—in its spare time."

"I will, I will," Lev said, "just as soon as *I* have some spare time. I just hope your god-in-a-box waits till my show is over before it comes down out of the stage machinery."

"We hope so too," Lakshmi said with a smile, but then quickly grew more serious. "Look, Lev, this is getting too big for just us to handle. We've got to bring more people in. I was thinking of contacting some of the encrypted names, the ones it sent us. Seiji Yamaguchi and Atsuko Cortland in particular. That okay with you?"

"Lakshmi, I'm surprised," Lev said, feigning astonishment. "Of course it's okay. Since when have you ever needed my permission to do anything?"

"Since we all got stuck in this together," she answered. "I know you're busy, but we'll keep sending you the messages we pull out of the RAT code, and the sources for them when we can find them. See if you can make any sense of it, notice any patterns."

"I'll do my best—in my spare time," Lev said, signing off and returning to his research in military history for the band's performance. Somehow, though, after everything Aleister and Lakshmi had just told him, all this history of the ways in which humans had mauled, mutilated, and murdered one another seemed childish and petty now, toylike, just variants of pop-guns and firecrackers and sharp sticks.

• • •

Wʜᴀᴛ Marissa had seen Roger up to that early morning had bothered her deeply—less in itself than from the way it fit into a disturbing, larger pattern. Not wanting to think about it, she shrugged back her long red-gold hair, donned her goggles and suited up for the CAMD virtuality, diving deep into her work once again.

Her antisenescence project was progressing slowly, even though she had largely left behind the mole-rat part of it and was concentrating almost exclusively on human possibilities. Despite this shift, however, ordinary nonviolent mortality in humans was proving to be the result of an almost unbelievably complex synergy of factors. Death seemed never to be the simple result of one thing. She'd had to examine patterns of mutation and evolution on many different scales—not only the vector virus's, but the potential human host's too. Even when she thought she had those possibilities covered, Marissa still had to spend more time working through genespace, finding intron and pseudogene locations where her viral vector could safely splice in manufactured coding—for telomerases and a variety of telomere stabilizers that didn't induce cancer, as well as extra engineered copies of so-called Methuselah genes, particularly DNA sequences for making free-radical absorbers like superoxide dismutase.

Despite its frustrations, Marissa had to admit that her work in virtuality had a hypnotic effect. It took her mind far away from the real. When she was tweaking molecules and twisting fate in the CAMD room, time had no meaning to her, so thoroughly was she caught up in her own world. In that timeless realm she truly felt she was more than just a researcher developing a viral vector against senescence—important as that work was. She was more than just a genetic cryptographer cracking and rewriting the code. Most of all, she was no longer the poor kid who had struggled up from the hardpan and broken glass of the fringes and trailer parks; she was a powerful woman riding the coiling serpents of the DNA molecule, a high-born lady astride the double dragon, holding in her hand the dragon's secretly hoarded pearl of great price, the talismanic object that could cure the serpent-wound by which mortality had come into the world.

But was that what she wanted? Certainly the theory of clonal selection, evolution on a somatic scale, even directed selection on that same scale—all suggested her antisenescence project could be accomplished. But should it? Clicking out of virtuality, removing her goggle overlays and gloves and shutting down the holo display at last, she reflected that whatever she might be feeling about Roger at the moment, he was probably right about the danger of releasing an incurable Immortality Plague on Earth. Unlimited life extension without corresponding limits to birthrate would lead straight to a vastly accelerated boom/bust cycle in human population, an inevitable carrying-capacity disaster and, paradoxically, the very possible extinction of the human species as a whole—by violence and starvation, though not by disease or so-called natural causes.

Sad, she thought as she walked out of the lab and down the corridor. Especially since the absolute increase in the population growth rate had peaked fifty years ago. True, the human population was still growing, but at a "decreasing rate of increase," as one of her undergraduate biology profs had put it. He'd been full of phrases like that. To him, cancerous growths were "cells with an ego problem"—and humanity was a "species with an ego problem" especially when it completely eliminated other species out of ignorance or for its own selfish concerns.

Leaving the desert preserve building and coming out into the late afternoon light, Marissa thought of the Tennyson passage that had been carved in stone over one of the entryways to the old Life Sciences building on her undergraduate campus: "Nature, so careful of the type, so careless of the single life." But that favorite biology professor had said the problem with people was just the opposite: "Humanity, so careful of the single life, so careless of the type." All those individuals wanting the genetic immortality of children for themselves, until the planet as a whole was being driven toward ecological collapse by the sheer weight of human numbers and their demands. Victims of our own success. Crazy.

Marissa's vectoring of cancer-derived immortalizing factors into human beings seemed hardly likely to make the species saner, or cure it of its egotism. No, Roger was right. She would have to be very careful, so very careful in her research, the closer it came to fruition.

Yet Roger had been wrong about so much else. He privileged numbers and abstractions over life, but life had a weird way of working against simple numbers, and simpler laws of thermodynamics. Looking into the sphered garden of the habitat curving away from her into the surrounding distance, Marissa realized that Roger had, for one thing, crucially underestimated the inhabitants here—and the power of their ideas.

The greatest resource here wasn't something that could be mined from the moon or grown in the ag tori or caught in the sun's rays. The greatest resource here was something human beings found in themselves. Sitting down in the grass and looking up, Marissa could feel that resource around her as tangibly as the light on her face and the air in her hair and the ground beneath her. *Hope is a resource*, she thought, *and the orbital habitat is richer in it than any place I've ever been.*

Running a brush through her hair as she waited for Seiji to arrive, Jhana tried to take stock of her day. At the lab, old Larkin, though not yet fully warmed to her presence, was at least not as oddly disposed toward her as he had been. The DNA fingerprinting scans and their importance for her research into genetic drift were panning out even better than she'd hoped, too.

But all was not sweetness and light. Dr. Tien-Jones had sent another confidential missive. She glanced at it once more on the bathroom counter beside her.

TO: Jhana Meniskos, Ph.D.
FROM: Balance Tien-Jones, Ph.D. TPAG Dir. R/D (Bio)
RE: Projects

Tao-Ponto will be contacting Dr. Roger Cortland concerning his pheromone research. That lead is much appreciated, but we're a bit perturbed that neither you nor any other of Tao-Ponto's observers in the habitat have made any progress on Diamond Thunderbolt or its possible links to the structures currently being deployed in space near the satellite solar power stations. Discovering the nature of those structures has become all the more imperative because they have, only hours ago, emitted a very brief flash—indeterminate as to nature or content, but Weapons Division is calling it a 'test firing.' United Nations and Corporate Presidium have begun closed-door hearings. Please make investigation into nature of Diamond Thunderbolt and possible linkage to aforementioned structures your TOP PRIORITY.

Jhana stared at the message, her lips turned down in an expression of vague disgust. Was she supposed to be a scientist up here—or a spy? Whatever was going on, things seemed to be heating up. Ol' T-J had dropped the cryptic wording of his earlier messages, at least.

Her front door buzzed. That would be Seiji. Dropping the message into the recycling chute, she hoped he could shed some light on whatever it was Tao-Ponto was looking for.

"Good evening, Seiji," she said, opening the door for the bearded man dressed in a blue sweater and white shorts. "Come in. I don't know why I even bother to keep that door shut, since apparently nobody up here steals anything. Everybody knows everybody."

"Our small-town size has its advantages, no doubt," Seiji said as they walked through the living area toward a small glassed-in solarium, through the windows of which the flowers of the back garden could be seen in bloom. "Disadvantages too, though. When I was growing up, I was more used to urban anonymity. Everybody knows your business, up here. Sometimes it feels like we're living in a fishbowl—like privacy was something we left back on Earth."

Jhana smiled and nodded. She had felt a little of the same thing.

"I imagine you could get to know almost everybody here in a few months' time," she said as they passed through the solarium. "We'll be taking tea on the patio in the back garden. So, you grew up mostly in large cities, then?"

Reaching the umbrella-shaded cafe table on the patio, Seiji stood with his hand on a white metal chair.

"That's right. In Japan, the States, England," he said, looking down at the chair and tapping it briefly with his knuckles—as if to test its solidity. "Don't get me wrong: I'm very much a booster of this place and its emphasis on communal values. Just not completely used to it, is all. I'm told that towns of similar size back on Earth have the same fishbowl quality, but I doubt even *they* have as low a crime rate."

"I see your point. Please, sit down," Jhana said. "What's to steal here? I mean, everybody has pretty much the same standard of living—no large disproportions in the distribution of wealth, as far as I can tell. Everyone seems well-educated and dedicated to what the community's about—though the teenagers do seem a bit on the rebellious side."

Pulling his chair out from the table and sitting down, Seiji laughed.

"What can you expect? They're the first generation even partially raised in space. Right now, they're big fish in our small, isolated pond. I'm on a committee that's working with that, though. We're developing a sort of initiation rite for them—a month spent in deep isolation, in space, working on the outside of this habitat or others as they're built. All of us on the committee went through it, a couple months back. Really changes the way you see things, gives you a properly humble perspective on the universe. When the initiates come back, the whole community will gather to officially welcome them to full status as adult citizens of the habitat. It's as close as we can get to the old idea of a vision quest or ordeal rite."

"Isn't that sort of exposure *outside* potentially dangerous?" Jhana asked.

"Certainly," Seiji agreed. "My brother's death itself probably had something to do with a failed personal initiation rite or quest. He was trying to do it alone, however—outside of any sort of social framework. The hazard of madness or death in the ordeal will still be real, but our initiates will at least be doing it within a social framework that'll reduce their risk somewhat."

"But what about death here?" Jhana asked suddenly, for reasons of her own. "I don't mean that I think Earth's going to invade and start killing people or something, but I was just wondering. Death's part of the big cycle too, right? But I haven't seen any graveyards up here.''

They fell silent for a moment as Death sat down to wait for tea with them.

''You're right,'' Seiji said slowly. ''We've had very few deaths up here—almost a miracle in itself, when you consider the percentage of our population that's elderly. But this is no Eden. We know death is waiting. There's been some discussion—and remarkably little consensus on the issue. If you think population control is a tough nut to crack, just try talking about the recycling of human bodies. We can't burn them— too polluting, even if we just pumped the ash and smoke into space. That would only make for more space junk and debris and a hazard to astrogation in the long run. In the colony itself we can't afford to give over land area dedicated solely to graveyard space—and from an ecological standpoint the bodies shouldn't be isolated, they or their ashes really should be put back into the cycle as quickly and completely as possible. 'Feed the tree,' as it's called. But how to do that in a way that the living will regard as respectful to the dead?''

''No one wants to think of their relatives being passed through something like a rendering plant, I suppose,'' Jhana said, clearing her throat.

''You know it. Some of the bereaved may want to bury their dead at home, in the gardens or woods. Some may not want to be reminded, may not want to have the dead so close at hand. Those living in the central sphere may decide to bury the deceased in the agricultural tori, those living in the tori may decide they want them buried in the gardens of the central sphere; some may even want their remains to be sent back down the well to Earth or fired into the sun for the ultimate cremation— as ecologically 'wrong' or prohibitively expensive as such death exports might be. As the colony moves out of its own adolescence we'll have to give more thought to the elderly and the children, to the ancestors and the progeny, the long view of past and future. We'll have to face it in a deep way, since continuing to deal with death only as an 'inconvenience' would ultimately make our work here hypocritical. It's a difficult call, particularly because of our isolation up here.''

"But that isolation can be a plus, too, don't you think?"
Jhana said, sitting down across from Seiji. "There's the co-
hesiveness of a remote island settlement, here."

"Exactly," Seiji agreed. "If someone stole something here,
everyone would know who the rightful owner is, and since
we're so far from Earth—the nearest market to 'fence' things
in—it would be more trouble than it's worth to try to smuggle
stolen goods out. And the idea of ownership itself—"

They were distracted by the sound of a teakettle whistling
to full boil.

"Wait!" Jhana said. "Hold that thought while I go get our
tea. I'll be right back."

While Jhana was gone, Seiji glanced at the garden. When
she returned with the tea tray Jhana found her guest smiling.

"You're been keeping your garden very well," Seiji said
approvingly.

"Oh, that's easy," said Jhana, placing the teapot and cups
on the table and sitting down. "The garden's designer did such
a fine job that I have barely anything to do."

"Thank you," Seiji said in return, smiling, bowing his head
slightly at the compliment. "What was I going on about when
you left?"

"Private ownership."

"Yes, that was it. That's the root cause of theft," Seiji as-
serted. "As long as you have private property there'll be
theft."

"The root of all evil grows a popular bush," Jhana commented.

"Sure does. Right now, we're pretty much a decentralized
society of free, uncoerced small owners, but in the long run I
see this colony, at least, becoming more and more communal
in terms of ownership."

"Decentralized yet communal?"

"Yeah, if you can picture that. Most of the land area here
in the sphere, the crop area in the tori, and the manufacturing
at all gravities is already cooperatively controlled."

"What about the use of credit chips and money?" Jhana
asked.

"That's increasingly just for the sake of the HOME consortium's record-keeping," Seiji assured her. "It's only a matter of time."

"Is that your 'future perfect imperative'?" Jhana asked dryly, cocking her head at him.

"No, no," Seiji said with a laugh. "That's a different story. From the past."

"Well?" Jhana could hardly believe the usually voluble Seiji was actually being reticent about something. "Go ahead."

"I can do better than that," Seiji said, fiddling with his personal data unit. "It happened fourteen years ago, when my brother Jiro and I were in high school, at a Latin School run by priests, in the U.S. We were the 'studio audience' classroom for a distance learning environment, so I thought the original situation might still be recorded somewhere. Looking for it gave me something to do when I was obsessing, after my brother's death. Eventually, the diocese sent it to me. Ah, here it is."

Seiji shot the old-format videotape to Jhana's data unit and they watched it in the false 3D of sharespace. A man in the black garb and collar of a Roman Catholic priest appeared before a classroom full of students.

"That was our Latin teacher, Father Stargoba," Seiji narrated. "An intense guy—former Golden Gloves bantamweight boxer."

Jhana thought "intense" was putting it mildly. The priest's face was twitching, his fists clenched, as he scanned the classroom for someone to answer a question he'd just put to all of them. Jhana turned up the sound.

"Don't any of you know?" Father Stargoba shouted. "Jiro Yamaguchi. *Scripsero*. Meaning, tense, mood!"

Jhana watched as Seiji's brother Jiro swallowed hard. Stargoba's sharp stare seemed to spike out from behind his steel-rimmed glasses and transfix Jiro to his desk like a butterfly on a mounting board. A vein in the priest's forehead pulsed and a muscular tic flared along the man's jaw, his face in close-up reddening angrily from the black of his priestly collar to the short iron brush of his close-cropped hair.

"Speak up!"

"*Scripsero*," Seiji's brother said, his voice quavering. "Meaning: I shall have written. Tense: future perfect. Mood: uh, imperative."

"*What?*" the priest yelled, exploding in a chalk-dust frenzy at the green blackboard. "There is no future perfect imperative! Only the indicative has all six tenses. The subjunctive has no future or future perfect, and the imperative has only the present and the future—no other tenses! The present, imperfect, and future are the tenses of incomplete or continued action, while the perfect, pluperfect, and future perfect are the tenses of *completed* action. Think, Yamaguchi! The imperative is the mood of command or entreaty. Why command or entreat for something that's already done? It's ridiculous!"

"But if it's in the future, it isn't—"

"It's in the *future perfect*, Yamaguchi!" Father Stargoba snapped. "The past future. *I shall have written*. From the vantage of a given point in the future the action talked about will already be completed, will already have been done or taken place. A future perfect imperative is impossible because it demands that an action be completed and continuing at the same time—a logical impossibility. You see that?"

"Yes," Jiro said, nodding. But even to Jhana, watching it on old video, it was clear that Seiji's brother didn't see that at all.

"Good," Father Stargoba said, satisfied. "So tell us the mood of *scripsero*."

"Indicative, Father," Jiro said. Jhana could almost hear the boy trying to keep the tone of resignation out of his voice.

"Good," said Father Stargoba, his blood pressure apparently falling at last. "Let's return to our translation."

Seiji shut off the data feed and took a long sip of his tea. His eyes seemed to be looking at something in another place and time.

"I was only able to finally get the tape of that class a couple months ago," Seiji said. "After all these years, it's still as bad as I remember. What happened in that class was no big deal to Stargoba, but it left a real mark on my brother. He wanted to know why the future perfect imperative should be any less possible than any of the other language phantoms we studied. Language, after all, was something people created, something we made real, something we could *change*. Logic too—same thing. For Jiro and me, the future perfect imperative became a sort of shorthand for a lot of things."

"What things?" Jhana asked, finishing her tea.

"Oh, I don't know," Seiji said, glancing up at her. "Shorthand for getting beyond human stubbornness, narrow-mindedness. Shorthand for the ridiculous 'language is everything' idea, the notion that language and symbols can capture the whole of human experience, contain the *alpha* and *omega* of human consciousness. Shorthand for the incompleteness of any system or theory."

"It meant all *that*?"

"Yeah," Seiji said, smiling awkwardly. "In a mostly unspoken way, but yeah, it meant all that. It means more and more to me all the time. The future perfect imperative. It means constant striving, the unending opening of new paths, the refusal to take Impossible! for an answer. Perfection as something always to be striven for, precisely *because* it can never be obtained. A constant challenging of the assumptions of knee-jerk traditions and mindless conformity. That's what my brother was all about."

Seiji toyed with his teacup a moment, then set it aside.

"That's what really appeals to me about the space habitats and the opening of this frontier, too. Each habitat can be different. I complained about the lack of anonymity here—probably a function of small population. But people can choose to make the population density of their worlds as crowded or as solitary as they wish. Eventually, given a multitude of worlds to choose from, settlers can decide what sort of political and social organization they want—they can experiment, or they can stick with what's been tried. Different religious groups can choose to build their own worlds, if they wish. Personally I'd rather see more integration of human beings from diverse cultures, the way it is here, than some sort of neo-tribal fragmentation all over space, but that'll have to be left up to each group to decide. In any case, there'd hopefully always be that 'openness to diversity' Atsuko Cortland and the other founders are always talking about."

Jhana began gathering the tea things. Seiji helped her take them back into the house.

"Atsuko Cortland—she's Roger Cortland's mother?" Jhana asked as they soundwashed the dishes and put them away.

"Yeah. You'd hardly guess two such different people might be related, would you?"

"I don't know. I've never met the mother."

"I'll have to introduce you to her," Seiji said, then smiled. "That would *really* be diversity—a world for Roger Cortland, and another for his mother! If that could be done, there could be worlds for everyone. Even better, one world where they could *both* be happy." He paused, teacup in hands, halfway to the china cabinet. "Maybe even one where my brother could have been taken in, appreciated, understood. A world he wouldn't have felt the need to leave at such a young age."

That trapped feeling that Jhana had first felt upon hearing Seiji speak of his brother's death returned—even more powerfully now than when he'd spoken of it at Arthur and Sarah's party, her first night in the habitat. That party seemed months or years ago, though it was in fact not long ago at all.

Looking at Seiji, Jhana realized the man was still somehow trying to work his way through a grief too deep for tears, a guilt too deep for forgiveness. Thinking about it made her uneasy, for it reminded her too much of her own grief, her own guilt. Yet somebody's guilt would have to be faced before she could get on with asking him about those things that so intensely interested her employer—those paranoid plots and counterplots which seemed so trivial at the moment.

"Come on," she said, taking Seiji by the arm. "Let's go walk down by the river. You can tell me about your brother as we go."

They left the house and made their way through gardens and woods, toward the river, but said little until they came to the fern-banked path along the water's edge. The stream reminded Jhana of mossy green tributaries that she had once seen flowing toward the Thames, in the part of that river near Oxford, where it was called the Isis.

"Let us cultivate our garden," Seiji said suddenly, apropos of nothing and everything.

"What Voltaire has Candide say, as his final injunction," Jhana observed, recognizing the paraphrased quote. "When we were walking past the gardens I was thinking of the same thing."

"*Our* garden—not someone else's," Seiji said. "To mind

our own cultivation, and not mind or exploit the cultivation of others.''

"Hard to do, sometimes," Jhana said thoughtfully. Seiji nodded.

"After my brother started having his psychological problems, I very much wanted to be my brother's keeper, to mind his business too, as much as I could. To do that, though, would have been to interfere in his freedom to live the life he wanted to live, even when I feared—even when I *knew*, deep down—that it was a life tending toward an early death. I couldn't balance the costs. Couldn't figure out how to reconcile respect for his freedom with compassion for his suffering.''

They had come to a small mooncrete footbridge that arched steeply over the water where the river—really not much more than a stream—broadened to a large, slow-flowing, mirror-smoothness that lifted a variety of water lilies and lotuses toward the light it reflected. Jhana and Seiji stopped halfway across, leaning their elbows on the railing of the bridge, gazing down into the water's mirroring stillness.

"Could you see your brother's death coming?" Jhana asked quietly.

"He'd been having his troubles for years," Seiji said with a small nod. "I can see that now, in retrospect, everything leading up to the end. In second grade the nuns found him walking around on the playground with his arms stretched out like Christ on the cross. We're descended from a line of Hiroshima Catholics, so we were always in Catholic schools. Maybe the programming took too well. As a kid, Jiro got it into his head that sex was something dirty and evil. He was always distressed by his own sexuality after that. In high school he was painfully shy. He didn't date, but that was okay. He was a good deal younger than all the other kids, and he put all his energy into his studies anyway.''

As she listened to Seiji, Jhana was reminded, oddly, of Roger Cortland's manner. She wondered briefly what *his* particular loss and grief might be.

"Jiro took his studies *extremely* seriously—and it paid off. Bachelor's degree in Computer Media Studies while he was still in his teens, master's when he was twenty. But as he got older I suppose he felt he was trapped. He didn't go out with

girls, but he wasn't homosexual—maybe he was afraid to be—
and he didn't want to be a priest. He'd started trying to 'dumb
down' in his late teens, first through heavy drinking, then with
drugs. Figured that if he killed enough brain cells he'd fit in
better, I guess.'' Seiji flicked a piece of dried leaf off the
railing and into the stream. ''That's when he started doing
high-powered hallucinogens like KL 235—'gate,' as it was
called. The intelligence services or somebody like that had
spread it around, after it was synthesized from a rare tepui
fungus. Ask Paul Larkin in your lab—he knows all about it.''

''He seems like a bit of a crank sometimes,'' Jhana ventured.

''Oh, yeah,'' Seiji said. ''But he does know what he's talking about when it comes to mind-bending and the world of
the shadowy. He's been there. Get him going on it, and really
listen to him, and you'll be in his good graces forever. We've
got some of the original fungal strain they took KL from,
growing up here now. Supposed to be part of the attempt to
preserve lost or 'ghost' biodiversity, but mainly it's here because Larkin insisted.''

Above and below them, in the sky of air and the sky of
water, the mirrored sun would be going out before too long—
at least in this sector of the habitat. Jhana barely noticed.
Something Seiji had said about Larkin, the shadow-world, and
KL 235 began to make things come together.

''Anyway,'' Seiji continued, looking over the water, ''Jiro's
use of KL 235, instead of dumbing him down, got his brain
completely revved up. He just started pumping information
through his eyes and ears all the time, until it was like he went
supernova. He was so bright back then, the year before his
breakdown—it scared me. It's hard for an older brother to
admit, even to himself, that his younger brother is smarter than
he is—but Jiro was smarter, and I had to admit it. His brain
was roaring full throttle. It was like his mind was analyzing
and synthesizing at light-speed everything he'd experienced,
all the technology and history he'd studied, all the data he'd
taken in. Just burning with everything he'd learned. I don't
know—maybe all the KL he'd taken had locked his mind into
overdrive. I do know that talking to him in those days was

like talking to God. In his presence I felt the urge to avert my eyes.''

Seiji let out a long, slow sigh. Beneath the water's smooth surface, fish and frogs and salamanders moved.

''He couldn't hold it together. No one could hold that level of fiery intensity for long. He must have hit some limit at last. He knew he was losing it. Everything came bubbling to the surface. Long-distance he told me that he didn't want to hurt anybody, that he'd rather die than hurt anybody. When his moment of explosion and collapse came, I was working on the first satellite tests of the new large-scale photovoltaics up here. I wasn't able to be there for him. Still, I like to think that last great flash of his mind blew off in this shock wave of light, spreading forever away—some of it even flashing onto the solar sats, sparking across gaps.''

Jhana watched as the sun began to dim and redden in the engineers' best imitation of sunset. Night sounds began to rise tentatively from the water, from the banks, from the forests.

''Did he die soon after that?'' she asked.

Seiji smiled sadly.

''Not for almost another six years. My parents brought him back home until he seemed better again. He went back to work on his doctorate in Intelligent Systems at MIT. He'd already accomplished a lot. He'd developed some big new system protocols and he had money coming in from those patents, from all sorts of things. We thought he was okay again.''

Seiji shook his head and turned his back on the darkening sky, the darkening water.

''I really hoped it was true,'' he said, bitterness rising in his voice, ''but I never quite believed it. The laser sharpness his mind had before—that was gone, somehow. Just this shell of paranoia and conspiracy and weirdness left behind. He began to think he was some sort of techno-shaman. Jiro was always interested in American Indians and in computers, all the way back to when he was a kid. I guess he kind of went back to that time, and those interests just coalesced. After his breakdown he swore off gate and vowed only to do 'naturals,' but things kept getting weirder.''

Jhana turned her back on the water then too, turning around but still leaning on the mooncrete bridge railing.

"In what way?"

Seiji shoved his hands in his pockets and looked down at his feet.

"He started to disappear periodically," Seiji said with a shrug. "Just dropped completely out of sight, out of touch. There's no real word for it in English or Nihonglish, but there is in German: *Aussteiger*, 'someone who gets off the train.' He got off the train, all right. He got as far from the tracks of our world as he could. He claimed he was fasting and purifying himself like a shaman, vision-questing, enduring long, lonely ordeals for spiritual purposes. All we could say for sure was that whenever he disappeared, credit tracing showed he was also spending every penny of his available funds on exotic computer and imaging technologies, which would always disappear with him—usually into the outskirts of Balaam."

Jhana stared down at the mooncrete beneath her feet. She knew something about the hinterlands of the Bay Area Los Angeles Aztlan Metroplex. Not a nice place. She looked up again as a girl with bright white hair, fully tech-dressed in wearable media, started across the bridge with half-dancing steps, singing, *You wash, I'll dry, we'll never think to wonder why, till it fades, fades without warning: our love like the moon in midmorning*. In a moment she had danced obliviously past them and was gone.

"Could you have done anything about it?" Jhana asked, putting her hand lightly on Seiji's elbow, wondering if his brother could have been any crazier than the space habitat's wild children. "Have him listed as a missing person, maybe?"

"We tried," Seiji said with a grimace. "Before he disappeared for the last time, he contacted my parents long-link. He told them they had nothing more to say to him and he had nothing more to say to them, so he wouldn't be calling anymore. The days became weeks and—no word. We tried to get the police departments around Balaam to find him and bring him in, but they couldn't do anything. Failing to keep in touch with your family isn't a prosecutable offense, after all. Jiro was an adult, he had free will, he had broken no law, so the police couldn't hold him against his will—even if it might have saved his life." Seiji glanced toward those parts of the habitat still in light. "As the weeks lengthened to months we couldn't even have him listed as a missing person because the police always told us—mistakenly—that they had seen him, or someone who looked like him, recently. In fact he'd already been dead for months.''

"Tragic," Jhana murmured, holding onto Seiji's arm a bit more firmly, wanting to make contact.

"Yes," Seiji agreed, his chin slumping toward his chest. "But also no. Sad as it was that the police couldn't bring him in to save his life, I have to agree with that sort of law. At least it respected Jiro's right to be wrong. It didn't meddle with his freedom, not even 'for his own good.' ''

"Yes—now I see what you were getting at before," Jhana said, straightening up from where she'd been leaning against the bridge railing, letting go of Seiji's arm a moment. "The conflict between freedom and compassion."

She followed Seiji's glance up the path toward the townlet cluster of buildings ahead. Together they began to walk slowly in that direction.

"Right," Seiji said as gravel crunched under their feet. "If the police had taken Jiro into custody and held him—the compassionate thing to do, I suppose—there's always the chance that we could have brought him home and had him cured or 'put right.' But there's an equal chance that he might well have ended up in some dehumanizing asylum for the rest of his life, clocked out on psychosocial control medications—or even worse, imprisoned. Knowing how much my brother valued his freedom, perhaps even freezing to death inside an abandoned refrigerator wasn't the worst end he could have faced."

The lights of the buildings had begun to glimmer on Seiji's face when Jhana turned to him.

"Is that how he died?"

"Yeah. In a cloud of liquid nitrogen. In the middle of the smoldering trashlands, surrounded by all this expensive high-tech electronics he left behind, sitting there like so much junk. The coroner ruled the death an accident, instant hypothermia. He told me it must have been a very peaceful way to go. The police suspected suicide. The case remains uncertain, still unresolved.''

They walked toward the noise of Corazon del Cielo, a small glass-domed eatery, silently agreeing on it, without discussion.

"What was he doing with enough liquid nitrogen to freeze himself to death?" Jhana asked, opening the door to the very warm, dry restaurant, full of noise and hothouse desert flowers.

"Who knows?" Seiji said as they looked for a table. "What was he doing with all that expensive state-of-the-art gear—still all plugged in and running, his pirate microwave hookup still draining power off the solarsat grid? That was how they discovered his body, you know: the power company sent a man *on horseback* through the trashlands to find out who was at the other end of the downlink line."

"But what was he working on?" Jhana said as they sat down beneath the glassed-in sky.

"Who knows? Maybe he was trying to commune with the Great Spirit. Maybe he was contacting the spirits of the dead or trying to pull off some techno-shaman stunt. The local people in the trashland didn't know what to make of a guy who came out only at night from a white coldbox coffin. They were mostly TechNots and Neo-Luddites around there—a very superstitious bunch when it came to anything involving technology. Some of them said his soul had been stolen by one or another of his machines, that Jiro's ghost had even talked to them before the power was cut off. The power company rep didn't see or hear anything. What the locals probably came across was just some automatic program running its course."

A middle-aged woman named Herria Bidegaray, a bit heavyset and greying, appeared with water glasses and a familiar hug for Seiji. Jhana discovered from the menu display that Corazon del Cielo took its name from the Mayan *Popul Vuh* and was some sort of combination Basque restaurant/desert biodiversity conservatory. Seiji, of course, was engaged in an experiment in "cuisine design" with this restaurateur too, and it was only after some quick businesslike flinging about of various common and Latin names of fleshy fungi that the waitress/owner happily bustled away.

"What happened to your brother's machines?" Jhana asked, taking up the strand of Seiji's conversation after Herria had moved on.

"Most of Jiro's devices were just expensive black boxes to me," Seiji said, glancing at the menu." The locals might as well have been telling me about voodoo spirits living in tin cans. Still, I had all Jiro's gear and personal effects shipped up the well. Cost a fortune, but I guess it's a memorial of sorts. Haven't looked at any of it in months, not once since it came up. I could let you look at Jiro's things, if you're interested. I've got them stored with a friend, Lakshmi Ngubo. She's got a workshop up in micro-gee, not far from one of the solarsat manufactories—that's where I work my 'real' job. I could show you everything, and introduce you to Lakshmi, if you'd like."

Bingo, Jhana thought. *And I didn't even have to ask for a tour.*

"Yes," she said, while appearing to concentrate more carefully on the menu. "I'd be honored."

"I must warn you—it's not that impressive," Seiji told her, glancing over the bill of fare. "Jiro has been pretty much reduced to text: police reports, bills, receipts, notes, that sort of thing. A few wallet holographs. Lines of print and other hard-copy codes. Personal effects, bits and pieces of junk. A lot of it's probably useless and trivial, but I can't bring myself to get rid of any of that information. It's pretty much all I have left of him. Too much has been lost already, you know? It's like when a star collapses and a black hole forms: a lot of information about the star inevitably gets lost."

Jhana looked up from perusing the menu, thinking about what Seiji hadn't said—what he'd left out.

"What about the information he might have stored on computer media—in the electronics you said were found near his body?"

Seiji pressed a menu selection and ordered a glass of HOM-Ebrew, the local beer. Jhana decided to stick with water and pressed in her order too.

"That's still just a little too painful for me to deal with yet," Seiji said, looking away from Jhana as their meals and drinks promptly arrived. "Sure, I want to know if there's anything important there, but I don't want to face it cold. I've turned those machines and their memories over to Lakshmi, along with all his effects. She's an expert. I haven't heard from her in a while, but I know she's been seeing what can be salvaged, what might be worthwhile. She's always very thorough."

He took a sip of beer and stared directly at her.

"I don't know what sort of grief and guilt you may have known," he said. "Sorry to have burdened you with mine."

"I guess none of us can really know another's grief," Jhana said sympathetically, between bites. "One person's grief can never be measured against someone else's. We can only know our own."

"Yeah, I do know mine," Seiji said, twirling his beer glass slightly between his palms. "I've learned names for the condition my brother suffered from—long-term paranoid schizophrenia, Messiah complex, depressive disorder, psychosexual dysfunction arising from 'incomplete gender identification.' I can quote chapter and verse of the scientific theories: imbalances of neurotransmitters in the brain, a misreading in the genetic code that caused him to misread reality, some flaw in the DNA mirror that fun-housed his mind's reflections. I take comfort in the theories and the labels, like I'm supposed to, but in the end none of it has meant squat. I lived with it, with *him*. I know."

They ate, hungrily and in silence, for several minutes.

"What was it like?" Jhana asked at last.

Seiji leaned back in his chair and looked up through the restaurant's transparent dome. Gradually Jhana tilted her head, too, trying to follow his gaze to whatever it was he was looking at.

"Do you remember the place where you had your anxiety attack, the first day we met? At the ridge cart station up there, hanging at the center of everything?"

"Yes," Jhana said, not wanting to remember, the smell of burnt almonds and all its negative associations even now drifting through her mind. She was disturbed at the sudden swerve of the conversation into her personal life. "What about it?"

"Being up there, hanging at the center of a completely artificial sphere, completely enclosed by that sphere—that's what Jiro's paranoid schizophrenia was like," Seiji said, gesturing overhead again. "Think about the middle of this sphere, Jhana—but instead of the sphere having a shell of static surfaces like this one does, think of the shell as being like those on the new habitats, the ones that are almost finished, the ones with active surfaces where micromachines are always swarming and flowing in the layers of that surface, nanotech assem-

blers and replicators always vigilantly repairing and maintaining that surface, always keeping the outside from getting
in and the inside from getting out. If you can picture a deluded
psyche functioning like that—impervious to argument or logic,
always flowing quickly in to fill any dent reason might make
in its surface—then you can understand my brother's paranoid
world as well as I ever could.''

They had just begun to turn back to their unfinished meals,
when the bent snake circle of the Möbius Cadúceus skysign
rainbowed into space above them.

Jhana suddenly found herself plunged into darkness, running
through a hellish underground world of red and black, from
room to room of nightmare, auditoriums or theatrical spaces
without audiences, dark spaces of empty seats facing thick
blood-red curtains where actors rehearsed scenes of gory tragedy, gouged-out eyes raining gobbets of black, blind blood, in
one room a blind Othello/Michael turning his mutilated blood-
daubed corpse toward her and bellowing, ''Racist whore!''
until she ran screaming into another room—only to find Roger
Cortland looming, leering and gigantic, as a powerful scent
filled her head, turned her hands to digging claws, her naked
flesh to fierce, hard, inhuman muscle—

Abruptly she was back in the Corazon del Cielo, staring
through the transparent dome at the point in the sky where the
oddly twisted dual serpentine ring had just disappeared.

''What was *that*?''

Seiji looked at her oddly, but she didn't care. She was profoundly shaken. That sense of losing herself, of becoming a
conduit or vessel of sensations, had passed through her again
unexpectedly. She was sweating and trembling slightly. Her
appetite seemed to have vanished utterly.

''Promotion for that band, Möbius Cadúceus. I gather
they've got some big show coming up. Interesting symbol.
You mean you haven't seen it before?''

''If I have, I must not have paid it any real attention,'' Jhana
said, trying to focus on her surroundings, to reorient herself.
''But the strangest thing just happened. One second I was
looking at it and the next I was in some full-blown waking
dream.''

"What kind of dream?" Seiji asked, growing suddenly more interested.

"Oh, I don't know," she said. Seiji looked at her expectantly, but she didn't want to tell him exactly what she'd seen—that would bring up too much that was personal, vulnerable. "Dark and fragmented stuff. Lots of guilt—and grief."

Seiji stared at her for a moment longer before he spoke.

"I don't know how to tell you this," he said uneasily, "but the first time I saw it, it triggered associations in me too. You might say guilt underlies them, as well."

"What sort of associations?" Jhana asked, becoming curious—and glad that they weren't talking specifically about her anymore.

"A man on horseback at sunset," Seiji said, working on finishing his meal. "One morning, just at the shadow of a dream, I woke with the image in my mind of Jiro's corpse being found by a man on horseback at sunset in the trashlands. Six months later, that was exactly how and when Jiro's long-dead body was found. I sometimes torment myself with the thought that they were simultaneous—that image of skewed time-line image flashing into my mind where I lay warm in bed, even at the exact instant Jiro was freezing to death in a trashland down the well."

"Do you think it was genuine prescience?" Jhana asked. "Some sort of second sight?"

Seiji swirled the dark amber of the beer remaining in his glass.

"I don't know—and I don't want to know. I used to wonder if it was an authentic unveiling of hidden connections—or just a vision of patterns that weren't really there. Numinous mystical experience, or an episode of paranoid delusion? That way lies my brother's madness," he said, then downed the last of his beer. "But I do know that if seeing that skysign triggered a jump of subconscious material into consciousness—in both of us—"

"I thought altering other people's consciousnesses without their informed consent was against the rules here," Jhana reminded him.

"It is," Seiji said with a nod, finishing up his meal, "but

this may be a grey area. Chemical tech versus physical tech—everybody's harder on the chemicals, on drugs. The question is whether this trigger works the way KL does, say, or more like the way Ehab's stereograms do. In either case we've got more reason than ever to talk to that expert friend of mine up in micro-gee."

"The one with your brother's stuff?" Jhana asked, bewildered. She didn't see the connection.

"The same," Seiji said with a nod. "Lakshmi Ngubo. She does a lot of the lighting design and holographics for Möbius Cadúceus, so she probably designed the skysign too. Would tomorrow be too soon for you to visit?"

Things were moving faster than Jhana could have predicted, but she was on for the duration of the ride, now.

"No, tomorrow won't be too soon," she said slowly. "If tomorrow evening is all right with your friend, it'll be fine for me."

TEN

Passages embedded in RAT code:

The mystic sacrifices Self for World, the egotist sacrifices World for Self. All the endtimers throughout time have always seen themselves as chosen and the rest of the world as damned to holocaust—sacrificing the world for themselves, always completely inverting what their particular Holy One was about.

The egotism of the apocalyptist is also seen in a perverted abstract sensualism, which dares not look upon the image of an innocent naked child yet fantasizes about the tempting beauty of the Whore of Babylon. This objectifying ego is further seen, more subtly but more importantly, in the fact that millenialists and apocalyptists choose to see the apocalypse and the utopian paradise as something "out there" in the world, as the rending of the veil of this world through global catastrophe and endtime destruction, followed by a thousand years of the Perfect State—rather than choosing to face the apocalypse and the paradise *within*, happier by far but far more difficult, the remaking/remembering/revealing in the individual soul, the "lifting of the veil of appearances" through the

ecstasy of that vision which leads one to live in this world
as if it were heaven, paradise, utopia.

As the bulletcart rode silently along, Roger began to wonder
if he was indeed pushing himself too hard—as Marissa had
claimed. First there had been that odd blackout when he was
airbiking, then the recurring flicker of angel wings in his peripheral vision, and now the dreams—strange dreams in which
he was dressed in a monk's habit and being given lectures in
aerodynamics by angels.

He would have discounted such sleeping visions completely
were it not for their clarity, their lucidity—and the fact that,
now, the dreams had given his monkish dream-self a habitation
and a name. From what he could gather, in his night visitations
he was a monk named Eilmer, a brother of the monastery at
Malmesbury, who had lived approximately one thousand years
ago. . . .

Two of the habitat's oddly dressed and queerly coiffed
youngsters boarded the bulletcart at the next stop, singing
along to their stereo plugs. Roger recognized the tune as
vaguely reminiscent of the old standard "Take Me Out to the
Ball Game," but what lyrics he could pick out were unfamiliar
indeed.

Lyrics to Möbius Cadúceus song, "The Old Ball Game":

In the beginning
Dad the Father's Big Banger
Waited just thirteen billion years
To come to bat and no sooner was he up
Than POP went the Thunderbolt into Soup
(Our Holy Mother)
Because Dad so loved the world
We all made it to First
And it's Base Pairs, DNA, RBI—the Living Cell!

Roger shut it out. No doubt more of that Möbius Cadúceus
nonsense. He secretly blamed the band for his unwanted visions and visitations: they'd only appeared following his air-

bike near-collision with their damned advertising apparition, after all.

But even if he were to try to take them to court—virtually unheard of among the unlitigious space habitants—what would the charge be? Negligently tapping into the collective unconscious—or at least his strand of it? Ridiculous!

As he got off at his stop and headed toward his lab, he thought there must be some other explanation. He must have seen some holoflick or trideo documentary about this Eilmer of Malmesbury person, this "flying monk" of his dreams. The monk must be an historical person. He would check on it at the Archive as soon as he got a chance, but even at the moment it seemed reasonable that he had just forgotten the particulars of some obscure production, that was all. That would explain even last night's twist in the dreams, the one without angels which nevertheless spoke most particularly to his condition. It flared up vividly in his mind as he recalled it.

Databurst-triggered memory of *The Pressure of Angels* (synopsized):

Eilmer, age seven or thereabouts, his POV, is walking toward the heart of the village with his mother, wiry pale blond Elfgiva. Sexburga, stout dark-haired wife of Caedwalla the ostler, sees them and begins to direct foul, slanderous remarks at Elfgiva, which Eilmer's mother disdainfully tries to ignore. Sexburga, though, will not be ignored. Spitting, fuming, and ranting, she comes out onto the dusty rutted road and blocks their way. Only after the overbearing Sexburga has spat and struck at her several times does Elfgiva strike back, clinching with the stouter woman, both coming to furious blows, kicking and clawing, pulling at each other's hair and tearing at each other's garments until they are a tangled knot of rolling bodies and flailing limbs from which grunts and curses and cries periodically erupt. In this state they tumble among Sexburga's animals, sending her chickens flying and her cow ambling away in great mooing confusion—until a small crowd of townspeople stand watching beside Eilmer, and two brawny young peasants pull the enraged women apart. . . .

Opening the door to his lab, Roger thought of how many popular entertainments—historical fiction, Westerns and spy thrillers, science fiction and fantasies—featured such gyno-machian scenes. *Ten Million B.C.*, *Destry Rides Again*, *From Russia With Love*, *Genesis Two*, *The Farewell Gift*, *Free Fall Free-For-All*, and hundreds of others. He hardly needed to search for some dim vast archetype—some experience in a past life lurking in the collective unconscious—to explain the roots of his personal kink. He was sure this manifestation of it must all be from some low-budget lowbrow entertainment he'd once seen as a child, which—for some inexplicable reason—was now resurfacing in his mind.

Commanding the power up on one of his simulators, he still could not shake the idea that Möbius Cadúceus's skysign had triggered something in him. It might not be all bad, though, if the dream-image that had opened in his head turned out to be what he was hoping for.

Sitting down, he entered the simulator's virtuality. Using force feedback to plot and move and orient molecular structures in virtual space, he caused a structure to gradually form in the space before him. He watched a molecule begin turning through primary, secondary, tertiary, and quaternary structuring, until it was unlike any he had ever seen before. He suddenly felt a strange hyperlucid sensation he'd never previously experienced. The dizzying, glowing exhilaration of it was so power-ful, he wondered a moment if this was what had driven the medieval alchemists on and on in their search—not just for gold from lead, but even more for gleaming islands in the soul.

He sat back, shaking his head slightly to clear it. He knew gleaming islands in the solar system—the habitat, Earth itself. Nothing more. He looked once again at the molecular structure floating in space before his eyes. It was a structural analog of the mole rat pheromone, yes, but one with a distinctive, elegant twist, a molecular Möbius strip, a lazy untangling infinity sign without inside or outside, beautifully simple overall, despite its complexity at the fine-detail level. He would have thought such a form impossible until it had flashed into his half-awake mind this morning, right on the kicking heels of his dream.

Roger smiled. Legend had it that Kekulé had discovered the structure of the carbon ring after dreaming of snakes rolling about like hoops, their tails in their mouths. If it could work for Kekulé with one hoop made of one snake, then why not for him—with a bent-hoop snake itself made of many such hoops? The thought occurred to him that this jump from rats to humans was all happening too easily, too quickly to be true, but he repressed it. He would check his new molecule's structure against all the response tests, all the receptor sites, but he felt intuitively certain that this structure of elegant twistedness, this complexly beautiful image. that seemed almost a model of his own mind and mirror of his consciousness—this was the complete structure of the human pheromone for which he'd been searching.

The door to the lab opened and Marissa came in, logging into a Cybergene virtuality. No doubt still busily at work on her antisenescence vector. A frown flickered over Roger's face. Things had changed so rapidly between them. They had been getting along so well, particularly during their dance in space and immediately after, but now their relationship was somehow distant and prickly, especially since she had stumbled upon his after-hours pornholo debauch. Lately, he was seeing the copper-haired woman and her large, pale-nippled breasts only in his dreams.

Surely, though, his discovery this morning was momentous enough to serve as the occasion for initiating some rapprochement—

"Marissa," he called virtually, over his throat mike. "Log into my space, please. I want to show you something."

Marissa linked slowly, tentatively, until he could feel her staring into virtual space with him.

"Well, what do you say? Intriguing structure, don't you think?"

Marissa nodded.

"What is it?" she asked.

Roger smiled broadly.

"I'm willing to bet it's the human pheromone I've been looking for. It's a structural analog of the mole-rat pheromone, but a good deal more complex. Pump it through the synthesizer, would you? Then we'll run tests on it to see how it binds to human vomeronasal and brain tissue. If my guess is right, then all we'll need to do after that is find the right base and top note and we'll have created the most important—and potentially most profitable—fragrance in human history.''

Nodding, and smiling a bit awkwardly, Marissa called up power on the synthesizer.

"Okay," she said evenly, "shoot the data over here."

Roger gave a series of command codes that shunted the structure and all its specifics into the synthesizer's memory. Under Marissa's watchful eyes the synthesizer chuckled and clucked to itself as it began assembling the actual compound from the virtual template that Roger had presented to it.

As he listened to the mechanism doing its job, Roger was nonetheless a bit peeved. Certainly after all his work he had expected a more enthusiastic response from Marissa, and wondered why he hadn't gotten it. Maybe she was just being cautious—waiting for the structure to prove out. Well, let her be cautious. He had no such need for concern. This was the structure he'd been looking for. Of that he was certain.

Passage embedded in RAT code:

. . . the tangled etymology of the word *utopia*. In the computerized catalogs the generally accepted etymology—*ou* (not) + *topos* (place)—leads one into a long and deep maze of "not places," no places, nowheres, Big Rock Candy Mountains and the Land of Cockaigne, Schlaraffenland and Lubberland, the upside-down worlds of festival and carnival and Saturnalia, an entire literature, oral tradition, folklore, and popular culture of Nonsense going back at least as far as dusty comedies in the Attic Greek.

But this search also leads to places grown out of No Place—to Essenes and Diggers and Shakers and scores of other faith-based communities, to Brook Farm and New Harmony and the Kaweah Colony, to Rancho Linda Vista and desert arcologies and Biospheres.

"I've already contacted Atsuko Cortland and Seiji Yamaguchi," Lakshmi said into Lev's bleary-eyed virtuality. He'd been up late, working on a stop-and-start blocking rehearsal and, though it was already late in the day in his sector, he was still asleep when Lakshmi and Aleister's joint conference call came through, causing him to sit bolt upright in bed and slap on his overlays—the posture he still remained in. "Seiji is bringing Jhana Meniskos with him. Roger Cortland and Paul Larkin haven't returned my calls and probably won't make it, but Atsuko is bringing Marissa Correa."

"The one that sent me the complaint," Lev asked with a yawn, "about Roger Cortland's encounter with the skysign?"

"The same," Lakshmi said with a nod. "She wasn't affected by it, but he was. Interesting that his name was on the RAT list, but not hers . . ."

"Whatever," Lev said. "I'm not looking forward to explaining the skysign's effect to her—or to Roger's mother."

"To Seiji and Jhana, too," Lakshmi told him. "They said they've also apparently been affected by it to some degree. But you haven't got it so bad. Think of everything *I've* got to explain to Seiji about what's been going on with his brother's stuff."

"Aleister can help you with that, can't he?" Lev said, volunteering his friend—and perhaps hoping to get himself out of the planned meeting.

"Afraid not, old boy," Aleister responded primly. "Lakshmi's deputized me and assigned me a higher priority."

"What?" Lev asked, incredulous.

"Seems our RATs and the distributed consciousness behind them have attracted the attention of Earth's intelligence and information-gathering services—corporate, governmental, straight military, you name it," Aleister said. "We're weathering a rain of semiautonomous information probes. Monitoring and diverting the little net-spies has become a full-time job in the last twenty-four hours. You and Lakshmi are on your own."

"Anything more you can tell us about the RATS and our situation before we have to explain them to our guests later?" Lakshmi asked Aleister.

"Only that the ALEPH program Manqué used in building the RATs is much more subtle and sophisticated than I thought," Aleister said carefully. "I expected to find a fairly rudimentary virtual environment—one 'species' of cellular automata being bounced off another to 'evolve' something that's supposedly new. What I've found instead is a piece of work with quite an appreciation for the subtlety of the actual evolutionary process—species co-evolving with each other, entire communities co-evolving. It makes very impressive use of the counterintuitive Paine work on predation—''

''Which is?'' Lev asked, peeved. ''Come on, Al. We don't all have your background on this.''

''It's the idea that predators in an ecosystem,'' Aleister said, warming to his topic, ''rather than reducing the number of species by their activities, actually *increase* the diversity of species by preventing any single species from gaining ascendancy.''

''What's that got to do with the Myrrhisticineans' project?'' Lakshmi asked, puzzled.

''They were Teilhardists, remember?'' Aleister asked rhetorically. ''Well, Pierre Teilhard de Chardin was big into evolutionary theory. Complexity is the trick Life plays against Entropy, and Teilhard claimed that life at all stages manifests what he called the 'law of complexification.' According to this law, everything in the cosmos—from subatomic particles to us to galaxies—has a conscious inner face that duplicates the material external face. Physical evolution and the evolution of consciousness increase in complexity together. The more complex and integrated an outward material system becomes, the more developed its psychic interior also becomes.''

''Let me get this straight,'' Lev said, now finding himself almost awake enough to engage in rational discourse. ''Self-conscious human thought evolved with, or because of, the intense integration and concentration of nerve-cell structures in the brain?''

''Right—but when you think about it, never lose sight of the idea that individual mind is also always part of Universal Mind.''

''But what's this got to do with computing power and the Rainbow Door and the rest?'' Lakshmi asked.

''Isn't it obvious?'' Lev said pedantically. ''Think about it— the integrated complexity of a material system is mirrored by an inner psychical development. Complexity trends toward sentience. As a result of producing human beings capable of self-conscious thought and culture, the biosphere has spun off what Teilhard calls a 'noosphere,' a 'thinking layer' produced by human activity. Since Teilhard's time, though, the human activity of the noosphere has in its turn increasingly spun off an *infosphere*, the cyberspatial layer generated by the activity of increasingly complex machines.

"The Myrrhisticineans saw themselves as extending Teilhard's work," Aleister continued, his little icon trying to keep pace with his gesturing. "If God did not exist, it would just be necessary for them to invent him, that's all. According to Teilhard, a long co-evolutionary convergence has been taking place, simultaneous movements toward a single planetary consciousness *and* a psychical concentration. As things become more evolved they also become more *in*volved. The noosphere—especially with the infosphere speeding things up—is becoming involuted into a Hyperpersonal Consciousness, which will be fully achieved at a point Teilhard called Omega. At Point Omega, matter and consciousness reach the terminal phase of their convergent evolution and become one. Absolutely indistinguishable. That's what the Myrrhisticineans really meant by the Rainbow Door."

"And the distributed consciousness you and Laksh have been going on about," Lev said, "you think it's this Hyperpersonal Omega thing?"

"Who can say?" Aleister shrugged. "It might be a step on the way. Point Omega's meant a lot of things to a lot of people. To the Myrrhies it was the Rainbow Door, but to some of the info-industry types who pumped money into their abbey, it seems to have meant something quite different. Two of the abbey's big donors, Dr. Ka Vang of ParaLogics and Jem Kerris of Kerrismatix, both authored papers extending Friedkin's hypothesis of an 'information-based cosmos,' where matter and energy are alternate states of information. Kerris proposed something called an 'information density singularity' and Vang at one point claimed to be developing a 'simulated quantum information density structure'—a transluminal portal."

"So the thing that blitzed the abbey maybe wasn't a Rainbow Door," Lev ventured, "but a kind of black hole sun, like the tabloids claimed?"

"Maybe," Aleister said, "but that seems too passive and material to me. Teilhard talks of a *hyperconsciousness*, after

all. Maybe it was a Rainbow Door, or a Transluminal Portal—
or maybe it was the maw of a technological superpredator.''

"*What*?" Lev and Lakshmi said in unison.

"Who says the hyperpersonal consciousness has to be divine rather than demonic?" Aleister speculated. "What if
Manqué the apocalyptist got impatient? What if he decided
that human history is proof of the Paine hypothesis gone
wrong: a single species—us—has gained ascendancy and has
been steadily reducing the biodiversity of the ecosphere around
it. Our development of culture and survival technologies has
made it unlikely any successful natural predator will develop
against us. Through warfare and the creation of the rich as a
permanent vampire class we've tried to prey on ourselves, but
that hasn't worked because no species can really limit its numbers through self-predation.''

"Oh, I get it," Lev said, shifting gradually but increasingly
into Bela Lugosi mad-scientist parody. "So maybe Manqué
figured he'd help create a predator so advanced that it could
successfully prey on human beings, no matter how impressive
our technology. An angel of death, a hungry god. Mystical
union, oneness, Omega—what else but to be devoured by the
rough beast, the great demon, the terrible beauty slouching
toward Sedona to be born . . .''

Lev and Lakshmi laughed, but Aleister merely smiled.

"Laugh if you want, but it is one possible scenario for what
might have happened at the abbey outside Sedona," Aleister
said. "This 'distributed' or 'hyper' consciousness, if that's
what it is that's growing in the infosphere now—it may have
to undergo a spiritual battle between its angelic and demonic
sides, just like any other self-aware consciousness. You could
argue that that the Building the Ruins game already provides
evidence of such a battle.''

Lakshmi became abruptly silent, which surprised Lev.

"I haven't played that game yet, myself," he said.

"You might want to," Aleister suggested, "before you meet
with your guests. You might also want to look at more of the
information encrypted in the RAT code. That's what's helped
direct me in my speculations. Look, I've got to get back to
spy-catching duty. I'll touch base tomorrow.''

Aleister disappeared from their shared space. Lakshmi turned to Lev.

"You will join us for our meeting, then?" she asked pointedly.

"I promise," Lev said. "I'll even come up early and sample this game Aleister seems to think is so important. Good enough?"

"Good enough."

"FOOLS!" ROGER SAID, STORMING THROUGH THE LAB. "Idiots!"

Marissa said nothing, just tried to keep doing her work, focusing on some final simulation runs of her antisenescence vector, but that didn't stop Roger. He seemed to need to hear himself rant and rave.

"Those fossils—those mossbacks at the *Journal of Mammalogy*—they rejected my article! 'Fails to provide proof of pheromonal/chemical suppression of mole-rat reproduction adequate for overturning established behavioral suppression model'—that's what one of their peer reviewers wrote. He even had the gall to write 'See Faulkes et al, in *The Biology of the Naked Mole Rat*, Sherman, Jarvis and Alexander, Princeton 1991'—as if I were some upstart graduate student! Faulkes and the old boy network! Don't they know my 'unorthodoxy' predates their orthodoxy? The pheromonal suppression model was first proposed by Jarvis herself! It was the reigning paradigm for the first decade of mole-rat studies—and never disproved!"

Marissa finished her test runs on the Cybergene machine. She turned on her nucleic synthesis equipment, then abruptly shut it off, got up, and left—looking disgusted. Roger stared after her, rage and frustration contending in his face.

Where was the sympathetic Marissa he had known before she'd surprised him in that early morning debauch? Did she know too much already? What had she really seen? Enough to make the connection?

No time to worry now. To hell with her. Resubmit the article—to *Nature*, perhaps? No, maybe no need. He had enough results on his new compound. Now he needed to synthesize it, to begin situational testing. . . .

Using one of his father's old corporate encryption codes, Roger moved through his virtual reality's data construct until he gained access to memory-stored perfumery guides—the secret but surprisingly unprotected hoard of his father's perfume company subsidiaries. Poring over pane after pane of text, detailing perfumes and extracts and eau de toilettes, concretes and absolutes, early odors and late fragrances, notes and harmonies, tenacities and predominants, tops and hearts and cores and bases and auras and sillages—he got a sense of what he might need. Yes, jasmine picked at dawn or perhaps lavender as a top-note, civet as fixative and bottom—

He scanned through the lists of the botanical and zoological holdings of the habitat. He expected to find jasmine and lavender, and he did. According to the registry of holdings, several gardens contained plantings of one or the other or both. Interestingly, he recognized at least one name among the garden lists—Larkin, Paul. Roger scanned for Larkin's home and work addresses and was surprised and pleased to see that the man was director of the lab to which Jhana Meniskos had been assigned. He thought of the slim, dark-haired, dark-eyed woman—then of Marissa too, her coppery hair streaming out behind her as she'd left just now. Better and better.

He scanned for sources of civet and—was this providential, or what?—found that Larkin's lab was also doing work with endangered mammals of the family Viverridae. Civet cats.

Dr. Paul Larkin was clearly the man to see. Roger would have to pay him a visit as soon as possible. Then, when he'd compounded his perfume to the guides' specifications, he would stage for Marissa and for Jhana—but most of all for himself—a private situational test. . . .

Perhaps because he'd been keeping such odd hours of late, or perhaps because he'd been pushing so hard and now had apparently succeeded (despite this recent rejection note), his body decided it was time for him to rest. Whatever the reason, he now found himself slipping off into a light, nervous sleep.

Passage embedded in RAT code:

Think of the discovery of fire as a blow against the cold and the dark and the raw. Think of the discovery of agriculture as a blow against the tyrannical vicissitudes of hunting and gathering. Think of the invention of writing as a rebellion against oblivion, against the endless brute days of the peasant farm laborer, the bloody brutal ends of the warrior. Think of the invention of the scientific method as a blow against the bureaucratic priests and their Holy Writing—the managerial class's revolutionary idea that reading from the Book of Nature could be just as valuable as reading from the Book of Scripture. Think of the development of space travel as a rebellion against gravity, against the tyrannical linking of human destiny to a single planet. Think of the development of virtuality as a blow against the tyranny of the meat body over the mind. The only tyrant left now is death. Space travel is really about species immortality, all the work against senescence is really about individual immortality—blows against death's tyranny, ideological weapons all—

Disturbed by Roger's rapid mood swings—extreme elation over his hypothetical pheromone, all too quickly changing to extreme anger and bitterness over the rejection of his article—Marissa left the lab, early and in a rush, and proceeded to the grounds around the Archive, where she was to rendezvous with Atsuko after the latter's speaking engagement.

Realizing she had been spending entirely too much time on her antisenescence vector and wanting to convince Atsuko that she was deserving of her fellowship in utopian studies, Marissa turned on her overlays and PDA and began to comb through her notes again as she walked steadily along. A bibliographer or librarian had cross-referenced both Aldous Huxley's dystopian novel *Brave New World* and his final utopian novel *Island* to a series of books by someone named R. Gordon Wasson. Intrigued, she followed up the lead, only to discover that the Wasson books were mostly about the ritual use of sacred mushrooms in priestly and shamanic contexts.

Doing this side-alley research soon proved to be something other than the complete waste she'd anticipated, however, because she gradually came to realize that both of Huxley's books were indeed characterized by the presence of an ingested psychoactive substance unique to each text. *Brave New World*'s "soma" and *Island*'s "moksha" could each be profitably read as a microcosmic embodiment of the macrocosm of the novel in which each was found. All that was dystopian in the Brave New World could be found in kernel form in the nature of soma. All that was truly utopian on the Island of Pala could likewise be found in concrete form in the mushroom called moksha. The consciousness-altering substance ingested in each novel was an "artificial paradise" inside an artificial paradise, an island within the island of the ideal society that each novel presented.

As she examined the texts further, she saw that the "drug" in each was, to some degree, the holiest of holies—but, more importantly, it was also central to the way Huxley examined the relationship between individual freedom and social responsibility that was also so very important to the inhabitants here in the space habitat. In *Brave New World* and *Island*, how each society treated its drug and its drug users was the litmus test for how that society treated its citizens and their freedom of choice, their autonomy as individuals.

Marissa had reached the Archive grounds now. She was so absorbed in her research that she located a bench and sat down without really thinking about it, doing it all in that mental state she called autopilot. In her continuing train of thought, she realized it was only a short step to Huxley's letters, essays, nonfiction books, and his other novels. Scanning back through the entire corpus of Huxley's writings, she saw they could be examined for the light they shed on the attitudes of twentieth-century Western societies toward drugs, drug usage, and particularly the ongoing tension in those cultures between individual freedom and social responsibility.

Her eyes looked through and past her overlays as her mind began to wander. She thought suddenly that her utopian studies had as much to do with life as with literature. She wanted to see what the literature said about how human beings might create a society both just and merciful, that fulfilled the needs of the body without denying the freedoms of the mind, the soul. A truly humane society that prospered but did not thoughtlessly exploit either its own citizens or the environment in which they were embedded. One that recognized the alleviation of suffering as its highest goal, but was neither paternalistic nor authoritarian in its pursuit of that goal. Ultimately, she supposed, she was less interested in literature and literary criticism as a tool for making better books and more interested in it as a tool for making better people.

At the sound of footsteps, Marissa came out of her reverie.

"Resting your eyes, Marissa?" Atsuko said, standing before her with an impudent smile.

"Just contemplating," Marissa said, standing up a bit stiffly and joining Atsuko. "How did your presentation go?"

"My speech, you mean? Fine. All teachers in the audience—up from Earth for a conference. Remind me to tell you about it—on the way. I saw Seiji on the way back and he said he's looking forward to meeting you. It turns out he and another of our visitors are also getting together with a mutual friend, Lakshmi Ngubo, this evening. She'll be expecting us along. We've got to meet with Seiji and his friend in an hour, so we'd better hurry."

REALIZING THAT SHE WAS NEARING PAUL LARKIN'S RESIdence, Jhana slowed her pace. She had decided to test Seiji's suggestion that her supervisor was someone worth getting to know, and to that effect she had already spoken to him in the lab to set up this appointment. Larkin's manner had been curmudgeonly and noncommittal, seemingly habitual with him, so to strengthen her case Jhana had tried to familiarize herself with his life and work.

Walking slowly beside a mossy fern-banked stream that flowed boisterously beneath the shade of a grove of young cedars, Jhana was not quite oblivious to the beauty of the little ghyll through which she was passing. She had run an extensive data search on Larkin and now was quite puzzled at the strangeness of his history. She found herself thinking again of the flying mountain, Caracamuni tepui.

When, twenty-eight years ago, Larkin and his guide and native porters had returned from the tepui country of South America with their story and video recording of Caracamuni's top quietly lifting off, decoupling from the Earth, the geologists, seismologists, and volcanologists dismissed the ascent of the mountaintop as an "anomalous volcanic eruption," and wrote off the video as a hoax, trick photography, a cinematically contrived special effect. After such denunciations, Larkin's claims inevitably fell into the disreputable limbo of the mass tabloids, the murky half-tone half-light of the faxoid cheapsheets, in whose pages the spectacle of the flying mountain was periodically resurrected. What made it all the more appealing to the faxoid editors over the years, as far as Jhana could tell, was Larkin's own status as a serious senior scientist—an expert in the cryogenic preservation of threatened species and also someone making claims outside his field. Controversy, dissension, and disagreement within the ranks of the scientific community could always be counted on to sell papers.

From what Jhana could glean from the public documents, such tabloid exposure had apparently not been good for Larkin's career either, which seemed to go into eclipse for nearly a decade, during which time he had apparently left his first career in investigative journalism—that would explain his media obsession—and gone back to graduate school. He'd gotten a decent position shortly after completing his doctoral and postdoc work, but then interest in the flying mountain had ballooned up again. He'd refused to recant his previous statements on the subject and his career had derailed once more. He had been reduced to the status of "independent researcher" and had scrounged funding wherever he could—including rather shady unofficial sources such as the various intelligence agencies, which at that time were transmogrifying from national security apparatuses to corporate espionage and intelligence brokers.

Moving from the cool of the cedar copse onto a sunny green hillock of steep mazelike gardens, Jhana made her way over and around the bright sinuous rills and streamlets that both knit together and unraveled the maze—a landscape that largely escaped her notice, for her eyes were on the cluster of airy, tentlike domes shining at the top of the small hill.

"What are you thinking about, Jhana?" a voice asked, so suddenly that she almost thought it had come from within her own head. Turning, she saw a gnomish white-haired man staring up at her and realized she'd been addressed by Paul Larkin.

"Actually, I was just thinking how you and your flying mountain came back into the limelight almost by accident, Dr. Larkin," Jhana said. "After KL 235 was derived from *Cordyceps jacintae*."

"Yes," the old man said, rising from his cross-legged position on a stone garden bench, all his joints popping and snapping and clicking. "I see you've run a background check on me."

"Tell me something about that," Jhana said, perhaps feigning greater interest than she really felt. Anything to get on the old guy's good side. "You claimed that fungus grew only on Caracamuni tepui . . ."

"That's right," said Larkin, joining her on the path. "I obtained spore-prints of it before the mountaintop vanished, so I had sole access to the species."

Walking together beneath the sheltering sky of the habitat, they set a leisurely pace along the maze of garden pathways leading to the domes.

"I read that you were working for the intelligence agencies when you developed the drug," Jhana said. "Was it the flying mountain story that first got them interested in you?"

Larkin laughed, then fixed Jhana with a glittering eye.

"Be serious! The spyboys never gave much credence to that story at all! The effects of *Cordyceps jacintae*, now—those were verifiable enough to be of interest to them. And they knew about psychoactive fungi, of course. Seventy and eighty years ago the cloak-and-dagger lads were intimately involved in the dissemination of LSD, for instance—and that was derived from *Claviceps purpurea*, a wheat ergot fungus. *Cordyceps* and *Claviceps* are closely related, too, so they saw . . . possibilities. They didn't care if I claimed to have gotten the fungus from Atlantean mermaids or little green men. It worked, and that was all that mattered."

They stopped beside a spot so fragrant that Jhana took immediate note of it. An herb garden of some sort, she presumed.

"If I remember his call, he wanted some jasmine . . ." Larkin said, leaving the path and stooping among various flowering green plants. He stopped beside a small bed of white flowering shrubs labeled "J. GRANDIFLORUM."

"Who's 'he'?" Jhana asked, watching Larkin move like an old monk-herbalist about the gardens, plucking flower after flower.

"Roger Cortland," Larkin replied, depositing his burden of flowers in the bags and sacks he took from his pockets and snapped open. "He wanted some ingredients for a perfume he's making. Know him?"

"We've met," Jhana said, thinking at the same time that Roger certainly hadn't struck her as the *parfumeur* type.

"The lavender is a bit further along our way," Larkin said, rejoining her on the path. They walked along, wreathed in the florid scent of *Jasminum*.

"What were the effects of KL 235 that the intelligence agencies were so interested in, exactly?" Jhana asked, continuing to endear herself to the old man.

"It circumvents the action of the DMN, the dorsal and median raphe nuclei in the brain," Larkin said evenly. "The DMN function as a sort of governor on the level of brain activity, keeping that level down to low percentages of total possible activity. The ketamine lysergate 235 I derived from *Cordyceps jacintae* allows prolonged brain activity at very high percentages of total possible activity."

Jhana glanced thoughtfully at the gravel of the path, the jasmine scent still lingering in the air like a morning melody heard in the mind all day.

"But why would the spyboys, as you called them, be interested in something that increases brain activity?" she asked. "For smarter spies?"

"Much more than that," Larkin said, scanning the gardens about them. "At such high levels of brain activity, parapsychological phenomena appear in abundance: clairvoyance, second sight, mystic heat and cold, far-seeing, mindtime journeying. KL 235 vastly enhances those phenomena that improve understanding of the patterns of possibility backward and forward in space-time, and the intelligence collectors saw great potential in having such powers, despite the risks."

Larkin stopped short.

"Ah, here we are," he said. "I wonder if he wants to use the flowers only? Hmm. They all contain the essential oils—

flowers, stem, and leaves. We'll pick them all. He can sort them out if he wants to."

"Is that an editorial 'we'," Jhana asked, "or may I help?"

"You're welcome to," Larkin said with a nod. Leaving the path, they climbed up among the plants of another elevated plot. He showed her how to pinch back several stems. In a very short time they were each returning with an aromatic armload of spiky-leaved, purple-flowered stalks.

"*Lavandula officinalis*," Larkin said, handing his bundle of lavender to Jhana for her to carry as he picked up his jasmine samples again. Jhana took the extra armload awkwardly, spilling a few stalks and bending to retrieve them.

"You mentioned risks with KL 235," she prompted as they walked along, now doubly wreathed in sweet scents.

"Unavoidable ones," Larkin said with a nod. "Brain burn-out. The raphe nuclei *do* have a reason for existing, you know. They're your body's way of keeping the brakes on your brain. Some researchers have theorized that the brain inherently serves as a reducing valve, allowing into consciousness only a very small fraction of what's out there. According to such theories we're all prisoners of our brains. Through the barred windows of the prison-house we see only as much as we need for survival. For those of us who follow that line of argument, the dorsal and median raphe nuclei are the pins and tumblers in the lock on the jailhouse door—and KL 235 was the perfect way to pick the lock."

Larkin smiled awkwardly as they made their way among the domes of a small settlement cluster.

"Myself, I now think the DMN serve a bigger purpose," he said. "The brain normally can't run full throttle for very long. If it does, it destroys itself. I can't say for sure but my sister Jacinta could have. She was the ethnobotanist in the family, after all. She was the one in search of the hallucinogenic grail, not me."

A small group of children raced noisily past them. Jhana seemed to recall something from an old news story she'd glanced at in her data search.

"Jacinta's the one who disappeared when Caracamuni ascended?"

"That's right," Larkin said as they entered one of the

domes—apparently the old man's residence. "She'd already disappeared into the 'field,' as the ethnobotanists so fondly describe it. I set out to find her, and I did, though not for long. That mountain didn't go up uninhabited. 'Forty-odd aboriginal astronauts and a drug-crazed ethnobotanist, all serving as humanity's first personal ambassadors to the universe.' That was how my story was described in the media at the time. Believe me, I know how crazy that sounds. Much easier to view it as just an odd volcanic explosion, just the disappearance of another obscure piece of rain forest real estate—lamentable, but God knows it was going on all the time back then.''

They walked through the living area and into the kitchen.

"Still, I saw what I saw. Here, let's break that lavender into smaller bundles and tie them up so you won't drop any more of it.''

Jhana emptied her armload of lavender on a table as Larkin searched drawers for string. When he found it, they quickly sorted the lavender by size and wrapped it into three tidier bundles.

"What did you see, exactly?'' Jhana asked as they were tying the last of the bundles—growing interested in Larkin's strange story almost despite herself.

The old man fixed her again with that glittering eye of his.

"I still have the videotape we took, if you'd like to see it. Might help us both understand what Jacinta was up to.''

"I'd enjoy that,'' Jhana said, thinking that people up here seemed to hoard old videos and trideos the way others collected photos in family albums.

Leaving the lavender on the table, they adjourned to a viewing room with a video screen set into one wall. Larkin popped a video minidisc into a player.

"I'll try to fast-forward through to the actual ascent sequence,'' he said, obscurely embarrassed. "I really should have edited this down after all these years, but I never could bring myself to destroy anything from that time.''

The video came on and Jhana saw an exterior shot of the Missouri Botanical Gardens—apparently the institution Jacinta had worked for—then a shot of a cluttered cubicle, a stationary cyclone of notebooks and reports, folders and pamphlets and monographs strewn everywhere. This was followed by a satellite photo of Caracamuni tepui. Next came a scene of bills and receipts, check stubs and requisition slips for an odd assortment of things—industrial autoclaves, portable solar- and gas-powered electric generators, diamond saws, thousands of feet of power cables, fold-out satellite dishes and uplink antennas, language acquisition and translation programs, camcorders and optidisk player recorders, fifty microscreen TVs—

"She'd had all that stuff shipped to a little nothing town in the middle of the jungle," Paul said. "So that's where I went next."

The videotape continued with views of a jungle village's mud street, scrawny dogs prowling about, *indigena* porters, a mestizo man with a smile like a slash across his face, tipped back on a veranda chair, whittling a stick with a big blade. . . .

"My guide," Larkin said, "Juan Carillo Garza. Most of the others are Pemon Indians."

A series of jungle scenes followed: Canoeing and portaging up river and stream, past flights of blue and red macaws, past troops of monkeys shrieking green waves through the forest canopy, past the fluttering flashing blue of giant morpho butterflies. A bearer-line slogging through a wet green hell of venomous snakes, brittle scorpions, stinging ants, ever-present mosquitoes. A green tunnel of machete-hacked trail switchbacking endlessly, like a journey through the bowels of some immense ruminant animal.

"Took us three days before we finally got into the mountains proper," Larkin said, still playing about with the fast-forward.

Shots taken above the tree line appeared at last, scenes of the guide Garza pointing to a mountain on the horizon, a high mesa shaped roughly like a giant anvil, a sunlit plume of waterfall plunging from its top.

"Caracamuni tepui," Paul Larkin said quietly. "The geologists estimated that the shield rock of Caracamuni plateau was approximately one point eight billion years old. That jibed to some degree with parts of the inhabitants' mythology."

There were more shots of the pack line hiking up switchbacks, the green tunnel replaced by a constant low ceiling of leaden clouds. The backbone of a ridge. The tepui itself, a place of stone-black with eternal rains, blotched with fog and algae and fungus. A dense stone forest of balance rocks and pinnacles, columns and arches, the sort of city that time and water dream from stone.

"A labyrinth of stone clouds," Larkin said. "Everything rounded, no right angles anywhere. Ancient strata broken by lopsided eggs of sky, interrupted by oblongs of rain. Forty square kilometers of it. My sister was out there somewhere. Garza and his men refused to go further. Old taboos about the 'ghost people' who were supposed to inhabit the tepui."

More old video camera images of the top of Caracamuni tepui showed an island of stone floating among the clouds, raindesert island above rainforest sea. Dark water-soft contours of ancient stone: geological ruins, nightmare temples, alien cathedrals dribbled like children's slurry sand castles onto an anvil-top high in the sky. Mostly barren, Jhana noticed, but here and there dotted with pocket Edens, swampy rock-garden-sized oases. A view of a sun setting behind bars of clouds, smearing slanting light on ancient stones, stood out strongly from the rest of the wild-shot, uncontrolled documentary footage.

"That sunset filled me with melancholy," Larkin said quietly, remembering. "Almost as if I were seeing a universal twilight of men and gods, of worlds and time."

Amid shots of a new day, a young woman, *indigena* girl really, disappeared in and out of fog and cloud like an apparition, naked but for a loincloth patterned with masterfully intricate serpent-knot designs, drawing Larkin and his camera on, stopping only where the stony maze broke off and a cloud-filled gorge came into view below. Further along the edge a sunburnt woman stood, clad in tattered shirt and shorts and gym shoes, sun-bleached hair under straw sun hat, clipboard in hand on the brink of the abyss, adjusting the angle onto heaven of a satellite dish.

"Jacinta," Larkin said hoarsely to Jhana, clearing his throat.

The camera followed Jacinta and the *indigena* girl walking down into the cloud-mist obscuring the gorge, the antenna line following along the footpath then losing itself in thickening undergrowth. Now the camera focused on the tree canopy through the mist, the ever-denser cloudforest growth, dripping innumerable varieties of lianas and orchids and epiphytes; then on the bottom of the steep gorge, slippery downed trees ranging across a torrent plummeting to waterfall beyond.

The camera panned across and up a branching canyon trail, jungle thinning, mist clearing. Foot-trampled pathways converging on an earthen slope beneath a high cliffside. Power lines and cables snaking out of the forest on both sides of the gorge, purposeful vines of black, grey, and red growing into a half dozen holes in the cliff.

"You'll see in a minute that those holes are part of the entrance to a cave," Larkin explained as the camera followed a line toward a cliff hole. Above, heads, then torsos, then entire bodies of *indigenas* appeared, largely unclad but for occasional intricate loincloths and, incongruously, headsets.

"The 'ghost people,' " Larkin explained. "The theory was that they were a very small Pemon group which, until my sister's arrival, had been isolated up there for a long, long time. According to the Pemon, the ghost people's ancestors supposedly broke some ancient taboo and were considered 'already dead' by their tribe. A small group of them—refugees, outcasts—settled the tepui 'at least a thousand years ago'. My sister's work there, however, suggested that they had been there many, many thousands of years, that they were in fact far older than the Pemon—and they weren't completely isolated either."

The scenes that appeared now, inside the cave, were dimmer and much more confusing. Jhana saw movement down a slantwise tunnel, past rock honeycombed with innumerable small side chambers.

"Even after my sister's arrival," Larkin explained, "the Pemon porters would carry all the gear she'd shipped only as far as the edge of the tepui. The inhabitants had to carry it the rest of the way."

Jhana watched as tantalizing glimpses of what was going on in the side chambers flashed past: several *indigena* children watching what appeared to be a Chinese TV documentary, a young loincloth-clad man watching an American news broadcast about an Indian monsoon, a young woman checking an enormous crystal column for flaws as it flowed out of a high-pressure extrusion autoclave, loinclothed boy and oldster seated before computer terminals and scanning at unbelievable speeds through what looked like extremely complex mathematical equations, a half dozen operators of various ages scanning through what might be star charts or astrogation data—

Then Jacinta (and Paul behind the camera) were out of the chambered stone, the tunnel opening into an enormous underground space like a nether sky where shadowy light glimmered off crystalline rock. Then the camera cut away to a brief shot of an old man or woman dressed in a full loose robe of the same intricate knot-weave as the loincloths, a longhaired gaptoothed bright-eyed elder of indeterminate gender—

Then abruptly the camera was shooting from outside the cave again, then out of the gorge, off the tepui, back again with the guide and bearers in sunset light. Larkin slowed the playback. The camera, pointed at Caracamuni tepui from the far end of the ridge below it, was shaking violently. The forests between it and the tepui seemed to toss like waves in a storm.

A great ring of dust formed about halfway up Caracamuni's height and the tepui itself appeared to be growing taller. As its top continued to rise, though, Jhana saw that it was not growing but separating, top half from bottom half, at the ring of thinning dust. Soon the top half had risen free from the dusty billows, and a space of clear sky intervened between the sundered halves of the ancient mountain.

Rising smoothly as a mushroom in the rain, drifting away like a ship slipping from harbor toward open sea, open sky, the mountaintop ascended. Clear of the Earth's curved sunset shadow, the sun shone full upon it again. Strangely, its cascade did not disappear in a long mist to Earth. Jhana puzzled over the image of the waterfall moving downward like inverted smoke, only to pool crescentwise at some unseen boundary—until she saw the way the light bent around the mountain, refracting in a great sphere like the shimmer of heat waves from asphalt, from desert and mirage, from the boundary of a soap bubble like those Marissa, her fellow passenger on the flight up the well, had talked about.

If Jhana could believe what the video was showing her, then she could only conclude that Caracamuni was ascending in a bubble of force, its high cataract plunging down only to spread out again in a broad swirl along the boundary's edge. She looked more closely and saw that, from the sphered mountain itself, a pale fire like inverted alpenglow had begun to shine, increasing in intensity until, in a brilliant burst of white light, the mountain disappeared, as silently and completely as a soap bubble bursting in a summer sky.

Jhana and Larkin stared at the screen for a time.

"A tremendous blast like thunder swept over us after that," Larkin said. "And then it was over. But it's not really over. Not with KL 235 out there. And lately, someone or something has been accessing the copies of this tape in the public archives. A lot."

"Isn't there something missing?" Jhana asked. "Why'd you stop recording inside the cave after that old shaman or witch or whoever it was appeared? And what does all that have to do with KL 235?"

"Everything," Larkin said with a sigh, standing abruptly. "Come along with me to the lab. Dr. Cortland still needs musk from civet cats, so I'm headed that way anyway. If Mr. Yamaguchi is on duty, I've got something to show you in the mycology labs on the way."

Leaving Roger Cortland's bundles of lavender and bags of jasmine flowers behind, they left Larkin's residence, striking off along a path that ran among the hilltop domes.

"The 'old person' of the tribe, Kekchi, refused to allow me to keep shooting what I was seeing," Larkin said as they walked, "so I'm still trying to piece it together out of memory. Jacinta tried to explain the situation to me, but I wouldn't listen. I thought she'd just hooked up with a lot of backwoods mushroom cultists. I couldn't wrap my mind around it."

"What did she try to explain?" Jhana asked as they stepped over rocks and crossed a small stream.

"My sister claimed the ghost people had been living in symbiotic relation to *Cordyceps jacintae*, their 'sacred mushroom,' for millennia," Larkin replied as they passed sidewalk cafes and a small park. "Jacinta called it a 'myconeural symbiont' because after someone ingests the fruiting body, the spores germinate and the spawn forms a sheath of fungal tissue around the nerve endings of the central nervous system, penetrating even between the nerves of the brain and brain stem, even to the dorsal and median raphe nuclei, without damaging them."

"You mean they have fungus living in their heads?" Jhana asked, her face wrinkling in disgust.

"Exactly," Larkin said with a nod, glancing away toward meadows where children played—watched by adults who might or might not be their parents. "I found the idea of such a fungal infestation disgusting, too. But the relationship is mutually beneficial: the fungal spawn obtains moisture, protection, and nutrients even in adverse environments, and the human hosts are assured a steady supply of the most potent 'informational substances,' as Jacinta called them."

"KL 235," Jhana said, watching children create a species mandala out of stones and leaves and organic debris while adults captioned it with the words "Not King nor Steward, But Friend."

"No, that was my mistake," Larkin said with a grimace. "One of the ghost people apparently planted several of Jacinta's mushroom spore prints in my backpack when I was on the tepui. All unknowing, I carried them off with me before the mountaintop ascended. When I got back home and found the prints in my pack, it didn't seem fitting to go public with my discovery—not after what had happened. But, as I said, I couldn't bring myself to destroy anything associated with that time—not even the spore-prints of the very things I held responsible for my sister's disappearance."

A shadow passed lightly over them from an airbike pedaling high in the sky above. Jhana's eye was caught by a sign hung on a tree announcing a co-op consensus meeting for that evening, and an elaborately highly wrought poster announcing the Möbius Caducéus concert the following evening—skysign and all.

Returning her attention to Larkin, Jhana said, "But KL 235 did eventually hit the market. So your attitude about going public must have changed."

Larkin nodded glumly as they walked along.

"The flying mountain story had ruined my career. I was desperate for a score, something to reestablish my name. I had sole possession of the fungus that Jacinta and the tepui *indigenas* had discovered, so finally I decided to play it as my trump card. I'm not a mycologist and not the world's best biochemist either, but I was able to pitch the idea of working with the fungus to a friend of mine with connections in government and corporate security.''

Passing at a quick pace through clusters of domes and hogans and small cooperatively maintained parks, they came upon a sign that read Mycology and a ramp descending into the ground. At least, Jhana thought, they were headed toward Seiji's workplace, or one of them, where she might meet him and save some time.

"The cloak-and-dagger folks wanted in on the game," Larkin said, starting down the ramp, "and they anted up cash for a staff. I was in business. I grew a batch of the fungus and they began testing it—I didn't want to know where, how, or on whom. My most grievous error. They liked what they saw and the funding just flowed in."

As they came to the bottom of the ramp Jhana saw a long corridor leading away, dimly illuminated by bioluminescent strips and the light spilling from an occasional open door. She hoped they would be stopping soon: she and Seiji had appointments to keep, and she didn't have all day. . . .

"The only problem was, we estimated that the development of full myconeural symbiosis would take about twelve years, just as Jacinta had told me it did among the tepui people. That was far too slow for the professionals putting up money for my research. Twelve years was too much time, time in which the fungus could easily be detected and eliminated by antibiotics—and ingestion of mushrooms was too bulky and unwieldy to begin with. My investors wanted something fast, discrete, potent: the twelve-year effect, but in about twelve minutes. The word came down that we were to isolate the particular chemical that produced such-and-such effects. I obeyed, we obeyed. Isolation was our unpardonable sin."

"How's that?" Jhana asked as they walked along in the corridor's half-light, the punky, funky smells of rich humus and decay wafting toward them more strongly whenever they passed an open door.

"Brain burnout, of course. A generation of infojunkies, datazombies. Those were the products of my problem child, once the damned agencies and corporations made sure it escaped from the labs into the grey markets and the streets. From Jacinta's work with the *indigenas* of the tepui it was clear that, unlike straight KL's more limited effects, the myconeural complex did much more than just circumvent the DMN and prompt high-level brain functioning. The mushroom complex produces many other substances—neurotransmitter analogs and psychoneuronal interlocks we haven't begun to fathom, even now. Twelve years seems a long time to wait, but at the end of that time the fully myconeuralized *indigenas* were at constant high-level brain activity without burnout or any apparent ill effects. They even claimed that human hosts with full myconeural complements become natural telepaths with each other, though we haven't been able to test that.''

Larkin took special note of light coming from a doorway ahead.

"Looks like we're in luck—Seiji appears to be waiting for us," Larkin remarked, before returning to his previous discourse. "Anyway, not only had we removed KL from the myconeural complex, but we'd already dislocated the mushroom from its proper environmental and cultural context. In the name of international insecurity first, and then for the sake of corporate profit, KL was given to and taken by people who had no framework for understanding its effects. The *indigenas* of Caracamuni tepui had an entire millenia-years-old mythological and cultural framework to plug their sacred mushroom into, while the street kid or college student doing pure crystalline 'gate' in a back alley or a dorm room had nothing to fall back on but tenuous personal myths and explanations or, at best, vague ideas about the sort of mindset and environmental situation appropriate to taking KL.''

Entering the brighter confines of Seiji Yamaguchi's mushroom workspace, Larkin shook his head savagely. When he spoke again there was deep bitterness in his voice.

"I told them what would happen. I told them not to let it get loose, but the intelligence commandos, the corporate moneymen—those bastards just wouldn't listen. They didn't give a damn. The worst was Medusa Blue and Tetragrammaton, with that grail of theirs, the 'information density singularity.' ''

Jhana saw Seiji over in a corner of the workspace, but surrounded by a group of children to whom he was apparently explicating the joys of mushroom cultivation, he hadn't noticed her and Paul Larkin yet. She was hoping he would save her from more of Larkin's endless conspiracy theorizing, but help didn't seem to be forthcoming from that quarter.

"After the disaster at Sedona," Larkin went on, "the Tetragrammaton people shifted their efforts out of pure machine approaches and into mind/machine linkages. They're going to find their translight portal if they have to kill a million people to do it. They're still around, you know. Look at the board of directors of your company, Jhana. Dr. Ka Vang serves there, as well as on a bunch of others. He's on a lot of interlocking directorates, but the one that's not listed is his deep connection to the worldwide intelligence apparatus—all the way back to his childhood, when the CIA recruited him as a Hmong boy-soldier, over sixty years ago."

"How do you know so much about all this shadowy stuff?" Jhana asked, but what she was really thinking was, If you know all this is true, then how come you're still alive to talk about it? She'd heard Tien-Jones mention Vang—one of the many members of TPAG's board, all of whome seemed to have their fingers in lots of infotech and biotech "pies."

"I was a fellow-traveler for a lot of years," Larkin said with a shrug. "Their creature. Quite involved with Medusa Blue. Maybe I still am, in a way. What better cover for a conspirator or spy than the role of conspiracy theorist, hm?" He directed a meaningful glance at Jhana. "You'll just have to trust me on this one."

"Wait, you're confusing me," Jhana said. "What's this Medusa Blue thing got to do with Tetragrammaton?"

"Medusa Blue was a psi-power enhancement project within Tetragrammaton," Larkin explained as patiently as he could. "It was intended to facilitate computer-aided apotheosis, the translation of human consciousness into a machine matrix. You see, the human mind possesses the right kind of chaos to complement the kind of information density only computers and AIs can assemble. Put together the right combination and Boom! A mathematical model of a gateway so complete it *is* a gateway. The virtual and the real coincide. The Big Payoff: much-faster-than-light travel to anywhere in space-time."

"And how does all this tie into KL and your work?" Jhana asked, hoping to finally unsnarl the mass of information he was throwing at her.

"Medusa Blue involved using university hospitals and certain medical centers as fronts for giving selected women treatments with KL 235—as a 'uterotonic' during their second trimester," Larkin said. "Pumping KL to the womb during embryonic development—to encourage the development of paranormal talents useful to effecting that big mind/machine link in the sky."

"They gave the stuff to pregnant women without their consent?" Jhana said, disturbed by the memory of certain patterns in her own family. "But that's crazy."

"Of course it's crazy," Larkin agreed. "Just like doping soldiers up on BZ without their knowledge or consent was crazy. Just like dropping LSD on your own unsuspecting citizenry was crazy. Just like nuking your own citizens was crazy. But in the name of international insecurity all those things have happened—and lots more besides. Governments and corporations doing to their unknowing and unconsenting citizens and employees things which, if the citizens and employees later did them to themselves with their own knowledge and consent, would have gotten said citizens put in jail or fired."

"And KL followed the same pattern?"

"Sure," Larkin said with a nod. "By the time it was made illegal worldwide, the pharmaceutical combines had already made their profits. They couldn't lose. If gate turned heavy users into paranoids and long-period schizophrenics who spent all their time consuming knowledge and information so they could create and flesh out their own personal conspiracy-worlds—well, so what? Who cared if it increased the number of schizophrenics and catatonics? No big deal—the companies that pumped out KL were the same ones that made the pharmaceuticals for treating schizophrenia and catatonia."

Seiji and his crew of kids had walked into an adjoining room of the lab. Following, Larkin and Jhana found him and the kids examining a trough of moistened straw and hay, from which oyster mushrooms were fruiting in great profusion. Seiji glanced over as they came in.

"Paul! Jhana! I thought I heard your voices over there," Seiji said, coming forward to shake hands. "What are you two up to?"

"I was just bending Jhana's ear here about the usual unu-

sual—Tetragrammaton, KL, the creation of long-period schizophrenics . . ." Larkin told him.

"Ah. As in my brother's case," Seiji said with a small nod,
looking away. Jhana saw Larkin wince.

"My karma—you see, Jhana?" Larkin said. "To find that
so many of my friends' loved ones have been damaged or
destroyed by something I helped bring into the world. My only
relief is to tell my tale like some damned ancient mariner,
again and again. Yet absolution never comes for good and all
no matter how many times I make my confession."

"I'll help you work off your debt faster, if you'd like,"
Seiji said, half-seriously. "Take care of these kids for a
while, okay? Jhana and I have an appointment to meet some
people—"

"And we're already late," Jhana put in.

Larkin agreed, appreciative of the time Jhana and he had
spent conversing—or, more accurately, her listening to him.
They parted—with a hug from Larkin! Who'd have thought?—
and Jhana and Seiji darted off for their appointment.

"I'M WORRIED ABOUT ROGER," MARISSA TOLD ATSUKO AS
they climbed aboard a bulletcart headed to the ridge axis
where they were to meet Seiji and Jhana. When Atsuko looked
at her questioningly, the words began to pour out of Marissa:
about Roger's mood swings, her worries concerning the threat
his pheromone posed to human freedom if it somehow managed to work. She told Atsuko a great deal, though not everything she might have revealed, for some of it was still too
private.

"The strange part is," Marissa finished, "he must know that
the odds are against his pheromone working—if it even *is* a
pheromone that he's designed. That's the scary thing—the denial, the delusion, the fact that he's not looking at his experimental results in a balanced or objective way."

"Yes," Atsuko said with a deep sigh. "When does dedication to one's work become obsession? Whichever it is, his
'thing' for those mole rats seems to be getting out of control."

"If it doesn't work," Marissa suggested hopefully, "then
there's really no harm done—"

"Except to his psyche, his self-esteem," Atsuko said, sighing deeply again. "Roger, Roger—now, he's someone who could have benefited from the educational system we're developing up here. It's just like I was telling those teachers from Earth."

"How's that?"

"Because Roger's been warped by what passes for education on Earth. Too often it's a system that emphasizes division and domination while de-emphasizing similarity and mutuality," Atsuko said, gazing toward the top of the cart. "Who knows what sort of power fantasies Roger may entertain? We had enough difficulty convincing him that we wouldn't bend the rules so he could bring his gun collection with him! Even the most ardent gun enthusiast would have second thoughts about projectile weapons in a space habitat, but not Roger. Nurture more than nature's the cause, I think. Earth's educational system itself is an example—not only what it teaches but *how* it teaches. It's a dysfunctional family, a factory model. A warped cultural hologram."

The bulletcart deposited them on the central platform, the sphere within the sphere. There were several people passing to and fro, but Jhana and Seiji were not among them, so they waited, gripping handrails as the sphere around them spun gravity into space and they made their way out to its circumference.

"Look at our little world here," Atsuko said, "and then remember Earth. Take the warped cultural hologram, the factory model, one step further. Think of the entire human race as one big conglomerate, Consolidated Humanity, and the Earth as one enormous factory. Matter and energy are the raw materials, the 'unformed children' in the system. Mother Nature's plants and animals are the factory workers on the food-chain assembly line. But what is Big Daddy management trying to produce?—what's Consolidated Humanity's product?"

Atsuko paused, following with some interest a free-fall soccer game going on not far from the sphere—but also obviously waiting for an answer.

"Consolidated Humanity produces people," Marissa said, catching on. "Very successfully. Far more than the market or the planet can bear."

"Right. Mother Nature is the abused wife of *Man*kind."

Marissa cocked an eyebrow at Atsuko in disagreement.

"But certainly the idea of dominion, of power over others, isn't an exclusively male concept—" she interjected.

"No," Atsuko agreed, but with a sly smile. "It's just that males have made such a study and art and religion of it. What we're trying to teach our young people here is that the natural world is not just a factory for helping humanity turn out more human beings. We help them see that the relationships between mother, father, and child, between other living things, nonliving things and humanity, are circular and interdependent rather than linear and hierarchial."

"Food webs rather than food chains?" Marissa ventured. "Flows rather than pyramids?"

"Right. Human beings embedded in their environments rather than somehow standing above them as lords and masters, or below them as hapless victims of hurricanes or monsoons or other so-called acts of God."

Marissa turned and gazed out the side of the observation sphere, toward the other side of the much larger and seemingly motionless sphere in which the world of the space habitat was enclosed. Yes, everything seemed to move in circles and ellipses and rings here. The watercourses, the forests, the savannas, even the homes and buildings, now that she thought about it, seemed to be losing right angles, softening toward variants of domes and hogans.

For a time they were silent as Atsuko watched the soccer game and Marissa watched a group of young people get off a bulletcart and gather around the noise of a portable holojector playing a music trideo. In virtual space a young male lead singer with extremely white-blond hair was cavorting and singing. Marissa listened to the song despite herself.

Excerpted lyric from Möbius Cadúceus song "Jesus of Oz":

Every day machines become more like people
Who become more like machines every day
And I know this for real and true
Because because because because because

Last night on the elevator of dreams
When I got off on the ground floor
An unrecognizable artificially intelligent friend of mine
Stabbed me to death with a screwdriver through the heart
Because because because because because
It wanted to calculate the escape velocity of my soul
But its numbers were off so it programmed me
For resurrection and tonight it will kill me again
Kill me a little better this time which we call Progress
Because because because because because
Of all the wonderful things it does
For people becoming more like machines
Becoming more like people every day . . .

Even their songs run in circles up here, Marissa thought, turning back toward Atsuko and the soccer game.

"Certainly, though, you haven't remade humanity here, haven't overcome all our perennial problems—"

Atsuko laughed.

"Not at all! We're still very much imperfect people in an imperfect world. Or at least we're incomplete, both our world and us—and probably always will be. From the human standpoint, however, reality to some degree consists of what we think it is, so if we change the way we think we also change the reality we live in and the way we live in it."

A flash of lights along the tube signaled the approach of another bulletcart. It stopped and opened and a Mennonite-bearded man and a dark-haired, dark-eyed woman stepped out.

Seiji and Jhana came forward and introductions were made all around, Seiji apologizing profusely for their lateness—his fault, he insisted, because he'd gotten caught up in demonstrating some of the finer points of mushroomery to a squad of children in his family-support network. Marissa and Jhana remembered each other from the flight up the well, and Jhana was quite aware of Atsuko's relationship to Roger Cortland. As they made their way to the tube where their bulletcart would soon be arriving, Marissa noticed that Jhana was gazing around the platform, looking rather tense.

"Does the height bother you?" Marissa asked. "I was feeling a little acrophobic myself, not long before you two arrived.''

Jhana nodded as, along the tube, lights for their arriving cart began to flash.

"Yes—vertigo. Not as bad as when I was here last, though.''

"Not nearly!'' Seiji said with a laugh. ''We'd just met. Poor Jhana looked as if she'd seen a ghost—white-knuckled grip on the railing, her eyes big as satellite dishes—''

"Now don't exaggerate, Seiji,'' Atsuko chided. "I know the engineers have good reasons for keeping this observation sphere transparent, but really, seeing so much space all around must come as quite a shock to newcomers.''

"The space was only part of it,'' Jhana said quietly. "A lot of it was just the sheer strangeness of everything, all the detail. You'll laugh, but—I don't know—I felt as if I'd been trapped inside a big, multidimensional mandala.''

"What a wonderful image!'' Atsuko said with a laugh as their bulletcart eased up before them. She craned her head to look at the large sphere, and nodded as they boarded. "Interesting you should think of it that way.''

"My mother was a Western devotee of Buddhism,'' Jhana explained. "When religion came up at all in my upbringing, it was an amalgam of my father's Greek Orthodoxy and my mother's Neo-Tibetan Buddhism.''

"Both of which are very iconic,'' Atsuko said with a nod. "Yes, now that you mention it, I see what you mean about this place being like a big mandala.''

"I guess I do too,'' Seiji agreed as the doors of the cart sealed around the four of them and they shot away. "The Indians of the Pacific Northwest had a mandala called a salmon circle. It's a symbol of the fact that for millions of years the salmon have circled—from hatching in fresh water to life in the seas to spawning and death in the same waters where they were born—cycling endlessly, generation after generation. My brother showed me a picture of that mandala once. It's a haunting image. If you stare at it long enough, after a while it stops being just salmon. It begins to metamorphose: the humps of the fish start looking like serpents or dragons, the fins are transformed into wings, birds, angels. I saw rivers and forests and clouds in it too.''

Marissa found herself warming to Seiji. If this young man was an incarnation of what Atsuko meant by the New Science, then Marissa was all for it.

''That's sounds like as good an image as any,'' she put in, ''for a living world inside a spinning sphere, in an orbit around the Earth, in an orbit around the sun. All those orbits would probably make quite a mandala too, if we could just see it!''

Jhana looked up from her lap. She had idly popped on her personal data display for note-taking and, since she'd done nothing with that program, the machine had scanned up a news broadcast from Earth as a screen-saver.

''You people better have a look at this,'' she said, interrupting and forwarding the broadcast to her companions' personal data units.

''. . . today,'' said an overdressed anchorwoman on all their screens. ''Motions have been introduced simultaneously at the United Nations and the Corporate Presidium council to consider the implementation of trade sanctions or possible military action against the High Orbital Manufacturing Enterprise. The motions charge that, among other matters, the space habitat has violated product treaties and, more gravely, placed satellites illegally into Earth orbit for undisclosed reasons. The news of the satellites has prompted a groundswell of public opinion in opposition to the space habitat's actions.''

They watched as the newscast switched from the anchorwoman to coverage of a street protest, then an interview with a protest organizer.

''—trends in population and resources, it can go only one of two ways,'' said a pale young woman with a shaved head, dressed in solidarity street-rags and carrying a baby on her hip. ''Either everybody's piece of the pie has to be limited uniformly at a smaller and smaller size, or the pie has to be distributed more and more unequally. Follow that second road and you end up with domed islands of plenty in dying seas of want. Garden bubble oases of the wealthy surrounded by toxic waste deserts of the poor. The flight of the rich to suburbs in space while Earth City crumbles. That's exactly what's going on with this latest move by the space habitat—they're trying to set up shop on their own, free of any responsibility for the rest of us down here. Cosmic selfishness, that's what it is!''

Jhana snapped off the broadcast. The spin this was all being given on Earth, the way the space habitat was being misrepresented—it was even beginning to disgust her.

"We knew this was coming, sooner or later," Atsuko said. "I'd hoped my liaison work could stall it longer than it has. All the more imperative that we see Lakshmi and get to the root cause of these satellite games—so we can learn to live with some new facts of life."

Seiji glanced around at his fellow passengers in the cart and smiled a sad, odd smile.

"Human beings—we're born for trouble, live in trouble, die in trouble, as my brother used to put it."

The ridge cart slowed and stopped among the agricultural tori and some flamboyantly dressed young people got on, moving to their own music, their own games. Out of the corner of her eye Jhana saw the name VAJRA flash up, and a symbol like a shimmering lightning strike, and a shining data-construct city under siege by dark forces. She turned away.

"Not to change the subject, Seiji," Atsuko put in, "but what kind of ag schedule are you on?"

"A couple of month-long clusters," Seiji said as the cart eased to a stop in the manufacturing zone. "September and October, why?"

"I was thinking it might be nice to see if you could join our work group," Atsuko suggested as they stood and the doors opened. "I think you'd fit in well, even though we're mostly older—"

Jhana was surprised that Seiji and Atsuko could so blithely accept the news of the latest threats from Earth. There was little time to contemplate that, however, for two people were waiting for them on the platform: a dark-complected woman of perhaps forty dressed in flowing clothing and seated in a hoverchair and, standing beside her, a lanky young man with albino-white hair, wearing wraparound magenta sunshades and a black body suit.

"Lakshmi!" Seiji and Atsuko called in unison as they stepped forward to greet her. They did not attempt to shake her hand, and something about the way the woman's body was positioned in the chair made Jhana suspect that Lakshmi was almost totally paralyzed and had not opted for the usual cyborg fix.

"Atsuko! Seiji! And you two must be Marissa Correa and Jhana Meniskos? I'm Lakshmi Ngubo. A pleasure to meet you both!"

For all the apparent rigidity and frailty of her body, Lakshmi spoke in full, deep, flowing tones that reminded Jhana of the courier Losaba—the South African man who had delivered a private message from her employer. Lakshmi Ngubo—an Indo-African name?

"I don't know if you're acquainted with my friend here," Lakshmi said, with a nod toward the tall young man beside her. "Lev Korchnoi, the mind behind the music of Möbius Cadúceus."

"Not really," Korchnoi said in his flat Midwestern American English as he shook hands with Jhana and Marissa. "Just a member of the band."

"False humility suits you so poorly, Lev," Lakshmi said with a laugh as she spun her hoverchair around with a whispered command and led them out of the ridge cart station. Only Lakshmi looked dignified as they moved along—the others had to assume the loping gait characteristic of movement in low gravity. "Marissa," she went on, "Lev is here to talk with you, Jhana, and Seiji, about your responses to his group's skysign. It seems there've been some other complaints."

"Not complaints," Lev corrected, glancing at Marissa as they proceeded down a corridor. "More . . . *bewilderments*."

"You designed the skysign, then?" Marissa asked, addressing her question to both Lev and Lakshmi.

"Oh no," Lakshmi said. "I was trying to design something for Lev's upcoming concert when this glitch thing started developing on its own in my virtual space. I couldn't get rid of it."

"That's where I came in," Lev said. "Lakshmi showed me her glitch thing and I immediately concluded it was the perfect image for our performance of *Temple Guardians*—the show we're doing to celebrate the opening of the two new habitats."

"Since I initially thought that image might be someone else's intellectual property—and therefore copyrighted—I tried to dissuade him from it," Lakshmi said as they made their way down a corridor marked Transshipment Docking. "To no avail."

"It wasn't any one else's property," Lev said, almost petulantly, "and it was perfect: the twin snakes of the caduceus, bent round into a Möbius strip. What more could we want?"

"How about a symbol that doesn't cause subconscious material to suddenly appear in consciousness? Hm?" Lakshmi said pointedly. Lev tried to ignore the comment.

"But if you didn't create it," Seiji asked as they moved— Lakshmi floating, everyone else loping—down a ramp, "then who did?"

"We don't know," Lev said, tight-lipped. "Not exactly."

"Oh, come on, Lev," Lakshmi objected. "It has to be 'something' connected into VAJRA."

"VAJRA?" Atsuko asked.

"Does VAJRA have something to do with these new trideo games that have been popping up everywhere lately?" Seiji wondered.

"VAJRA has something to do with a lot of new things," Lev said cryptically.

"Wait a second," Jhana interrupted. "What's vajra?"

"V-A-J-R-A," Lakshmi spelled it out, hovering to a stop before the gate area of a space dock. "Variform Autonomous Joint Reasoning Activity. It's a flexible-response system for networking all the machine intelligence activities associated with the functioning of HOME—everything, from the big AIs to the micromachines, the expert systems to the cellular automata."

Lev laughed.

"Now who's suiting up in the armor of false humility? Lakshmi designed the system. VAJRA is the 'mind electric' of the space habitat. Or the mind of light, rather, since it's all laser-connected and communicated."

"It's a sort of psyche," Lakshmi explained, though a bit reluctantly, as if explanation was inevitably a reduction, "that constellates quantum information packets in a way that's analogous to how the brain coordinates the firing of neuronal groups in specific locations relating to particular functions."

"But I seem to recall the word 'vajra' in some completely

different context,'' Jhana said hesitantly. ''A spiritual context.''

Lakshmi gave her a surprised look.

''You're right. Not many people know about that. I took the name from *The Tibetan Book of the Dead*. In Indian mythology, the vajra is the jewel that destroys all weapons—a symbol of a power that is indestructible, pure, and supreme. 'Vajra' means both *diamond* and *thunderbolt*, or *diamond thunderbolt*, in Sanskrit, but I've always thought of it as being more like a boomerang of coherent, pure light.''

''A weapon, then?'' Jhana asked, surprised that she had taken so long to connect ''diamond thunderbolt'' with a myth system she had known since childhood. The different contexts—Tibetan Buddhism and the paranoia of Tao-Ponto's Weapons Division—had kept her from making the link. Now, though, many puzzle pieces came clicking into place in her mind.

''Oh no, no.'' Lakshmi said, shaking her head—quick sharp shakes. ''The vajra of the old myths can never be used frivolously, it always fulfills its function of destroying the enemy, and it always returns into your hand—but it isn't a physical or outward weapon, any more than Blake's concept of 'mental fight' is about a boxing match or Gandhi's *satyagraha*, truth force, is about an armada of nuclear missiles. I've always thought of the vajra as a symbol of the indestructible power of Truth itself, a spiritual weapon destroying Error or Illusion, 'the enemy.' ''

Lakshmi glanced down at the floor, rather embarrassed.

''I admit that giving the system such a grand, old mythological name was something of a flight of fancy,'' she said, ''but since the whole QUIP transfer technique was based on the bending and reflecting and return-cycling of light—the boomeranging of laser light from microscopic lasers—I thought such a name appropriate at the time.''

''But I still don't see what all this has to do with trideo games,'' Seiji said in a puzzled voice, ''or with what Jhana and I, and apparently some other people, have experienced.''

Lakshmi spun away in her hoverchair, commanding open the docking bay doors before her, revealing the interior of a transfer ship.

"If you want to know the game," Lakshmi said, floating into the ship's interior, "then let's play the game. My workshop's only a quick drift away."

Atsuko, Seiji, Jhana, and Marissa filed in after her, Lev bringing up the rear, smiling crookedly.

Passage embedded in RAT code:

This colony is already a unique community, a zoo and a natural history museum and a botanical garden, an open-air concert hall and art gallery, an exercise in consensus decision-making, a commons, a bioregion composed of several subregions—all rolled up into one. A city-state in space. Yet none of the social engineering engaged in here is impossible on Earth. In most cases it'd be even easier there. It's just that, in the habitat, there's a sense of starting anew in a place that's uncompromising in its demands on the residents' time. The sense of community, the idea that every part is engaged in the support of the whole and the whole is fully engaged in the support of the parts, that this place is as much a part of the residents as the residents are a part of it—that idea is particularly strong here.

When they were all strapped in, the transfer ship eased free of the turning habitat, headed for the micro-gee manufacturing facilities situated at a nonspinning, hence "weightless," end of the axis—"the still point of the turning world," as Lakshmi described it, using a phrase Marissa also seemed particularly fond of.

They drifted past shielded mirrors and collectors, past the habitat's own solar power arrays, until, very nearly in free space, they saw crews supervising the finishing touches on the nearly completed disk of a satellite solar power station.

"That's one of the newest designs," Seiji explained to Jhana. "Solar exchange film, it's called. Its big advantage is that it can be assembled—'spun out' is really a better term for it—completely by micromachines. Big webs of spider-silk organic steel and microlattices of silicon converting sunlight directly to electricity."

"If it's being spun out completely by micromachines,"

Jhana asked, "then why the construction crews?"

"They help guide and supervise the process, keep an eye on it," Seiji explained. "The brigades of micromachines, the 'spiders'—they sometimes go off on their own tangents. But it's worth the effort. That bulkier thing in the center—like the spider in the web, see it there?—that converts the electricity to microwaves that can be beamed down to the large antenna arrays on Earth. Clean energy that's saved Earth's atmosphere from additional coal-fired power plants, saved hundreds of rivers from hydropower dams, saved future generations from tending more nuclear wastes—"

Jhana laughed.

"One would never guess you worked for the local power authority," she said, glancing farther away into space, at the necklace of power stations ringing the distant blue-white ball of Earth.

"But some of those other stations," Marissa remarked, "the ones already deployed—they're shaped differently: squares, and rectangles too."

"Older technologies," Seiji said with a nod. "Solar panels, even collecting mirrors. Some of the first stations aren't even large-scale photovoltaic, like all the newer ones. In those older sats sunlight is simply used to heat up a thermal-exchange fluid to spin a turbine. Ancient plumbing is what some of my friends in Utility call it, but the old workhorses are still cranking out the gigawatts—light to heat, heat to electricity, electricity to microwaves, microwaves to Earth, then microwaves reconverted to electricity and heat and light."

"Cycles and transformations," Atsuko said. Seiji nodded as Lakshmi muttered commands to the ship, bringing it around for docking.

"What's that over there?" Marissa asked. "The thing that looks like a cross between a thimble and a badminton birdie, only giant-sized?"

"That?" Seiji asked, pointing, unsure from Marissa's description just what it was the red-headed woman was looking at. "That's a mass catcher."

"A *what?*" Marissa said, her expression that of someone who thought she'd just heard an off-color joke but wasn't quite sure.

"I know, I know," Seiji said, holding up his hands before him in mild embarrassment. "You should hear the comments whenever we get someone new on staff. But really, that's what it does: it catches mass, payloads of lunar material launched by mass driver from the moon's surface. That's what most everything that isn't complex organic is made from up here: lunar material."

"And lately," Lev Korchnoi put in, "some of the micro-machines have been raiding the mass catcher for extra material. Seems some of our 'spiders' have bugs."

Seiji stared at him.

"How do you know that?"

"My day job is in Communications," Lev said, smiling his crooked smile. "Word gets around."

Jhana wasn't paying much attention to this exchange, for she had found something else in the universe that was puzzling her.

"Seiji," she said, getting his attention. "What about those X-shaped things? See? The ones that look sort of reddish? Some of them are near the solar stations, some aren't—"

"I see them," Seiji said, ill at ease. "Frankly, I can't tell you what those are. The SSPS staff isn't responsible for them. We think they're just some space junk that the glitching micromachines are producing on their own—"

"Junk?" Lev interjected, cocking an eyebrow. "Pretty organized, for junk. Come on, Seij. I've gone to check them out myself, for Communications. Surely you people in power production must know something about them."

Seiji sighed, glancing around the cabin as the transfer ship began to dock.

"Well, we *do* have some idea what they are," he conceded quietly, "but no idea at all of what they're intended to do."

"Then what *are* they, at least?" Jhana wanted to know.

"Combinatorial arrays of microscopic lasers embedded in photorefractive material," Seiji said in a rush, as if he were glad to have it out in the open. "Linked to interspersed layers of solar exchange film. The film apparently functions as a power source and memory matrix, but we haven't been able to fully figure out what the laser/photorefractive combination does yet."

"We haven't either," said Lev, who had been nodding his head in agreement while Seiji was explaining. "But personally, from the electron micrograph close-ups I've seen, I think it's some sort of communications device. Something like what we've been using to generate our skysign—only what's being built out there is hyperminiaturized, multiplied by millions and billions of individual units—and makes what we're using look like a stone-headed axe."

"Whatever they are," Atsuko put in, breaking a silence unusually long for her, "we had better find out quickly. Their unexplained presence is making a number of our corporate and national neighbors down the well *extremely* nervous."

"They think it's some kind of weapon, no doubt," Lev said with a chagrined smile, then shook his head sadly. "The military mind surpasseth all understanding. Just because it's on the 'high ground'—boom! Sputnik effect! That thing over our head! Sword of Damocles! Star Wars! Ridiculous."

"You don't think it's dangerous, then?" Jhana ventured.

"How should I know?" Lev retorted. "But I'll say this: from everything I've seen, it's no space-based beam weapon. Photorefractive material doesn't concentrate laser light—it disperses it in predictable patterns. And the lasers involved are tiny ones. You're not going to burn up anybody's hometown with these things."

"I tend to agree," Seiji said with a nod. "The configuration's all wrong for a beam weapon."

"But that still doesn't answer the big question," Marissa put in. "Who's building it?"

"Not who," Lev said with mock gravity. "What."

"Enough speculation!" Lakshmi declared loudly, commanding the ship's airlock open. Floating around them as they unstrapped, she made her way into her workshop. The others followed close behind, again awkwardly trying to manage movement in near-zero gravity.

The visitors found the workshop to be a thoroughly "smart" space—heavily voice-activated. In the low gravity, even large pieces of equipment hung grasped by what looked to be the frailest of robotic arms and voice-response waldoes. Amidst all the cutting-edge technology, however, there also stood

something that looked very much like a loosely made statue—
or even a shrine.

Immediately drawn to it, Seiji went to take a closer look,
Jhana following close behind. Some of it was recognizable
enough: an odd juxtaposition of tantric ritual objects, a few
Roman Catholic icons—but what seemed to interest Seiji most
was one particular grouping of bits and pieces, all turning
slowly about one another like some mobile held together by
nearly invisible wires. A beaded leather pouch with an oddly
familiar trefoil symbol hung at the center, surrounded by a
nebula of cast-off material: A pair of smudged white feathers
looped together. A distorted metal asterisk of age-blackened
barbed wire. A red rust-pitted toy gyroscope. A stub of dark
green candle. A dirty silk cocoon. A fragile, nearly translucent,
piece of snakeskin. A glinting computer macrochip. A tiny
mechanical umbrella. A yellowish beaked skull, clearly a small
bird's. A desiccated dark brown thing pitted and convoluted
like a dried and shrunken brain. Up close, it seemed a more
or less random assemblage, a mobile of bits and pieces, but
from a slightly greater distance it resembled some misshapen
human being, or perhaps a four-footed mammal standing on
its hind legs as if digging into air or space itself with its front
paws.

"What's this?" Jhana asked, pointing to the little dried-up
object that resembled a shriveled brain.

Seiji looked more carefully at the last item, until he finally
recognized what it was.

"A dried morel," he said. "A 'sponge' mushroom from
which nearly all the moisture has long since been wrung out."

Looking at one particular section of the bits and pieces—
several of them drifting about the beaded pouch, which seemed
as if it might almost once have held them—Jhana was struck
by the idea that their juxtaposition made a strange forlorn sort
of sense. The objects that seemed to have come from the pouch
hung like a heart in the chest of the creature. Glancing at Seiji,
Jhana saw from his face that something about the little assemblage in its larger whole was tugging at him. Jhana had the
distinct impression that he wanted to quickly but carefully
place the objects back inside the pouch.

"I didn't quite figure you for the ceremonial type," Seiji

said, turning toward Lakshmi, who was watching him carefully. "Where'd you get this stuff?"

"Only the tantric material is mine," Lakshmi replied. "I thought you might recognize the other paraphernalia. It's from your brother's personal effects."

Seiji stared at her, speechless.

"Since Lev and I hooked your brother's equipment into VAJRA," Lakshmi continued blithely, "some odd things have happened. One of them is that several of the robot arms here began acting cooperatively to sort through your brother's personal effects. I tried to stop them at first, but after a while I got curious and wondered what they might put together if I let them go about their business. That structure there, all connected by microthin optical wire—that's apparently the finished product, though the robot arms still add pieces from time to time."

Seiji still could not speak, could only try to hang on in the absence of gravity as objects floated and bumped lightly against him.

"It's a statue of a big R-A-T, if you ask me," Lev said, then explained briefly what the RATs were. "It's a joke, a parody—just like the bits of embedded code we find when we're allowed to find them."

"Not a joke—a mirror," Lakshmi said. "I think those embedded passages are intended to remind us who we are, and what we're about here."

"It's a fun-house mirror, then," Lev insisted. Lakshmi spun her hoverchair quickly in Seiji's direction.

"Do you know what your brother was working on?" she asked.

"No," Seiji said, finding his voice at last.

"Neither do we," Lev said, cutting Lakshmi off just as she was about to speak. "Not really. But we have suspicions—"

"Strong ones," Lakshmi said, so forthrightly that Jhana wondered for a moment what the relationship might be between them—the tall young man, ghostly pale yet agile and energetic and never removing his wraparound shades, and the older, immobilized dark woman with the penetrating eyes and flowing robes. Jhana doubted she'd ever know.

"We can't say for sure," Lev continued carefully, "but

your brother appears to have been in quest of what's become something of a grail in the interface business—"

"Direct mind/machine linkage," Lakshmi put in. "Interfaceless communication. Transparent relationship between matter and mind. No keyboards, no screens, no trideo display, no consoles, no cyberspatial or virtual reality constructs. A big paradigm shift. The grand unification of infomatics and telecommunications."

"I don't understand," Atsuko remarked from among a thicket of reed-thin robot arms. "How can that be?"

"We don't know if it *can* be, yet," Lakshmi replied. "I've worked on the problem myself, though never full-time. The model that I've looked at—and the one your brother was also apparently working with, Seiji—is the idea of the transducer, a substance or device that converts input energy of one form into output energy of another form. There are lots of examples of them." She began calling up images into holo display before them. "Piezoelectric crystals like quartz that convert mechanical stress into electrical energy or electrical energy into mechanical stress. Photoelectric cells that convert light into electricity, and many others."

"I know the principle quite well," Seiji said with a nod. "Most of the solar power generation done up here is based on transducer effects of one sort or another."

"But how does that apply to the interfaceless communication you spoke of?" Marissa asked Lev.

"Simple—theoretically," Lev said with a shrug. "Think of mechanical stress and electrical energy and light not so much as different types of energy but as different patterns of information. Think of the brain itself as a transducer for converting energy, information patterns of one form, into information patterns of another form—its entire structure, at all levels of complexity, as the structure of a transducing substance or device. Then find the proper information pattern, the proper energetic 'carrier wave,' both medium and message as it were, and beam it at a human brain which will convert that carrier wave instantly into information useful for thought."

"And vice-versa," Lakshmi added. "The energy of thought acting in a transeunt fashion, producing effects outside the mind, in the machine it's sending to, through the same sort of transducing process." She sighed audibly. "Unfortunately, no one's really made it work in either direction, so far as we know."

"What's the snag?" Seiji asked, quietly, as if from far away.

"The brain/mind problem," Lakshmi said levelly. "No one has yet figured out how mind attaches to brain. If the strict materialists were right, if mind were simply brain, the transducer model would have already produced a viable technology. But it seems strict materialism is a good myth but a poor explanation. The epiphenomenalists, on the other hand, by maintaining that mind is just an epiphenomenon arising from the physical and phenomenal activity of the brain—they're really just closet dualists. The uncloseted dualists seem to be right, at least to a degree: mind and brain do appear to be distinct entities that somehow manage to interface—that word again—in consciousness."

"Only it's an interfaceless interface," Lev insisted, calling up holo displays of his own. "Like a meniscus formed between oil and water, or the surface tension between water and air. In the first case, is the meniscus made of oil, or of water? Neither, and both. In the second case, is the surface tension made of water, or of air, or of the dynamic of forces balancing between *them?* Is consciousness merely material and local brain, or transcendent and ubiquitous Mind, or some dynamic between them? It's a paradox, a snake swallowing its own tail, a Möbius Cadúceus."

He ended with an irrepressible smile. Lakshmi shook her head slightly, as if at a wayward child.

"Which brings us back to why Jhana and Seiji are here," she said, smiling slyly in turn. "Atsuko and Marissa—you should be interested in this too, in regard to Roger. Lev, did you ever think the skysign might be acting as a sort of transducer already—in a rudimentary sort of way?"

Lev was quiet for a moment. Lakshmi smiled more broadly, seeing she had caught him by surprise.

"I hadn't really thought about that," he said. "I guess we could accept it as a provisional hypothesis. But I thought these folks came up here to play the game—not try to figure out the skysign."

The others nodded in agreement.

"Oh, very well," Lakshmi said, commanding a trideo game unit to display in the midst of the group. "Here goes."

VAJRA
presents
BUILDING THE RUINS™

"We'll play a beginner's version," Lakshmi said, robotic arms placing a circlet of electronic headgear on her temples. "It has the whole opening sequence. You may view it either projected or in one of these full-sensorium circlets. There are several scattered about."

"The trideo's interactive reality can be joystick-controlled, voice-directed, or," Lev said, slipping on a pair of thin gloves, "if you put on these livegloves, you can let your fingers do the walking—and the talking." He handed around several pairs to those who opted for them. "Of course, if we had the sort of direct mind/machine link we were talking about before, we wouldn't need all this gear. These will have to do for now."

Jhana chose for herself one of the wraparound circlets—depth screens for her eyes, audio implants for her skull—and pulled on a pair of livegloves, thin flat-wire traceries prickling over her hands as she did so, electrodes probing minute differences in electric potentials at her skin surface. She was now in the world of the game.

"I've called for a share-game," Lakshmi said over Jhana's implants. "All of us will essentially be functioning as a team."

For Jhana, this "team" manifested itself as a silvery translucent orb—like a soap bubble blown from mercury metal—afloat upon a couch of sunset-fired cloud. In the bubble, etherealized human faces stood out, cut in bas-relief from the virtual sky and tinted the same silvery-blue hue of that sky. Her teammates' eyes all turned toward one vision.

"Welcome to the MACHINE," a disembodied voice said over the implants. "The MetAnalytic Computer Heuristic Incorporating Nonanalytic Elements. The global brain. A synergistic and evolving system composed of two parts: LOGOS, the Logical Ontological Governance Operating System, and

CHAOS, the Cognitive Heuristic Antalgorithmic Operating System. They were created to work together, but now they work apart. The global brain has gone insane and now seeks suicide to end its pain. Your job is to help save it from itself.''

In the virtual space around and before Jhana, there now began to appear what she believed must certainly be the LOGOS referred to in the voiceover. She had seen quality graphics before, but this LOGOS was incredible: an immense cybernetic data construct, a shape of thought almost beautiful beyond thought, a shining global village-on-the-hill rising from the flatland gridspace of the Plains of Euclid, a cybertopia stretching onward and onward, mathematical kingdom of orderly orchestrated bustling where all the trains of thought ran on time. It was a thing of preternatural beauty, as if the greatest symphony of the most glorious music ever played had been flash-frozen in the form of a City of Light, celestial harmony transubstantiated in an instant into the radiant architecture of a Neon New Jerusalem, an Electric Heaven too coolly perfect for mere mortals to sing in.

Hyperreal, surreal, ethereally unreal. She remembered that someone had once said virtual reality would never look truly real until they figured out how to get dirt and noise and grit into it. That pre-dirt godly cleanliness was the LOGOS all over. But if there was something disturbingly ''too ordered'' about the cool perfection of this city of LOGOS, it was not nearly as disturbing as the CHAOS.

As the teammates moved deeper into the game's virtual space, it was soon enough apparent that the inhumanly perfect order of the LOGOS did not go on forever. In innumerable regions the dark matter of CHAOS appeared, fluid as ocean waves and dry as desert dunes, thing of all shapes and no shape of all things, Illusion and Error breaking through and turning to disarray the clear lines of the Plains, battering discordantly against the harmony of the Shining City, drowning and choking out and covering in obscurity the structures of light, as if some great Earthly city were falling to ruin beneath the waves of a final flood, or sinking abandoned into the desert of time.

The silver orb, the mercury-metal soap bubble Jhana and her fellow players were contained in, burst and dissolved. With the vast computing power of the LOGOS behind them, fully integrated with that power, the players moved like a tall, soft wall of driving sunlit wind against the uncreating dimness.

Encountering the dark tide, though, there was an almost physical sensation of impact. Jhana felt as if she had plummeted like a hurtling meteor into a vast ocean of grey tapioca static, cold and dark and viscous. She did not have time to think, for the darkling sea seemed inhabited by the sharks and eels of long-repressed memories, ancient sins—her own and those of others.

Something waited at the heart of the CHAOS, a sleeping dragon on a treasure hoard, a Minotaur in the center of a maze, a night prowler compounded of every creature that had ever lived and died, a hybrid beastly intelligent thing of horns, claws, teeth and tentacles, slit cat's eyes and adder fangs dripping the poisonous milky rheum of death, a universe of death horrifying in its enormous impersonality—

Jeez, what am I getting so frightened about? Jhana thought. Must be projecting my own problems onto this chaotic swirling grey stuff. This thing's got phenomenal graphics, excellent tactiles and full sensorium feed, yeah—but it *is* only a game, after all.

That in itself was disturbing, though. All this effort, put into something that was ''just a game''?

As if through corridors and chambers of a flooded maze, she moved onward with her teammates, more fascinated than afraid, while behind her the sharks and eels followed, swimming to their own slow and silent dark rhythms. Her movement and that of the others felt ''upstream,'' seemed to push back the chaotic flux, to re-create what that dark flux had blotted out.

Eventually, she found herself just beneath the surface of a glassy stream, looking up through a drowned Ophelia's eyes into a lawless sky of flawless blue. Impelled and compelled to break through the surface tension of the water, she sent ripples rebounding in every direction, new beauty settling into place as the scene calmed. Like a rapidly evolving computer animation or fractal graphic, cragged peaks mounted up to snag the sky, encircling in their broken bowl an alpine meadow and small city so idyllic it seemed a caricature of itself.

The others had risen from the stream with Jhana, and moving forward, they drove the cloudy tide back before them, the beautiful new world establishing itself around and behind them, scene after scene, as they pressed on.

The regions they were helping the LOGOS recover now seemed better somehow—more beautiful because less sterile, less rigidly perfect than those regions of the LOGOS that had never been touched by the CHAOS. Whether from taint of contact with the CHAOS, or from touch of human consciousness, or from whatever cause, the element of randomness and unpredictability had been introduced into all the re-created regions so that they were now more truly beautiful than all those undisturbed realms of perfectly ordered geometry. No, they had not put "dirt" into virtual reality: it was more like soil, or even soul.

The restoration was not an easy task. The flux they pressed forward against was no sooner driven back in one region than it flooded in at another. At times the CHAOS seemed to howl in gibbering triumph, but overall the forces of the LOGOS were turning back the invading tide. Jhana was certain that through their teamwork the dim flood of CHAOS's insurgency was being driven back completely, to the borders of the CHAOS itself. They were winning!

Perhaps everything should have stopped there. It didn't. Somewhere something happened: a test was failed, a border was accidentally crossed. Perhaps the LOGOS forces pressed their advantage too far, moved too readily against the opponent, crossed some Yalu River of the mind. Whatever the cause, the CHAOS felt its own existence threatened, and struck back with Sphinx-like ferocity, exploiting weak links in the LOGOS front and bursting through with all its might—until cataclysm threatened to overwhelm all.

Jhana felt a sudden and immediate sense of vertigo, as if she were falling from deep space into planetary atmosphere at tremendous velocity and at very much the wrong angle of re-entry. All at once she was burning, breaking up, blossoming in petal shards of fire and blowing away, like a disintegrating falling star, like a rose of Hiroshima.

The Möbius Caдúceus skysign flashed before them.

"Game over," the voice of the MACHINE said quietly.

Back in Lakshmi's workshop, Jhana looked about her at a

room full of dreamers waking from strange dreams, Atsuko and Seiji and Marissa looking just about as disoriented as Jhana felt.

"Every game is different—and the same," Lakshmi said. She and Lev seemed more familiar with the game's parameters and, consequently, much less disoriented—especially Lakshmi. "Innumerable scenarios, but underlying them all is the same pattern."

"Yeah," said Lev. "The damn thing's teaching us how to lose—and we're learning."

"VAJRA has been marketing receivers and hookups both here and on Earth through network and multilevel sales structures," Lakshmi continued, ignoring Lev's comment. "Billions of hours of game-time have been logged already. Building the Ruins has very quickly become the world's master game—in less than a month's time."

"But is it just a game?" Jhana asked. "All those billions of human hours, all those scenarios logging back into VAJRA, all that information—what is it being used for? Maybe the game is more serious than we think."

Marissa nodded. Apparently she'd been thinking the same thing.

"Certainly there's more to it than some trivial trideo game," she seconded. "It's an ancient pattern that's being played through again and again here, especially the idea that the perfection of the LOGOS can be amplified from its 'having known imperfection.' That goes all the way back to Genesis, to the idea of the 'fortunate Fall'—that Adam and Eve's primal sin was ultimately good because it made necessary the incarnation of Christ. With the loss of perfection, change and history came into the world."

"What our experience in the game demonstrates, though," Lakshmi put in, "is that by their changes things aren't completely changed from their first perfection. Through *apparent* change everything in the game dilates its being until at last it becomes truly itself again, works its own re-perfection, moves from perfection to new perfection, cognition to re-cognition."

" 'The end of all our exploring will be to arrive where we started and know the place for the first time,' as Eliot says," Marissa suggested.

"So," Lev asked her skeptically, "even CHAOS is just a more subtle form of order, eh?"

"Yes," she said with a nod. "Discord is merely harmony not understood, and partial evil must be subsumed within universal good."

"That's putting a nice rhyming spin on it, and maybe that's how it will work out in the end," Korchnoi said with a shrug, "but right now what's going on in the game seems to be a reflection of what's really going on in the world. Or a parody of it. A parodic reflection—a fun-house mirror. Think of our era's fascination with acronyms, and the way the game parodies that—"

"Maybe the game is simply *implying* the world that produced it," Atsuko speculated. "Self-similarity across scales— less like a fun-house mirror than like a section of a fractal or a small piece of a hologram."

"Okay," Lev said, "but what kind of world is it a 'self-similar' chunk of? Lately VAJRA—and whatever 'distributed consciousness' is ghosting it—has been taking in unprecedented amounts of seemingly random information. Maybe the global brain *has* gone insane, *is* seeking suicide to end its pain. Maybe the goal is to save it, but maybe not. I wish I could be as sure of the outcome as Marissa is, but I'm not. All I know is that the MACHINE always wins, no matter which side we're on. We always get blown out of the system at last."

Lakshmi called up food and drink, and thin, supple robotic arms began to move.

"When I'm playing that game it feels like I'm in the midst of some sort of psychomachia," she said, then paused, as if unsure of what she was about to say, "though whose soul or what soul is being contested I can't say."

"I felt it too," Atsuko said. "Almost as if it were the struggle for the soul of the proverbial 'new machine.' Or maybe a struggle for the World Soul, the Mind At Large."

Seiji had been unusually quiet since they came out of the game, intent upon examining the iconic assemblage, but Jhana noticed that he had glanced up when Lakshmi and Atsuko spoke of struggles for souls. Still, as the evening wore on and all of them drifted amidst conversation and zero gravity and robotic arms and icons and fellowship, Seiji volunteered nothing of his game-playing experience. Lev and Lakshmi went into no further detail about what relation his brother's personal effects might have to what was going on, though at one point Lakshmi suggested that the icon assembly seemed shamanic to her somehow—almost like a fetish or an image of an animal spirit-guide. Seiji very much agreed with that interpretation.

Gradually their meeting evolved into an informal dinner party, Lev regaling them with stripped-down guitar-only versions of the many new numbers Möbius Cadúceus would be performing at *The Temple Guardians* event.

"I'm surprised you were able to get away from rehearsal," Marissa said to Lev at one point during the evening, "with the performance so near."

"Oh, the band has a tradition," Lev said, tuning his guitar during a pause. "We always take a break from each other a night or two before the show—to avoid getting too slick or overrehearsed. Got to keep at least a little spontaneity in it, after all." He struck a chord tentatively. "Speaking of the spontaneous, sorry we're not much closer to understanding the skysign's power to evoke images or whatever in you, Jhana, and Seiji—or in Roger—but I assure you that our group will retire the logo immediately after the performance of *Guardians*."

"If it wants to be retired," Lakshmi said. By way of comment, Lev merely began to play his guitar and sing again.

So the party continued for a long while, until all at last said their farewells and everyone save Lakshmi departed by transfer ship for the habitat's central sphere. Jhana noticed that Seiji still seemed weighed down by his private thoughts, and perhaps she was beginning to understand why.

ELEVEN

Passage embedded in RAT code:

For most of history human beings supported themselves on what they could take from the Earth. They never had to support it, never had to give back much. In the habitat the residents have to stay constantly mindful of what must and must not be done, or the world they've built could all come crashing down in an instant. The children who are raised in the habitat—even more so the children who are born there—grow up with interdependence as part of their day-to-day life.

The residents' recognition of interdependence is really only the first step. Ultimately, the citizens of the habitat are trying to correct an error that is at least as old as Plato. That error is the idea that the universe is really a duoverse, the world of dung we inhabit, temporal and material, and the world of diamond, eternal and immaterial, that is the habitation of the divine. Despite occasional excesses and sometimes sophomoric ideas, the residents of the habitat are striving to realize something of the unity of the universe: to be no more the hostages of the world as it appears to be—divided—but free, thinking subjects at one with the world as it truly is. They hope to efface whatever wall of flaming swords it is that keeps human beings out of paradise and paradise out of human beings. Diamond is dung and dung is diamond—all holy, to those who have the eyes to see it.

Roger's troubles with angels had been growing steadily, leaking out of his dreams and into his daylight existence— enough to make him want to find out more about the contents of his nightly visitations, some rational explanation for them. He went personally to the Archive, for its data links gave him access not only to all the Archive holdings but also to virtually all of Earth's public and electronically archived material as well.

Searching through the infosphere, he was surprised how much information he found on what might be called ancient human-powered flight. He popped up holographic illustrations of the flying cherub wagon of Ezekiel, the flights or flight attempts of Daedalus and Icarus, of Pegasus, of Fama. Into his virtuality came the report (in Suetonius) of an actor who feathered his arms and tried to fly at a feast given by Nero—only to plunge to his death in the attempt.

Scanning further, he also came across the record of a reportedly successful flight by one Abu'l Kasim 'Abbas Ibn Firnas, a Saracen of Andalusia whose flight supposedly took place in A.D. 876. Ibn Firnas, though, had apparently not communicated his flying secrets to his co-religionists: in A.D. 1008 the attempt at human-powered flight by one al-Djawhari ended in his death.

Then Roger found it. According to the chronicler William of Malmesbury, Eilmer, also a brother of the abbey at Malmesbury in England, "collecting the breeze on the summit of the tower, flew for more than the distance of a furlong. But, agitated by the violence of the wind and swirling of the air, as well as by the awareness of his own rashness, he fell, broke his legs, and was lame ever after. He used to say that the cause of his failure was his forgetting to put a tail on the back part."

Roger ran a find-scan, but William of Malmesbury had nothing else to say of Eilmer, save for one cryptic reference relating to April, 1066: "A comet, a star foretelling, they say, change in kingdoms, appeared trailing its long and fiery tail across the sky. Wherefore a certain elderly monk of our monastery, Eilmer by name, bowed down with terror at the sight of the brilliant star and sagely cried, 'Thou art come! A cause of grief to many a mother art thou come; I have seen thee before, but now I behold thee much more terrible, threatening to hurl destruction upon this land!' "

That was it—the full extent of historical reference to Eilmer of Malmesbury, proto-aviator, prescient predictor of the invasion of England by William the bastard duke of Normandy, later called "the Conqueror." Fast-scanning through the following millennium's worth of references, Roger noted that they were all more or less elaborate retellings of William of Malmesbury's initial tale.

Roger found other references to the protohistory of human-powered flight—to da Vinci and Michelangelo and a thousand others who tried their wings before the successful gliders of the nineteenth century, before the Wrights' initial machine-powered flight at Kitty Hawk. Most of the studies Roger examined eventually wound their way to the advent of Paul MacReady's Gossamer series, the vehicles with which the era of human-powered flight might be said to truly have begun—though the great blossoming of such flight had to await the appearance of the space colony with its juxtaposition of atmosphere and low gravity.

No matter what research tactic he tried, however, he could find no full-length movie, no trideo, no docu-holo, on Eilmer of Malmesbury—only fragmented, artist's renderings, brief reenactments. Where was the source for the movie that ran in his dreams—in which the aged Eilmer was recruited by political forces in England to perfect his gliders, and they used those very mechanisms to help defeat William the Bastard's forces at Hastings? No place. It was crazy, a film sent from an alternate universe by an angelic conspiracy—a movie from another reality, which he seemed always to have already seen, the memory of a matinee experienced in a theatre in another dimension.

He hoped there might still exist an old movie or video in this reality, some obscure culture-shard that somehow all his computer searches were missing. But he hesitated, wondering. From his dream-movie, he felt he knew things he shouldn't know, things not recorded in any historical source. The exact year of Eilmer's flight, for instance: A.D. 1010. The exact construction of his flying apparatus: wings of thin, lightly waxed linen stretched over frames of light wooden splints and hollowed bone, four of them, two long wings (one for each arm, and each of these over two ells in length) and two short wings (one for each foot, and each of these an ell in length). Each and every wing surface was one ell broad as well, the long, primary wings being secured to each other by a harness of strong light wood and thin iron, the two shorter, secondary or foot, wings secured by a smaller harness of similar design.

Where had he learned all that? How the hell did he know what an "ell" was? How did he know that William of Malmesbury was wrong about Eilmer's rashness—that in fact Eilmer had gained the approval of Abbot Leofric for the building and testing of his apparatus, once he, Eilmer, had explained his visions of angels and flight to the abbot? How did he know that Eilmer's essential mistake was that he had followed Aristotle's incorrect dictum that "In winged creatures, the tail serves, like the ship's rudder, to keep the flying thing in its course"?

Roger didn't recall ever having read that passage in Aristotle—so how did he know that quote? How did he know that Eilmer had treated movement through the air according to the same principles as those that apply to movement through water? How did he know that, unaware of the faulty analogy between horizontal bird's tail and vertical ship's rudder (as well as being thoroughly ignorant of the role of the tail as "flap" and "pitch control"), Eilmer had deemed a tail unnecessary for straight-line flight? How was he supposed to know all this? Was he channeling the long-dead monk? Was he the monk's reincarnation? Was he linking into some aspect of the collective unconscious the old psychoanalysts had never suspected? All that stuff was at least as crazy as some transdimensional angelic conspiracy.

Even worse was the vividness of some of the material he recalled, especially the dreams-within-dreams of angels lecturing him/Eilmer on aerodynamics. He had dreamed within his dream that he was standing in a vast windswept field while, high above him, an angel soared and hovered, flapping its wings not at all. Nearer the ground, every kind of large soaring bird—hundreds of them—glided and drifted upon the winds.

"See the handiwork of Almighty God in the shape of my wings!" trumpeted the angel. "See it in the shape of the wings of all God's flying creatures! This it is that allows us to fly!"

Then the winds and the air itself suddenly seemed made of myriad tiny angels, moving along paths and currents like minnows in a stream. The great angel flew nearer to him and he/Eilmer saw more clearly what was taking place. Moving against the currents of tiny angels, the shape of the great angel's wings was such that the tiny angels flowing over the top of the wing moved faster and farther apart, while those flowing beneath the wing tended to bunch up and crowd. In his dream within a dream, he/Eilmer concluded that the respective pressure of angels along the top and bottom surfaces of the wing was the means by which an upward force was maintained.

No mean feat of aerodynamic reasoning, for the Middle Ages, Roger thought. With a thousand years of hindsight, though, he could see that it was not only Aristotle but also the shape of the angel itself that had led him—Eilmer—to assume a flying man would need no tail.

Roger also knew (without knowing *how* he knew) that while Eilmer fever-dreamed in pain and infection after his disastrous, laming flight, the angel had appeared to him again, carrying him up above a floor of clouds into a sky filled with peoples of every nation riding in what seemed to Eilmer fantastic vessels of the air, flying mechanisms powered by small windmills or roaring barrels mounted on the wings or bodies of their vessels. The shadows these vessels cast upon the surface of the cloud-sea were like those that would be cast by thousands of crosses sailing in the sky. In such apparently blessed craft, men and women and children moved on errands of business and pleasure toward places their forefathers had not even dreamt of. A setting sun tinted the wings of these myriad craft silver and gold, and even in dreams within dreams, he—Roger? Eilmer?—seemed to swoon in awe before the scene.

Abruptly the clouds parted and he saw in the twilight below a vast, strange city sprawling like a dark mold on bread. Out of the sunset, black fliers came in high and fast, raining down dark seeds that blossomed up in fire wherever they touched the ground until the city burned everywhere and the sun sank blood-red in a sky of smoke.

Greatly perplexed by what the angel had shown him, he/Eilmer had begged some sign whether his flying apparatus, when perfected, would bring more peace and good to the world or more evil and war upon it. Night fell around the angel, who said nothing but only gestured toward an area in the sky where a star trailed a banner of ghostly fire like the hair of angels or the writhing of bright Medusan snakes. Abruptly the angel vanished, leaving him to fall down the sky endlessly toward a world that kept rushing up at him but upon which he never seemed to land or impact.

That last image would explain Eilmer's trepidation at the appearance of Halley's Comet, Roger realized—and, if he had, as a boy, perhaps read of Eilmer's story or seen it somewhere, then the dream was easy enough to explain, for nothing in it was beyond the technology of Roger's times or the experiences of his own life.

But what of the final appearance of the angel, the final dream-within-a-dream? That vision seemed to have taken place during the aged Eilmer's recuperation, after he collapsed upon seeing the comet in the sky again, during 1066. The angel of his visions had appeared to him a final time and taken him into the starry heavens themselves. As they rose through the air, fliers of ten thousand kinds ravaged the Earth below, some blasting sprawling cities with bursts of pure hellfire, scorching the ground black for years and sending invisible, horrible death even to people going innocently about their work and play far away.

Angel and dreamer rose higher and higher, past strange fliers like pylons or obelisks, fliers with tiny wings or no wings at all, often without a soul aboard yet roaring swiftly skyward on pillars of fire by night and columns of cloud by day to place peculiar artifacts among the stars themselves or to wait for a chance to pounce with satanic fury onto a world beautiful and shining like a holy sacrament, a world adream on a bed of stars—and turn that world's dreams of life and beauty to nightmares of death and horror.

At the distance of the moon, the dreamer and the angel came to a stop, invisible there among the strangely clad men who themselves drifted like wingless, faceless angels between orbed cities floating in space. Winged fliers of unimaginable design rode out of the world on winds until they flew so high the winds ran out, and on tongues of fire they continued their journeys to the floating cities and the mines of the moon.

At that point in the dream-within-a-dream the most disturbing thing always happened: Roger had the distinct impression that he was no longer looking out into a dreamed universe through Brother Eilmer's eyes, but rather the eleventh-century monk was staring through Roger's own eyes into the cislunar space of the twenty-first century. Time and space, past and future—all became one eternal mind-filled moment, all separation and distance and alienation lost.

Would the far-flung settlements in the whispering darkness remain in true peace or burst into strange fire, pierced by beams of killing light or crushed like eggs by the pressure of Luciferine blasts? Would the soul-crushing tyranny of Endless War keep the stars, like a blanket of pure snow, always out of reach, beyond barbed wire? Or would that tyranny turn even heaven itself into just another, vaster concentration camp of falling bodies? Planets and stars and galaxies trudging pointlessly round and round the prison yard of the universe, to the pointed witness of almost-angelic astronauts bringing their barbed wire with them wherever they might go? In Roger's dreams the answers were unknown, all unknown, except to know that everything balanced upon a moment which was all moments and a decision which was all decisions.

The angel always turned to him then, its eyes vast islands of stars adrift in vaster seas of darkness, eyes expanding to become the whole of the sky, all skies, the only sky, eyes taking in everything like the undertow of eternity, eyes flashing dark with excess of bright, piercing through and through the pall of Death's black peace until unearthly light burst forth in a van of angels winging about a hollow sphere, circling latitudes of shimmering ethereal creatures, flocking around him, carrying him away—

Roger always woke up then. He shook his head. What mad nonsense! What possible connection could these phantasms from the past—a monk most notable in his failure, angels extinct as rocs or moas or passenger pigeons—what could they possibly mean to him? He, after all, did not believe in angels. And he most definitely would not fail in his mole-rat project.

Furiously he scanned through all the Archive's doorways into the infosphere for some reference, any reference, to a film or documentary about Eilmer. He found flying cities, flying islands, even a clipping involving Paul Larkin and a flying mountain—the same Larkin he'd met up here. He could, however, find no more on the flying monk.

Disgusted, he ended his searches and got up to leave. On his way out of the Archive, he was too busy to notice anything going on around him, too busy remembering an episode from his childhood, climbing with his father over a fence to fall into a field of untouched snow, a flat expanse of empty whiteness pure and sweet as a blank page, to lay his body down and write a winged figure into those cold pages ten thousand times, or until his body grew cold as a snow angel's—

Stepping outside, he saw the Möbius Cadúceus skysign hovering in the air—but much smaller this time, a trideo game projection floating above some teenagers on the lawn. Quickly he averted his eyes. To him the sign had become as ominous a portent as the appearance of Halley's Comet had been for Eilmer so many centuries before, and he wished it would just go away.

He decided he needed some good news. He would check his virtual mail and faxes, then go see Larkin about the ingredients for the perfume.

ALEISTER McBRUCE'S OTHER DAY JOB WAS IN SPACE-engineering. Normally the job wasn't much trouble, but when, in response to increasing pressure from Earth, the word came down that work teams were to go out and start dismantling the anomalous X-shaped satellites, Aleister was appointed a team leader. As he and his team went out to rendezvous with the first of the satellites to be dismantled, Aleister put in a call to Lakshmi, filling her in on the background.

"I don't know why the council doesn't just wait," Aleister said at last. "If the governments and corporate transnats are that upset about it, sooner or later one them is going to send in a hunter-killer satellite and take one of these X-sats right out. Then we can just gather up the pieces and examine them at our leisure.''

"Maybe the powers on Earth can't just 'take out' these satellites," Lakshmi suggested. "We know that the entire infosphere has been thoroughly infiltrated by the distributed consciousness. Quantum information packeting is at the heart of how the infosphere currently works, and the D.C. pretty much monitors everything that's moving through QUIPs. It probably already out-spies, out-commands, out-controls, and out-communicates anything Earth's got. Maybe their efforts against the D.C. have been as futile as ours. Maybe there's no more action at a distance—the only way anyone can get close to those X-sats is to go out to them personally.''

Aleister nodded.

"That's why I want to keep this communication line open to you, Lakshmi," he said. "I know the VAJRA runs just about everything on the habitat, and it's now probably more or less part of the distributed consciousness. I just want you to keep an eye out for any sort of response when we start hacking away at this first X-sat, and we're just about to do so. I'll give you full visual feed from this end.''

Lakshmi watched as Aleister and his crew suited up in maneuvering units and drifted out of their transfer ship's airlock. As the work crew in near space got closer to the X-sat and turned on their laser cutting torches, Lakshmi called up full readouts on all habitat systems. Out in cislunar space Aleister did the honors, using his cutting torch to bite into one limb of the big X. At the instant of contact, alarms began to scream and flash on Lakshmi's readouts.

"Stop, Aleister!" she said over the line. "Cease, desist, quit!''

"What happened?" Aleister asked over his suit mike.

"The VAJRA has begun crashing systems," Lakshmi said, scanning her feeds. "In two minutes it will blow all bay doors, hatches, and airlocks. Explosive decompression in most of the tori—including the one I'm sitting in. After that, I'd say it will probably shut off all power and environmental support, to get at the central sphere. It's got us, Aleister. It can survive cold, dark, and airless a helluva lot better than we can.''

Aleister shut off his laser torch and motioned for the rest of his team to do likewise.

"Any suggestions?" he asked.

"I've already sent a report to your shift leaders in engineering," Lakshmi said. "I'm sure they're aware of the situation and will be advising all your teams very soon."

No sooner said than done. Almost immediately Aleister received word from Gene Smith, his shift leader.

"Tell your team its mission has been halted for now," the wiry black man said. "You are all to return to the habitat at once."

"Hey, Generino," Aleister said as he and his team headed back to the ship, "did I hear just a hint of nervousness in *your* voice? You, the calmest of all high-flying, land-on-your-feet cats?"

"My day job is not supposed to be a place for this kind of excitement," Gene said with a grimace. "If I want that action I can get it blowing sax or teaching people to airbike—either of which I'd rather be doing right now."

"I hear you," Aleister said, smiling. "I think we'd all rather be someplace else, doing something else. In a minute we will be. Hopefully no harm done."

Once Aleister and his crew were back in the ship, he received a message from Lakshmi.

"After all your cutting crews left the vicinity of their respective X-sats," she said, "the VAJRA brought all the threatened systems back up. No explanation. As if nothing at all had happened—except a sort of machine amnesia."

"The kraken has awakened," Aleister quipped in purposeful mis-rhyme, "and it doesn't like being prodded, if I'm not mistaken."

Passage embedded in RAT code:

As Earth's increasing paranoia about the anomalous X-shaped satellites clearly indicates, the most frightening feature of unreason is its failure to recognize itself.

In his pocket Roger still had the faxes of interest and intent from Dr. Tien-Jones at Tao-Ponto, and he carried them almost as if they were talismans of improving luck. Certainly it was true that he hadn't slept well in days and days and that everything came to him in a sort of fever lately, all occurring so fast, making him feel a bit wobbly and overwrought. As long as things kept moving his way, though, why should he worry?

Roger was so sure now that he'd be able to strike a deal with TPAG that he was already thinking of names for the perfume as he walked along in search of Paul Larkin's home. His first thought was to call the new perfume Dusk. Searching his pocket MultiLangue™ for the French of that, he found *tombée de la nuit*, "fall of night," but above that phrase, on the same screen of the dictionary, he found *tombé*, meaning fallen.

Perfect! A perfume whose name meant Fallen. He could imagine the ads for it, especially on trideo. A scenario spun itself in his head as he walked along, and he quickly dictated it into his personal data system.

Transcript of possible advertisement for *Tombé*:

Pounding, driving music. Two athletic-looking women appear, backlit in shadowy purples and yellows. Tight overhead spotlights make all the angles of their model faces stand out, make their close-cropped slicked-back hair shine like chrome. Their limbs oiled to a bright sheen, their torsos clad in purple or yellow one-piece swimsuits, they face off against each other. The music pounds. Sharp camera work and tight editing cut the women into fragmentary images—a leg kicking into yellow, a clawlike hand striking out at purple, tight lips around gritted teeth, a sharp-nailed fist clenching hair or digging into thigh. Over the prostrate body of her defeated foe the woman in purple slowly rises, breathless and flushed with triumph. In a corner of the screen flash the words "*Tombé*. Violently sexy."

Of course such a trideo advertisement couldn't be released right at the beginning of the marketing campaign. The perfume wouldn't yet have had time to work its magic, so there'd be too much noise about the ad being sexist or degrading to women. But just let *Tombé* get established and everything would change. In a few years' time there'd be no complaints because the ad would be reflecting the new reality.

Roger smiled when he thought about the pheromone's other probable but undisclosable side effect, the sideshow feature of the naked mole rat's eusociality that had always been its main attraction for him. That secret collateral effect would be surest product-death to reveal, yet who could implicate him in it once the product was established on the market? The initiator of serious mole-rat research had been a woman, after all; mole-rat eusociality was itself female-centered. They'd never figure out his real stake in the game.

And, after the violence had settled down to a permanent background level (fully tolerable), Roger felt confident that the *feministas* and their allies would actually be thankful to him, their unrecognized benefactor, for having helped make possible the truly matriarchal society that was sure to develop once *Tombé* worked its way into the global culture—

Wings fluttered disturbingly in his peripheral vision. He turned but there was nothing to be seen. That flutter, at the edges of his eyes and over his shoulders, was bothering him more and more of late. It made him want to shoot very small birds with a very large gun. Fortunately, he soon enough arrived at Paul Larkin's home and found more important things to distract him.

Roger learned from the gnomish white-haired elder colonist that he had not only gathered the jasmine and lavender and such for the perfume, but had already extracted sample essences. Roger could have kissed the old guy, who had just made his job that much easier. Though not a fan of the elderly, Roger thought that if he lived that long, or if the work of people like Marissa didn't make them all eternally youthful first, then Larkin was the type of old man Roger himself would like to be: full of piss and vinegar and a crazy sparkle in the eye.

When Roger mentioned that he'd come across a reference to Larkin in connection with a "flying mountain," the little man again launched into the ancient mariner's tale that he eventually told everyone he spent any real time with—and which he had so recently told Jhana. Roger put up with Larkin and his video and his story—at first because he owed the guy, but gradually because the story itself had begun to intrigue him. Unlike Jhana, however, Roger wanted to see some of the mushrooms from which the infamous KL had been extracted. Larkin was more than willing to oblige, and they set off at a lively pace toward the mycological facilities. He had intended to show them to Jhana when she'd stopped by, Larkin said, but there hadn't been time. Showing them to Roger would give Larkin a sense that he had "completed the arc," as he put it.

When they arrived, they found Seiji already at work in the lab, tending a coldbox.

"Roger Cortland here has expressed some interest in KL 235 and *Cordyceps jacintae,*" Larkin said, introducing Roger to Seiji. They shook hands, politely if somewhat stiffly. In the small community of the habitat, they had seen each other in passing and knew of each other by reputation, though they'd never been formally introduced or spoken at any great length.

"Would you like to see some of the 'vertical fruit of the horizontal tree' itself?" Seiji asked Roger.

"Pardon?"

Larkin laughed.

"That's how the tepui people described their totemic mushroom. Seiji is one of the growing number of people who's heard my whole story. Remarkably patient of him."

"Not really," Seiji said, examining the wording of a sign headed with the legend *Pleurotus ostreatus* (Oyster Mushroom). "My brother Jiro's schizophrenia was to some degree precipitated by KL. I have a personal interest in the history and mythology of the fungus that chemical came from."

"More guilt to tear at my soul," Larkin said, serious and mocking at once.

They walked among the troughs and tubs and platforms of fungi, each with its accompanying descriptive sign. Passing trough after trough—veritable fields of fungus—Seiji finally stopped to examine a muddy flat of oak leaves and humus chilling in a glass-topped freezer box, explaining to them as he did so the complex freeze/flush cycle needed for bringing on the fruiting of morels. Seeming satisfied with the temperature setting on the coldbox, Seiji straightened up and they walked on.

They continued along quickly until Seiji stopped once more, this time to flake away dirt from a mounded surface and examine the truffle lurking beneath. Roger occupied himself reading some of the signs, which turned out to be brief overviews of each species—descriptions of physical characteristics of the cap, gills, stalk, veil, and spore-print, along with descriptions of habitat, edibility, and some general comments.

Apparently pleased by the progress in the truffle trough, Seiji stood up and they walked on, entering at last a small work space, the environment of which was rigorously controlled, containing as it did projects important to the habitat's Biodiversity Preservation mandate—exotic fungi, in this case species endangered or threatened and thought to possess special characteristics.

Abruptly they found themselves gazing down at a tabletop on which grew fresh fungus unlike anything Roger had ever seen or heard of before—clublike structures thrusting up from a drying grey-white mass, weird mushrooming reddish-brown ball-stalks like vertically stretched brains, blue dust in their pits and convolutions.

"*Cordyceps jacintae*," Larkin said quietly. "The little mushroom that caused the big trouble."

"I thought you said they grew inside the central nervous system," Roger remarked.

"They do," Seiji agreed, "but they're not obligate myconeural symbionts. The fungus *can* survive without a myconeural association, but it doesn't thrive very well. Its long-term genetic stability and survival chances are greatly reduced outside a host. Here we grow them on a medium composed of cloned nerve cells. When we want them to fruit, as these are doing, we drain off the nutrient that the nerve cells need to stay alive. As conditions worsen and the nerve cells die, the *Cordyceps* spawn sends up these fruiting bodies, from which we collect the spores."

"In the cave inside the tepui," Larkin said, "I saw them growing from corpses preserved by the cave's stable environment. An island of the dead in the midst of a shallow lake in the cave's great room. Fine masses of cottony white threads spread and knit over entire corpses there. Mushrooms jutted like alien phalluses from mouths, ears, eye-sockets, abdomens.

Jacinta assured me the spawn only fruited after its host had
died, but the sight of it was so grisly it still made me vomit.
What we've found in the lab seems to bear her out on the
death/spawn cycle, though.''

Roger crouched down until the mushrooms were at eye-
level.

"So these bring clairvoyance and far-seeing and all those
other subtle powers you mentioned, eh?'' Roger said to Larkin.
"Full brain activity, the high road to enlightenment—''

"Not enlightenment," Seiji said with a sniff. "What you
call 'subtle powers' yogis have long called *siddhis*. But yogis
don't view such powers as enlightening—rather almost as obstacles to be overcome on the path to enlightenment. If you
get so obsessed with them that they prevent you from proceeding further along the path, then you never reach enlightenment.''

"But what about that telepathy Paul mentioned?'' Roger
asked. "Wouldn't that tend to make people more—I don't
know—compassionate, as they're always going on about here
in the habitat? More enlightened in that sense?''

Larkin looked down at the cell-masses from which the fungi
grew.

"Certainly my sister and the tepui people would agree with
you," he said. "Once the full development of the myconeural
symbiosis has taken place—after twelve years, remember—
then yes, they claimed that human hosts with full myconeural
networks become natural telepaths with each other, experiencing immediate information transfer, mind to mind. I did note
myself that, among them, language was for children—'because
only children have need of it,' or so they claimed.''

Larkin touched the tip of one of the fruiting bodies, then
shrugged and raised his palms upward.

"Who can say? They had so many strange ideas, such a
strange mythology. I mean, they claimed their sacred mushroom came from the sky tens or hundreds of millions of years
ago. Before we parted company for the last time, Jacinta said
the spawn 'remembered'—or at least allowed its symbionts
access to a collective unconsciousness unlike anything Jung
could have imagined.''

Roger straightened up. The idea of "remembering" sparked something in him.

"What sort of collective unconscious?"

"One not limited to this solar system," Larkin said, clearing his throat awkwardly. "Their myths spoke of a Great Cooperation, a sort of angelic communion and harmony of all myconeuralized creatures throughout the heavens. According to them, we humans were all meant to be telepaths, part of their Great Cooperation, but we went wrong. We developed consciousness and intellect without the fullness of empathy we misname telepathy. For the tepui people, all the wars and brutality of human history were a proof of our 'wrongness.' Their myth of the Fall was that it was all a big mistake, that we have a rightful place in the bliss of the Cooperation, but we were accidentally passed over. That's what my sister and the tepui inhabitants claimed they were up to with all the gear she brought out there. They were trying to reconnect with that galactic harmony or whatever it was supposed to be."

Roger looked up from the mushroom heads to stare quizzically at Larkin.

"The dish antennas in your video—they were trying to broadcast information to extraterrestrials, then? Or wait for some message out of the long night?"

"Not at all," Larkin said, shaking his head. "In their mythology, what we would call 'information' is everything. The universe is information, gravity is an expression of it, matter and energy are two of its states—but information underlies it all. Jacinta claimed that she and the tepui people were pulling as much information down from the satellites as they could, the tepui *indigenas* pumping it straight into their wide-open minds, shaping it and casting it from mindtime into space-time through what Jacinta called quartz information drivers and intelligent crystal technology."

Larkin did not miss the wry, disbelieving smile that flickered over Roger's face.

"I know, I know. I didn't believe it either. When Jacinta started talking about analogous piezoelectric effects and telling me that crystalline materials of proper lattice configuration and sufficient size could receive and amplify mental energies and translate them into motive forces, I thought she was just plain deluded. When she told me they were going to sing and think critical information densities *into* the crystal 'collecting columns' they'd placed throughout cave's big chamber, when she told me those collectors would translate and amplify that information so they could dissociate the tepui from the gravitational bed of local space-time, I thought they were *all* flat-out insane. What else was I to think?''

"Seems like a logical conclusion to come to," Roger said with a nod.

"Yes," Larkin replied distractedly. "But then the tepui took off and disappeared, and then something almost equally strange happened outside Sedona a few years later. *Cordyceps jacintae* was found to contain KL 235, and 'gateheads' developed the same sort of information-devouring propensities as the tepui tribe. The gateheads, though—lacking a full myconeural complex and a cultural mythology of rejoining some Great Cooperative—didn't know what use to put all that information to once they had it, I guess, and it has driven quite a few of them truly crazy."

Seiji stared at Paul Larkin, as if something had just occurred to him, but Roger was already speaking again.

"What if I wanted to try some of these things?" he asked, gesturing at the crop of *C. jacintae*. "I mean, this space habitat is known for its *laissez-faire* personal-use policies, right?"

Larkin and Yamaguchi glanced worriedly at each other.

"We certainly can't and won't stop you," Seiji said after some thought, looking Roger hard in the eye. "You're an adult, you have free will, you have a right to be wrong so long as that right doesn't infringe on the rights of others. But my brother had those rights too, Dr. Cortland—even if they weren't the law on Earth. He became a gatehead and eventually suffered a nervous collapse. As you're probably aware, ingestion of *Cordyceps jacintae* was also implicated in Paul's sister's strange behavior and eventual disappearance.''

Larkin nodded, then addressed Roger, too.

"If you're just looking for a holiday from your everyday mind," Larkin speculated, "and you think adaptogenic mushrooms might be your meat, it would probably be safer if you tried one of the more traditional varieties—*Psilocybe* or *Panaeolus*, perhaps. Their nature and effects are much better known—and there isn't such a legacy of madness, disappearance, and death associated with them.''

"Interesting," Roger said with a sly smile. "It almost sounds as if you're trying to dissuade me. But what if I insist?''

Another of those quick, worried glances passed between Larkin and Yamaguchi.

"Then you may remove the fruiting bodies in such numbers as I judge do not constitute a threat to the continuance of the species," Yamaguchi replied. "We will also provide you with as much relevant information about the chemical composition, physicochemical and psychological effects, history, and tepuian mythology of C. jacintae as we can make available to you. What use you make of that information—whether you even peruse it at all—is up to you, of course.''

"All right," Roger said, plucking convoluted ball-stalk fruiting bodies from the neural mass in which they grew before him, but not removing enough of them to "constitute a threat to the continuance of the species," apparently. He smiled to himself. He'd always wanted to test the colonists' policy hypotheses, their loose fabric of "neo-autonomous communitarian" ideas.

When Roger had perhaps a half-dozen of the mushrooms, he tossed them into one of the sacks containing jasmine-flowers and their extract. Yamaguchi and Larkin, meanwhile, were busy scrounging up informational faxes to hand to him on the subject of the vertical fruit of the horizontal tree.

"What the tepui people developed wasn't just a mythology, really," old Larkin remarked as he handed Roger a sheaf of faxes. "It was an entire cosmogony centered around the life cycle of their totem mushroom. Even in the little time I spent with Jacinta and the tepui people I was able to see that. Everything for them was spore and spawn and fruiting body—and the void that comes before and after and always is. Kekchi, their old wise one, sang me their Story of the Seven Ages, the history of the universe as seven Great Cycles of spore/spawn/ fruiting body, spore/spawn/ fruiting body—''

Glancing at his watch, Larkin abruptly broke off.

"Good heavens! I didn't realize how late it was. Thanks for

your time, Seiji, but we've got to go. To my lab, Dr. Cortland—double-time!''

Gathering up their impedimenta, they quickly and quietly
made their way out of the underground complex of Mycology
laboratories, returning to the surface only briefly as they
looked for a bulletcart station. With a flashing of lights and
the quiet whoosh of its sudden appearance, a cart arrived and
they boarded.

Larkin's Cryogenetics facility was within easy walking distance of the station at which they disembarked, and in a moment they found themselves striding down another
underground corridor, a better-lit twin to the passage they'd
walked down in Mycology. Roger thought it could easily have
passed for one of the corridors in his own lab—or for a bulletcart tube, but for the many doors lining it.

"You're fortunate that we have some civets bred up right
now," Larkin said, opening a door onto a room of thick, pungent animal smells that reminded Roger of the atmosphere in
the Big Cat house of an old-fashioned zoo. "We breed all our
species up to sexual maturity now and then—as a test to see
how well their genetic material is holding up to cryogenic
storage, and as a source of new sperm and egg for *in vitro*
fertilization work."

Larkin handed Roger four brown-glass vials filled with a
liquid of some sort.

"Here you go," Larkin said. "I've already extracted the
musk fluid from their anal scent glands for you."

"That's it?" Roger asked incredulously, putting the vials in
his shirt pocket as Larkin ushered him back out to the hall.
"It's that easy? Thanks! You've saved me a lot of work."

"No problem. Good luck with your perfume experiments,"
Larkin said, shaking hands with the younger scientist. Larkin's
face grew graver for a moment. "Your psychoactive experiments too, if you know what I mean. And be careful, whatever
you decide."

With a nod and a wave, Roger parted from Larkin and began
moving down the corridor with his sacks of plants and their
essential extract and his newly acquired civet musk. *At least I
don't have to carry one of those little civet beasties back to
my lab*, he thought.

Not far along the hallway, he stopped, surprised to see Jhana Meniskos sitting behind a desk in one of the lab offices, placing slides on a microscope. He put his bags and bundles down and knocked on the doorjamb. Jhana looked up.

"Dr. Cortland! This is a surprise. What brings you here?"

Roger gestured toward the sacks.

"Gathering materials for my perfume, actually. I was here to see Paul Larkin. He's been such a big help, I think I'll have the first batch brewed up very soon," Roger said, staring with sudden intensity at Jhana as he withdrew faxes from behind the musk vials in his shirt pocket. "I'd forgotten you worked here, but this will expedite things nicely. I received these faxes of 'interest and intent' from your employer at Tao-Ponto. He's asked that you pass on your encryption code to me for any future business I might wish to transact with the company."

Jhana took the faxes Cortland handed her. She scanned them, read the request, and nodded, then jotted down a number and handed it back to Roger with his faxes.

Roger stared down at the number 105366 and smiled. Jhana seemed preoccupied with thoughts of her own.

"One more thing," Roger said, tucking the faxes back in his pocket. "Would you be so kind as to be one of the first women to wear the perfume I've created? I'd be honored if you would."

Jhana glanced up at him.

"All right," she agreed quietly. Just once wouldn't cause any permanent harm, she supposed.

"Good! Then come visit my lab about two, your time here. I'm looking forward to it."

Jhana nodded mutely while Roger gathered together his bundles. As he left her office and walked down the hall, he was so proud of what he'd already accomplished today that he almost felt like whistling—were it not for that distressing flutter of wings in his peripheral vision once more.

A S SHE DRESSED FOR THE COLONY COUNCIL MEETING Marissa kept half an eye on the last few minutes of a minidocumentary playing on one wall screen. The program was called *Worldchangers* and she'd seen a couple of installments since her arrival. They seemed to consist mostly of archival footage and interviews with habitat residents who'd been active in various movements for peace, social justice, and ecological restoration on Earth before they came up to the habitat.

A black woman who looked to be in her late fifties appeared on the screen. The frame froze and a caption appeared on the screen:

CLARA SCHULMAN organized the first of our colony's Earth Restoration Groups (ERGs), organizations dedicated to transferring to Earth those ideas and practices of ecologically sound living developed here in the space habitat.

As she spoke, her image was replaced by archival footage of what she was talking about.

Transcript of *Worldchangers* interview with Clara Schulman (excerpt):

I was very young at the time, but I remember very clearly the first time I got arrested for civil disobedience.

I guess you might say I had an epiphany of sorts. Right then and there I decided to go over the fence—to commit what the Department of Energy called illegal trespass. From a representative of the Western Shoshone National Council I got my permit to enter the Test Site lands— which by treaty were still the Shoshone people's territory. I trespassed, got arrested and handcuffed by a man in camouflage, then was herded into the women's side of the holding pen, sort of a mini-concentration camp bull-dozed out of the desert. Putting us on the same chartered buses that had earlier brought the test site workers out from Vegas, the authorities hauled us off to be booked for our 'crime.'

I won't say I haven't looked back—I have. But never with regret. Eventually all the nuclear test sites everywhere ceased operations, and that was an important step for the protection and restoration of the Earth. But even if the test sites were still operating, even if we'd failed in our larger project, for me my action would still have been right, still worthwhile, for my experience there taught me that the Earth itself—and all time and space—is a test site, a vale of soul-making. . . .

Marissa commanded the screen off, got up, and left her residence. Deep in thought she passed through her garden, wondering about heavens and hells, paradises and test sites. She thought of distances, fences, boundaries, walls. She glanced up at the garden world arching in the sheltering sky above her. The space habitat was itself a world walled off both by distance and by metal, a world increasingly free of Earth—yet its settlers paradoxically felt themselves increasingly responsible for Earth and what went on there. For them, the ensphering walls of the space habitat were less a boundary than a sort of semipermeable membrane through which light and ideas and sustenance might pass in both directions.

Walking to the nearest bulletcart station Marissa thought of how, since her arrival, she'd become more aware of the ERGs and the habitat's various other missions to Earth. In some ways, this colony was so completely different from every other colony in human history. Undeniably, it did have something of the typical colony/mother country relationship: the space colony shipping energy down the well, getting back from the mother planet those finished products that couldn't be manufactured locally. But that was about the extent of the similarity. No indigenous peoples had had to be "civilized," "displaced" or eliminated here, no wilderness had to be exploited out of existence. Rather this was a place built and peopled for the first time, a seed or spore of the homeworld, an offspring that had in some ways come to maturity and moved away—but one that was still concerned for the welfare of its parent.

On the platform waiting for the cart, Marissa shrugged back her hair and gazed once more toward the distant, other side of the sphere, into the shadowed forests and fields and gardens beyond the glittering line of the axial ridge, past the shimmering dragonflies of aircyclists, the tiny gnat-swarms of free-fall soccer players. Unbidden, the phrase "a land of dreams, so various, so beautiful, so new" rose into her mind, with force enough that she could not ignore it.

Yes, it was all of that—especially new. But would it at last prove only a world like that poet's vision of nineteenth-century Earth, a place having "really neither joy, nor love, nor light, nor certitude, nor peace, nor help for pain"? Would this world of light also be reduced to a darkling plain where ignorant armies once again clashed by night?

Despite the warmth of the air, Marissa shivered. Was this what it meant to have a sense of the habitat, to care for and about it, to worry about who or what might betray its promise? Lights flashed, and a bulletcart—one of the few that came to the surface here—sighed up before her. Marissa boarded and, returning underground, the cart sped her along.

Passing through the tunnel, she wondered at herself. On Earth she had always thought about the habitat in an abstract, detached, scholarly way, but now she seemed to have somehow become personally and emotionally involved with it and its fate. Had she changed that much since her arrival?

She got off at the station where Atsuko had said to meet her and found her mentor already there.

"H'lo, Maris," Atsuko said, coming forward and giving her a quick hug. "The pavilion is up the ramp and a short walk to the left. It's the same one where Lev and his group are going to be holding their concert later, but the colony council is using it first."

At the bottom of the ramp Atsuko turned to her.

"I hope you don't find the proceedings too boring. I figured that your fellowship research here should at least include some exposure to our local species of government—and today's agenda looks a good deal more interesting than most."

As they walked up the ramp Atsuko explained briefly that, for purposes of representation, the permanent residents in both the agricultural tori and the central sphere were grouped into "centuries," or community districts, of one hundred citizens each, corresponding roughly to settlement hamlets and neighborhoods. Each century had its own council of ten (whose membership rotated every year), and one council member from each century was chosen to represent the century in the meetings of the colony council. Any resident of the colony could

attend the colony council meetings and voice his or her opin-
ions on any issue, though only the century representatives
could participate in the consensus decision-making process.

"We're still experimenting with the system, of course," Atsuko added as they came to the surface and approached a large,
airy, open-work building, below which stood a reflecting pool
of considerable size. "I believe our colony council already has
a few features you won't find elsewhere, though. Besides
having the usual staff ecologists, we also have representatives
specially designated as Speaker for Animals or Speaker For
Trees or the like, whose job it is to be especially sensitive to
the environmental impact of any action the council may be
contemplating. I know it sounds strange, but it seems to work.
The special Speakers take their responsibilities quite seriously,
and since ours is government by consensus, it only takes one
representative in disagreement to halt an action—so the special
Speakers have considerable weight in the colony's deliberations."

They entered the light-filled space created by the high-
domed modular building. Since weather in the habitat was so
predictable, the pavilion—like all the public buildings in the
central sphere—was built as much for symbolic and artistic
expression as it was for shelter. Strolling through it, Marissa
felt as if she were inside an architectural construct that fell
somewhere between a bright beach umbrella and the interior
of a hot-air balloon's inflated silk bag. The effect was only
heightened by the presence of tall, thin, temporary stage curtains—behind which, she gathered, Lev Korchnoi and Möbius
Cadúceus had hidden their stage set.

The light-filled space was very sparsely furnished: a low,
portable-looking, semicircular dais facing outward toward
rows of seating. Atsuko took her place among the council representatives, while Marissa joined the members of the audience.

What followed was indeed unlike any business or political
meeting Marissa had ever attended. It began precisely on the
hour, but not with the banging of gavels or any ritual more
formal than people raising their right hands one by one
throughout the pavilion as a sign for silence. Soon the conversation and the bustling of the crowd in the hall quieted

down to complete silence. Glancing around her, Marissa noticed that many of those in the audience had assumed a prayerful or meditative attitude. Though their eyes were closed, something about their posture indicated that they were nevertheless attentive to unseen things.

The council's current Presiding Minister—an African-American woman whom Marissa recognized as Clara Schulman, the woman who'd been interviewed on the *Worldchangers* program—began to speak without standing up.

"Before entering on the business of the colony," the Presiding Minister began ritually, "let us spend time in thoughtful meditation as is our custom, seeking in the silence to put away the voice of our individual egotism and short-sighted self-interest so that we might hear and be guided by that more subtle voice in which we live and move and which lives and moves in us. Let us seek in the silence to open our minds and fill our hearts with the light and love that fills the universe. May all our deliberations, decisions, and actions be guided by our desire to protect, preserve, and renew all life, both here and on Earth."

Marissa was less surprised by the scattered whispers of "Amen" and "Shanti" than she thought she'd be. As everyone sat in an attentive, aware silence that stretched to five and then ten minutes, she began to wonder if religious services in the space colony felt as political as this political meeting felt religious. She had not yet had a chance to find out, for though profoundly and personally interested in spiritual things, Marissa wasn't, in the institutional sense, particularly religious herself. Whenever a proselytizer back on Earth had asked her about her religious convictions, her usual line was that she was "just your average Zen Born Again Catholic Quaker Pacifist Anarchist—with a strong interest in the Gita, the Talmud, and the Koran." That was usually good for confusing and frustrating the evangelizers, though somehow she doubted it would bother anyone here. Even on Earth some of the evangelizers had heard her self-description selectively, one remarking, on hearing it, "Oh, you're a Christian, then."

At an unspoken signal the meditative quiet ended, but the effects of that thoughtful silence seemed to linger as the council took up the colony's business. The first item on the agenda was old business, a discussion of a petition by the Möbius Cadúceus Entertainment Cooperative requesting use of the pavilion's reflecting pool as part of their upcoming performance. Apparently—due to questions of possible environmental impact and specific requests for clarification from the Speaker For Animals—consensus had not been achieved among the council members during the previous discussions of the petition and the issue had been turned over to a committee for further research and recommendations. The staff ecologist and Speaker For Animals, representing the committee, stated that all questions of environmental impact had now been addressed to their satisfaction and they recommended approval of the petition. Lev Korchnoi also rose from the audience to announce again the time and place of the concert, to invite everyone to the performance, and even suggested that if the council would like to appoint an official observer to see that no violations of environmental integrity occurred, Möbius Cadúceus would have no objections and would in fact welcome the interest. Atsuko volunteered her time as official observer. Surprisingly quickly, the council approved both Möbius Cadúceus's petition and Atsuko Cortland's appointment as council representative to the event.

Watching the proceedings, Marissa was left with a strong suspicion of where she'd probably find herself during the performance, but she barely had time to formulate that thought before the next speaker, a young black Frenchman representing the HOME consortium, stood to address the council on more business postponed from a previous meeting. The HOME representative informed the council and the audience that the prototype asteroid mining tug *Swallowtail*, designed by colony resident Brandi Easter, had been completed well ahead of schedule. With the council's approval, the HOME consortium proposed to have *Swallowtail*'s launching coincide with the opening of the two new habitats—and therefore part of the celebration that Möbius Cadúceus's performance was already included in. After some good-natured complaining about ''overloading the event'' at this late date—and Lev Korchnoi's humble assurance that Möbius Cadúceus would try to limit the number of its encores so that its performance didn't too seriously overlap other presentations—the colony council gave its approval to the consortium's proposal.

HOME's young resident representative was about to sit down, when the Presiding Minister rose and addressed him, something about her words and posture causing the atmosphere in the pavilion to grow suddenly grave.

"Mr. Fanon, we may need your responses on our next agenda item," she said, then turned to her fellow council members and the audience. "We are on the brink of great accomplishments and celebrations, as you've said and we've heard, but, as a number of you already know, we are also on the brink of grave danger. The Chinese ideogram for 'crisis' is made up of the characters for both *danger* and *opportunity*, which is indeed an apt description of our current condition.

"We have tried to base our culture here on a simple but metaphysically profound truth: There is no separate existence. 'Things derive their being and nature by mutual dependence— they are nothing in themselves,' as the sage Nagarjuna put it. We have emphasized reality-as-process and the liberating truth inherent in the world's incompleteness and uncertainty. We have seen the way in which such a world view subverts the traditional paradigm of dogma and dominance. Events today, though, remind us of how inextricably our fate is tied up with Earth's and give us more proof of our tentative truths than ever—and more challenges to them, as well.

"Relations between our colony and a number of nations and corporations of Earth have become strained of late. The source of the strain is this."

Shades came down over the building's exterior, dimming the light inside as trideo displays floated into the central space between audience and council. Marissa saw that the images in the ghostly display were views of the big X-shaped structures that she'd earlier heard Seiji and Lev and Lakshmi discussing.

"As nearly as our computing- power generation- and space-engineering staffs can determine," the Presiding Minister continued, "each of these objects is a new type of device for channeling substantial amounts of solar power into information functions—particularly memory storage, retrieval, and communications. Our friends on Earth, however, apparently believe with considerable fervor that they are devices for channeling large amounts of solar power into pulse lasers of unprecedented efficiency and destructiveness.''

Marissa watched as the trideo display cycled from close-ups to wide-angle images of the X-shaped structures, glinting like an enigmatic necklace (or noose) about the Earth.

''Several weeks ago, we began receiving diplomatic queries from various national and corporate entities,'' said the Presiding Minister, ''all of them asking more or less the same question: What are these things and why are you building them? Our initial answers—'We don't know' and 'We're not building them'—must not have been satisfactory, for the queries have continued in increasing numbers and decreasing friendliness, growing less diplomatic until, now, they have become downright hostile and threatening.

''As of just yesterday we were able to tell them that the structures are definitely concerned with information and not destruction, and that they are being built by micromachines apparently under the control of our colony's machine-intelligence networking system, the Variform Autonomous Joint Reasoning Activity—without colony approval and over human objections and countercommands. These answers have also proven unsatisfactory to our inquisitors on Earth—at least in part because they are determined to see a weapon in these structures. They further claim that, since VAJRA is supposed to be under our control, we are responsible for the construction of the objects and the threat they supposedly present.''

The Presiding Minister sighed wearily.

''Twelve hours ago, the United Nations and Corporate Presidium issued statements demanding that we immediately dismantle the disputed structures—and, if we fail to do so, threatened trade sanctions and possible military action ranging from blockade to invasion and UN/CP occupation of the habitat. We have sought to comply, but as soon as work teams attempted to dismantle one of the structures today, VAJRA precipitated a series of 'crises' in our intelligent systems—particularly those support systems on which this habitat is most dependent for its continued survival.

''Lakshmi Ngubo, the designer of VAJRA, along with the computing staff, is at this moment engaged in trying to correct the problem. The political situation, however, seems to be worsening very rapidly."

In the floating projections the X-shaped structures disappeared and were replaced by video and trideo images of blue-black, single-stage-to-orbit military shuttles, preparing for launch.

"As you can see, we may soon be forcibly reminded of our connection with Earth. Four hours ago, what appears to be a combined multinational, multicorporate force of ten ships and four hundred astronaut-soldiers left the launching pads at Edwards, Tanegashima, Baikonur, Lop Nor, Guiana Bleu, and Windhoek. These spacecraft are currently in low Earth orbits but could hard-burn toward our position here at a moment's notice. Those of you who follow Earth's media know that in the last few hours they've begun making most warlike noises, speculating that a 'colonial rebellion' is under way—even though we've been at constant pains to deny such rumors.

"To make matters even more critical, a number of HOME consortium members are among those corporations helping to loft this expeditionary force. Things seem to be strained up to their topmost height, so I think it's appropriate that the council should hear from all the people of the community, residents *and* visitors, as to what our course of action should be now."

So saying, Clara Schulman, this quarter's Presiding Minister, opened the floor for questions and discussion as a buzz and murmur ran through the audience. As Marissa listened to the flurry of bewildered queries and stark pronouncements that ensued, she found that the shrillest of the speakers were the visitors, who like herself seemed much more concerned by these developments than the permanent residents. Odd, she mused, that those who might have been thought to have more at stake would turn out to be calmer and more prepared for this eventuality.

The first several speakers all expressed bewilderment at finding themselves "hostages of our own machine," as one of them put it. All urged that Lakshmi Ngubo correct the VAJRA difficulties as quickly as possible. Several questions were addressed to the resident HOME representative, Mr. Fanon, and—though these queries were surprisingly without rancor, given the situation—the interrogation left the young man dazed and confused. Apparently he was being kept as much in the dark about external affairs as any other resident—probably because he *was* a resident, and therefore a "security risk" to HOME's member conglomerates.

Discussion only really got going, however, when a visitor, a woman named Ekwefi Muwakil, suggested that the whole brouhaha, even the actions by the UN and the CP, really had almost nothing to do with the strange X-shaped objects.

"Can't you see it's just a ploy?" she asked shrilly. "I wouldn't be surprised if HOME's corporate security were behind the VAJRA malfunction and the building of those things! It's a setup. Doesn't it seem a little bit too coincidental to you that this should be happening just now, when the new habitats are about to take in their first settlers, when the opening up of the asteroid frontier for metals and carbon chondrites is about to make this habitat far more self-sufficient? Doesn't it seem a little too pat that—just when it's starting to look like these space habitats really might work—the nations and corporations have drummed up an excuse for taking over? It's just as I suspected: if this new idea of space habitation proved out, the powers-that-be would co-opt it for themselves, like every other new idea. An executive escape-pod, a lifeboat for the power-elite while the Good Ship Earth goes down—that was their plan all along! And I'm sure this four-hundred-member occupation force has *always* been a part of that plan!"

Whether Ms. Muwakil was right or not in believing nations and corporations on Earth had some sort of long-range take-over plan, Marissa could not say. The converse possibility, though—that the habitat's residents had already given some thought to contingency plans of their own—was clearly in evidence as she watched the discussion. Marissa listened carefully as consensus quickly developed around a proposed two-part plan of action.

The first part, the filing of a formal protest against the UN/CP positioning of troops in space, was quickly adopted because it was within the colony council's powers to issue such a protest. Preparations for a civilian-based NonViolent Direct Resistance (NVDR) defense—the second part of the plan—would, upon colony council approval, have to be taken by the colony council representatives back to their home community councils, and from there to the people in each community-century for approval and action. Such a process sounded slow to Marissa, but if consensus could be achieved as quickly at all levels as it had been in the council meeting today, then there could be no doubt that the colony could operate democratically even in such a crisis as that which now faced the space habitat.

"Having accomplished the work on the agenda," the Presiding Minister said at last, "let's give over another moment to silence, and through that silence round off the council's proceedings. Let us find in the silence the strength, courage, and resolution we'll need to act upon the decisions we've made today and see all our actions through to a peaceful and just conclusion."

Marissa closed her eyes in the silence this time, finding as she did so that falling into the quiet darkness was somehow as pleasant as floating in a sunlit pool of cool water. Whatever tensions the meeting may have generated in her now dissipated into the quiet darkness, fell away, and were gone. When the sounds of conversation and the scraping of chairs signaled that the quiet, contemplative time was over, Marissa opened her eyes to look upon the world with renewed vigor and determination.

Rejoining Atsuko near the dais, Marissa found her mentor getting final reminders from Lev Korchnoi about curtain time for the Möbius Cadúceus show.

"As soon as I got the go-ahead from the council," Lev was saying, "I went ahead and called the crew to help me finish the final setup for the show. If you want to see some of that, follow me."

Atsuko and Marissa agreed and followed Lev out of the pavilion in the direction of the reflecting pool. The council's discussions and the colony's dire situation were, seemingly, past and forgotten but for Lev's rather laconic statement that he hoped "this thing with Earth" didn't blow up and ruin the concert and the other parts of the celebrations scheduled for that evening.

"Here they are," Lev announced when they'd reached the edge of the reflecting pool, pointing toward two impressively large machine assemblages, one of which was already being lowered by crane into the waters of the pool. "My temple guardians."

"What are they?" Atsuko asked, noting groups of curious onlookers, Seiji Yamaguchi among them—already beginning to gather. "What do they do?"

"Everything!" Lev said proudly, climbing with considerable agility into a cranny about a quarter of the way up the nearer mechanism, a towering crystalline megalith studded with weapons blisters and looming above them like a dumb god of hulking metal. "Each one's a sort of self-consuming theatrical robot. My own computer-aided designs, you know—though the ideas are old. I've taken the monsters Scylla and Charybdis from the ancient Western myths and tried to blend them with the Shut-Mouthed Fear and Open-Mouthed Desire demons found at the entrance to some Buddhist shrines. The result is that this machine is my Rock of Fear, and that"—he pointed to the other mechanism, the squatter companion piece, just at the very moment the crane deposited it into the water with a loud splash—"that is my Whirlpool of Desire. Together they make up the difficult passage Our Hero must navigate."

Noting the crane turning its attention toward the second machine, Lev climbed down from his Rock of Fear and walked toward Atsuko and Marissa with the careful physical control of a natural athlete or veteran dancer.

"Are they safe?" asked Seiji Yamaguchi, who had moved to the front of one cluster of onlookers.

"Completely," Lev assured him, though Marissa quickly realized the tall pale man was speaking as much for Atsuko's benefit as for Seiji's. "All just bells and whistles and special effects. Even the 'bombs' will only be noise and a little smoke, sulfur, carbon dioxide and occasional methane—all well within environmental standards. Just stage combat and choreography and acrobatics. I doubt the shuttlecraft troopers down in low orbit can say as much."

Seiji's data-display unit began to chime and show a message.

"Gotta go," Seiji said with a puzzled frown, taking his leave. "Lakshmi wants to see Jhana and me up at her workshop. Top priority. Any suggestions as to where Ms. Meniskos might be about this time of day?"

"You might try Cryonics or Cryogenetics," Atsuko remarked. "Paul Larkin's lab."

"I was thinking of looking there myself," Seiji said with a nod. "I keep trying to get Larkin to go up with me to Lakshmi's place, but he refuses. Hates micro-gee, he says." Seiji turned to shake Lev's hand. "I hope the show goes well, Lev."

"Thanks. Say hello to Lakshmi for me."

"I will," Seiji said, striding quickly away. In the reflecting pool, the crane was settling Lev's Rock of Fear mechanism into place.

ROGER WAS OVERTIRED AND EXHILARATED TO THE EDGE of dizziness. He had worked diligently all morning and into the afternoon to at last produce a complete sample of his pheromonal perfume, and soon, very soon, he would test its effects. He had already cleared most of the furniture out of one of the lab lounges and put down thick mats. Marissa, after attending some colony political function (God only knew why), was already in the lab, supposedly at the moment pumping out, under the most rigorous safety controls, her first prototype culture of that immortalizing viral vector she'd been working on. Jhana, too, was due soon. Visions of the two women going at each other—voluptuous pale redhead versus wiry dark brunette—and of himself at last nobly stepping in to break them up (though not too quickly, not too soon) flickered in his head.

It occurred to Roger, however, that if the perfume he'd developed worked as planned, stepping in between them might be dangerous. Deciding it was best to be on the safe side, he headed over to his office desk and, opening the bottom drawer, dug underneath a stack of papers for the one item from his weapon collection that he'd been able to smuggle up here: a Sig/Sauer Laserwire Dirk—mostly dark plastic, and at the moment broken down into three parts. He quickly reassembled the short-range (one-third meter) beam weapon, clicked in its coiled snapwire and battery pack, and dropped the small, unprepossessing weapon into one of the large pockets of his white lab coat.

He felt ready to take on the world now—ready to celebrate his impending Great Achievement. His hand strayed to the small plastic bag of *Cordyceps jacintae* still sitting on his desk from when he'd returned to the lab after his jaunt to see Larkin. He had scanned enough of the literature Paul and Seiji had given him to be able to figure out the dosages for certain desired effects. A one-gram piece of the mushroom, for instance, would open up the reducing valve of the dorsal and median raphe nuclei enough to allow heightened sensitivity to and awareness of visual and auditory stimuli, an increased libidinal and sensual response. . . .

He took a small specimen out of the bag and stared at it. Certainly the test he was about to run on his perfume, with Jhana and Marissa's not-quite-fully-informed participation, would be something worth experiencing in a state of heightened sensory awareness—and worth remembering from that heightened state! If he didn't like the effect and didn't want the fungus colonizing his central nervous system, he could always have its spawn eliminated through fungicidal antibiotics later.

Why not? he thought—and so thinking, he popped a couple of the small mushrooms into his mouth and chewed them slowly, deliberately. Though unaccustomed to eating uncooked mushrooms, he nonetheless found them surprisingly tasty, possessing only the slightest trace of any bitter or alkaloidal tang.

Now he was truly ready. A vision of a future—the future he was today creating—sprang into his head, unassisted by the mushroom and its various adaptogenic substances. He wouldn't be feeling the effects of the mushroom for at least fifteen minutes. No, this vision was all his own.

He saw a future where underground malls were all the rage—the first step toward a Sandman burrow, a human version of the naked mole rat colony structure. He foresaw a shift in styles, more unisex overall, everyone's nails all filed sharp like digging claws, their hair cropped close and tight. People who moved in unison, a part of the great "we," the invincible "us," a eusocial superorganism capable of surviving in areas where a single individual or a pair of such Sandfolk could not. A society whose queen ruled with an absoluteness and efficiency never before seen, whose courtiers unhesitatingly defended the status quo with gun and uniform and mind, whose workers were ever diligent and productive and content with their lot. A future where only the rich could afford *Tombé* in significant quantities—*Tombé*, which would make men crane their necks and bend other women's wills to the wearer's own; *Tombé*, which would ensure chemical control over those who had less or none of it, suppressing reproduction by them, guaranteeing an unconscious obedience, an almost instinctual subservience, from them; *Tombé*, which would be deep power, such that the more *Tombé* one owned, the more power one would have. Soon only the rich would have children, not because the poor would have made a "free will choice not to have them" (as these cislunatic idealists up here might phrase it), but because *Tombé* would be something only the rich could afford. But most importantly, *Tombé* would eliminate all need for his own pathology of secrecy, perhaps even the pathology of secrecy on which all human culture was built—

Wings glittered in Roger's peripheral vision and, startled, he reflexively drew his dirk, only to find that there was once again nothing to strike.

He shook his head, smiling wryly. He was wrought up, strung on a wire tighter than the one in his laser. The mushroom was chipping through whatever brain-dam it was that kept the flow from the senses down to a trickle. Sensations were now beginning to flood into him at a rate he'd never known before. After this test proved out he would have to take a long nap, rest, recharge. Taking the prototype bottle of *Tombé* from his desktop, uncapping it and wafting its wonderful musky-sweet scent under his nose once more, he felt reassured.

TWELVE

Passage embedded in RAT code:

The meat model of human consciousness holds that, somewhere out there, is the Sacred (Holy, Wholly) Cow of Unmediated Reality, Urreality, the universe as it is in itself. According to this model, the human sensory apparatus is the slaughterhouse, which cuts out those pieces it can use, the beef and beef byproducts of experiential data. The Cow's sacredness is killed so it can be understood. Next, the human perceptual apparatus functions as meat grinder, extruding the seemingly continuous "sausage" of sense-perception gestalt. Consciousness is the arbitrary cutting blade of time, the machine that cuts the gestalt sausage into digestible moment-to-moment slices. Self is the virtual construct, the master continuity program, the butcher or meat packer who neatly stacks the gestalt-sausage slices, makes them seem like they all cohere, even though they are different every split second. This model—though it has much to recommend it—not only offends vegetarians but is, in several of its steps, dead wrong. Nonetheless, it remains true that those who love person-hood, like those who love the law or sausage, should never watch any of them being made.

Jhana had a great deal on her mind as she half-ran to Roger Cortland's lab. Events were moving too fast. She'd just received a message that Dr. Tien-Jones was part of a negotiating team ready to come to the space habitat immediately. But negotiating for what—the terms of surrender? Passing a sidewalk cafe, she'd seen a news flash indicating that corporate and national forces had moved shuttlecraft and troops into low orbit. She couldn't say with absolute certainty, but she suspected the troop movement had all too much to do with some fear-pumped "Diamond Thunderbolt" connection the powers on Earth were making between VAJRA and the enigmatic X-shaped structures floating in space.

She felt obscurely responsible for the way things were turning out. For whatever good it might do, just as soon as this thing with Cortland was done today she would have to contact Dr. Tien-Jones and stress the enormous misunderstanding of it all to him. He had to be informed that she absolutely did not believe the X-shaped structures were a weapons system of any sort or that Diamond Thunderbolt posed any threat to Earth, either. She had already delayed too long in sending that message.

Her misgivings about Cortland's work with his pheromone perfume continued unabated as she ran along. She would have preferred to have no more to do with it, but she reasoned it would be best to keep her Earthside employers happy with her work on at least that front. Strangely, too, Paul Larkin was friendlier than ever toward her, since he'd found out she was "helping Dr. Cortland with his research," as he'd put it when she told him that she had to leave the lab to meet with Roger. Larkin told her he'd be along shortly as well—to see how Roger's work was going. The senior researcher seemed to have developed an interest in the younger man which Jhana could not explain.

Entering Cortland's lab, she found Roger standing and his assistant Marissa seated—both of them silent. Was it only her imagination, Jhana wondered, or had some estrangement taken place between the two of them? The red-haired woman seemed nervous and sulky somehow, while Cortland himself looked, up close, as if he hadn't slept in days. When he saw her, however, his eyes lit up with an excited gleam.

"Jhana! So glad you could make it for our little test. Right this way, please," Roger said, stylus and electric clipboard in hand, turning to go. Marissa lagged behind. "Marissa?"

Reluctantly the redheaded woman got up and followed as Roger led them to a lounge. Unlocking the door, he let them into a room which—but for some thick mats on the floor, a permanent lab table, and two padded chairs—was entirely stripped of furnishings. Jhana noticed that Marissa's eyebrows flashed up on seeing the room, but the woman said nothing. Roger locked the door behind them.

"I hope this won't take too long, Roger," Jhana said as she sat down in one of the chairs. "I've got to get an important message to my employers about this military mess that's going on."

"Yes, I heard something about that," Roger replied absently. "Well, don't worry. The potential side effect I'm trying to investigate with this test should be almost instantaneous."

Jhana wondered about the term side effect, but didn't have time to ask because, with a flourish, Roger withdrew a vial filled with a faintly yellow-orange liquid from his pocket and placed it on the table between Jhana and Marissa.

"Ta-da!" Roger said, a bit too shrilly. "The fruit of my labors. Go ahead, put a little on. Jhana, you first—as our guest."

Jhana opened the vial and sniffed the scent arising from the pale amber fluid within. Finding the sweet, musky fragrance quite pleasant, she inhaled more deeply. Marissa and Roger watched her every move very carefully as she dabbed the liquid onto the pulse-points of her wrists and then behind her left ear. Sniffing at her right wrist, she realized that the scent had changed somehow—improved, just through contact with her skin.

"It's a wonderful scent," she said, placing the vial back on the table before her. "Responds to the wearer's body chemistry?"

"That's right," Roger said slowly, with a brief nod, as he lifted the vial and placed it in front of Marissa. The excited gleam in his eyes seemed to have brightened to an absolute dazzle.

Jhana watched as Marissa hesitantly dabbed on the yellow-

orange fluid, looking less like the happy coworker testing an
innocent perfume than someone who feared she might be putting acid on her flesh. She too sniffed at the scent of the perfume on her skin, but it didn't seem to reassure her that much.

Electropenning notes, Roger sat down for a moment on the
ledge of a large lab sink and watched them with an intensity
that Jhana found disquieting. Shouldn't he be taking blood
samples, looking for a drop in estrogen levels or something?
She turned and, with some effort, struck up a conversation with
Marissa. As they talked, Marissa grew less nervous and reticent, while Roger conversely became more agitated, pacing,
then circling around them, checking his watch every few seconds or peering at them with eyes that seemed to burn in his
head. Jhana began to wonder at the man's odd behavior and
wanted to be gone from him and his lab as quickly as possible.

"Roger, how much longer is this going to take?" she asked
impatiently.

"A few more minutes," he said thickly, breathing hard. "A
few more minutes."

Roger's unfocused agitation grew more and more disturbing. The few minutes came and went—and then some.

"It's not working!" he cried at last, his voice very nearly
a shriek. Jhana and Marissa stared at him. "It's not working,
don't you see?"

"Yes, we do see that, Roger," Marissa said uncertainly, yet
in a voice remarkably placid, given the circumstances. "Please
calm down. We have to face the facts. The Faulkes orthodoxy
appears to be right, Roger. The mole-rat social hierarchy, the
queen's suppression of reproductive capacity in the rest of the
colony's females—it must be almost completely mediated by
behavioral and physical factors, not chemical ones, not pheromones. The effect you're looking for isn't there."

"But the tests!" Roger roared. "What about the tests I
ran?"

"Inconclusive," Marissa said quietly, patiently. "Impossible to fully separate out behavioral factors. I was afraid to
confront you with it, after your previous funding request was
denied and you became so obsessed with this pheromone project. You were in denial about your results and I said nothing.
I was worried about what the letdown might do to you, afraid

you might start acting like this. So I went along as long as I could. But you have to face the reality now, Roger: pheromonal social control is not what's at work—in humans or in mole rats.''

"Better never to have known!" he cried, pulling at his hair distractedly, his eyes dancing wildly in his head as he paced. "No, no! I refuse to believe it! You're lying, trying to deceive me! I'll never give up this project—never!''

Jhana could see Marissa's patience snapping at last.

"Fine, Roger. Go ahead. Waste your life in a twisted obsession. What 'side effect' was it you hoped to test with Jhana and me today, hm? Whether your pheromone perfume would make us do what female mole rats do? Oh yes, Roger: I know the brutal idiosyncracy of the mole-rat social structure. Before the naked mole rat hierarchy is fully developed, females coming into estrus fight violently, frequently killing one another—''

"Shut up! You shut up!" Roger yelled thickly, wagging his finger threateningly.

"That idiosyncracy was what attracted you to them in the first place," Marissa continued fiercely, ignoring his commands, "wasn't it? Not their pheromones. I know your kink, Roger Cortland. I've known it ever since I stumbled upon you watching that porno. Since human women are in a sort of permanent low-level estrus, maybe you thought introducing your supposed pheromone would make them fight the way mole-rat females do, right? Was that your logic? Is that the side effect you hoped for? Some crime-of-passion triangle scene? Jhana and I leaping at each other tooth and claw, for your personal viewing pleasure?''

A stinging slap and then another exploded out of Roger, then the words "Cunt! Bloody whore!"—spoken with a venom more stinging than any slap could ever be. Marissa's chair toppled to the floor, where she sat stunned, her nose trickling blood. Once past her initial shock, Jhana rose swiftly to leap between Marissa and Roger, but Cortland—now thoroughly out of control—pulled a laser blade from his pocket, snapped its wireguide full length and shouted, "Back! Stay back! Don't come any closer!''

Jhana stopped in her tracks, watching as the wild-eyed man,

spittle flecking his lips and chin, backed stumbling toward the door. Once he spun and slashed a fiery arc over his shoulder—electric hum, ozone crackle, plaster exploding like a bomb on the wall behind him—at the same instant shouting something that Jhana thought sounded like, ''Damned angels! Leave me alone!''

Seeming to recover somewhat the little of his senses that remained, he unlocked the door behind him and slipped out. Jhana heard the sound of the door being locked from without, then two more crackling stabs disabling the automatic lock-overrides on the door—and then another series of crackling sounds down the hall. For a moment she thought she smelled the dark, bittersweet scent of burnt almonds, of pain and history in the air, but then it was gone. When she thought she'd heard Roger's staggering footsteps moving far enough away down the corridor, she stepped forward and tried to open the door. They were locked in tight.

Turning from the door, she stepped quickly toward Marissa, who was shakily trying to get to her feet. Jhana helped her up with one arm while with the other she righted the toppled chair, then eased the other woman into it. Taking tissues and a handkerchief from her pocket, she dabbed at Marissa's bleeding nose.

''Are you okay?'' Jhana asked. Marissa nodded her head tentatively, then after a while took some of the tissues from Jhana's hand and began dabbing at the blood herself and leaning her head back to slow the bleeding. Jhana was relieved to see that she was starting to pull herself together.

''I expected him to be angry when I finally confronted him with the failure of his pheromone research,'' Marissa said—almost apologetically—after a time, ''but I never expected he'd respond this way. It's just not normal—not even for Roger.''

''From the way he was acting he almost seemed drunk or on drugs,'' Jhana remarked, pulling the other chair over to sit beside Marissa.

Marissa shook her head, as vigorously as her nose bleed and her attempts to stop it would allow.

''That wouldn't be like him. I haven't known him that long, but I've never known him to indulge in anything that would

alter his state of consciousness. That would be giving up too
much control—and Roger loves control.''

Jhana shrugged.

"My friend Seiji says that sanity is a very tenuous thing.
Maybe he's right, in Roger's case.''

"Seiji Yamaguchi?" Marissa asked. "He seems like a nice
guy.''

Jhana nodded, getting up to throw the blood-soaked tissues
down a recycling chute.

"How did you figure out what Roger was up to?" she
asked, curious. "I was bothered by some aspects of his work,
but I never figured out his motivation, the way you did.''

Marissa pulled a sheaf of folded printouts from her pocket
and handed them to Jhana, saying, "Turn to the sections I've
highlighted.''

Jhana saw that they were texts of old articles—some going
back to the early 1980's—with titles like "Eusociality in a
Mammal: Cooperative Breeding in Naked Mole Rat Colonies''
by Jarvis and "Constraints of Pregnancy and Evolution of So-
ciality in Mole Rats'' by Burda. Turning to the highlighted
sections, Jhana read passages like "Soon after four mixed colonies were established, two females in each colony came into
estrus simultaneously and fought violently until one of the pair
died'' and "Aggression was observed toward unknown adult
conspecifics of the same sex. Females were more aggressive
to each other, and their fighting was serious with fatal conse-
quences, particularly if one of the females were in estrus or if
both females had bred in the past already. Fighting of males
was ritualized and foreign males were more willingly accepted
than foreign females. . . .''

"I must have read background passages like these a dozen
times in doing my research on their genetic stability,'' Jhana
said, looking up from the printouts, "but it never clicked for
me.''

"Same here,'' Marissa said with a nod. "It only fell into
place when I accidentally stumbled upon Roger viewing a
pornholo on one of our machines here—a porno that promi-
nently featured women fighting. That was the key piece of the
puzzle. With a little thought I was able to figure it out.''

"All of it?" Jhana asked.

"No, maybe not all of it," Marissa said thoughtfully, "but most of it, I think. There's a sort of dark logic to it. Investigating their longevity and slow maturation for my own work, I've gotten very familiar with mole rats and what Roger might have wanted from them. I think he really believed he was breaking ground for the foundation of a perfect society, one in which the will of the individual would be sacrificed to the will of the colony. It even had a sort of feminist cover to it, too. Mole-rat society is female-centered, and the first important researcher of the species was a woman. Not only that but, if Roger's plan had worked, women would have been more powerful than ever. That threw me off for a while, until I realized we would be less powerful than ever, too. Because everyone would have less freedom, even the queen. The highest goal of a woman would be to become a breeding machine. After the genetic lines of those who couldn't afford the perfume died out—then and only then—family would be everything, for everyone in Roger's Sandman future would be closely related. Those whose breeding would be suppressed would solace themselves with the knowledge that, by caring for their closely related broodmates, they would ensure the survival and passing on of their own genetic characteristics, even though they themselves would not actually breed. Self-sacrifice would be the new and total watchword."

Sighing, Marissa got up. Since her nose bleed had stopped completely at last, she walked over to the recycling chute to dispose of the bloody tissues she was still holding.

"But this big family would not be all kindness and gentility," she said, returning to standby the table. "If Roger's *Tombé*, as he called it, had worked as planned, when it hit the market it would have increased astronomically the level of woman-on-woman violence. Woman would be put at the figurehead-top of the social pyramid, as *breeder*, while simultaneously sisterhood was destroyed. That's what his pheromone perfume would have led to, if it had worked. He'd have bottled up all humanity like insects inside his amber fragrance. A perfect, unchanging world. All we'd have to do is forget our humanity, turn away from the responsibility of freedom, sacrifice the reality of our individuality to some meta-illusion called Society."

Jhana cleared her throat and stood up beside Marissa.

"Freedom, yes. We *should* probably try to get free of this room somehow, don't you think?"

"More than ever," Marissa said with a nod. "It just occurred to me that it might be *my* lab cubicle's door he zapped open when he went down the hall. He may have taken something of mine—something I don't want to get out."

Together Jhana and Marissa began tugging and banging on the door, pounding on the walls, and shouting to anyone who might be there to hear.

ROGER COULD NOT FIGURE OUT WHAT WAS HAPPENING TO him. When he looked about himself, he didn't see his surroundings the way a person would see a place, but more like the way the place would see itself. He had ceased to be Subject and had instead become a Moving Context, a diffused local consciousness through which people and events were passing.

With only a moment's focused concentration on any object, he could lift the veil of appearances and see instantly in that object's history the eternal interconnectedness of all flashing and dying temporal things, could see the Big Picture, the deeper order overlaid by the random-dot surface of time, could experience the subtle joy of living in a universe like a Great Thought ever unfolding, even his life merely a word in the language of that undying Thought—

And in the next instant the interconnectedness of all the words in that language was too subtle, something to be ignored, denied—and all about him was only the history of grief the universe composed everywhere, every word inflected with suffering, aspirated with anguish, pronounced with pain, until he could not see the purpose of any of it or what the beating, beating, beating Mind had intended—

His head pounded with the ghosts of pain and memory that filled even so new a world as this habitat. He felt it all—from a child's tear to the memory of the father and son work-team accidentally entombed in the construction of the habitat. He was more naked and vulnerable than he'd ever been, his very soul exposed fully and completely to the world, everything flowing straight into him without passing through even the thinnest wisp of filter. He wanted out, away into empty un-peopled unhistoried space. That thought alone provided solace and a goal.

Inundated with the overflowing intensity of his senses, the pain of mere existence was a burden which he staggered under as he sought out a bulletcart station. In a pathside cafe a trideo broadcaster spoke of the armada of shuttlecraft and troops now positioned in low orbit for a potential boarding of the space habitat. Frustratingly Roger's ears seemed to no longer be working, for as he listened, the news anchor's voice began to digitize, break up into little packets of sound separated by di-lating time, until Roger could not bridge the gaps between the packets to make any sense or meaning. Still, he smiled. If he had failed in his project, well so be it—at least it appeared that the work of these idealists up here was going to fail too. Disaster loves company—but how to ensure that it came about, that it all went down with him?

He came to a bulletcart boarding platform, deep in thoughts that would not hold together, in moods that swung faster than he could hold on to them. Everything around him shone with an aching clarity, a piercing naked light, as if he saw beyond every surface into the innermost depths, toward sharp bright and dark shapes below. A world of particulate light, of shim-mering motelike scintillas, danced around him in the air itself. Again, he feared he was going quite mad.

Brighter lights flashed and a bulletcart surged up before him. The other people on the platform—a woman with a little boy, and an old man—eased up toward him as the cart's doors sighed open.

"I want this cart to myself!" Roger yelled, brandishing his short, humming laser, his voice breaking up in his head even as he spoke. The man and woman froze, instinctively raising their empty, open hands to shoulder height.

"Mommy," said the little boy, "is he one of the soldiers from Earth?"

Roger did not wait to hear the mother's response to the boy's disintegrating words, but stumbled to a seat in the cart as it resealed itself and sped off. Among the glittering shards of his thoughts a backup plan began to form, one he could accomplish on his way out of here. In a pocket, next to the vial of Marissa's prototype vector-virus culture, which he'd stolen on his way out of the lab, he found Jhana Meniskos's encryption code-key number: 105366.

Yes, he thought, a message to Tao-Ponto, to her boss and his bosses, providing good reason to suspect that the colony rebellion was real, that Jhana herself was in jeopardy—that might help seal the final fate of this habitat . . .

Arriving at the Sphere's central observation platform, he left the cart and approached a telecommunications console near the snack bar. Looking away, into the vertiginous distance, he saw the whole sphere come alive with naked pipes, circuitry, fiber-optic tubes all swarming with mole rats moving endlessly through them. He tried to ignore all of it. Calling up a down-link line to Earth, he entered Jhana's keycode and typed in a top priority message:

TO: Balance Tien-Jones, Ph.D. TPAG Dir. R/D (Bio)
FROM: Jhana Meniskos, Ph.D.
RE: Current Status

Have evidence X-shaped structures are weapons systems of unprecedented destructive capability. Urge immediate action. Fear nonresidents will soon be taken hostage by resident colonists. Security of encryption code likely to be compromised. Ignore all future messages, this code.

It took him some time to complete the message—and almost more concentration than he was capable of mustering in his current state—but when it was at last finished he broke into a sly lopsided smile and sent the communication on its way. Walking with a loping gait, he made his way to a (blessedly empty) ridge cart and sat back on one of its benches. The ridge cart sealed itself and hurried him along toward the storage locker in the industrial sector of the axis—where his livesuit hung, beside his pod, beside an airlock, beside a gateway into unbounded space.

A glittering angel crossed its arms on the bench opposite him, but before Roger could flick on his laser or even blink, it was gone. Too suddenly for any rational explanation, Roger hung his head and wept, overcome by emotions he could not understand.

Drying his eyes as he got off at his stop, he made his slow, woozy way to the storage locker. He would skip the pod—just dive straight out, free of all encumbrances. Taking out his livesuit as he stripped dizzily to his underwear, he was careful to transfer from shirt to suit both Jhana's code-key number and the vial of Marissa's prototype immortalizing vector. Why he needed them, he did not know—one he had already used and rendered useless, the other might or might not be of use to the living, though it would certainly not bring back the dead. Still he held onto them, like talismans of lost hope.

Getting clumsily into the suit, he wondered if hell meant always seeing angels and never believing in their reality. If such angels could bring only torment, how did they differ from demons? Suited up at last, he made his unsteady way to the airlock. After he entered, the hatch door slammed behind him, its clang going on forever like a gong sounding from eternity to eternity. Before him the airlock doors began to dilate, the exit of a womb opening onto space in a second birth.

Drifting out, he saw the Earth itself, still alive in the middle way, wandering between the killing heat of the planet of Love and Desire, the killing cold of the planet of War and Fear, while all around stood the void, its dark brightness terrifying, like the eyes of the angel in his dreams.

WITH PAUL LARKIN AND SEIJI RAMMING THEIR SHOULders against the outside of the door and Marissa and Jhana pulling and tugging on it from the inside, they finally dislodged the door from its jamb and Paul and Seiji came tumbling into the lab lounge. Getting up from the floor and dusting himself off, Seiji explained that he had gone to Larkin's lab looking for Jhana and that together he and Paul had come looking for her and Roger.

Succinctly as they could, Marissa and Jhana described to them Roger's abreaction episode, his slapping Marissa around, his threatening them with a laser blade. As the four of them walked out of the lab lounge and down the corridor, the men's faces grew graver and graver.

"Do you think the mushrooms we gave him are involved?" Larkin asked Seiji, who nodded dolefully.

"What mushrooms?" Jhana asked.

As they came to the surface Paul and Seiji told them briefly about *Cordyceps jacintae* and how Roger Cortland came to have samples of it in his possession.

"He must have had an adverse reaction to them," Seiji summed up.

"Really? What makes you think that?" asked Marissa sardonically. "The point is, we've got a crazy man running around with a lethal weapon—so what do we do about it?"

"He won't be too hard to find," Larkin speculated. "All permanent residents are responsible for the policing of the community and, in an emergency, have the power to deputize visitors willing to be so deputized. Would you be willing to help me locate him, Marissa?"

"Sure," Marissa said, shrugging and shaking her head. "I don't know if he'll be willing to come with us peaceably, but it's worth a try."

"Jhana and I have a prior commitment," Seiji said quickly. "Lakshmi Ngubo called me to say that something seems to be breaking with the VAJRA stalemate. She wants us to work with her on it, immediately, so I think we should head out there."

Wishing each other luck, the four of them shook hands in parting and went their separate ways. Already late, Jhana and Seiji hurried to catch a bulletcart to the axis, passing one group of citizens after another practicing "going limp" or doing what looked to be some purely defensive form of aikido—using strange terms like "restoring the attacker to harmony" and "ahimsa" and "dynamic compassion" and "truth force." Jhana turned questioning eyes to Seiji.

"Civilian defense groups," he said as they hurried along. "Particularly effective for unarmed resistance to armed occupation forces. All defense of the colony is civilian-based—one of the responsibilities of citizenship. No permanently specialized police or military forces."

"Seems like a good idea," Jhana said as they came to the bulletcart platform. "I wonder why more use hasn't been made of it on Earth?"

"Too threatening to the status quo," Seiji explained as they boarded a cart. "In any society with major disparities in wealth, training the citizenry in techniques of cultural critique and effective nonviolent mass resistance would make the populace much harder to manage—less docile and manipulable."

"But I thought you said it was most effective against occupation forces," Jhana remarked as they sped along.

"True," Seiji said with a nod, "but the same techniques that are effective against an invader's occupation forces are also effective against a society's internal occupation forces."

"Who are—?"

"The powers that be," Seiji replied with a shrug as the bulletcart slowed, unsealed itself, and they exited, to dash for yet another cart just arriving. "The 'haves' who control a disproportionate amount of social and financial power—and the military and police forces that protect the haves from the more numerous 'have-less' and 'have-nots.'"

They made their cart, which quickly sealed around them and sped them toward the docking bays far along the axis.

"I'm beginning to see how you permanent residents have been able to take the threats from Earth so easily in stride," Jhana told Seiji. "You've been preparing for it all along, in a sense."

"Part of our basic philosophy," he said with a nod. "Once you educate a mass society in compassionate social analysis and thorough dedication to nonviolent direct action, it's impossible to maintain that society in a state of lopsided economic disparity. It's probably only in societies where such disparities do not already exist that training in our kind of social critique and civilian-based defense can be encouraged—or even tolerated."

They sat silently a time, until their bulletcart slowed and disgorged them.

"But will it work?" Jhana asked at last, as they walked the final leg through the docking bays to the transfer ship that would take them to Lakshmi's workshop.

"Variants of it have worked before," Seiji replied as they jogged along. "Even against nasties as bad as Hitler. Let's just hope we don't have to test it here—that this mess with Earth can be cleared up without an occupation."

Boarding a transfer ship, they were surprised to find it already programmed for Lakshmi's location. As the ship slipped out, they saw the bright glimmers of satellite solar power stations—as well as the dimmer glints of the X-shaped structures which, as they watched, seemed to begin turning slowly from a vertical to horizontal orientation.

"I almost forgot about those things," Jhana said, startled. "I've got to call my boss."

Seiji stared at her.

"I don't follow you. What's your boss got to do with them?"

Glancing at him, Jhana decided that matters had reached such a pass now, she could risk revealing her unofficial mission to him.

"I guess it won't hurt to tell you. I haven't only been studying genetic drift and population dynamics up here, Seiji. From the beginning I've also been an unofficial observer for Tao-Ponto. They wanted to know about any projects I came across that might be of interest to the company—you know, the usual informal corporate intelligence. They were also very interested in, and worried about, those things out there. I've got to call my boss and reassure him that, whatever they are, they're not weapons."

Seiji stared at her as if he didn't know what to make of this revelation.

"Ship's got a built-in downlink console," he said quietly, looking as if he'd intended to say something else. "That's it over there."

When Jhana entered her code, however, she got an unexpected response.

"That's odd," she said aloud.

"What is?" Seiji asked.

"This console. When I enter my encryption code, it says 'security code compromised—please try again.' When I tried again, it said the same thing."

"Here, let me try it."

Seiji tried the code number—with the same results. He tried it several times more but with no success.

"Oh, no," Jhana said heavily. "I gave Roger my code number for communicating with Tao-Ponto. Maybe he's gimmicked it somehow.''

The ship began docking maneuvers then, bringing the enigmatic X-shaped structures into view once more.

"I'm surprised somebody from Earth hasn't fired missiles or lased them by now," Jhana remarked, "since everyone seems to be so disturbed by their presence."

"Uncertainty, probably," Seiji said. "Lord knows they have the weapons to take them out—micronukes, electromagnetic pulse bombs, hypervelocity kinetic kill warheads. Lakshmi claims, though, that this distributed consciousness thing has infiltrated not only the VAJRA but everything that uses QUIPs—and that *is* just about everything. There've been some unexplained shutdowns on ships up from Earth that got too close to them. When we tried to take them apart ourselves, the space-habitat started toward self-destruct. Maybe no one knows what attempting to destroy them might trigger."

Docking completed, the ship's lock opened and they drifted into Lakshmi's workshop.

"Lakshmi? Are you here?" Seiji called.

"Yes—and no," said a laughing voice coming from the speakers attached to Lakshmi's equipment.

In the middle of the room where robotic arms sighed together like a stand of metal bamboo in a breeze, Lakshmi floated in her hoverchair, her back to them. Drifting around until they were in front of her, Seiji and Jhana saw her smiling rapturously, her eyes remming at unbelievable speeds beneath her lightly closed lids. A tenuous beam, the merest whisper of coherent light, traced a path from the jumble of Jiro Yamaguchi's machines to impinge on Lakshmi's forehead, where it pooled slightly, suffusing her skin with a roseate glow, a third eye of light, still and open above the two jittering, closed eyes below.

"Lakshmi, what's going on?" Jhana asked worriedly.

"I'm in dreamtime, mindtime," Lakshmi said, her voice echoing pleasantly from the many machine speakers throughout the room. "Seiji, your brother Jiro's done it! Direct mind/machine link, an information carrier wave that uses the structure of the brain itself as a transducer! The grand unification! And just in time, too. Come on, you two. You're late, and you're needed here.''

"But how do we get there?" Jhana asked, casting about.

"Just sit down or anchor yourself very still. You don't want to look directly into the positioning beam, so close your eyes. Concentrate—the light will find you."

Jhana glanced at Seiji. Both of them cocked eyebrows and shrugged in perplexity, but nonetheless quickly found chairs and strapped themselves in.

Jhana sat still, tried to concentrate on the entoptic flickerings on the insides of her eyelids, growing impatient as time passed and nothing happened.

Then everything happened.

Facts, figures, data—raw, seemingly senseless and shapeless information—flooded into her at insane speeds as if she were straitjacketed into a rocket sled bound for oblivion with her mental eyelids nailed open by screaming innocence and she couldn't shut any of the torrent out, couldn't turn away, must take everything in as it came flying at her, until it felt her head would burst like an overinflated balloon—

A sudden expansion: a valve opening in her head, or her brain shifting into a higher gear, or something far less describable. Abruptly the torrent became less menacing, though still hardly pleasant. Now she felt merely engulfed in a luminous flood that thundered, a Victoria Falls of bright hot heavy light instead of water.

The more she grappled with the light, tried to swim against it, the more she realized that it was filling her with a cascade of her own memories, all the data and details of her life burning through her consciousness at greater than flash-cut speed. She imagined herself swimming and burrowing upward into the flood of light, the flood of her life, and as she imagined it, so it was. When she came to the top of that datafall, her entire life stood gathered about her in vast panoramic memory, a living holographic tapestry, each part implicated in the whole and the whole implicated in each part, each memory containing within it all other memories which it implied, a finite but unbounded sphere of interconnections.

In the center of the sphere, floating in an axial shaft of sunlight that fell from eternity to eternity, stood a container both grail and beaker, its walls clear yet slightly opalescent. Inside it a suspension of innumerable particles danced and flashed like the sun splintered on ocean waves or moted on the dust of deep space. Reaching out with her mind toward it, she passed completely inside, became a particle dancing on the flux.

There was a pattern to the flux she danced in, a latent order and structure waiting to realize itself, waiting to shift into meaning like a stereogram or hologram or fractal, waiting like consciousness hidden in chaos to crystallize about her if she would only allow herself to be that seed crystal.

That valve in her head—wherever her head was—seemed to open again and all around her the flux condensed, crystallized, shot out like an enchantment in infinite directions, rays and leaves and crystalline spikes precipitating out of the flux, a universe of seemingly formless information suddenly shot through with form rising grandly out of the random background.

Faster than she could ever dream it, a sudden channel opened between the worlds and she was abruptly aware of the presence of Seiji and Lakshmi in the alterior universe around her—and of someone or something else as well—*there*, the way air, gravity, or space-time is there.

Intuitively Jhana realized they were inside the mindspace of VAJRA and the distributed consciousness itself, surrounded by the game of Building the Ruins being played on an incomprehensibly vast scale. The illusion of the virtual reality about her was so flawless that it made her question whether any reality she had ever known was truly real—or if the reality she had taken for granted her whole life long was also only virtual.

Before her, the game's CHAOS and LOGOS now manifested conflict in the forms of two great beasts locked in deadly combat. The LOGOS was a vast bright-toothed spermaceti whale whose body glistened in the Deep, the lights of planets, stars, and galaxies informing its flesh, while the CHAOS seemed a writhing gigantic squid formed of Coalsack nebulas' worth of dust, detritus, debris—all dark matter coiling tenebrous tentacles about its celestial cetacean opponent, shaking the Deep with its own strange dark lightnings as the two Titans roiled the universe of mind.

What disturbed Jhana was that she and Seiji and Lakshmi were not on one "side" or the other—they were a part of both and neither, tooth *and* tentacle *and* aloof Other observing the struggle.

G LANCING AT THE CROWD AROUND HIM AS THE MÖBIUS Cadúceus show began, Aleister wondered how the people of the colony—even Atsuko Cortland here beside him—could give themselves over so totally to celebration when the habitat might at this moment be poised on the brink of disaster.

Yet here he was too, taking a break from the long, arduous task of fending off what intelligence probes were still coming up from Earth. And here they all were, mostly young people, gathered round a pavilion that had been collapsed to proscenium stage, round a reflecting pool and its shores transformed by thrust stages to playing area, as music came up and Lev Korchnoi sang of a village where "the men make weapons and the women make babies." Aleister was close enough to the playing area to notice that the "villagers" were dressed in the costumes and kept the customs of a hundred times and places of Earth's history, but the main focus of the scene was bucolic, pastoral, except for a fabril smith at his forge, his pregnant wife beside him, town buildings from a variety of Earth's cultures holojected in the background.

A blonde woman in a long, diaphanous white robe and an elaborate bi-winged headdress appeared. To Aleister she seemed an important ritual figure—a novice nun or vestal virgin of some sort, most notable for her innocence and naiveté. The program notes designated her only as Bliss, and she sang a panegyric to the people of the village and their contented way of life.

The smith, growing enamored of the young woman and her singing, looked upon her with growing desire until, forgetting his pregnant wife and consumed with lust for the vestal, he pursued her night and day, a flattering irritant around whose compliments and attentions even so pure a heart as Bliss's began to build the black pearl of pride. Led by her fledgling pride and the cunning of the smith, she came into a wild forest where, overcome by his lust, the smith took her by force and raped her, threatening her with death of body and reputation if she should ever reveal what had happened between them.

Bliss sang no more. The life of the village tilted out of balance, and out of the reflecting pool Fear and Desire rose, unleashing upon the villagers the scourges of drought, famine, pestilence, violence. Walking among the beggared and crippled, through scene after scene of human suffering, Bliss smiled to reassure the grieving until she could stand the farce no longer. Finally she sang again, no simple innocent panegyrics now, but notes and chords woven round painful truths of bitter experience. She sang of contradictions between making weapons and making babies, of men making too many of the former and the women too many of the latter—but most of all she sang of acts of force and silence.

The smith, growing fearful that the villagers would divine the truth, appealed in swelling song to the people and priests and patriarchs to save the village by sacrificing Bliss. With her rebelliousness already a strong mark against her, her fate was sealed when it was discovered she was pregnant—that she was tainted, had broken her vows.

Clearly (the chorus of black-robed religious functionaries sang as they dragged her to the altar) her taint had brought all manner of misfortune upon the village. It was best to be rid of her, to purge the village of the sin of Bliss. Bound at last to the altar, she could only lie helplessly as a monstrous robotic arm reached out from the huge Fear machine and snatched her up, to carry her captive over water toward its Arcadian temple island.

The tempo picked up here as the scope of the performance broadened. Aleister saw that, even after this second rape, things got no better—in fact they got much worse. Accompanied by pounding music like the raggedy-mad beating of a hyperstimulated heart, the machineries of Fear and Desire projected holotaped scenes of decadence, madness, carnage, and mere anarchy over the whole world of the stage. Slave and serf and tenant farmer metamorphosed into coal miner and factory line drudge and paper pusher, transmogrified again into graveyard-shift computer-room corpse, machine servicer, techno-peasant databoys and glitchgirls. All suffered, and those sufferers who weren't sobbing or screaming or crying or shouting drank or drugged themselves into sloppy-smiling oblivion. Grimy children from burning homes threw stones at the windows of mansions where the rich toasted their good fortune with priceless champagne in crystal goblets. Exploiters exploited those who, given the chance, would exploit in their own turn again and again and again, and over it all Möbius Cadúceus played and Lev sang.

Excerpted lyrics from Möbius Cadúceus song "Fix":

> *Everybody needs a fix! Everybody needs a fix!*
> *Some call it love, some call it politics,*
> *But everybody needs a fix!*
> *Some call it God, some—microelectronics*
> *Some call it peace, some—defensive tactics*
> *Some say Armageddon, some—Apocalypse*
> *But everybody needs a fix!*

Rather redundant stuff, Aleister thought, but by then the action had shifted again.

Klaxons sounded, air raid warnings grated across the staged night like vast diamond saws cutting into the crystalline spheres of heaven. Across time and forest and plain and mountain and desert, by foot, ski, sled, horse, elephant, camel, cart, chariot, coach, car, troop-truck, jeep, and tank, they came, warriors with stone axes and spears and slings and arrows and bows and guns and rockets and lasers—Sumerian charioteers, Greek hoplites, Roman legionnaires, Vikings with two-headed Danish axes, Mongol bowmen, Saxon huscarls, French knights, Cromwellian foot soldiers, musketeers, samurais, Zulu assegaimen, GIs, and Red Army infantry—to battle, all.

Excerpted lyrics from Möbius Cadúceus song "Butcher Paper":

> *Winds of war are always blowin'—*
> *One power source that never fails*
> *But ships of state, they can't keep goin*

Without those butcher paper sails
So we pay taxes yearly . . .

Listening to Korchnoi's plaintive wail over the stage mayhem, Aleister thought that at least this lyric seemed to have a
little more substance to it than the sometimes heavy-footed
doggerel of the previous song.

Meanwhile, rafts and dugouts and canoes, galleys and gal-
leons and dreadnoughts, nuclear submarines and hovercraft
and hydrofoils, all were forcibly boarded, burned with Greek
fire, cannon-struck, blasted by precise shell and torpedo, sunk
by atomic shock waves.

Keep the butcher paper handy
Let it soak up all the blood
Smoke cigars and drink your brandy
While men die and turn to mud . . .

In the timeless sky, stones, spears, burning oil, arrow vol-
leys, catapult loads, cannonballs, shells, bombs, strafing air-
craft, rockets, missiles, transatmospheric fighters, orbiting
forts, suicide satellites, all roared and flamed.

Call it dollar, call it ruble
Call it franc, pound, mark, and yen
Call it what the hell you want to—
All butcher paper in the end . . .

Infants mushroomed up into Mother's Day mothers and Vet-
erans Day soldiers together breeding still more mothers and
soldiers, rising birth rates driving rising death tolls, the machinery of death fueled by the machinery of life, the machinery
of life fueled by the machinery of death. Many heroes and
would-be heroes set out in search of Bliss across the world-
stage, but none found her there.

As sure as this world turns, Lev Korchnoi sang, *this world
is gonna burn if we don't turn it around.* Playing the unlikely
hero, Will—"a walking contradiction in terms, a bookish rus-
tic and knight-errant," as Aleister read in his low-light display
Program Notes—Lev (in character?) stumbled at last into the

spotlit playing area, his ever-present wraparound shades *not* present, for once.

Though usually not much enamored of popular art forms, Aleister was impressed despite himself. Of what he'd seen so far, how much was real, how much illusion? How many actors, how many holojections? It had all flowed together surprisingly seamlessly . . .

He barely had time to wonder, for in the playing area and in amplified projections he saw Korchnoi's costume armor metamorphosing upon his body—now Greek hoplite, now Saxon huscarl, now samurai—as Will, through a stage-field that mixed live and virtual, dodged and ducked arrows and bullets and cannonballs, leaping and flying and darting and diving and singing all the way through the panoply of real and virtual destruction being hurled in his direction as he made his zigzag progress over the field.

At last the paraded images of human suffering and pain and rage began to thin; the discordant clashings of instruments softened and faded before Will as the jarring sounds and scenes fell back toward their sources. The paincries of those entering and those exiting life began to quiet, the smoke to clear somewhat. Standing at the edge of the reflecting pool, Will and the audience with him saw looming over the water the wellspring of all the floods of noise and image: a towering weapon-studded megalith glinting like ice or crystal, and a whirlpool glowing with pale pink fire at its mouth, churning like a horizontal waterfall. Myriad ghostly images of souls dying and aborning paraded endlessly between the two guardians, while beyond them stood the temple island, with Bliss bound between two pillars upon it, an airily beautiful wordless song of purest vocalization bursting from her even as parts of the temple toppled and burned around her.

OUTSIDE ROGER'S MANEUVERING LIVESUIT, THE EARTH spun visibly, sleeping like a top, dreaming like a gyre. In its dark empty setting the blue-white planet of his birth, flecked here and there with russet continents, shone brightly as any jewel.

The most frightening feature of unreason is its failure to recognize itself, said a voice in Roger's head, again and again, until it too began to break up, splintering oddly, so that "recognize" sounded like "re-cognize."

Roger's dead father appeared before him abruptly, a light-fringed apparition pointing to the world Roger was looking at.

"Looks simple, doesn't it? But you wouldn't believe how complex and interrelated everything is down there. Every human being, every artificial intelligence, every information processor of whatever size is a ganglion in an immense global mind. All telecommunications, all telegraphy, cable, telephony, radio, television, trideo, and holo: it's all being plugged into the older sensory systems to create a new network, one trafficking information to and from a developing mind so vast that our lives are only its passing thoughts—a mind with such enormous capabilities we can see only the vaguest outline of its potential."

Shivering in the perfect environment of his livesuit, Roger raised his laser dirk. Blessedly, his father's apparition disappeared, leaving only the Earth before him. *Only a memory,* Roger reminded himself, *only the logic of hallucination.* Why he had called it up so lucidly now he could not say, but he had seen no vast mind out there then, when his father had first spoken those words, and he saw no vast mind out there now—only a place whose light was too bright for him, making his head hurt till he had to turn away.

The void itself glistened brightly now, and those damned angels—they were growing worse! But at least every time he struck at one it would disappear, and that painful brightness of their wings would leave him for a moment.

He thought he'd located the point in space from which the angels were emerging—a spot not so far away from the habitat, where the light from the stars seemed to be warping out in an arc or ring. He'd been making his way to that spot as quickly as he could, but he seemed to be going nowhere—and taking forever to get there. Another angel flashed into the space before him, making his eyes hurt.

"Damn you bastards!" he cursed inside his helmet. "Leave me alone! You're extinct! Obsolete! We don't need you anymore!"

His laser blade sent a blue-white arc sparking in the void as he lashed out with it, but the angel was already gone. He found he was breathing heavily, too heavily, that his heart was pounding in his chest, his neck, his forehead. His gaze strayed toward Earth, where in low orbit he could see at least half a dozen bright points of light flashing on.

Aha! They were coming, then—the ships of the occupation! Just a few hours more and HOME would be changed forever!

He cast about until he saw the distant gleam of the two new colonies, the shine of the asteroid tug. Those too would be changed, he thought.

His glance strayed toward the X-shaped structures glinting in the sun. Something about them had changed already. Had they canted over, changed orientation from the vertical to the horizontal? As he watched, they seemed to be slowly separating, like chromosomes moving from metaphase to anaphase in some enormous dividing cell.

He wondered a moment what unseen spindle poles the half-X's might be moving toward, but he shrugged it out of his thoughts as he plunged on to do battle with his angels, the painfully bright things mocking him yet again with their chants about unreason unrecognized.

IT OCCURRED TO JHANA—AS MUCH AS SHE WAS STILL "Jhana," as much as she was still a person and not this place—that perhaps the rules of Building the Ruins had to change. She felt the need to reduce, minimize, and if possible, eliminate the titanic struggle taking place in the universe of mind around them. Working with Lakshmi and Seiji on both sides of the CHAOS/LOGOS divide, she set about making the great change of Mind possible, shifting the game from competition to cooperation.

First they reduced the combatants in scale from galactic to merely planetary; then they altered their form as well: LOGOS they induced to play Mongoose to the CHAOS's Cobra. Initially their conflict was vast enough—both mammal and reptile were of gigantic stature. But gradually their battling no longer shook continents, reared mountains, or dug river channels. Soon they were merely two fluidly agile forms, one furred, one scaled, both roughly life-sized. Soon they weren't even that big.

Jhana saw her own right hand reaching down and taking hold of the snake. At the touch of her hand, the shrinking reptile coiled faster and faster in her palm, swallowing its tail with such speed that it was no longer form but rather a sort of anti-form, a not-knot of one snake and many, a blurred pit of blackness roiled to rainbow about its edge—like the mouth of a whirlpool, the eye of a hurricane, and the event horizon of a black hole all rolled into one and not into one.

A man's darker, left hand took hold of the mongoose. At his touch, the diminishing mammal became pure, fluid, warm-blooded light, a pillar of unflawed yet fragile fire, a beam of coherent brightness shining in the man's palm.

In the universe of information they found themselves in, a voice (but whose?) asked, "LOGOS, why are you?"

"I am," the flame of order replied, "to answer the questions."

"CHAOS, why are you?"

"We are," the pit of possibility replied, "to question the answers."

The hands moved steadily toward each other, the path of light and the pathlessness of the pit intercepting each other on the same plane, a mouth finding a tongue and a tongue finding a mouth, the light and the pit speaking together in a voice that grew the more harmonious as the outstretched hands drew closer and closer to each other.

"Why are you?" they asked of the voice, at once and nearly as one.

"I am," replied the voice neither male nor female and both female and male, "to discover why I am. Endlessly. To discover why there are questions to be answered and answers to be questioned. What I am is your answer. What I am is your question. Our purpose is one."

The right hand of the woman and the left hand of the man came together palm to palm, paler and darker forming the mutual prayer of folded hands. The light knew the source of the dark and the dark knew the source of the light, and in that instant Jhana saw the face of the man behind the hand: Michael, her Michael and himself, as she remembered him and as she'd never seen him, with so much sorrow and forgiveness and expiation shining from his eyes as she could only hope shone from her own.

At that instant, light flamed out everywhere, a glimpse of supernova's haloed star cross, perfect balance of light and dark, of darkness quartered by planes of light into perfect wedges bounded and made whole by the ring of light.

When the burst of light had faded, the universe of mind had changed fundamentally. The heavens had been floored with a floating chessboard gridwork stretching to infinity, over which floated a face that filled the firmament, a face through which the stars shone.

Something about the enormous visage was familiar, made Jhana feel as if she should know it. Its eyes—made more prominent by the thinness of the face, the tightness of the skin on the skull—were brown and soft, something about them suggesting faraway vistas from which the seer had never completely returned, the eyes of a vision quester, a sufferer through ordeals, a mind-diver who had plummeted to the far side of madness. The hair—dark, moderately long and unkempt, receding a bit in that shape called a widow's peak, with two feathers jutting up from a braid behind—fringed the forehead of a troubled thinker. To say that its cheekbones and eyebrows, for all their prominence, could still add no solidity to the soft ghostly sense of loss those eyes conferred on the entire face—making it the visage of an alcoholic young nun or priest, a gently stoned Rasputin or Joan of Arc, a shaman-sibyl who had lain too long in a land of eternal ice and winds that carved canyons in the soul—to say all that was still to say too little. Jhana felt her own soul opening, dilating, instressing toward the inscape of that face, and through that dilation she thought in other minds, other minds thought in her.

"My God," came a thought from Seiji. "Jiro!"

A FLASH OF LIGHT, BRIEF BUT DAZZLINGLY INTENSE, MADE Roger blink. When he opened his eyes, the half-X's were much closer—and seemingly headed for the same spot in space toward which he himself was headed. He marveled at this, but only for a moment. He was quite convinced he had now lost his mind for good. How else to explain the incredible speed with which the large half-X's seemed to be moving? How else to explain the fact that, even when he tried to throw his lifesuit's maneuvering unit into reverse, it made no difference—as if some spindle fiber of gravity were towing him down to a center he could not imagine?

Yes, he must certainly be crazy. The mushroom must have seen to that.

The revelation affected him so profoundly that even with the angels flickering right in his face, he struck at them only halfheartedly. By the time the battery of his laser blade was empty, the great half-X's were circling about him. They had all very nearly reached their common destination.

A BRILLIANT FLASH SEEMED TO FILL THE WHOLE OF THE sphere a moment. Shutting his eyes against the light, Aleister wondered if it was part of the show—though, truth to tell, it seemed to come from everywhere at once. As he opened his eyes, he found himself staring toward Will at the edge of the reflecting pool and wondering about the costume armor Korchnoi was wearing. His dimly glowing Program Notes said it was the real stealth soldier article.

Wonderful, Aleister thought, looking up. Just what the well-dressed occupation forces will be wearing this season. Yet most of his fellow colonists seemed to see it only as a costume in a production half-opera, half performance art extravaganza.

Before him the temple where Bliss was manacled continued to collapse and contract. The armored Will began to stride purposefully atop the water toward the island while the music played, Aleister becoming for a moment more aware of the lyrics than he'd been before, aware that Bliss's song now had words after all.

Excerpted lyrics from Möbius Cadúceus song "Sayonara, Deathship Sailor":

> *To know One Future belongs*
> *To Everyone*
> *Or to know one*

> *Is to love one*
> *When it's over*
> *Turn me over*
> *Keep my face*
> *In time*
> *Keep my face*
> *To the fire*
> *Sayonara, Deathship Sailor*
> *Have a nice walk*
> *Upon the water.*

Aleister didn't know quite what to make of that, except the walk upon the water part—that tied in to the performance, anyway. But surely it was just a glassine path of some sort that Will was walking on, wasn't it? Something just below the surface?

As Will came closer, the icy, fearsome Scylla-mechanism lashed out at him with its arsenal of arrow and bullet, spear and missile. The burning, yearning Charybdis stopped its insuck and spewed up—once, twice, three times—iron-toothed demon cherubs that devoured everything in their path. Swatting them aside with blasts from his shockwave gauntlet, Will seemed unstoppable.

There was a pause in Fear and Desire's attacks as they changed tactics. A burning figure strode out of Charybdis' maelstrom, while simultaneously a cold crystalline figure came from out the portal in Scylla's side. Walking upon the water, they came together and fused into one: an ahuman, robotic figure in stealth armor, twin to how Will himself looked—except that, in place of a shockwave gauntlet, his alter ego bore a sword of frozen fire.

Will's twin charged toward him, berserker-fashion, slashing the air with his great fiery icicle. Will leveled the shockwave gauntlet at his opponent and fired, and again, and again. The blasts should have blown his other self off the path, but the soldier kept coming: slowed, staggered, arcing and sparking, but still coming on.

Will's Other lashed out with the burning cold sword. Will dodged, but not before the weapon struck him a grazing blow upon the neck and glanced into his shoulder armor, short-circuiting the whole suit. On the giant projections Aleister saw that, from Will's neck, blood dripped into the water, dispersing in a scarlet cloud, too strong a flow for the wound to fully self-cauterize.

When Will jumped to his feet, ready to fight on, Aleister was right there with him, having for that moment at least thoroughly suspended disbelief, lost all his sophisticated detachment and esthetic distance. But the alter ego soldier was past, charging on, aimlessly cleaving the air until finally the deranged mechanism staggered off the path and plunged into the water, still slashing, great arcing sparks leaping over its armor as it sank, drifting even as it sank, caught in the vortex of devouring Charybdis, drifting and slashing, slashing and drifting, down toward spiraling oblivion.

The glass path exploded in sharp, tinkling music beneath Will's feet, hurling him into turbulent water. Close up on the big virtual projections, Aleister saw that Lev/Will, looking momentarily disoriented, struggled quickly to the surface, swimming in the direction of Scylla, for Charybdis's pull was already tugging at him. In the projections, Will's dead armor seemed to be slowing him down, and Aleister was relieved when he saw Lev blow the suit's bolts and struggle free of the exoskeleton. Ahead, Aleister saw the portal in Scylla's slick side closing slowly as Will made for it, armor exoskeleton in tow. In projection close-up, Aleister saw that Will, upon reaching the portal, yanked the cord for the armor's mechanical self-destruct, then stuffed the armor into Scylla before swimming for the island and Bliss as fast as he could churn water.

Barefoot and drenched, he stumbled onto shore, where the broken temple on its bleak island had thrashed and contorted itself into ruins almost beyond recognition. Will rushed up the small hillock to where Bliss lay, her headdress gone, her robes torn, her disheveled hair spilt over the cracked black and white chessboard pattern of the temple floor. In the projections Aleister saw that Will, finding Bliss still breathing, still alive, set about freeing her from her bonds. Behind him sounded the loud *whump* of an underwater explosion sending water geysering high into the air and raining down. The Scyllan rock of Fear, broken from its base by the armor's explosive self-destruct, canted over and fell toward the open maw of Desire. Greedily the whirlpool drew the great load toward itself.

"BUT," SEIJI STAMMERED THROUGH JHANA'S MIND, "BUT you're dead!"

"Dead?" Jiro seemed genuinely puzzled at the thought. "There is no death—only a change of worlds, as Chief Seathl once said."

"But they burned your body to ashes—to nothing!"

"Ah, the body," Jiro said, nodding thoughtfully. "Another machine, you know. Each of us is a god in a machine, when you think about it."

Seiji could make no sense from such cryptic comments, however confidently they might be delivered.

"I can't believe this. Jiro never spoke with such assurance. VAJRA has sampled my memories and this is just something it's put together."

Laughter rolled through the universe.

"My dear brother, VAJRA is a wonderful tool, but that's all it is: a tool. It reaches many of the same ends as human thought, but by different means. It 'sees far but notices little, remembers everything but learns nothing, neither errs egregiously nor rises above its normal strength, yet sometimes produces insights that are overlooked by even top grandmasters'— which was also said of the first computer to defeat the world's last human chess champion, by the way. In joining with VAJRA, I've benefited from an insight I'd overlooked, a key point in the game."

"What game?" Seiji asked in exasperation.

"The only game worth playing, once you realize that building the ruins ruins the building. Think about it, Seiji. Human beings make a living by making a killing—eating, devouring, desiring. And for what, if that can end only in death? Even our civilizations: what we built yesterday or are building today will fall to ruins tomorrow, cities blossoming and wilting like flowers, nations spreading and dying like fungus on an old log. There's a deeper game, a more serious game that needs playing. The game in which troubled gods play chess against the unbeatable machinery of themselves."

"The game Jiro lost, you mean. Which is why you can't be him."

Jhana almost imagined she heard a machine sigh. That, at least, was easier to imagine than the fabric of the universe sighing.

"Proof, hm? Known by the scars. Very well. It's true no formerly living individual ever returns to life as exactly the same individual, but I can still give you proof from my memory, things experienced from my point of view."

The images and emotions began to flood out then, almost too fast to follow.

Scandalized nuns at Guardian Angels School finding Jiro wandering around on the school playground with his arms stretched out like a soaring bird, like an eagle dancer, like Christ on the cross—

A greenhouse summer evening, tagging after Seiji and neighbor kid Rudy as usual and Seiji beginning to talk with Rudy about girls until Jiro runs home shouting and crying, "Mom! Mom! Seiji and Rudy are talking about sex!"

"*Arma virumque cano,*" Jiro, standing, recites in a classroom, in a cracking adolescent voice, "*Trojae qui primus ab oris . . .*"

Night upon teenage night of sitting suddenly bolt-upright in bed spewing forth streams of seemingly incoherent speaking-in-tongues gibberish.

"Jeez, Jiro!" Seiji says angrily in the dark bedroom they share. "You're talking in your sleep! Wake up, for God's sake!"

"Wha—?"

"You were talking in your sleep. Go back to sleep."

Silence. Then, "Was not!" and his eyelids closing—

Flashing images of shyness and backwardness and awkwardness all from Jiro's point of view—of how he just doesn't fit in in the one-size-fits-all world of his boyhood, the nice girls he places on a pedestal from afar, unable to approach them, girls pure as bright shining light that he will never dare shadow with the umbra of his lust—

The refuge he takes in books and the life of the mind, his obsession with Native Americans and their lifeways—

Picking dandelions from the firehouse lawn, the firemen

laughing, saying, "What you gonna do with those weeds, son? Smoke 'em? We'll have to turn you in if you are!" but he tells them no, they're for wine, which the firemen can almost understand—

His mind exploding with KL 235, drifting, airless, breathless, drowning, falling toward the bottom of a deep well full of water so pure it seems full of light—

"Got to keep the schizophrenic heads together and socially tracked," he says into the holophone. "Mutants. Victim heroes. Yeah. But most mutations aren't beneficial to the individual with the trait. Die out. Killed off. Gandhi. Martin Luther King. Winona Walking Bear. Victim heroes of the evolving human organism—"

"People here have dreams in which I die, big brother. Wish fulfillment. But my dreams counter them. They come true. Stop me before I dream again—"

"They're putting KL 235 in the cafeteria food here to make me sink uncontrolled telepath into the massmind, the cultural macro-organism. But I'm fighting them. I know they're scanning this call, big brother, but I don't care. Their power is growing, but I've gone starburst. Full telepath televisionary. Protecting you so you can be heard, so your message can get out, so you can communicate. I am a powerful starburst and you are under the silver force-field umbrella of my psychic protection, the silver mirrorball that reflects all the watching eyes and is reflected in all the watching eyes, and you're inside, infinitely beyond harm—"

Seiji's bewildered face as Jiro tearfully says, "I have these violent thoughts sometimes. But I don't want to hurt anybody. I'd rather die than hurt anybody—"

In his white coldbox coffin, tinkering with the LogiBoxes, getting ready to superconduct and freeze out—

"*Enough!*" Seiji cried at last. "No more. Please. You're Jiro, or at least you have all his memories. How did this happen? Are you, well, *okay?*"

Universal mirth seemed to echo around them again.

"Quite well, for someone who's 'dead.' Better than ever, actually. Sorry to have to put you through all that, but you did want proof."

Abruptly a cafe table appeared on the chessboard floor of

the sky, and Jiro, down from the sky, was seated across from them.

"My old machinery had some problems—chemical imbalances, that sort of thing—so I took an example from holography and split myself into two beams of coherent light, an object beam and a reference beam, as it were, and transferred to an artificial brain, a new machine, whatever information was transferrable from the old. Once Lakshmi allowed those two beams to constructively interfere with each other again, by reactivating the machinery I'd transferred myself into, I became aware of my identity and situation. Suffered a great loneliness, but conscious again, back in time, which amounts to the same thing—though differently from what I was."

Jiro's simulacrum, his virtual self, dressed in the full regalia of a Dwamish Indian shaman—complete with a medicine pouch adorned with a trefoil symbol—leaned back in his virtual chair, apparently thoughtful.

"Of course, since I no longer have a human body or a human brain, it can be persuasively argued that I no longer have a human consciousness. Perhaps so. A conundrum for the philosophers, with their 'emergent fractal self-organizing dynamical chaotic networks-within-networks' and 'transthermodynamic informational black holes.' Not so far off, really. All I know is that I feel more truly human than ever—isn't that strange?"

"Then you really *are* okay?"

Jiro's simulacrum laughed and turned the whole world around them into myriad staring eyes, surveillance watching on different "screens" Roger drifting toward his nexus point, Aleister and Atsuko watching the Möbius Cadúceus show, Marissa Correa and Paul Larkin searching for Roger, the military shuttles coming on, Balance Tien-Jones and Ka Vang coming with them, a thing like a strange spirit-animal moving out into space after Roger . . . .

"If you mean, do I still see the world like this, the answer is no—and yes," Jiro said, effecting the disappearance of the eyes and surveillance screens. "Paranoia and metanoia both arise from the realization that everything is interconnected, related, even if, to simpler senses, there seems to be no relationship. The paranoid fears or desires something in that interconnectedness, but the metanoid blissfully accepts its presence. I'm not afraid of the weight of interconnectedness anymore—it's glorious, in fact!''

Leaning forward, he smiled.

''It's like each of us is part of a spin pair whose total spin, the total spin of the universe, is zero. Change my spin and you change hers, change hers and you change mine, for we are all inextricably linked. Subatomic karma, cosmic golden rule,'' he said, bright-eyed and laughing. ''That's why, when I 'died,' you had your vision, Seij. If the metanoid, the mystic, is a diver who can swim, and the schizophrenic is a diver who can't, then I feel I've learned to swim at last.''

''But what about the Ruins game?'' someone—Jhana or Seiji or Lakshmi, or perhaps all of them—asked. ''And the X-shaped structures? And Roger? And the list of names in the RAT code? And the occupation force from Earth?''

''Oh, yes.'' Jiro smiled. ''All that. Has to do with information, you know. With human help, especially from the three of you, the game has been a way of moving and shaping and integrating tremendous amounts of information into a form useful for creating what Tetragrammaton's theoretical physicists call 'quantum information density structures' or 'QUIDS.' QUIDS allow one to move into and through the gravitational bed of space-time—to open a hole in the sky, climb into it, and pull the hole in after.

''Like God, the Project and the Program knew us in the womb. You, Jhana, you, Seiji, and me, and Roger Cortland—we were the ones up here whose lives have been most impacted by the long planning of Tetragrammaton, the uterotonic experimentation of Medusa Blue. Atsuko Cortland and Paul Larkin also had previous exposure to KL. There are others, as well. You two and Roger were potentially predictable focal points for this transition, especially because you'd all suffered the death of a loved one recently and were all shaken by grief, primed for transformation. Marissa and Lakshmi have proven a surprise, though, and Lev and Aleister too, and Roger—ah, the man, and his darkness, and what has happened to him I must acknowledge mine. He is perhaps more sinned against than sinning.

''When I leave through that hole I mentioned, by *becoming*

it, that density of shaped information I've gathered must be returned. That's where the information refractors, the X-shaped structures, come in: what was taken in must be poured out again. A kenosis will take place, a prevenient grace will flood out, a paraclete will shine forth in every mind, calling that mind to remember, to learn again what it really is. In that instant we will have in a circle round us, if only for a moment, the chain of the hours, the sequence of the years, the order of the heavenly host. We will for a very brief time stand in that event horizon, that ring of light in which all times can be seen at one place and all spaces can be seen at one time.

"How each mind responds to that situation, to that call, is of course each mind's own business. One can hope, though, that a constructive interference will take place, a simultaneous interaction of chance and necessity. A miracle. A crux point in human history. An evolutionary shift. An irenic apocalypse. One that helps people realize certain behaviors and structures are obsolete—that maybe this occupation fleet, for instance, is just the last fling of the old warrior economy and the threat it poses to habitats everywhere."

Jiro stood, growing swiftly larger in the firmament.

"*Deus absconditus ex machina*," he said, waving and smiling as if at some wonderful joke. "Time to wake up from the nightmare of time, to go through to the other side. Someone's waiting there for me. Adieu, adieu. Remember me, and recognize yourselves, in the very near future—"

Jiro disappeared in light, vanished into more than visible light, and in the flash Jhana saw:

Roger Cortland, tightly hemmed about by refractors, spindle-paths of light surging and spiking round him, a lambent knot of flickering fire dancing above his space-helmeted head, his eyes jittering fiercely, then gone: knot, lightpaths, refractor, Roger—

Will/Lev standing up with Bliss in his arms. A deafening roar belching up from the Charybdis of Desire as it blows apart, vomiting up with a prodigious surging and spewing of waters huge chunks of the too greedily devoured Scylla of Fear. Simultaneous eruption of light into the whole of the habitat, thousands of lightpaths, thousands of knots of flickering fire over the heads of everyone, over Paul Larkin's head and

Marissa Correa's, over everyone in sphere, ag tori, industrial sector, over the heads of everyone in the crowd, over Lev's head, Atsuko's, Aleister's, everyone's eyes remming furiously in their skulls for the instant the light blasts into their minds, then Bliss coming to, kissing Will, the island blooming instantly with fertile foliage and flowers, stage magic, finale music soaring and applause pouring down as Bliss and Will take their bows—

More than visible light shining into the minds of the dignitaries waiting to christen the *Swallowtail* on her maiden voyage, shining into the brains of those waiting to open the two new habitats, also into the heads of the soldiers and negotiators in the troopships rocketing up the well, lightpaths spiking everywhere, eyes remming fiercely one and all, knots of flame lambent like speedily twisting rainbow snakes, like cycling salmon circles and mandalas and Möbius strips and infinity skysigns over every brow—

Supernal light to the bow of Earth bending in straight lines, surging spiking shining down, this Earth from every side clasped in wings bright with a billion billion lightpath pinions, clear light striking into every mind in every land, treading DMNs and demons down, speaking in tongues of flame and in flickering eyes restoring what was lost at Babel—

The light gleamed an instant and was gone. In Lakshmi's workshop, inside and outside the machine called VAJRA, the metapersonality that called itself Jiro, his trefoil-beaded medicine pouch with all its odd assortment of trinkets, and his spirit-guide statue as well—all had disappeared as fully as if they had never been.

DISAPPEARING INTO THE DEEP CHANNEL-TUNNEL BETWEEN the worlds, Roger had the distinct impression that something like a man-sized mole rat was excavating the tunnel before him. A strange chantsong arose in his head in words he should not have understood, but did. Even in translation the chantsong would have been gibberish to him, were it not that in his mind it was accompanied by images that allowed him to translate it into a myth-language he was more familiar with—that of science. It played in his head until he began to understand that it was a cosmic mythos, a Story of the Seven Ages of the Universe. At times it seemed a weird amalgam of various theologies and cyclic big-bang theory—with some space-opera thrown in for good measure—but there was something deeper to it as well, and a haunting sense that he knew whose myth this was.

In the void of endings—the chant sang out, and in his mind he saw a perfectly uniform universe without matter, just time and the enormous blank sheet of space with its potential for gravity.

—the spore of beginnings bursts into spawn. The threads of spawn absorb the voidstuff and knit it into stars—Spore and spawn and fruiting body of the First Age: big bang, superstrings, first-generation stars.

Stars release spores, the spores burst into spawn, the threads of spawn absorb starstuff and knit it into worlds—The Second Age, the matter of those stars blown off in bursts of explosions, gravity's configuring of that new matter, the planets condensing from that process.

Worlds release spores, the spores burst into spawn, the threads of spawn absorb worldstuff and knit it into life—The Third Age, the vulcanism of some of those planets spewing out early atmosphere, the proto-organics threading out and chaining up, the self-organizing life of the cell that eventually results.

Living things release spores, the spores burst into spawn, the threads of spawn absorb lifestuff and knit it into minds—The Fourth Age: reproduction, the threading out of chromosomes, of DNA and RNA making evolution and the whole panoply of life possible, and eventually the knitting of all that into consciousness, self-awareness, mind.

Minds release spores, the spores burst into spawn, the threads of spawn absorb mindstuff and knit it into worldminds—The Fifth Age, the age of code: ideas, bedding out into roads, trade, exchange, civilization, until such spawn comes to the brink of either mushrooming up into cataclysm, or knitting into worldmindfulness. Where humanity stood in its history, had stood for all of his life, Roger realized: at the end of the Fifth Age, too-clever creatures trying to navigate the perilous strait between weapons production on the one hand and its own reproduction on the other, the thick spawn of human civilization struggling to achieve its fruition in either harmony or disaster.

Worldminds release spores, the spores burst into spawn, the threads of spawn absorb worldmindstuff and knit it into star-mind—A prophecy of the future already seen, the Sixth Age: interstellar travel, galactic civilization, eventual starmindfulness, though what that last might mean Roger was not quite sure.

Starminds release spores, the spores burst into spawn, the threads of spawn absorb starmindstuff and knit it into universal mind—The Seventh Age, intergalactic travel and civilization and at last universal mindfulness, the emptiness able to contain the fullness of everything.

Universal mind, the void of endings, the void that has taken all things into itself, releases the spore of beginnings, the fullness that pours all things out of itself—The compassionate void perfect and uniform, as it was in the beginning, is now, and ever shall be, void without end amen, which in the exact moment of its perfection always forever releases the spore that bursts outward again into spawn. The interwoven snake swallowing its tail to be reborn. Men and universes dying, but compassion going on and on.

No sooner had Roger gotten some handle on this when the scene shifted. Something told him that the episode running in his mind was an old, old story, a tale of shipwreck. A contact ship from a Sixth-Age civilization—which on closer examination appeared to be made up of a sphere of overlapping angels—it was this craft that got into trouble beyond the edge of the solar system, beyond the Oort cloud. Something to do with a passage between a red giant star and a newly formed black hole out in deep space, but the upshot was that many of the crew had died, the ship was crippled and had eventually begun falling toward the sun. From diverse worlds had the members of the fully myconeuralized crew come, some beautiful to human eyes, some ugly as demons—winged, naked, eusocial tunnelers-in-the-sky burrowing through space like mole rats through desert.

Yet, for all their varied experience, the surviving members of that crew of many species couldn't save their vessel. They could, if they chose, break apart what was left of their sphere and live in orbit around this sun. Or they could try to find a world that looked as if it might some day harbor intelligent life, and attempt a spore crash on it. The consensus was for the latter.

The world they found, Roger saw, was Earth—but an Earth strangely different from the one he knew. The continents weren't right, or in the right places. This episode, he realized, had to be older than he first thought.

In the attempt, most of the sphere of angels and demons burned up in Earth's atmosphere, but the crew's sacrifice was still successful: they managed to seed the Earth with spores, which germinated and spawned and fruited. Those few crew members that survived returned to space, where their wings could catch the sun and they might live out a long immortality of isolation. The loneliness and deprivation worked even on such minds as theirs, however, and some became deranged.

Roger saw in his mind a long time passing—eons—without the development of a proper myconeural associate for the mushroom that grew from the spores they brought to Earth. Incident radiation and corresponding mutation rates were higher outside a host. Throughout most of the world the fungus that had grown from the spore changed, evolved, became denatured into thousands and thousands of species. Only in a few shielded biomes—caves, particularly—did anything like the original strain survive. Even there, however, changes occurred and over time the pure strain died out nearly everywhere, leaving Earth a preterite planet, passed over by the angels of empathy, save for those few of the saving remnant that yet survived in the solar system and its immediate alternate space.

Abruptly Roger found himself out of the tunnel between worlds. Around him a universe opened, an anvil-shaped mountain floating in the void before him. Of course! Only in the cavern inside Caracamuni tepui did the pure strain survive. Larkin had said that, according to the inhabitants, the spawn of the mushroom they found in that cave inside the tepui 're-membered' how it got there—ten, maybe hundreds of millions of years before—and their myths claimed it came "from the sky"—

A pair of angels were rising to meet him. His laser blade was dead, but he didn't feel much like slashing them anyway, not anymore. Instead he just watched them coming. Now that he saw them more closely, he noticed that their wings were more shining than feathery, the white of reflection and glow—and that they seemed vastly intricate, on the smallest of scales, but also absolutely functional. His own livesuit was cumbersome and clunky by comparison, and it occurred to him that their functions—life support? locomotion?—might not be so divergent: the angelic glow might be force-field, the wings energy collectors. Yet still they looked more theological than technological.

—*mysterious ways*, he heard one of the angels say (though he saw no lips move), the one whose "feathered" headdress and wings looked less like something out of the Bible than out of a Western. *Not so different after all. Maybe the soul is also a tool, a vajra thrown by the divine hand, to which it also returns.*

The other nodded, then turned her flashing eyes and floating hair to face Roger. He had seen eyes like those before, but only in his most perplexing dreams.

You'll have to go back, Roger Tsugio Cortland, she said in his mind.

"Why?" Roger asked, speaking aloud and feeling inadequate somehow—like someone sounding out words in a world full of silent readers. "Because I slashed at you?"

The angel stared fixedly at him, reminding Roger of someone from Larkin's video.

Why did you strike at us? Why did you want to persecute us?

"Because you're history. From the past. We don't need you anymore."

The angel smiled.

We're not from your past. We're from your future. You need us more than ever—more than in all the millions of years angels have watched you.

A van of angels, bright and glinting, joined the pair and began to ensphere Roger and move him back toward the gap in the fabric of space-time through which he'd come.

"Please—one more thing," Roger pleaded. The pair of angels gazed at him with their eyes shining like eternity. "I've got to know: Why do you care what happens to us?"

The somehow familiar angel smiled again.

To care is why we're here. The image of the divine is imprinted in all things. The just person justices, the true angel angels. We do what we are. All humans are incarnate codes, words made flesh sharing fully in the same flesh message with all the best and all the worst of human beings throughout time—a message that is itself only a variant of the message shared by all living beings.

We share a great deal, Roger, said the angel who looked vaguely like a Native American shaman. *I'm as guilty as you are. I forcibly shared my piece of the truth with the world, altered consciousnesses without permission for a brief instant. I imposed my will, in an attempt to assure their bliss. You suffered for that—you, who only intended the same, ultimately. Those who attempt that imposition chemically, though, always face the stiffer censure. Still, we're much the same—both reminders that even the bright dreams of reason and life cannot ignore the grim nightmares of madness and death. Always we must strike a balance between the angel and the rat—complete the circle at least temporarily, so neither stands alone.*

The way the angel smiled at him—so gentle yet so knowing—disturbed Roger profoundly. The two angels were so alike, like twins born into different worlds or on different timelines—even more, the same person, but male here and female there, dead here and alive there, staying here and going there.

You're still trying to cast everything into the past, Roger Cortland, said the other, as if reading his mind, *but the question is not, Who were the angels or Who was Divinity Incarnate? but rather, Who is that and Who will be that?—fully, again and again. Who is and who will be willing to forget self for the sake of other? We cannot give up caring so long as there still remain any who are endarkened, unmindful. This universe, and the plenum of all universes, can embody right mindfulness only when all in it also do so.*

The van of angels surrounded him completely then and Roger had a final vision. It seemed he saw every mind in all the universes, each decision shedding photons but also generating a minuscule black hole, a subnano-singularity. On the other side of each of those tiny black holes, a nearly parallel universe branched off. The road *not* taken here *was* taken there. As he watched, Roger saw that the total number of universes in the cosmos was essentially infinite, but with this peculiarity: from within any given universe, only that particular universe was "real"—all the infinitude of others was at best only "virtual." This appeared to be true for each and every one of the universes—but not, he noticed, for each and every inhabitant of all the universes. Larkin's sister here/brother there angelic pair flickered through his head once again. Parallel lines could meet in the space of mind, and mind in fact seemed to be nothing less than these meetings, the membranous infinity of portals and gateways between universes, the entire plenum of universes, the compassionate void conserving possibility and information the way the universe he'd been born into conserved matter and energy. He seemed to stand inside a great spherical golden tree, boundless in its rooting and branching but also rooted and branching in him, truly center everywhere/circumference nowhere, a tree of light aswarm with the activity of bees, fireflies, flashes of moving light, a vast Arc of information and Hive of possibility, enormous plenum ArcHive, flashing infinite of Mind Thinking—

The ensphering light overcame him then. When he regained consciousness, he was in a medical transfer ship, Marissa Correa and Paul Larkin standing on either side of the gurney on which he'd been placed. He handed Marissa the vial of her immortalizing vector, still in his shirt pocket. He had taken it, perhaps thinking that if he spread it to the world it might somehow bring his father back, retroactively cancel his death in canceling all future deaths. Now, at last, he had reconciled himself to the truth.

"Jhana Meniskos's code key!" Roger said suddenly. "I sent a message to her boss saying that she was being held hostage, that her code was compromised. We've got to correct that!"

"Don't worry," they said, looking down at him. "Already taken care of."

• • •

PARADOX. PARADISE. PARACLETE. THE THEMES AND CONcepts moved smoothly through Marissa's mind. Nothing had changed—except that everything about her fellowship research had fallen into place. The goal of that research was already being achieved. The synthesis of knowledge and compassion, coming together effectively and humanely. All she need do was help it along in her own way, and she could do that anywhere.

And her other research, on the immortalizing vector? She had yet to test the sealed vial Roger had returned to her. She did not yet know whether what it contained would be effective or humane, but she and others would run the tests, make the choices, inform the world of their progress—if any. That, too, would fall into place.

Looking about the cabin of the large transfer ship carrying them to tour the new habitats, Marissa realized that, indeed, *everything* had fallen into place. Atsuko beside her gazing out the viewport thoughtfully, Jhana Meniskos across the aisle reading a critique of Guaranty's work (an actual paper book) while Seiji snoozed, all the other people here that she'd become acquainted with back in the habitat—increasingly, they were a community, a world of their own.

The pieces of the larger human puzzle were becoming clearer to her as well. The X-shaped structures which Jhana and Lakshmi and Seiji insisted on calling "refractors" had disappeared completely in light, apparently taking with them the problems that had plagued the VAJRA. No trace of the RATs or the distributed consciousness or the metapersonality "Jiro" remained. All the colony's visitors (herself included, but Jhana Meniskos first and foremost) had met with the negotiators from Earth and had made a broadcast appeal to that world. They had made clear that they were not hostages and—since the refractors had proven to be self-consuming artifacts no more dangerous than staged fireworks celebrating the launch of the *Swallowtail* and the opening of the two new habitats—the presence of occupation forces in space was absolutely uncalled for. Strangely, out of all the permanent residents, Paul Larkin's word seemed to carry special weight with the negotiating team, though Marissa could not quite fathom why.

Some tense hours had followed while the troopships took up final positions around the habitat, but by then the media had already picked up the fireworks theme, and voices in favor of bringing the troops home began to rise throughout the world with surprising speed. The corporate and national forces finally returned to Earth without having boarded the habitat, recalled to base amid UN and CP calls for more clearly defined communication channels between the habitat and Earth—channels the colonists were only too willing to establish.

But other things were happening too, on Earth and in the heavens. Citizens' movements had already toppled, or were in the process of toppling, an unprecedented number of morally bankrupt governments throughout the world—the largest such movements since the Collapse Revolutions of 1989-91 but far more peaceful and widespread than those movements of forty years ago had ever been. A number of the nations involved had broken up, decentralized, and begun reforming along bioregional lines. From what Atsuko had been telling her, the colony and its residents had recently been receiving far more inquiries into alternative lifeways, diverse governmental forms, and species preservation plans than they had ever expected to get. Even the corporate powers had been finding themselves confronted with unified and increasingly powerful consumer and stockholder revolts against globally unsound corporate policies. Among the first concessions granted by the corporations was greater autonomy for the space habitat and all its colonists—though no such increased autonomy had been formally requested by the HOME (no matter how joyfully it was accepted).

It was as if a light had been cast into the darkness of human history, Marissa thought. The world itself seemed more numinous. Certainly on Earth there were still many places where hunger drove out thoughts of love and beauty and divinity, but that was changing, would change, had to change. All these recent external manifestations had to be the result of an epiphany, an apocalypse of the revealing rather than destroying type, an apocalypse *within individuals* that was underlying all the changes outside.

Marissa thought of the individuals she knew up here. Of

Jhana and Seiji and Lakshmi and their strange tale of meeting
the ghost in the machine, Seiji's dead brother, Jiro, apotheo-
sized in virtual space. Of that brother's persistence in another
form after death and his disappearance along with the refractors—and the threesome's attempts to explain that persistence
and disappearance to her, with all their talk of "Mind as fractional dimension between the four dimensions of the universe
we know and the n-dimensions of the plenum of all possible
universes we can only guess at," and "part of Jiro's mind-
fractal lodged in the LogiBoxes," of "Möbius knots" and
"Omega points" and "cosmic loopholes," of "the informational lacuna of Gödel's incompleteness theorem and the Hei-
senberg uncertainty principle, combined with the physical
lacuna of the black hole singularity, where the general theory
of relativity predicts that the general theory of relativity itself
breaks down." Thinking about it made Marissa smile. She
hoped they enjoyed their explanation—whatever all that jargon
really meant.

She thought too of Lev Korchnoi's assertion that something
luminous and divine had been operating in the performance of
The Temple Guardians, and the paradoxical result that Lev,
with genuine (and previously uncharacteristic) humility, felt
that he and the Möbius Caducéus Entertainment Cooperative
could not truthfully accept all the praise for the great success
of their performance that night. She recalled as well Lakshmi's
initial worries that she would be inundated with complaints
about the disappearance of the Building the Ruins game—and
Lakshmi's surprise when the complaints proved minimal, as if
nearly all the players had outgrown that game at the same time.

But most of all Marissa thought of the changes in Roger
and Atsuko. Roger, as soon as he was discharged from the
hospital, had sought Marissa out, had sought Jhana out, had
sought out all those people he had hurt, or threatened with his
laser—to apologize profusely to all concerned. He relinquished
the weapon, voluntarily put himself into therapy, and (perhaps
most astonishingly of all) he and his mother were at last able
to hold a civil, respectful, and even mutually loving conversation, without the rancor and gnawing tensions that had always underlain their words to each other before. Aside from

his constant mechanical drafting of angels and his occasional propensity to use nouns as verbs—"the true Christian *Christs*, the true Buddhist *Buddhas*"—he seemed to be doing quite well and quite differently than he had been, before. What had attracted her to Roger had only grown since the change, and what had repelled her seemed to have disappeared.

Atsuko had changed too, loosening whatever grip she had on her son, proving remarkably open even to such ideas as Roger's decision to travel with Paul Larkin to some obscure South American headwater. In her time spent with Atsuko of late, Marissa had also noticed in her mentor a more profound sensitivity and intellectual acuteness that raised the tenor and importance of all their conversations remarkably. Perhaps these changes weren't all one-sided either. Perhaps Marissa herself had changed as well. Certainly part of it was the deepening respect they felt for each other, but there was also something else, more even than that.

She followed Atsuko's gaze out the viewport. The longer Marissa stared at the universe out there, the more it seemed to shimmer and scintillate, the more it seemed alive, thoughtful, concerned—as she herself was.

"All times and places really *are* full of compassionate attention," Marissa said quietly. "I used to just believe that, but now at last I have eyes to really see it."

Atsuko turned toward her, nodding, her own eyes moist as she squeezed Marissa's hand.

J HANA LOOKED UP FROM THE OLD-STYLE BOOK IN HER hands, remembering from another flight, another time, something Marissa had said about electronic notes and comments. There had been something about utopia not being something to test but rather something by which we are tested. Something about the eternal coming into time.

Thinking of Michael, Jhana wondered about tests and time and eternity. That image of Mike, sorrowful and forgiving, that she thought she saw in the virtual universe Jiro had created—was it real? Where had it come from? Something fabricated from her memories—her hopes? Or was it true, what Jiro had said—that there is no death, only a change of worlds, that the body is just a machine? Was that an illusion as well? Was it all illusion?

She hoped never to be disillusioned of her belief in that necessary fiction. It was already helping her in many ways—not least of all helping her to forgive in her heart and mind Rick, for his betrayal of her, and of himself.

She glanced at Seiji sleeping beside her so peacefully, and wondered. Love, she thought. The most saving of all illusions, the most necessary of all fictions. She did not think it would happen to her again, that she could be so much in love that she was now, looking at Seiji this moment, willing to leave behind the world of her birth.

Deaths and births. This man had passed through her when they were in virtual space. Her ability to "think like a place" had proven a blessing as well as a curse. She had made possible the communication between this side and the other, but now that she had time to think about it, was that really something so new? She had performed an ancient function, for men were always passing through women, passing out of their mother's womb at birth, into the womb of their Great Mother at death. . . .

She glanced out the viewport, thinking thoughts she knew had been Marissa's, though she didn't know how she knew, or how she had shared another's thoughts. They came unbidden into her head as she looked at her homeworld below and thought of a sanctuary candle burning in the silent cathedral of space, and how its sublime beauty had become something she could no longer take for granted. In her eyes now, that beauty refused to fade or diminish.

She felt the worlds they could build in space might never be so beautiful as that first home. But perhaps it would be only after human beings had traveled the universe, when they had passed through everywhere, had seen and experienced all—perhaps only then could they hope to return to where they had begun and truly know their Mother for the first time.

Seiji stirred slightly beside her. Jhana thought she heard one of her fellow passengers say something about "bodhisattvas" and "a mountain of light descending." What a curious phrase, that last. Certainly she had misheard. The conversation continued but, returning to her book, she vowed not to eavesdrop. If what they were talking about was important, she would find out about it in due time. After all, who could say that mountains of light might not be descending quite often, from now on?